FINDING SOLACE

S.L. SCOTT

Nothing heals a broken soul like the love of a true heart.

Published in the United States of America

ISBN: 978-1-940071-97-8

Cover Designer: RBA Designs
Photographer: Amanda Rose
Advanced Review Copy
Editing:
Jenny Sims, Copy Editing at Editing4Indies
Kristen Johnson, Proofreader

Original Team:
Marion Archer, Editor at Making Manuscripts
Karen Lawson, The Proof Is in the Reading
Marla Esposito, Proofing Style

ALSO BY S.L. SCOTT

To keep up to date with her writing and more, visit her website: www.slscottauthor.com
To receive the Scott Scoop about all of her publishing adventures, free books, giveaways, steals and more:

https://geni.us/intheknow

Join S.L.'s Facebook group here: http://bit.ly/FBSLGroup

https://www.slscottauthor.com/audiobooks/

Read the Bestselling Book that's been called **"The Most Romantic Book Ever"** by readers and have them raving. We Were Once is now available and FREE in Kindle Unlimited.
We Were Once

The Kingwood Series
SAVAGE
SAVIOR
SACRED

PROLOGUE

Jason Koster

It's pouring rain, but that doesn't matter. I can't look away from my past. *Or her.*

Delilah Noelle.

Damn.

We shared many shameless kisses with our bodies covered in the slick love we'd made. Carefree hair blowing in the wind. A sunset captured on the back of a rowboat. We were all the good things that first love brings.

Yeah, we were wild in love back then with no cares in the world. Whether by choice or circumstance, all good things must come to an end. Nothing good can last. It's been a hard lesson to learn, but one that finally sank in.

A love so pure, so innocent like ours could never survive. *And didn't.*

The motorcycle's too loud to be considered stealth, so I'm sure she hears me coming. A bike like this, even custom and almost costing as much as a small house, will never impress her.

How do I know? Because *I* never impressed her.

Guess that's why she left me.

Or did I leave her?

I know the truth, but sometimes, I pretend the facts are fuzzy. Hazy facts or not, four years is a lot of time to pass without living with your other half . . . your better half.

She'd called us soul mates at one time. Maybe she was right, and I've been living without half my soul all this time. That'd make sense, though it can't cleanse the soul I have left, if any.

Now I'm back in the same town I once hated, sitting in front of the same house I once visited daily. And I'm not thinking clearly, much like a night I'd like to forget.

I don't know what I was thinking coming back here. I don't know what to think at all.

Maybe . . .

No. She's not an option. She's married.

She's off-limits.

It didn't stop *him* back then, but it should stop me now. Crazy memories fill my brain—holding her in my arms and making her promises I intended to keep. *Too young to make those kinds of promises.* Naïve for thinking I would be her guy forever or she'd be my forever.

Rumor has it *he* hits her.

If I'm not careful, he'll never take another breath if we cross paths again. The thought of anyone laying a hand on her kills me inside, but do I have a right to those emotions when it comes to her?

Gossip has gotten back that she visits my mom on occasion to reminisce. That she misses me.

Fuck.

Rumors. Fucking rumors.

Delilah is still so damn beautiful. I see that same look in

her eyes I remember from back then. The one that brought me to my knees the first time I ever laid eyes on her.

As I look at her standing on that front porch now, I can't deny that she makes me feel the same. Her smile, her small wave . . . two things I've craved. *Missed.* I scrub my hands through my hair and question everything I'm about to do.

Why am I here?

Unfinished business or feeling sentimental about a past I can't reclaim?

What am I doing?

I have no fucking clue, but I do it anyway.

I swing my leg off the bike to find out and then cut the engine to the black Harley. Shoving my hands into the pockets of my leather jacket, I start walking across a lawn I've walked a million times in another life.

The railing wobbles under my hand, and chipped paint pops off. I prop one foot up on the bottom step and stare at her.

Many things in life catch us, distract us, keep hold of us. I'm not one easily caught, though. But the one thing I never seemed to be able to get *uncaught* in is Delilah.

It's been too long since I've laid eyes on the beauty standing before me or felt a heart I thought had been lost on some dark highway. Here it is, beating to life just from being near her again. I take a deep breath, and say, "Hi."

Her shoulders drop, the tension falling away as if she's been waiting for this day and found relief in its arrival. "What took you so long?"

1

Jason

New York is always an option. I hate Manhattan, but I could live in a borough. I could blend into the city life and disappear among all the other ghosts that inhabit the area. I pass the exit, the city no longer a choice, and keep driving south.

I never felt as if I belonged there anyway.

I've traveled this country from Maine to Los Angeles, Alaska to Key West. I've stayed a few days in a motel outside Atlanta and swum in the Gulf along the Mississippi coast. I've drunk whiskey in the open air of Joshua Tree and slept under a blanket of stars in Texas.

~~I lived.~~

I survived.

But all roads seem to lead me back to Solace Pointe.

My jersey number still graces the beat-up old sign along the highway. The billboard is just before the exit that leads you to a one-stoplight town with a pharmacy still serving ice cream at the counter and Wilbur Macy rocking in a chair at the corner of Main and First.

It's the kind of place where you'll find the entire town at the stadium on Friday night and then in church on Sunday morning, leaving just enough time to sin on Saturday.

I laugh when I spot the sign I used to shoot my BB gun at while driving by: *This is God's country. Don't drive through it like hell.*

The devil himself has returned to town.

This time, I actually slow down. It might be the first time. I don't want the attention or Whaley, the local deputy, pulling me over. I've managed to avoid the law for some time now, so there's no need to cause trouble in my hometown, especially when I've earned a few new scars and inked my skin. He'll have a problem with my tattoo, and he'll judge me from that alone, but I also have a backpack of stuff I don't want to explain, much less travel down memory lane or tell him where I've been.

Unfortunately, I have to cruise down Main to get home.

Home.

My home was never a place but a person. It's funny how time changes things. I don't think about Delilah as much anymore. I'm really good at pocketing those disconcerting feelings away, but damn if being here doesn't drag them all back to the surface.

As familiar as this place feels, it doesn't feel like home.

Glancing down First when I pass under the green light, I'm tempted to cruise by her house. I wave to Wilbur instead —glad to see he's alive and still rocking on that corner—and keep driving. I should really say hi to my mom, but my throat is dry, so I pull into a parking spot a few down from Red River, the main bar here. I don't want to see anybody I know, but I will, so I might as well get it over with and put some rumors to rest.

Pulling open the door, I walk inside. It's dark, and my

eyes aren't adjusted, but I know this place by heart, so I keep walking until everything comes into view.

Front door. Top half glass.

Back door through the small kitchen in the left corner. One large window.

One window in the men's and two smaller windows in the women's restroom.

Five booths.

Six people.

Ten barstools.

Five taken.

Nodding to the bartender standing at the far end near the three beer taps, I take the one vacant stool at the end of an occupied row. "Daryl and Billy. Should have guessed you'd be taking up space here." Looking down, four guys stare back at me.

The bartender, McGilley, swings his towel over his shoulder and rests two hands on the bar top in front of me. "Look what the cat dragged in. If it's not Mr. Eight himself, Jason Koster. To what do we owe the pleasure, your high and mighty-ness?"

"I haven't been that guy in a long time, much less that number. How about a Heineken?" That entertains the guys, and they start laughing, mocking me. If I didn't stand out already, my beer choice just did it. "Never mind. How about a Budweiser?"

"You sure about that?" McGilley asks. "That's a working man's beer. Might be hard on your stomach."

"Serve the fu—" I catch myself. I can't talk like that around here. I'll end up in a fight and spend the night in jail. "I think I can handle it." I put a ten on the counter. "Keep the change."

"Big spender." Daryl asks, "Where've you been that you

decided to come home and spend money like it doesn't matter?"

Daryl Satters grew up down the dirt road from me. He was one year ahead of me in school and got a job at the plant right out of high school. All-around asshole. I'm not surprised to see him here. I figure his ass is parked on a barstool at Red River by five each night, drinking his sorrows away just like his dad. He once dreamed of being a pro-baseball player, but that took a dedication he never had for the game. Ironic how he's worked at the same industrial plant for eight years. *That* takes dedication.

My beer is set down, and the money swiped from the bar. I take a long pull before answering. "All over."

Billy lines up and fires his question next. "What have you been doing for work?"

I always liked Billy Langston. A tick older than me but we were in the same grade. At one time, I called him one of my best friends because he always had my back. Curious to see if that loyalty still stands.

"It's good to see you, Billy."

"You too, Koster. Rumors have been flying for years about what happened to you. Did you return to put 'em to rest?"

I'm suddenly feeling the need to clamp my mouth shut. I don't owe anyone anything, much less access to parts of me I'd rather keep buried. "Nah. Let them gossip." I down my beer and set the empty on the bar when I stand. Not looking to entertain an interrogation, I'm ready to go. This might be a record. Ten minutes and I've already had my fill of this town.

The darkness I carry hangs heavy over my head. My carefree football days are long gone, so I don't need to be here any longer. "I'm heading out."

"Going to see your ma?" McGilley asks.

"Heading there now." I tap the bar top and head for the door. "See you around, gentlemen."

The sun is setting when I head down Main Street and take the curve out to the small two-bedroom house with faded blue wood siding. It's dark when I pull up the dirt drive but can tell it's not changed. I cut the engine, surprised the sound of the Harley didn't drag my mom to the window. The lights are on inside, and a few of the shades are still open. The TV is muffled but heard through the thin walls of the old house. It needs some care. If I stay more than a day or two, I can help her out, make sure things are in good working order before I leave again.

I think about walking in the back door like I always have but then decide against it. She hasn't heard from me in a few months and hasn't seen me for years, so I head to the front and knock like a stranger.

The dented metal door opens, and she pushes the screen door with her hand before leaning against the frame. A mischievous smile appears, tipping up one side. I've been told I smile the same way. Guess I learned from the best. Her hair is pinned back, but some strands from a long day of work have fallen. She's dressed like she has someplace to go, but I know better. She's a homebody by choice. Meredith Koster just likes to look good. Crossing her arms, she says, "Well, if it isn't my long-lost son. What brings you to town, kid?"

The kid reference makes me smile. It also makes me miss the innocence that the name suggests. "Just thought it was time for a visit."

She drops the hard-ass act and opens her arms. "Come here." Hugging me tight, she adds, "I've missed you so much. I don't know why you like to worry me like you do."

One front door. Two deadbolts. One chain. A screen door.

Back door. Three small windows. Two locks. Fourteen windows in total.

It feels good to hug her again. I'm way bigger than she is, having grown taller than her by the eighth grade, but she still hugs me as if I'm her baby. Backing into the house, she says, "Get on in here and close the door behind you. You're letting bugs in."

The screen door screeches closed, and I shut the front door, locking it behind me even though I've never considered myself the paranoid type. I probably should be, considering what I've been up to, but I've never felt unsafe being here.

She moves into the kitchen as I drop my backpack on the floor. Peeking out, she says, "You sure are traveling light these days."

"A couple of changes of clothes. The basics are all I need." I leave the rest out and start for the kitchen. Sidetracked by the framed photos on a bookcase, I take in my graduation photo. It's hard to miss, being she ordered the largest size. Another photo of me as the quarterback my senior year and one from my Little League days stand beside it. I don't linger too long since it reminds me of breaking my arm in college, which ended my glory days.

Bending down, I see a smaller five-by-seven from prom. I touch the glass, wishing I could caress her face again. Delilah Noelle. The belle of the ball. The queen of my heart. The town darling. We made a good-looking couple, a match in every way—good grades, big dreamers, determined to leave this town. On the surface, she was the head cheerleader who fell for the football star. *So unoriginal.* We were so much more than that to each other.

People used to say we were so sweet together we gave them a toothache. Chuckling, I lower my hand and take a breath.

"I can't seem to pack it away," my mom says.

Sounds a lot like my feelings for Delilah, despite how hard I've tried to outgrow them.

Glancing over my shoulder, I see my mom coming with two glasses of iced tea. "How long are you staying?"

She respects my privacy, homing in on the fact that I have no intention of talking about the girl in the photo or the woman across town.

I take a glass. "How long will you have me?"

"As long as you need." She curls up on the couch and takes a sip.

"I'm not hiding out, Mom."

"Okay, as long as you want then. I've cleaned your room, and you have plenty of clothes in the closet and in the dresser. I can take you out shopping tomorrow for anything else you might need."

"I don't need you to buy me things. I can afford what I need."

"How is that exactly? How do you earn money? What do you do, Jason?"

Vague is best. "Odd jobs. Here and there."

She stops pushing for answers I'm not going to give her. Standing, she asks, "Are you hungry? I was just about to make some pasta with sauce."

"That sounds good."

"You go settle in and clean up, and I'll make dinner."

I grab my bag and head down to the hall but stop when she adds, "It's good to have you home, son."

Home.

There's that word again. It's a word I haven't known in some time. *Am I home?* I'm not really sure anymore, but my mom has always been a haven, so she deserves to hear that from me. I return to give her a hug and a kiss on the cheek. "It's good to be home."

2

Jason

My childhood bedroom is a memorial to my golden years—the football star, devoted son, all-around class favorite. The whole town had their hopes and dreams pinned on me, so my fall from grace was inevitable. I was set up for it with every win, trophy, and accolade I received.

I take off my shoes and clothes, leaving my briefs on as I make my way down the hall to the one bathroom in the house. It takes a week for the water to warm up, but when it does, I let it pound the stiffness from my shoulders. With one hand propped on the tile and my head lowered, I'm still wondering why I came back. Why do I bother?

My mom?

Sure. It's always good to see her. Doesn't matter what I've done or how long it's been since we talked, she opens her arms and smiles, still proud of me. She's a good woman who works too hard. I'm going to change that and give her the life she deserves.

No one else in this town mat—lies. Lies. Lies.

Everyone knows it's a lie. I saw it in their faces down at Red River. They can see through me when it comes to Delilah.

My only true weakness. *Even after all this time.*

The one weakness I can hide when I'm *not* here.

Married . . . *fuck.*

I push the thoughts of how I got my feelings all fucked up back to the dark compartment I keep them hidden in. I think that's my heart, but I'm not sure anymore.

Can a man who's killed another man really have a heart? It's a mystery, even to me, if I'm not allowed to feel anything other than remorse. *Remorse. Regret.* I can't seem to reason those emotions into my psyche, not when that same man wanted to kill the people I care about. I remind myself that it was a part of the job but not the job I signed up for. Who did I become once I left home? And is that guy truly gone forever like I want to believe?

The water rains down. I hope to have some sense of myself once the wicked is washed away, if it can be washed away. I have my doubts.

After showering, I wrap the towel around my waist and head to my room. I dig through old drawers until I find some boxers and flip through the hangers, choosing a black T-shirt that's not too faded. Grabbing a pair of black jeans from a stack on top of a crate in the closet, I pull those on too. Black fits me better these days than the gold of my old uniform.

The leather of my shoes is wet from the road, so I pad to the living room like I still live here. My mom sets down two plates with the hot pasta on top of the coffee table.

She smiles, looking surprised. "And here I thought that dirt was freckles."

"Ha. Ha." Sitting on the couch, I lean forward over the

coffee table, ready to shovel it in. "This looks good. Thanks, Ma."

"It feels good to cook for someone else again."

Despite the distraction of dinner and *Wheel of Fortune* playing on the TV, I can feel the slight tension in the room. I spin my fork around on my plate, taking a big bite. As I continue to eat, I don't have to make small talk with her. We're casual people, the kind that manners matter, and when we slip up, we're forgiven. I keep eating and glance over at her. "What's on your mind?"

That catches her attention and gives her the opening she's been waiting for since I showed up on her front porch. "Are you going to tell me why you're home, and why I didn't get a heads-up?"

"Can't a son visit his mom?"

"Any time, any day. You're always welcome. I haven't seen you in a long time, so I didn't know if I should be worried or not."

I take a drink of my tea, the ice crashing around the glass, then reply, "No need to worry. Just stopping by on my way through."

"Through to where?"

"Not sure. I don't have plans right now."

Reaching over, she pats my leg. "Then stay a while."

"I might. Not sure yet."

She sits back with her glass, staring at the TV. "Aurora borealis."

"What?"

"The puzzle," she answers with an all-knowing grin. "It's aurora borealis."

I smile. "Sure is. Good job." She always was underestimated in this miserable town.

An hour passes with ease, but my body is starting to give

up the fight to stay awake. I'm weary from being on the road, and the thought of that bed in the other room is heaven. I gather our dishes and clean up the trash. I refill Mom's glass and get her the blanket from the couch, helping her settle in for the night.

"You staying up?" I ask.

"There's an old Cary Grant movie coming on that I want to watch, and I'm halfway through a very intriguing book. Are you going to bed?"

"I am. I'm tired."

"Tomorrow's Saturday."

"I want to help out. Anything I can do around here for you?"

"I appreciate that. I have a list we can start on if you don't mind."

"I don't mind," I reply, walking toward the hall.

"Maybe we can talk about the subject you're so eager to avoid, too."

Maybe not. I'm not used to having anyone care about my thoughts. That probably won't or shouldn't change while I'm here. "Yeah, maybe. Night, Ma."

"Good night, Jase."

After readying for bed, I climb under the covers and let my body sink into the mattress. It's a cheap bed, but it's worn in all the right spots to fit my body. Delilah used to complain about rolling into the middle. Secretly, I loved it. I loved holding her close like that, my lips against the back of her neck, my nose full of her scent—like a citrus summer and a warm vanilla winter—and my arms cradled around her with no space left between us.

I didn't expect to have such a visceral reaction to being home again, especially while lying in this bed alone. It almost feels like I never left.

Almost. Until I remember what I've been doing the past four years, what I've done . . . It's a life I can never drag anyone into much less my mom *or* Delilah. Not like she's an option anyway, considering she's married.

Why the fuck do I keep having to remind myself of that fact? I just can't seem to wrap my head around it.

I get up and squat down next to the mattress. Lifting it, I dig around a few dirty magazines until I find what I'm looking for. The blinds are cracked enough to let a little moonlight drift inside the small room. I lie back down and hold the photo above me. Those little summer dresses Delilah wore back then drove me wild.

Easy access is the term that comes to mind, but it wasn't like that with us. She was never easy in my eyes . . . I'm not sure how our relationship got out of hand so fast. After four years of dating, almost to the day, we were breaking up. Junior year in high school to junior year in college.

Football season.

One minute, we were fighting about me getting a full-ride scholarship to a university on the other side of the state and transferring the next semester. Then she was walking back to town with me driving behind her, begging her to get back in the truck.

She never did.

That whole situation was a clusterfuck. It didn't matter how many times I called her, texted, or stopped by her house; she shut me out. As a last resort, I poured my heart into a letter I never had the fucking nerve to send. Billy brought the beers. The letter became a part of the night when I threw a match on top. I watched it burn as though I was watching my heart catch fire. The ashes floated toward the sky, and I wished the pain I felt inside would go along with it.

I was almost convinced I could move on from loving her, but four years isn't easily forgotten, especially in a small town where everything held a memory of happier times.

On a cold day just before New Year's Eve, almost three months after the worst day of my life, I detoured by her daddy's farm in one last sad attempt to talk to her.

I then realized why my best friend had been too busy to hang out. Cole Cutler's truck was parked proudly in front of her house. I'd been wondering why he hadn't returned my calls, and why he wasn't hanging out with the guys when we went out. He stopped showing up for our Sunday fishing trips. Cutler also got called out in football practice for unnecessary roughness against the quarterback—aka me.

I didn't get the chance to confront him or talk to her before they made their couple debut on a Friday night at Red River.

Billy remained by my side, the only one I trusted. He hung out with me all summer. He didn't discuss Delilah but let me when I felt the need. I realized it wasn't about the quantity of friends I had, but the quality that mattered. We built my mom a new fence with all the spare time we had to burn before I returned to college in the fall.

I said goodbye to my mom and almost took the long route out of town, passing by the Noelle farm. *Almost.*

Instead, I took Main and hit the highway. I was gone and had no plans to come back. I would play college football on a scholarship and then get drafted into the NFL.

Sometimes, life doesn't go as planned.

Sometimes, you don't end up playing pro ball.

Sometimes, you don't get the girl.

Sometimes, you find yourself living a life you never expected.

Sometimes, you wish you could go back and change the things you regret the most.

Wiggling the lock on the window, I test its strength. The blinds are bent, but the seal is solid around the glass. The house is safe, but I'll double-check it once my mom goes to bed.

Because sometimes, you become a man who has an exit plan to escape the life you created.

I drop the photo on the nightstand, giving it more respect than being forgotten among my old stash of magazines and start to wonder if I should stop by the farm while I'm in town.

3

Delilah Rae Noelle

Jason Koster rolled into town as though he still owned it. He just might, considering he's the talk of the town after only being back a week.

Just like old times.

It's not as if the locals have anything better to gossip about, but I don't like being thrown into the mix. I've managed to keep most of my drama at bay despite Cole's best efforts. But here I am at the center of everyone's chatter because I once dated the hometown hero.

And then he broke my heart.

I felt a surge of giddiness when I first got wind he was back. That flew out the window when I started to worry how Cole would react. I've finally found a peaceful co-existence with him in this godforsaken town, but now this will stir everything right back up.

From the time they were five and catching tadpoles out on the shores of the lake, Jason and Cole had been best friends until I came between them. Insecurity and immaturity sent me into the arms of someone who should have never been more than a friend.

Among other hard lessons, I've learned the word catastrophe is also spelled C-O-L-E C-U-T-L-E-R.

I've made amends with myself over my role in that relationship and marriage. Amends with lingering regrets. I made things as right as I could with the people I hurt—the people I always loved and who cared about me, like Meredith Koster. She'd been like a second mother to me when my own mother passed away.

My sister, who'd endured snide comments about what a whore I was. *Endured*, minus the time she knocked Sabrina Smith right in the kisser for calling me a slut. Shelby Noelle had never been in a fight prior, much less clocked someone, but everyone has their limits, and Sabrina Smith pushed my sister's that day. Sabrina still crosses the street when she sees the Noelle sisters. She was a mean girl all through school, so it's not a loss to us.

Billy Langston is one of my constants. If you would have asked me at fifteen if the geeky kid who had lanky legs and a really bad sense of humor would one day be the only man I relied on, I would have laughed all night. Now I know better. Sometimes, the underdogs become the true heroes.

He's been there more times than I can count and has stood by me. I've never asked him why. I often wonder what his answer will be, but I'm afraid to ask in case it changes things. Both he and Daryl were caught in the middle of this ugly triangle back in the day, but while Daryl firmly took Cole's side against Jason, Billy is a trusted ally of mine.

I've dropped more than a few hints to my sister about possibly hooking them up. Billy's outgrown those gangly legs, and his sense of humor is better than I remembered. He has made me laugh more than I imagined possible.

Now that Jason's back, I'm curious how that might affect my relationship with Billy. I've noticed he's not around as much, but I don't say anything. Jason is one of his best friends. I imagine they've picked up as if no time has passed at all.

It's times like these I wish my sister still lived here. She'd stop me from getting in my truck, or she'd go with me to keep me from stopping by Meredith's house. Here I am, cranking the key, begging my old truck not to start, to give me a reason to control my curiosity. It starts, and I roll my eyes. At the entrance to the farm, I'm greeted by Billy's familiar truck blocking my exit. We stare at each other for a second before he gets out and comes toward my door.

Gripping the steering wheel, I feel hot as though he can read my intentions. "Hi," I say, trying to sound casual.

"I just picked up the order from the feed store. Where ya going?"

"I, uh, wanted to get to the market before they close," I lie, hating myself for doing it, but my pride keeps it alive. "I'm craving ice cream."

He checks his watch. "They closed fifteen minutes ago."

"Oh," I start, turning my attention out the windshield. "Well, go on in. I'm just going for a drive then."

"Is everything okay?"

My eyes return to his, feeling even guiltier. "Fine." My fingers stiffen from holding the steering wheel so tight. I loosen my grip and stretch them. "Want to go with me?"

"Yeah. I can drive if you want or hop in your truck?"

It might be best to let him drive. At least I won't end up at the Koster residence. "I'll ride with you."

I pull my truck to the side as he turns his around. When I get in his cab, I turn on the radio, needing the distraction while he rolls down both windows. "Where to?"

Shrugging, I say, "Into town?"

"You got it."

He turns up an old country song that I haven't heard in so long. Something about wasting the summer away with someone you love until fall comes around, breaking your hearts. I relate too well. "Do you mind if I find something less . . . familiar?"

"Go for it." Signaling ahead, he says, "Cut through past Main?"

"Sounds good." He's so on to me. It would be a good time to fess up, but I find a good melody to sing along to and turn it up instead. My gaze lengthens when we near Meredith's block. I force it away, and say, "Thanks for picking up the order."

Billy's eyes are fixed ahead and mine soon follow to see the little blue house up on the right. "No worries. I was picking up mine as well."

I turn down the music like an idiot when I see the fancy motorcycle parked on the side of the house. "I heard he rode a motorcycle."

Billy finally turns to me. "What are we doing, Delilah?"

Shaking my head, I reply, "I have no idea."

"Better think fast because Jason just came around to the front of the house."

"Oh, shit." I duck, the top of my head hitting his leg. "Don't stop."

"Too late. He's looking at me. What am I supposed to do?"

"Gun it home, Billy. Don't let him see me." I hit his leg. "Why are you slowing down?"

"He's coming toward the truck. I can't just leave him in a trail of dust."

"Yes, you can."

"Hey," Jason says, his voice with some distance from the truck. My heart beats heavy in my chest, and I close my eyes, savoring the sound of hearing him again.

"Hey. Looks like you're settling in," Billy says.

"Yeah, doing what I can to help my mom out." God, he was always so good to his mom . . . to me. "Want to come in and have a few beers, catch up?"

"I need to drop some stuff off at the farm before it gets too late, but I can come by later."

"That works," Jason replies. The truck starts the slowest roll forward ever just as he adds, "Bye, Delilah."

My breath stops in my throat, my eyes squeezed closed as I pray for Billy to end this torture. "Bye," I mutter, mortification washing through me.

"See ya, man," Billy says. The road is bumpy when he pulls away, the rocks grinding under the wheels. Touching my shoulder, he starts laughing. "You can sit up. We're in the clear."

I sit up, fresh air whipping through the window and my hair. Turning to him, I pop him in the arm. "Remind me never to rob a bank with you. You're not exactly stealth."

"You're too good to rob a bank, but also, I'm very stealthy. Jason's just intuitive when it comes to you. There's no sneaking around when it comes to him."

"Can we not talk about him, his intuitiveness, or what just happened, please?"

He twists an imaginary key to his lips and then tosses it out the window. That lock can't hold. I know Billy too well. I also see that goofy grin he's wearing. "You do remember that we have to pass back by, right?"

Crap. He's right. It's the only way back to my farm. I won't hide this time despite how his voice made me feel— holy damn! His voice is one thing, but seeing him is a whole other thing. I'm not prepared. My jaw slacks open, and Billy reaches over to close my trap. "You might want to wipe the drool."

I don't have it in me to hide my reaction from him, though.

Jason Koster was incredible-looking back in high school and college, but now . . . he looks like a model from a magazine. His dark hair is long enough to lie to the side, but short enough to think that's the style he chose. A heavy dusting of stubble shadows his jaw while the intensity of his eyes pierces me, pinning me to the seat. And holy all that is great in this world, why does he have to be shirtless? Good God, I have great memories of his athletic body, but damn, how is it possible to be even better now?

"How should I know? Guess he works out," Billy replies, shrugging.

Crap. "Did I just say that out loud?"

He chuckles. "You did."

Jason's standing with a hose, watering his mom's lawn when we drive by. With a raised hand, he waves as we drive by, the water spraying high into the air. "So showy and phallic." I wriggle on the leather, tugging on my seat belt to make sure it's nice and tight.

"Now, that's where I draw the line. Don't put me between yours and Jason's pent-up sexual tension."

"What? No. That's not what I meant at all. It's like—"

"I don't want to know what it's like." He pinches the bridge of his nose. "Can we end this?"

"That's what I've been saying." Jason already knows I'm in here, so there's no point in hiding. He's wearing that stupid grin that used to do my heart in every time I saw it.

My heart doesn't swell, but it does still flutter for the man. *Why does he have to be so damn attractive?* I roll my eyes, making my own show of things, and look in the opposite direction.

Petty?

Sure.

Immature?

Definitely.

I just . . . I don't know how to feel about him being back, much less waving to me like we're old acquaintances who left on friendly terms. We didn't, so a second chance at anything—friendship or love—isn't going to happen.

Stopped at the light at Main, Billy looks across the cab at me. "That was awkward."

"It sure was."

The light turns green, and as he shifts his truck into gear, he adds, "Why do I feel like this town just got a whole lot smaller?"

I have the same feeling . . .

4

Jason

Roosters crow in the distance as I walk around the back of my mom's house to inspect it. She's almost paid it off, but I'll help her out since she wants to live here for the rest of her life. I need to make sure it's in good shape for the long haul.

My mom's been the one constant in my life. When I graduated from college, though, I didn't look back. Well, I didn't look back until thirty-six hours ago. I drove away from Kingwood Manor at peace with my role in that situation. It was a job, but it stuck with me. I'm aware of every choice I've made over the years, and I have found peace after getting a paycheck. But that one, that last job, and the friends I made, the family they became in a way, have stuck with me.

Even a good night's sleep, last night being one of the better ones in quite a while, can't erase what I've done. That's why I need to be here, grounded in the place with people who bring me back to simpler times.

Seeing the sun's rays shining over the roofline reminds me of Delilah, my *Rae* of sunshine, and I grin. She's not so sneaky, hiding in that truck like I wouldn't see her. Billy got caught up helping his dad at the farm and couldn't split a six-pack last night, but I have every intention of getting the details of that drive-by out of him soon.

Kicking a loose board on the side of the house with the toe of my boot, I mark it to replace and move to the front. As I keep checking for loose boards, I can't keep my mind off Delilah, though. And the honeysuckle bush growing wild at the corner of the porch doesn't help. Honeysuckle . . .

Delilah has spent the better part of an hour creating a floral halo, and the flowers grace her head like a crown. Her beauty is what drew me to her, but her heart—so open and loving—has me wanting to marry her.

Hovering above my head, she's upside down and smiling at me. "What are you doing, Jason?"

"Watching you." Lying on my back, I reach for her. "C'mere."

She moves around and kneels next to me. Plucking a flower from the wreath in her hair, she says, "Want some nectar?"

"Thought you'd never offer."

The flower is between her fingers when she starts to gently pull it away from the stem. I lift to rest on my elbows and watch as a satisfied smile appears. But when she offers the nectar to me, I say, "You taste it first, and then I'll taste you."

My favorite pink—Delilah blush—covers her cheeks. She has my full attention as I watch the nectar touch her tongue. Then she teases, her eyes on me, her lips tantalizing. I sit the rest of the way up and run my hand through the back of her hair. "My honeysuckle." I kiss her, tasting her honey mixed with the flower's sweetness.

. . . The screech of the screen door cuts through the mire of my thoughts. "Are you hungry?" my mom calls.

"Sure am."

"C'mon. I made eggs and bacon."

I add the front steps to my list. They need replacing before I leave again. Inside, I wash my hands and am told to sit at the table. I'm served a glass of apple juice. It's just like old times, which makes me smile. I could really use a cup of coffee but don't ask for it. My mom wants to serve her son, and I'm happy to play that part for a few days.

She sits down after setting a plate in front of me. I take a big bite and then look up. "Are you not eating?"

"I ate while I was cooking." She smiles, but I recognize that look in her eyes. It's the one that's usually followed by a compliment that I probably don't deserve, like how proud she is of me or how handsome I've become. Mom stuff. I'd hate for her to know who I really am on the inside. Elite security isn't usually a parents' chosen profession for their kid, considering the dangers of it.

I'm about to take another bite, but it's time we talk. I set my fork down and swallow some juice. "Let's do this so we can get past it."

She's always direct. I like that. I've been called direct, and I guess I got it from her. "Are you going to see her?"

Okay, not where I thought this was going. "You want me to drive over to the farm and just walk up those steps like I have business there? Mom, she's married."

"She's not married."

I hear the words, but they don't make sense. "What are you talking about?"

Resting her arms on the table, she sighs. "She's not married, Jason."

"But you told me—"

"Well," she starts while fiddling with the loose threads of the placemat, "she was married then. Now she's not."

I get up for coffee. Apple juice isn't strong enough for this conversation. If it weren't seven fifteen in the morning,

I'd be filling this mug with whiskey. With my back to her, I can feel the tension behind me as I fill the mug with hot coffee. I look back over my shoulder. "They're separated?"

"Divorced."

I lean on the counter, my palms pressing into the tile as I stare down at the stained grout. Mentally, I add this to the list of things to fix, right after I add Delilah Noelle. I don't think that can be fixed by a visit to the hardware store, but it's tempting to find out.

She says, "Finalized two months back. They separated more than a year ago. She's out on that farm by herself again. Cole moved across town to a rental behind The BBQ Shack."

"Why are you telling me this? I'm not going to be here long enough to spend my time thinking about the past."

"I think you already are. I also think she might be the reason for this spontaneous visit."

"She's not." Turning to face her, I cross my arms defiantly over my chest and lean my ass against the counter. "I thought she was married."

My mom shrugs. "Call it kismet. I think something inside you was unsettled, and we both know the best way to get settled is to visit the one that caused the uproar in the first place."

"I'm not visiting her. We left on bad terms." That's not how it went down. She left me. She left me with no explanation. But I'm not one to throw someone under the bus.

"*You* left on bad terms. She's been here all along, and if I know her at all, which I feel I know her pretty well after all these years, I think she's been waiting for you to return."

"She was married, Mom. The very definition says she wasn't waiting for me, so why fill my head with this nonsense? We both know I won't be here long, and adding that crazy back into my life won't turn out well for anyone."

She stands and walks around the table. "You're caught up in your anger and your pain. I understand, and I wish I could take it away, but that doesn't change the fact that I know you still care about her." With her mug in hand, she heads for the back door. "You know the truth now. You're the only one who gets to decide how you use it."

Before she leaves, I ask, "What about kids?" *Fuck, why'd I even ask?*

Looking back at me, she smiles. "What about them?"

"Just tell me."

"No," she replies, shaking her head. "No kids." Pushing the screen door open, she leaves, the door slamming shut behind her.

Delilah Rae Noelle isn't married. Not having any kids also surprises me. I don't have anything against the little humans. I dated a woman with two cute ones. But it takes a lot to step into the dad role. I wasn't ready to settle down at twenty-three, and the job ended, so I had to go. But I find some serious satisfaction that the world is safe, *for now*, from Cutler's offspring.

Despite the adrenaline rushing through my veins in an attempt to move my feet toward that door and drive out to the farm, my grip on the counter tightens. "No. I can't get tangled up when I'm here to untangle some of the mess I've made of my life."

Why am I talking to myself? *Fuck.* This town is already messing with my head. I grab a few more bites of breakfast, shove my list into my back pocket, and head out to the bike.

My mom comes out and tries to hand me money. "Here."

Folding her hand closed, I say, "I don't need your money. Keep it. You've been getting the money I sent, right?"

"Yes, and about that, I have it saved in a box hidden in the house." She shifts with a tilt of her head. "It's yours. Not mine."

"No, it's yours. That's why I sent it." I swing my leg over the seat and settle into the leather while righting the bike.

"Honey, I don't need your money."

"Save it for retirement then."

Taking a step back, she eyes my bike. "That motorcycle looks expensive. Harleys aren't cheap. I've worried a lot about you over the years, but do I need to worry about this?"

"No. I've done okay the past couple of years," I reply, trying to avoid what I've really been doing. "I wouldn't bring trouble to your doorstep. I'm heading down to General Hardware to get a few things."

"You might want to take the truck then." She walks to the garage and punches in a code. The door slides up, and there's my old truck. "You're not going to be able haul more than a few nails on that Harley."

She's right. I move it to the side out of the way and get off. Tossing me the keys, she says, "You can charge everything to my account there. I'm sure Fred will remember you."

He'll remember me all right. He busted Cole, Billy, and me stealing a tractor to joyride through the fields one night. Deputy Whaley let us go after a few hours, saying he was tired of our laughing. We were disturbing the peace of the jail. Coach came down to haul us to the field that night and worked us hard until the sun hit high noon. We'd dropped and lay there until my mom and Delilah showed up with turkey sandwiches and water, giving us just enough energy to get our sorry asses home. I pulled the drunk card.

Bad move on my part.

I was grounded for a week—no after-school fun, no

phone, and no Delilah—and learned my lesson. Don't be a dick and don't screw up. Stay on the right side of the law, although that one didn't sink in the way it should have when I reflect on the past few years of my life.

An hour later, I have everything loaded into the back of the truck and pay Mr. Carver for the supplies. There's no way in hell I'm sticking my mom with this bill.

"Say hi to your mom," he says.

I give him a glare similar to the one I've used with the guys right before they were fucked up for whatever offense they committed against my former clients. Getting into the truck, I'm about to leave when Billy shows up in his beat-up old Dodge and parks next to me. With my window down, I say, "I can't believe that old clunker still runs."

He gets out and leans on the open window of my truck. "Yeah, she's sweet when she wants to be."

"Sounds a lot like Lou. How is Lorraine these days?"

"Married to some accountant two towns over."

Shaking my head, I shift into park. "I always thought you guys would make it."

"Some could say the same about you and Delilah."

"Yeah, some could, but we all know how that turned out."

Looking inside the cab, he says, "She's in good shape."

"I didn't get a good look yesterday, but she always was."

He barks out a laugh. "The truck. Your mom has kept her in good shape."

"Oh, yeah. She keeps her in the garage and drives her around every now and again."

Silence slips in, an awkwardness that never used to exist back in high school. He finally says, "About yesterday—"

Leaning forward, I look through the windshield. "I should get back. It's gonna rain."

Looking up at the sky, he says, "You need help getting that wood covered?"

"Nah. I got it."

Backing up, he says, "Beers later? I'll even bring the fancy stuff."

Considering I have no idea how long I'm staying, I keep thinking it's best if I keep the people at a distance. But he makes me laugh, and I could use a few more. "Yeah, come over later. I don't know about fancy. I'll drink a Pabst or Bud with you if you prefer."

His keys jingle as he shoves them in his pocket. "I'll bring some over."

"Cool." I shift the truck into reverse and look through the back window. "Come by whenever."

He taps the top of the truck. "See ya, man."

Eyeing those gray clouds in the sky, I should head straight back, but my better senses left me the minute I found out Delilah's divorced. I take the scenic route out toward her house. There's a white truck parked in front of the Noelle house when I drive by the farm. It's not practical in color, and the rain is going to ruin that just washed shine, but if that truck's hers, I like that she's damning the elements of this town. If it's not . . . I swallow hard, my ego caught like a lump in my throat.

I keep driving, wanting to get the wood unloaded before the rain sets in.

5

Jason

After unloading the back of the truck and covering everything with a tarp, Billy pulls up. "Perfect timing," I say sarcastically.

"You didn't want my help, remember?" He's got a six-pack of Heineken in one hand, so he's forgiven.

Since he has a bouquet in the other, I add, "If you're looking to get laid, you came to the wrong house."

"I brought your mother the flowers, fucker."

I cross my arms over my chest defensively. "Umm, back up there. Why?"

He starts laughing. "I'm not hitting on your mom. She may be pretty, but yeah, not my speed." He hands me the beer. "Brought your girly beer for you. The flowers are for the last time I was here. I ran over her flower bed, and she was pissed."

Chuckling, I say, "I remember that."

"Figured I'd make amends. Better late than never."

Amends. Can a sinner of my stature make amends, or am

I a boot too deep into hell already? I force my thoughts back to the here and now. "Come on."

After he schmoozes my mom with the flowers, we pop the top on two beers and grab a seat out back. He sits on the patio steps, and I sit on a plastic white chair near the rusting swing where I used to sit with Delilah.

Her fingerprints are still on every part of my old life. It's only a dumb swing from my childhood, but the only memories I seem to recall are the ones where she sat next to me, resting her cheek against the cold metal while the tips of her sneakers dug into the dirt.

She'd been the only one who could get me to open up about my feelings. I shared so much with her—my fears about football, the loss of my father, my worries about my mom. We saw shooting stars sitting on this swing. We laughed, and we fell in love. I thought those times mattered to her like they did me, but I guess having your first love break your heart is just another part of growing up.

One good thing about Billy is he never needed to fill the quiet. I didn't, either. Still don't. We talk when we have something worth mentioning. Other than that, it's just good to have the company. I finally ask, "What are you doing these days?"

"I'm part-time coaching out at the high school. Assisting the offensive line coach."

"No shit?"

He laughs. "Yeah, no shit. The extra money saved my parents' place from foreclosure."

"What's going on with the farm?"

"They were turned down a few years back for an extension on a loan. I was already full-time at the plant in Cedars, so I sold my stuff, moved back home, and added coach onto the résumé."

"Sorry to hear about your folks. How's everything now?"

"Good. Besides the coaching, I'm still working at the plant but moved to supervisor, and I help a friend out on their farm as much as I can. We gotta look out for our neighbors."

"Yeah," I say, nodding. That small-town spirit shines in his words. "Congrats on all that. It's good to keep busy."

"It is. We've changed our crops. We used to be straight corn. Now it's all about the soybean. At least this year."

"Wow, that is a big change."

"Corn syrup's out. Soy milk's in."

"We do what we have to do to survive." I know this better than anyone.

I'll never forget finding that sweet girl I met in the mountains curled on the gravel, on the paler side of death. Any innocence she'd managed to hold on to was gone as she gasped for life. That fucker stole her hope and nearly her life.

It's the only time my professional life became personal.

The actions of vengeance have a way of sticking with you. That fucker who shot her slept with his arm stretched toward the nightstand. I could put money down that his gun was in the top drawer. I took the shot. No, I'll never forget, but I refuse to sink into the abyss of guilt or remorse. He deserves neither.

I'm starting to think I sold more than my soul that night, if surviving was only something I did physically.

He finishes a beer and grabs another. "So, what have you been doing?"

For anyone else, this would be an easy question to answer, but for me, it's one I'm always thinking about how I'll answer. I give him the rehearsed response, "Odd jobs here and there. Worked on a fishing boat in Alaska and a mini-mart in the northeast. Hauled lumber in Northern California, and worked on a cattle farm in Oklahoma."

"Never used your business degree?"

"You know," I say, thinking about this harder than I should, "I kind of use it all the time. I just don't get the bragging rights around the water cooler."

"Ah." He drinks more and then leans back on the screen door.

I'm not sure if the chair is going to hold much longer, so I don't tempt it by readjusting. "What happened with you and Lou?"

"Too much to remember. It's just easier to say we were together too young, and I couldn't give her the life she wanted." He doesn't sound as regretful as I feel over my screwed-up relationship with Delilah.

"Yeah, sometimes I wonder . . . *Ah, fuck it*. It's not worth the effort to worry about what could've been."

"That's for sure." He tosses the first can toward a bin a little ways away from where he's sitting but misses. "I still see Cole every now and again." His humorless laugh leaves me curious, but he adds, "Not by choice."

I toss my can from across the yard and make it in the bin. "What an asshole." I laugh. I thought I could hide my disdain better. Guess not.

"Every time I see him, I wanna punch his fucking lights out. Hands up." He tosses me a beer.

"You should, the fucking wife beater. If I'd been around —" *Fuck*. I crack it open and chug the first half, trying to drown the anger growing inside.

He lifts his hat and scratches his head. "I hear ya. I paid him a visit two times to make sure the shit would stop."

"Apparently, it didn't work."

His eyes hit mine. "She was good at hiding behind lies."

"Can't hide bruises," I snap back.

"She wasn't my wife, and I wasn't inspecting her body. You got a problem with me, Koster?"

My hand starts crushing the can. I've learned what I'm capable of. I've learned that it's hard to come back from the darkness once it gets a hold on you. Anger is a surefire way to have me seeing red, to dig deep and let that darkness back in. That red will turn to gray, and the rest of the world will fade away, except for one thing—my target.

Cole Cutler.

My former best fucking friend.

He saw his chance to take my place and took it, stabbing me in the back like we didn't have a long history behind us.

I may not have had many years with my dad, but his life always revolved around my mom, me, and his love of sports. From coaching me in T-ball at three to tackle football at five right before he died, he told me to always work hard and to do my best, but if you're not having fun, then it's not worth it.

When he died, I did my best. It helped that playing sports was the only fun I had left. It became my escape, and I became even better. Thinking back on those sports and every team I played on, Cole had always been right there next to me. Football was an escape for Cole. My house. Our friendship. He'd made for a good partner and a great teammate. He'd been someone I counted on. His father had been an asshole, but we'd been like brothers. Why the fuck he went after Delilah . . . *Can't go there.*

We make a beer run just after eight and keep driving like the days he might recall as the good old days. I'm not feeling nostalgic quite yet, but I can get on board with a few good times we had. I look over at Billy, and suddenly, I feel like I'm eighteen again with the world at my feet. "Remember when we used to go fishing every Sunday? The sun hadn't even come up, and we'd be heading out."

"We were still drunk."

"Were we ever sober?"

"I don't know," he replies. "I was too drunk to remember."

His Dodge slows to a crawl, and he switches the headlights off. I don't have to look out across that field to know where we are. I know this route better than any. I know *her* like the back of my hand.

The truck stops, and he turns off the engine. I take a long pull of my beer before I turn my attention to the farmhouse. The living room and kitchen lights are on, and the TV casts a blue tint across the corner windows.

Letting my gaze wander up a story to the second floor, I see her bedroom light on and the bathroom connected to it lit up. She owns that farm now, her parents long passed. Does she still sleep in that room? The one with pink-striped wallpaper and a full-sized bed atop a squeaky metal frame? I can't see the side of the house where I used to climb up the trellis to the roof and run across to sneak into her bedroom. Wonder if that trellis is still there?

He looks at me, his jovial mood wiped from his eyes. "I'm sorry."

"Why?"

"I took her to the emergency room once."

I'm not ready to dig this deep, but since he's brought it up . . . "Why?" My stomach tenses as my grip around the can tightens, crushing the aluminum before I toss it out the window into the bed of the truck.

"I should have stopped him."

"Were you there?"

"No, but my warnings weren't enough. I knew he had a

drinking problem. He'd picked a fight with me earlier that night outside Red River. She'd just gotten back into town, so I guess he decided to take it out on her later."

Staring out the window, I avoid looking at him. I don't want to hear his confession. I don't want to see his guilt. Because then it'll become mine, and I don't owe anybody anything.

Lies.

Lies.

Lies.

I owe her. I owe her better than she got. I was across the country when I first heard the rumor. *Cutler hit his wife.* The same girl he claimed to want enough to screw me over.

Back in school, Cole never struggled to get a girl's attention if he wanted it. He'd tell everyone how he hooked up with the popular girls and then ventured across county lines for what he called fresh meat. He was the guy who bragged in the locker rooms and teased you relentlessly if you didn't score with a girl.

Except for me.

We had a silent agreement—the bullshit put on for others didn't fly between us. I knew beneath that attitude he was a good guy. He'd only slept with two girls, but I kept his secret safe to protect his rep.

"He knew we had a fight. He was waiting for that moment and then pursued her. But after kicking my heart to the sidelines, why did she want him?"

She still owns parts of me that others will never see, and I'm left wondering why. Why him over me? Why didn't she fight for us? Those questions were packed away with the baggage I carried with me. The details weighing down my rucksack with emotional bullshit I've tried to shed across the miles.

"I don't know." Billy says, "The night he hit her, he only spent one night in jail for it."

"One night?" I repeat. One fucking night for hitting the love of my life.

Why'd she fucking stay?

She had eight hours to get the fuck out of there, but she stayed. I rub my hand over my forehead in frustration. "I don't understand why you didn't get her out. He hit the woman I love."

He glances my way but then turns toward the steering wheel. "Love?"

"Huh?"

"You said the woman you love."

Love. *Present tense.* Shit. "Loved. Anyway, this is about you. He hit a woman you've been friends with for years."

"Delilah's forgiven me."

"I haven't."

"Join the club, because I haven't either."

The cicadas fill the air, and we've drank enough. Too much has been stirred up for one night. "We should go."

6

Jason

The love of my life has bounced around my head since the errant thought last night.

The love of my life.

The love of my life.

What the . . .? *No.*

It makes no sense. I loved Delilah, but the love of my life? I'm twenty-six. I have a lot of life left to live. It's a stretch to call the girl I started dating when I was seventeen the love of my life. My logical side can argue that it was nothing more than teenage lust mixed with hormones. That makes sense. *But love of my life?* Not so much.

That thought mixed with the pouring rain has really put a damper on my day.

Sundays are supposed to be lazy, but I'm not used to sitting around. I only bought supplies to fix the issues out back, so by four o'clock, I'm going stir-crazy. Standing abruptly, I accidentally scare my mom in the process when I storm through the living room. She jumps, her book flying from her hands. "What are you doing?" she asks, holding her chest over her heart.

"I'm going for a ride."

Turning behind her, she looks out the window, then turns back. "It's pouring out there."

"I'm used to riding in all kinds of weather."

"I don't want you getting sick, Jason."

"I won't. I just need to burn off some of this energy. I'm not used to sitting around doing nothing."

She's staring at me with concern written through the soft lines of her face. "You can relax here, son."

My shoulders drop some of the burden they were holding. "I know. I'm just going for a ride." After working all those years for my last boss, hanging around and watching, I should have gotten used to being still. Patient. But not here. My mind is active and on alert as though I'm still on someone's payroll. I don't feel like I'm *home*. Not like I used to. I need something to alleviate the restlessness in my veins. I need out. Fresh air. A new view.

"Okay. Will you be home for dinner?"

"I'm not sure. Don't wait for me. I can always make a sandwich when I get back."

"All right." She's done trying to talk me out of it, and I appreciate the space she's giving me. Kicking her feet on the coffee table, she opens her book again. "Be careful. Those curves get dangerous when wet."

"Don't worry."

"I always worry," she replies.

"Sorry about that."

"Don't be sorry." Her eyes return to her book. "Just be safe."

I slip on my leather jacket and tighten the laces on my black shoes before leaving. The loud muffler of my Harley is a musical masterpiece, owning the chorus of the road while I ride.

The thing about small towns, though, is they're small. There aren't a lot of places to get away from it all unless you find a cranny down by the river to hide inside. Or you own property that doesn't back up to the main roads. No, privacy isn't a specialty of small towns, so I decide it's time to stop hiding and make my presence known. With my chest puffed out and my emotional armor in place, I drive straight to the Noelle farm.

I even rev the engine when I drive up the muddy driveway as if to prove some point I've already forgotten.

She always loved rainy days, so I shouldn't be surprised to find her outside. The bike is stopped before I take a good long look at her sitting on that front porch.

Delilah Rae Noelle looks younger than her years. Always did, but damn, if seeing her now doesn't make a million memories come back as if they were yesterday.

Her hair is twisted on top of her head, but that blond still shines. She moves to the railing, leaning against it as if she sees me every damn day. Even from here, I can see that sparkle in her blue eyes, an expectation I always hoped I could fulfill when she looked at me. I would have done anything for her.

Except the one time I didn't think twice, never thought of her or how my choices would affect us. I was selfish, but I've learned a lot since then. I'm curious whether she still smells of vanilla, or if she's changed to her usual summer scent. I run my fingers through my hair, hoping to tame what must look a mess from the rain and riding, and take a deep breath.

When she smiles and waves at me as though we're old friends, I cut the engine and swing my leg off the bike.

Shoving my hands into the pockets of my wet leather jacket, I start walking. With only four steps dividing us, I grab the railing. It needs a good paint job, and it's unstable. I add it to my mental list of tasks to take care of, though I know good and well that taking care of her is no longer my job.

Four years is a long damn time not to see the beauty who stands before me. Not even knowing why I'm here, I say, "Hi," to see where it leads.

She rocks back on her bare feet and smiles so wide the rain has trouble hiding her sunshine. "What took you so long?"

"I got here as fast as I could." I take another step up, and she turns as if I'm welcome on that rickety old porch of hers. "With a few minor detours along the way."

"I'd say."

I cover the last two steps, which leaves only a few feet between us. Leaning her backside against the railing, she says, "I never thought I'd see you again, but here you are, looking like all sorts of trouble in all black."

Little flowers against a white background, straps that wrap over her shoulders . . . I shouldn't like the sight of her as much as I do. "I like your dress."

Her cheeks pinken like the color of my mom's roses in her backyard. "Well, are you gonna give me a proper hello, Jason Koster, or are we going to pretend we never danced in the moonlight?"

There's my Delilah.

He didn't destroy her.

"No pretending over here." I go to her and wrap my arms around her, my eyes closing, my senses on high alert. She always awakened all of me, and today is no different as my whole body responds to her. Vanilla with a hint of orange—

the perfect combination. She smells so good, like home and sunshine. But she's not my home to lay claim to anymore.

I feel her cheek rub against my neck before she lowers back on her feet and our arms return to our sides. Her eyes are cast down when she steps back. I want to lift her chin, to touch her again just to feel the surge through my body, but I don't.

"I'm all wet."

"Sorry."

"It's okay." It sounds like it is too. When she finally looks up, she asks, "I heard you were back and had to see for myself. What brings you by the farm?"

Gossip. It spreads as fast as a phone call in this town.

I rest my shoulder against the column, smiling that she tried her best to hide that curiosity when she and Billy drove by yesterday. "Figured I should since rumors were going to be spread anyway."

"So you came by to nip it in the bud or to start the rumor mill spinning?"

The right side of my mouth lifts higher. "Maybe a little of both."

She smiles, but it falls quicker than it appeared. Her eyes are set on her toes, a dark pink dotting the nails of each. "You know, Cole's going to hear about this." The change is fast, her sunshine gone. Does she fear Cutler finding out that I visited?

"Not if you don't tell him."

Her gaze flashes to mine. "I don't talk to him unless I'm court ordered."

"What kind of court is ordering you to talk to him?"

The rain has become the most fascinating thing around when she turns away and reaches out to catch a few drops.

"You've been gone a long time. I think you've forgotten what it's like to live here."

"Yeah. Maybe." I reach out and take her hand in mine, bringing it under the shelter of the roof. Tapping the water that pooled in her palm, I say, "Maybe you can remind me."

She pulls her hand away, the last drops falling to the wood floor. As if she caught herself in a compromising position, she backs away from me and gives me a cold shoulder. "You know," she starts, staring out over the long drive leading up to the house. "It was good to see you, Jason, but I think it's best if you go."

What just happened? "Why?"

Her smile is gone, and an unfamiliar sadness creeps onto her face. She lowers her head for the third time in the past few minutes, and it looks all wrong on her. She moves across the porch, opens the screen door, and steps inside. "It's getting late."

Before it has a chance to slam closed, I catch it. "Talk to me, Delilah."

I see her chest rise and fall with a heaviness that wasn't there in the lighthearted moment we shared a minute earlier. "Don't say my name like that."

"Like what?"

"Like you still care."

"I do," I reply too quickly to replace it with the lie I should have told.

"Then don't." She tugs the screen door, and I release it, letting it slam shut. "I think it's best if you don't visit me again." She moves into the darkness of her house, and the front door is closed.

One lock.

Two locks.

One chain slides into place.

I'm tempted to ring the doorbell, but I'm in shock by the turn in her demeanor. Remaining there too long, I finally turn away when it's obvious she's not going to open that door again.

I mount my bike and start it, but before I drive away, I glance back at the house. She's quick to hide to the side of the window, but not before I caught her spying. What's going on? *Why the sudden change?* Is it Cutler? He scares her, but he doesn't scare me.

I leave because I'm over being wet and the path to her farmhouse will become a mud pit if I don't get out of here soon. I maneuver around the watery potholes on my way to the street. Once I'm on pavement again, I take off as if I have someplace I'm supposed to be. I don't. Delilah made it clear I'm not welcome around here, so why stick around where I'm not wanted?

It might be time to start mapping out a game plan. I have about a week's worth of stuff to do around my mom's house and then what? Where do I want to go? What do I want to do?

Jobs always found me after landing in LA. I was spotted by a scout at the beach working out. Boom. I was hired for stunt work. Then by an actor I met on set. We grabbed a few beers and partied together on the regular. He made a few headlines around Hollywood and asked me to cover him. The money was good, but then I was a free agent and scooped up by referral by a visiting dignitary.

I liked working in the private sector with my last boss, but almost getting killed several times over wasn't fantastic. The thought of just hanging around a bit and working on things that don't have me sleeping with one eye open sounds nice. I'll put a few feelers out.

I arrive at my mom's still hell-bent out of shape over that

farewell with Delilah. I dash inside and shake my jacket off just inside the kitchen door. My mom comes around the corner with two towels. "Looks like the rain won this round."

"I wasn't in the mood to fight." *With Delilah,* but I let it reside as if that response fits her comment.

"Take your shoes off and let them dry out here. I'll hang your jacket up to drip dry in the bathroom. Go change and bring me these wet clothes. I'm starting a load."

Toeing off one of my shoes, I look up at her. "You don't have to wait on me like I'm a kid."

"You don't have to be so resistant to help. We all need it every now and again."

"Is this really about clothes? I have a feeling it's not."

She takes my shoes and moves them off to the side of the door. "Everything I say doesn't have to mean more than the words I choose."

"Fine." I strip off my wet shirt and cut through the kitchen to the laundry room to dump it into the washer. "You were actually talking to me about wet clothes." I strip off my soaked socks and add them in too. I pass back through the kitchen and head for my room.

"Jason? What's wrong?"

Shutting my door, I strip off the rest of my clothes and pull on some pajama pants and a T-shirt I yank from the closet. When I return to put the rest in the washing machine, I pass my mom as she sips a glass of tea. Her eyes follow me, but she doesn't say a word.

When I return, I do. "She told me not to come around anymore and shut the door in my face. Is that what you want to hear?"

Her glass is set down, and she angles her head to really

look at me—right in the eyes. "No, that makes me sad to hear. I'm sorry."

Leaning back against the opposite counter, I sigh. "You don't have to be. I wasn't planning on staying long. Just long enough to help you out, and then I'll be out of your hair again. Delilah obviously wants nothing to do with me, so she can go about her life as if I never stopped by at all."

She crosses the small kitchen and hugs me, resting her head on my shoulder. "I don't want you out of my hair, Jason. I like you being home. I miss you and wish I saw you more, not less."

I lean down and look at my mom. She's always been strong—a single mother since my dad died when I was five—and worked full-time, even if it took two jobs to get the hours. Never missed a Friday night game of mine—whether home or away.

She's the one person who would be most disappointed to know the depths I've sunk during my time away. Somehow, even with mother's intuition, she hasn't seen the black of my soul. She's looked past the dead in my eyes, in my heart, that allowed me to do my job—*and do it well.*

Detachment was key. When I finally thought I could befriend someone, it put them at risk. Is it safe to attach myself now—to her again, to this town, and the people here with so much unsettled? "I'm not running out the door. Not yet anyway."

"I'll take what I can get. Or I'll bake your favorite cake to tempt you to stay."

Embracing her again, I say, "I never could resist your chocolate cake."

"Good. Now that it's settled, and you're going to stick around a bit, can I get you something to eat?"

Giving in to her dream is easy when I'm around her. "I'd like that."

"Head into the living room and find us something to watch tonight."

I do as I'm told and settle on the couch. As I flip through the stations, my eyes keep shifting to the right, straight to that prom picture. When everyone looks dated and awful, there's Delilah Noelle looking gorgeous even in her sister's hand-me-down prom dress. I get up and set the frame face-down and return to the couch. Continuing through the channels, I stop when I reach a Marvel movie.

The problem is, I'm still too distracted. I'd like to blame the frame, but I know it doesn't matter whether I can see the photo or not; that woman is ingrained in my brain. Delilah may not have been the reason for my return, but she's suddenly become the reason I'm staying. That, and my mom and her chocolate cake.

Getting up once more, I position the frame the way it was before and return to the couch just as my mom comes in with a plate of snacks. Glancing between the photo and me, she's about to say something, but I cut her off before she has a chance. "Just let it go, okay?"

"I wasn't going to say anything."

I look up with raised eyebrows, contesting that last statement with just a look.

Rolling her eyes, she confesses, "Fine. I'll wait until tomorrow."

"Thank you."

"You're welcome."

"I'm talking about the snacks."

"Oh," she says, then laughs. "You're welcome for that, too."

God, I love my mom.

7

Jason

After only five days of being back, I'm already feeling like I could hang around a little longer. Sure, Delilah has kept her distance, and I've kept mine, but it's been nice working around the house during the day and kicking it at night with Billy. I haven't felt as restless. Working with my hands has been calming on my mind. It keeps my attention focused on the task at hand instead of the million angles that someone might be playing to feed their greed like in previous jobs.

I've managed to avoid Cole Cutler, *thank fuck*, due to our schedules running opposite so far. The evening starts off casual, and I'm catching up with McGilley while Billy keeps the tab open. I've never been one for loose lips, but the easy nature of being parked on a barstool like the guys beside me have been for the past four or five years, I find myself talking about some of my adventures. I leave the illegal parts out. The talk is light with laughter as good times are being re-lived.

The door swings open, and I hear a few guys call out his name. "Cutler."

That's what I get for getting cozy in this town.

I'm tempted to turn and look when the conversation goes quiet, but I keep my focus on the pint glass in front of me. One by one, I hear him greet the guys, and then he's behind me. Billy says, "There's a free stool at the other end of the bar. I reckon it would be best if you take a seat down there, Cutler."

Cutler ignores him, his eyes already burning a hole in the back of my head. I feel it, every nerve in my body ready to fight. I still won't give him the satisfaction of my recognition. Fuck him.

"Well. Well. Welllllll. If it ain't the great number eight himself, Jason Koster." His hand lands hard on my shoulder, and he squeezes. "It's been a while, old friend."

Cracking my neck to the opposite side, I pick up my glass and down a swig before turning and looking back over my shoulder. "Not long enough."

"Nope." He slides in on the other side of me and pats the bar. McGilley already has a pint ready and sets it down. "It's on Koster," he tells him. With a fake smile plastered on his face, he leans closer. "Thanks for the beer, bud."

"You can thank Billy since he's buying."

He holds his glass up. "Thanks." Not wasting time, he gulps it down like it's water. Making a production, he pushes it toward McGilley. "Another." His breath is heavy, his shoulders weighing him down.

I can tell this is going to turn into something more, so I swivel to leave. My shoulder is smacked down again, and he says, "Here to visit your mom? Your girl? What dragged your sorry ass back to town?"

"Here we go," Billy says. "Cool it, Cutler. We're just catching up on old times here. No harm. No foul."

Bopping his head, he adds. "Oh, that's right. You don't have the girl. She's mine."

Maybe I'll stick around a little longer. I take another pull from the glass, and then reply, "Not from what I've gathered."

"What did you say, Koster?"

Turning to Cutler for the first time, I look him dead in the eyes. "I said, not from what I've gathered."

My shoulder is shoved, but I catch myself before I fall. Billy is on his feet and pushing Cutler back against the bar. "Get off me. Fucking assholes." He shrugs out of Billy's hold, giving up the fight before it ever really began. Sneering at Billy, he spits, "Where's your loyalty, Langston? Or are you brainwashed into bowing down to this fucker, too?"

His insults don't hurt me. Him breaking bro code pisses me off. "Loyalty? You don't know shit about loyalty."

"This has been a long time coming. Outside, fucker."

"Yeah, take it outside, boys," McGilley adds.

Fear is something I haven't possessed in a long time. So after finishing my beer, I slide off the barstool and head for the door. The bell above the door rings as I walk out. Moving down the sidewalk, I hear the shuffle of feet behind me and move to the corner before turning around. A calm I've come to expect washes through me. I've wondered many times if I've become desensitized to violence, almost looking forward to the release. My hands fist and then I flex my fingers.

I have to remind myself where I am. Causing trouble in this town means trouble for my mom, and that's the last thing I want. Billy comes toward me. "Walk away, Jason."

"Why?"

"Because he's drunk."

Cutler comes stumbling toward me with his fists raised. What the hell? I stare at him, crossing my arms over my chest. "You're fucking sad, you know that?"

"Get him outta here, Langston," McGilley yells down the way.

Billy wrangles Cutler backward as he yells, "Fuck off, Billy. This is a long time coming. I'm going to kick your ass, Koster, and set the record straight once and for all." He charges me. "I own this town. I own Delilah."

I don't lose my temper easily, but he manages to push just the right button. "Fuck you."

He's just about to hit me, but when he's within arm's reach, I take him by the throat and slam him to the ground. His face turns red, the veins in his neck begin to bulge, and his pulse pounds under my fingers. I could end him right here. I could look into his eyes and watch his life leave them.

This asshole doesn't deserve death. If this piece of shit doesn't get out of my sight, he's going to find it, though. I lean down so he hears me clearly, and say, "The more you fight, the more your throat will close on you. Relax if you want to live."

Pushing off him, I back away and tell Billy, "I'll see you tomorrow."

Cutler is left gasping for air while Billy stands there in shock. My buzz is gone, and I go around to the side of the bar to get on my bike.

I take the long way home.

Cutler's not the guy I knew growing up. Something's changed him over the years. Jealousy that grew into anger and then expanded into hate. Hitting women. He's become his father, who he regularly saw hit his mother.

Some fucking example he was.

Everyone knew what happened behind closed doors, yet his mom stayed. My mother was the only one who reached out—*repeatedly*—to his. Eventually, that relationship ended when his father decided he didn't care for people knowing his business. *No wonder Cole's so fucked up.*

I need the dark of the night to relieve the aggression I found too easily tonight. The cool night air clears my head. With clarity, I see through the fog that's been crowding my head. I turn around and head for the Noelle farm.

It doesn't take but a few minutes to get there, but I stop at the entrance and cut the engine. The lights are out except one in that upstairs bedroom. If I had her number, I'd text her to see if she's awake or wants to talk. Maybe she'd come outside and say hi again, even if only for a second.

The light is switched off, and a little hope goes with it. I start my bike and head home. I was stupid for thinking I could invade her night. I'll see her again. I know that much. Doesn't have to be a big deal, just to talk, to settle the wild thundering of my heart. To put the issues between us to bed. We're not those same kids in love. We're adults with problems to match.

I sneak inside, locking up behind me. My mom's bedroom door cracks open, and she says, "You okay, Jase?"

"Yeah, I'm fine. Go back to bed."

"Will you come to church with me in the morning?"

Leaning against the doorframe to my room, I say, "I don't think that's a good idea, Mom. Jesus and I aren't on good terms these days."

"That's exactly why you should come with me."

She's tired, and I'm not looking to argue. "I'll go. Now get some rest."

With a smile, she says, "Good night. Love you."

"Love you. Good night."

WE CATCH the only light in town, naturally. I come to a stop at the red and tug at my tie, which is feeling too tight. I haven't worn a tie in a long time. My mom is talking about what she calls the gossip girls and how they're going to lose their minds when I walk into church.

But I'm looking around at this tired town, the streets nearly empty on an early Sunday morning. Glancing into the rearview mirror, I watch as a familiar white pickup pulls up behind me. I'm pretty sure she recognizes my mom's car by how she's looking everywhere other than at me staring back at her.

A smile threatens to break the frown right off her face. Delilah might have broken my heart, but sitting here, I realize she has the power to do it twice.

I used to think she couldn't resist me, but she had no problem earlier this week. Let's see if she can this time. I have a few tricks up my sleeve when it comes to Ms. Noelle that I've been thinking about all night. "I'll be right back."

"What?" my mom asks, watching me get out of the car. "Where are you going? The light's going to turn green at any second."

I keep walking.

Delilah sees me. She lowers her sunglasses from the top of her head, but I imagine her eyes are probably damn wide right now. Reaching for the lock on the door, she pushes it down with her finger just as I arrive. She can kid herself all she likes, but she knows damn well the most I'll do is pressure her into giving me a little of her time.

Standing on the other side of her door, I knock. Delilah finally looks up and points at the light. It's green. I shrug, but then make the lame twist of the wrist roll-down-your-window motion with my hand because I have a feeling she might not understand if I pretend to push a button to roll it down.

"Get back in your car, Jason," she says through the glass.

"No. Roll down your window." To sugarcoat it, I add, "Please."

I can see her eyes through the lens. "Why?"

"What do you mean why? I want to talk to you, and I don't want to shout through the glass."

Huffing, the glass slowly slides down. "What is it?" She keeps her hands on the steering wheel, and her grip seems to tighten just a bit.

When her eyes settle on mine, I say, "I want to see you."

"You're seeing me, Jason, so if that's all there is, I'll be going now."

The glass starts to roll up, but I clamp my palm over it. She releases the button and looks up at me. "I don't know what happened the other day, what turned your mood so quickly, but I'd like another chance to talk."

"It's not a good idea."

"It's a great idea, actually." I can see the smile tugging itself free. I grin in response. "All you have to do is say yes."

"No."

My smile tilts into a smirk. "You haven't changed much."

"Then you haven't been paying attention." She sighs. "Red light."

"I have three minutes to change your mind."

"Why do you want to talk, Jason? Just let things lie the way they're meant to be."

Meant to be . . .

She and I were once *meant to be*. Maybe that's why this notion keeps making itself known. Is there still something between us? "I want to come by this afternoon. I'll bring lunch."

Shaking her head, she looks down at her lap. "I can't."

"Delilah." Her eyes return to mine, and the glass is level with the car again. I rest my hands on the door and lean down. "Let me see your eyes."

Another car pulls up behind her car, and I wave. It seems like the courteous thing to do.

Her body gives her debate away, her chest rising and lowering—her breath deepening. She gives in and moves her sunglasses to the top of her head and looks into my eyes. "What are you doing, Jason?" she whispers.

"Is that you, Jason Koster?" a woman calls out, sticking her head out of the car window.

"It is. Good morning, Mrs. Robertson."

"You're going to make us late for church if you don't get a move on."

"I'd love to get a move on and not be late for the Lord, but Ms. Noelle has refused me the pleasure of her company, so I thought I'd see if I could change her mind."

Delilah's blush spreads across her face and starts down her delicate neck. I know where it's heading, and the memories of her bare chest against mine cause me to shift.

"Jason, please?" Her voice is so quiet as if she wants to say yes without anyone hearing, except me.

I don't care what's happening around us. As I stand here, it's just me and her—our worlds colliding again.

Matching her tone, I say, "Please what, honeysuckle?"

"I've not been your honeysuckle in a long time."

"But it was so good when you were." She stares ahead, trying to pretend her body doesn't react to me like mine is reacting to hers. Leaning even closer, I rest my arms on the door. "We can play games all damn day, but you and I have unfinished business to tend to. So how about that lunch or better yet, dinner tonight?" A car horn blares, causing me to look back. Mrs. Robertson shrugs, but it wasn't her honking.

It was the car behind hers. That's when I notice a trail of them stacked behind us. The horn is honked again, and then my mom leans out the window and shouts, "Cool it, Janice. You'll survive if you don't get there in time to flirt with the choir director."

Go, Mom.

I have to see who this Janice person is, and I recognize her the minute I see her. She's one of the gossip girls my mom was talking about. When I turn back to Delilah, a finger tapping on her thigh has her appearing anxious. But I can stand here all day long if that's what she prefers. "We've got quite the lineup of anxious churchgoers."

She looks in her rearview mirror and then back at me. "You're not going to give up, are you?"

"Nope." I tap my watch. "The service starts in two minutes. Do you really want to be the cause of a church delay?"

Sighing loudly, she gives me a glare. "Dinner. One less thing I'll have to worry about if you're bringing it over. Seven o'clock and don't be late."

She should know me better than that. I've never been late when it came to her. Tapping the roof of the truck lightly, I smile from ear to ear. "You got it. See you at seven, *honeysuckle.*"

I return to my mom's car to the sound of applause. When I sink into the seat, I check the mirror again and see Delilah smiling. Prettiest sight I ever did see.

My mom says, "You sure know how to give them something to talk about. You've stirred up all kinds of trouble."

She's totally worth it. "She's single. I'm single. There's no harm in us being single together tonight."

The cars pulling into the church parking lot late causes a bigger stir. Grumbles are heard as a large part of the congregation finds a seat. It's really quite amusing. Even my mom struggles to hold in her laughter. At one point, she leans over, and whispers, "It's good to have you home. You're just what this town needed."

The moment Delilah walks in, the sun shines a little brighter through the stained glass windows that line the sides of the church. I watch her move down a row and sit between two families. I can't imagine she doesn't know them since everyone knows everyone in this town, but she keeps to herself.

Although I'd rather stare at her, being here in a holy place has me recounting my sins. I don't have as many as I carry the burden of, but the few I have are major. When everyone lowers their heads to pray, I don't. Instead, my eyes find the only other person who remains the same.

Delilah turns and looks at me over the bowed heads dividing us across the church. A little line forms between her eyes as if I'm a puzzle she can't figure out. Just as I raise my hand to wave to her, the minister clears his throat—harshly—and my eyes meet his irritated ones. "Amen," we say in unison.

Fully delighted, Delilah finally lets that beautiful smile show. With everyone listening to the minister, I lower my head this time and chuckle before settling in for a long lecture.

After the service, I get tired of nodding, shaking hands, and updating what feels like the entire town on what I've been up to. I toss out my regular spiel—traveling around the country and working odd jobs.

Since sinning sends you to hell, sinning in church must get you a fast pass. I tell my mom I'll meet her at the car and walk out the wide-open double doors into the sunshine. I veer left when I spot the minister ahead, but I'm not stealth enough because I hear, "So glad you could join us today, Mr. Koster."

I stop and turn around. "I am too, Minister Polk?"

He pats me on the back as he turns us toward the church. "You can call me Stephen. You're not a kid whose mother forced him to attend Sunday school anymore."

"All right. Stephen." I wonder if he detects the sarcasm. "How are you?"

"I've been good, son. How about you?"

"Good."

"We've seemed to have lost touch with you for a few years. I'm hoping you carried God with you on your journeys."

Anger feeds the finger that pulls the trigger. One shot to the head and I know he's dead without having to shoot again. I'm fairly certain that signs my fate after death.

The bodies differ in size and shape, but their souls are long gone. I don't think about it anymore. I just act. I grab the black plastic from the trunk and get to work.

Another body to hide—when did I become the expert in cleaning scenes? I need to get out of here, to leave this city and this life. Just because I can stomach the work doesn't mean I should do it. It's messing with my mind. The guilt digs deep, creating crevices in my soul. I need to leave before my soul becomes blackened from the depravity of my actions. I'm starting to think it's too late to save me.

"Jason?"

My eyes lift to find the concerned gaze of the minister. I

reply, "Yeah? God." Knowing the crimes I've committed, I can't honestly say I carried God with me.

He pats me on the back again. "We should talk sometime."

"Okay."

"Good to have you back."

"Thanks. It's good to be back." I'm an expert at giving the appropriate responses. Although this time, I've already found some peace in this one. I'm not sure if Solace Pointe is where I belong, but I'm beginning to want to stay.

8

Delilah

I'm being ridiculous.

I set the prom photo back in the shoebox and put the lid on. Tucking it in the back of my closet, I shake my head at myself. Why am I nervous? Why am I giving hope room to grow? I have so many thoughts about what happened, and they're muddling together as if to form a new scenario.

How?

He didn't love me any longer. That much was clear. So why does he want to see me, to talk to me now? More importantly, why did I invite him over for dinner? I know. I roll my eyes at myself. This is a big mistake, one that I could have avoided.

Damn Jason Koster, that cute grin, and the way his voice hums through my body, touching parts of me I thought would never be reawakened again. I always was a sucker for him.

I slip on a pair of flats and then stop to check my outfit in the mirror before dabbing a bit more gloss on my lips. My makeup is light but pretty, my dress cotton and cool for the warm day, and my legs freshly shaven.

Wait, what?

I roll my eyes again and walk away from the mirror with visions of his face years ago coming back like a torpedo. Much like his approach today.

If I'd really looked at him that day, I could've seen how broken he was. He promised me we'd be fine, but that was a lie. Jason had no way of keeping that promise, much less making it. I thought he loved me as much as I loved him, but clearly, I was wrong. Someone who loves you wouldn't make a decision about your future without consulting his or her partner.

Partner.

That's the problem. I wasn't a partner in that relationship. I was only a girl holding him back. Taking a deep breath, I try to rid my mind of that memory and the pain I still feel to this day. I grab my phone, head out onto the front porch, and call my sister. I need a new perspective or a reminder of how bad things were.

After texting her earlier about Jason, it doesn't surprise me when Shelby answers right away. "Hey, sis."

"Why do you have to live so far away?"

She laughs, but it's light as both of us are well aware of the reason. "Are you nervous or excited?"

"I'm undecided how to feel about him. On the one hand—"

"Oh, here we go."

"Hush. It's true. He hurt me, and that pain is tangible even now, and it has been four years."

"But?"

"I'm getting there. But he does look good, even better than I remember, and more charming if that's even possible." Smelled amazing too, just like he used to. I was tempted to touch that clean-shaven jaw of his, to run the tips of my fingers over the veins in his hands as he gripped my door like I'd escape if he didn't. He was intense. Determined. On a mission. Powerful. I struggle to swallow, remembering how imposing his body was, and how he leaned in, leaving me no room to say no. I wasn't scared. God, it was hot. I start fanning myself with—

"Jason Koster could charm a porcupine out of its needles. Your panties never stood a chance."

"Stop teasing." I'd like to argue her point, but she's right on the money. I won't tell her that, though. She'll hold it over me because Jason was everything—handsome, charismatic, talented, intelligent, and sexier than any man ever should be. But I thought I was his everything as well, and I wasn't. *So what do I know?* "Did you book your flight?"

"Yep. You have one week to clean the house and get that farm back in order." She laughs. "Do you have a few minutes to go over invoices?"

The sound of tires grinding against the gravel driveway alerts me to a visitor. "Actually, he's here, so I need to go. We can go over them tomorrow."

"Call me then and don't sleep with him tonight."

"What? There's no way in hell I'm sleeping with Jason. If that's what he thinks he's getting for dinner, he'll be sorely disappointed."

"How much do you want to wager?"

"I am not sleeping with that man, Shelby."

"All right. All right," she replies incredulously. "One of your homemade pies?"

"I'm not sleeping with him." She's ridiculous. "Fine. I'll wager a pie."

Giggling, she adds, "Good luck, little sis."

"I don't need luck. I have the remains of a broken heart as a glaring reminder."

"*Annnd* on that note, have a good time and call me tomorrow."

I hear the judgment in her tone under her laughter. This is no laughing matter, though. "Fine. Talk tomorrow." At least it wasn't to my heart four years ago.

But here I am, still running to the bathroom to check my appearance when I hear a knock on the front door. I smack my lips together to spread the gloss while I make my way to answer it. It's like I don't have a care in the world despite my whole body and mind caring too much, siding with my sister.

I will *not* sleep with him, making this the easiest wager in history to win. We're not the same people than we were four years ago. Considering I'm not even attracted to Jason Koster anymore, I should have bet money. I swing the door open, my confidence still buzzing.

Holy. Hell.

Lord, help me. I'm in trouble.

The color brown was never fitting for Jason's eyes—vibrant and full of life, joy, and love. Those words always seem to fit his shade better. Those words still light up that color, though I could never pinpoint the perfect descriptors with basic adjectives. Standing with the screen door open and now face-to-face with him, I see a new emotion hidden inside near the darkness of his pupils. I'm thinking it's life. It gets to us all at some time or another, but his concerns me. *What has stolen the light from his eyes?*

"Hi," he says with a smirky grin. Shelby was right. My panties never stood a chance. *Poof.* Yup, he's still got it.

I walk out, definitely needing to keep him outside and as far from the bedroom as possible. "Hi there, yourself." Leaning against the railing, I keep a few feet of distance between us, between me and those eyes and that smile, and from how amazing he smells. "So why did you want to have dinner together?"

His gaze lengthens toward his truck. "Because we have to eat. You hungry, Delilah?"

Honestly, I have nothing to prove, and my sister would never really make me pay up on any wager, fictional or real. But when I hear my name roll off his tongue as though he just tasted the sweetest ice cream he's ever had, I'm reminded of when he used to say it prefaced by three little words I don't say anymore. My body and mind remember that deep tone all so well as if it was just yesterday. With my heart jumpstarted, I swear my fingers tighten around that old white wood railing.

"You okay?" he asks.

"Good. Yeah. Fine." I wave my hands in front of me, but when it looks like flailing, I pretend to swat the air. "Damn mosquitoes."

Looking around, he furrows his brow. "Oh wow, I didn't notice. Do you want to go inside?"

"No!" I shout. "I mean," I add, lowering my voice, "no. Outside is good." He's staring at me. I bite my lip, shake my head, and dash down the steps. "I'm starved. What'd you bring?"

I make it to the truck before discovering that Jason is still standing on the porch, his head tilted down, his eyes watching me while he scratches the back of his neck. "I'm sorry."

"For what?" I ask, leaning my hip against the bumper.

"I didn't intend to make you so uncomfortable."

"What were your intentions then?" Holding my arms out, I ask, "You made a show of things in front of the entire town."

He descends the steps with an ease in his body and a confidence in his stride. "To feed you. I can go if you like." Would I like that? Or should I take this opportunity to get a few things off my chest as well? Walking right up next to me, he stands with his keys dangling around a finger. "Do you want me to go, Delilah?"

What am I doing? "No," I confess. "I should kick you off my farm and tell you never to return, but I can't. I won't. You want to talk? Let's talk."

Reaching into the bed of the truck, he holds up a picnic basket. "And eat? I was thinking we could sit down on the pier."

"That pier is long past safe these days, but I can grab a blanket or chairs for the grass."

Holding up a blanket, he adds, "I came prepared."

"Oh, I bet you did," I mumble under my breath.

"What was that?"

"Nothing."

He walks around to the passenger side door and opens it for me. "Hop in, honeysuckle."

Honeysuckle.

I wish I didn't like that so much, but the memories of how I got the name warm my insides, the taste of his kiss still lingering on my tongue after all this time. He offers me a hand, and I take it without thinking. If I had been thinking, I would have prepared for the current flowing between us like a live wire. I would have remembered how my body always came alive under his touch, and I would have remembered to breathe as my body brushed against his. Hell, if I were thinking at all, I wouldn't have accepted this date. But I wasn't, so here I am, sitting in the cab of his truck with so many good times flashing back.

"I didn't realize your mom kept your truck," I say.

"She didn't have to," he says, starting the engine. He drives across the property as if he never left. "She even takes her out for monthly drives."

"I once saw it driving through town. Figured I must have been seeing things."

He smiles, but it slips away when his eyes spot the lake ahead. Shifting the truck into park, he rests his arms on top of the steering wheel. "Wow, it's exactly the same."

The lake doesn't get the same attention from me since he's stolen all of mine. He turns to me, catching my eyes on him. Looking content, he says, "Hi."

Jason's sweet enough not to embarrass me. "Hi."

"You were staring." Okay, maybe he's not so sweet, calling me out.

"I'm sorry."

"Don't be. I like when you look at me." My cheeks heat because he not only likes me looking at him, but he noticed me staring. I open the door, needing to get out of the close confines of the cab of his truck. Before I can climb out, he calls, "Hey, you're making me look bad. Stay there." He hops out and runs around. Offering me a hand to get out, he stands close, not leaving much room between us.

Though I accept the offer, I say, "You don't have to worry about me. I can take care of myself."

When my feet land on the ground, we release our hands. He's quick to shove his in his pockets. "You were always very independent, so I know you can take care of yourself. But no matter how independent you are or how many years have passed between us from then to now, I will always worry about you, Delilah."

My racing heart calms as if I was tucked under his arms like I used to be. It's wrong, and my head is swimming in confusion, but it feels good to feel cared for again.

9

Delilah

Staring.

I'm staring at him again. The way his muscles work fluidly together, the veins popping out with the least bit of effort he puts into a task.

His arms . . . they're better than any porn I can imagine.

Jason Koster was always gorgeous. Tall, dark, and handsome was envious of what that man possessed. His body is hard, the fittest I've ever seen him, and he was fit when he played football. But this is different. This peak physical perfection makes me even more curious how he stays in shape, and why to this degree. "Do you still play football?"

He stops and stomps a plank of the dock with his heel. When he glances up, he replies, "No. Billy and I have tossed the ball around a bit, but that's all really."

"You got a tattoo." I eye the design on the underside of his arm. I move closer and reach out, unable to resist the urge to touch him. I'm quick to run my fingertips over the ink but realize I've crossed a line I shouldn't have. When I start to pull back, he covers my hand with his.

My heart rate kicks up, and my breathing quickens. I stare at our hands when he says, "Two years ago . . ." He pauses. Releasing me, he takes a deep breath. "It's a design I saw graffitied under a bridge in Seattle. I took a pic. I wish I knew the artist so I could show them."

"Why did you choose that design?"

"It spoke to me. If you look closely, the detailing of the clouds mixed with the darker sky. Blurring the night with the day." He shakes his head gently. "Can the light fight the dark? Can it survive?"

"Is that how you feel? Are you surviving the dark?"

He asks, "Right now? I'm living. For the first time in a long time, I'm living."

"That's surviving." Looking satisfied, he comes back to me . . . *back to me* . . . and stares deep into my eyes. I can't look away, especially when a smile crosses those full lips. "Can I have the blanket, Delilah?"

His request snaps me back to reality, and my eyebrows shoot straight up. "Oh, yeah, sure. Here." I shove the blanket I was holding like a lifeline into his hard, brick-like abs. Peeking down, I can see the muscle beneath the button-up shirt, that six-pack calling my attention right to it.

With the blanket bunched in his arms, his eyes lower to my lips before he leans forward. "Oh my God, are you going to kiss me?"

He chuckles. "I was going to cover you back up since I saw goose bumps on your arms."

Heat blooms through my chest and starts covering my cheeks. "Of course," I say, shaking my head. "I was kidding."

With the blanket wrapped around me again, he whispers, "Did you think I was going to kiss you?"

Still mortified, I jerk my head back. "No!" *Yes.* "Not at all." *Oh, my God!* This is so humiliating. I was going to let him. Not just let him but kiss him back. I know I was. Oh, good gracious. Desperate much? Yes, I sure am.

I walk around him and point at the dock like that is actually going to deflect the shame creeping across my skin in a fiery, blotchy haze. "Is the dock safe?"

Staring. *He's staring again.* "Yeah." He chuckles when he speaks. "It needs a little work, some planks replaced sooner than later, but for tonight, as long as we don't jump up and down on it, it's good to go."

I'm not even cold. It's just him causing these goose bumps. I toss him the blanket and watch as he spreads it across the planks. Grabbing the picnic basket from the truck, I can't believe I almost kissed Jason Koster. That is, if he would have kissed me. The man is magnetic, and I'm weak to his pull. *Will this never change? Even after he broke my heart?*

Reaching in after me, he grabs a small cooler and a few pillows, and follows me to the dock.

The scene is set, the sun going down. The cicadas get louder as early evening rolls into twilight. He's thought of everything, including wine. I pull the containers out of the basket as he fills two glasses with Sauvignon blanc. He's pleasantly surprising me. "I'll admit, Koster, I expected beer, but you went all out."

"I wanted to."

I pause midair with a large container in my hands as his tone draws my attention. "Why?"

I'm not granted his warmth, but he does seem to struggle to keep his gaze on the glasses in front of him instead of on me. "Do you like chicken salad?"

He may have avoided the question, but I don't point it out. "You know I love it."

With a nod, a rogue grin spreads on his face, and he finally looks up. With the sunset caught in his eyes, they shine with that light that used to live there. "My mom taught me how to make her recipe. She makes the best with grapes and celery."

"She always did. She's a wonderful woman, Jason."

He takes a baguette from the basket and rips it in half. "She says the same about you."

The compliment makes me smile, but the baguette fascinates me. "Where did you get that? I know Smally's Grocers doesn't sell French bread."

He glances up, his darker eyelashes highlighting the golden centers of his eyes. "I ran over to Kerbyville. They have a bakery this side of downtown."

"That's forty-five minutes away." I'm not so much asking a question as questioning why he drove so far.

Returning to the bread, he shrugs and hands me half. "It was the closest bakery."

"But it's bread."

"You don't like it?" He rips his piece lengthwise.

I struggle to comprehend why he would drive two towns over for specialty bread. "I love it. I just . . . you really didn't have to go to this much trouble, Jason."

"I had some time to kill this afternoon." He takes the lid off the container of chicken salad and then spoons some into the crevice of the loaf. "Did you know Smally sold the store?"

Smiling, I reply, "Yes, I live here. It was big news when he announced it. Raina Smith and her fourth husband bought it a few years back after promising Smally they'd keep the name."

"It is a legend around here."

"Well, Raina's fifth husband disagrees, but I heard she filed for divorce last week, so he won't have a say anyway."

He laughs. "Wow, she's only in her fifties."

"She brags she's had one husband for each decade of her life." I laugh now, feeling silly talking about this.

He chuckles, and it's a good laugh. The sound is a trigger of happier times in my life. I split my bread, and he spoons the salad inside, silence seeping in. I notice how his eyes take in the area as if he's scanning more than casually looking around.

"It hasn't changed at all out here," he finally says.

"The whole world seems to except this little plot of land, which forever remains unchanged."

"I like it. It's exactly how I remember." I look up when I feel his gaze lay heavy on me. "You haven't changed either," he adds.

My head lowers, and I feel self-conscious. I hate that my cheeks heat under the most innocent of comments. It's been a long time since I've been complimented. Setting my sandwich down, I tug at my skirt with one hand and pick up my wine with the other. A single finger touches the base of my chin and lifts it up. "I like seeing your eyes and your sweet face."

"I don't feel so sweet these days."

His hand returns to his side of the blanket, though there doesn't appear to be defined lines with my legs stretched over to his side and the arm supporting his weight on my side. "Can I ask you something, Delilah?"

I know what it is. It's always the same. People are baffled with how I ended up with my boyfriend's best friend. Gullible. Naïve. *I was so stupid.* Something about Cole or the divorce.

Coming out on the other side of this nightmare I survived, I see how he twisted the truth and made me believe I wasn't good enough to hold on to Jason's love, to keep his attention when he would soon be surrounded by so many girls and then the NFL would call. I stood no chance at all. Sabrina taught me that jealousy makes women vicious. I'd be an embarrassment on his arm. My accent would be mocked. He'd eventually see what he could have would be better than what he had at home.

Cole did a number on my head, which destroyed my heart. I don't understand why Jason is back, but I can't deny I still have feelings for him. *Does one ever get over their first love?*

"God, I'm the most boring person ever, Jason. What could you possibly want to know about me?"

"Why are you still here?"

Easy. "I live on the farm." I have nowhere else to go . . . not an easy thing to admit, not even to myself.

"No, why are you still in Solace Pointe?"

I take a sip of wine, the cool liquid counteracting the heat of the evening. I like how I feel less pressure with a little wine in me, more relaxed, or maybe it's that Jason puts me at ease. He used to. I never had to be on guard with him.

Not like with Cole.

Cole made sure I stayed on my toes, and the few unfortunate times I forgot that lesson, I paid the price.

"It's complicated," I reply.

"I have the time."

With the food forgotten, he settles in as if this story is worth his full attention. "It's not exciting."

"I've had enough excitement. Now I want to hear about you."

I want to redirect the conversation away from me, but I

have a feeling he's much better at this game than I am. He always did make me feel important, until the end when I didn't understand where I stood with him. "When my dad died, he left the farm and all fifty acres to my sister and me. The hard work he put into keeping the farm was what killed him. I wish I would have known that he was working so hard to get out of debt."

"I'm sorry to hear that. Your father was a good man. I know he thought hard work was the answer to everything."

"He had to let everyone go, and after that, he struggled to keep up with the crops. We inherited that debt, and now I struggle to keep up." Pointing across the property, I add, "We only have two working plots left. The others have gone to weeds."

"We?"

"Shelby and I. Oh, and Billy. He helps us more than he should."

"He's a good guy."

"Yeah, I've been trying to get my sister and him to go on a blind date." My giggle bubbles up. Damn wine. Damn Jason for treating me like I'm still cherished.

"I don't think that's how blind dates work. They've known each other their whole lives."

"They still see the gawky sides of each other," I start, my excitement to hook them up taking over my voice. "They need to see each other the way they are now. It's been a few years."

He finishes his sandwich and leans back on one elbow, facing me. "Where is Shelby?"

"After college, she went to New York City. We thought she was starting her career, but what she ended up doing was saving the farm."

"How so?"

"Although the debt was overdue, the bank gave us a five-year extension to pay it off. Kindness of a small-town farmer's credit union. We have one year left. She works and pays money toward the loan." The burden that weighs down on me returns. "I can't bear to lose it, so I gave up leaving to stay here and work it."

"Is it what you want?"

"I used to. It gets really lonely, though." I laugh humorlessly and then raise an eyebrow. "That's not a hint, by the way."

"I didn't catch it if it was."

"I have a feeling you don't miss much." I finish my wine. "Tell me about what you've been doing since I last saw you."

"Hmm . . . the last time we saw each other was when you walked into Red River holding Cutler's hand. That was all I needed to see. I knew right then that nothing was keeping me here anymore."

Ouch. If he only knew the truth. I missed him so much that I ached inside as I withered away. It was easier to pretend I'd never experienced pure love than to experience the burn from it. My sister was so worried about me, but I still couldn't bring myself to confess what was happening behind closed doors. The humiliation of them finding out the strong girl they once knew was weak.

And then Jason was gone. He disappeared into thin air, like the memories I held on to. I say, "Your mom was here."

Lying all the way back, he rests his hands under his head and stares at the sky. "My mom can take care of herself."

"*I* was here," I whisper.

"You were being taken care of by somebody else." He pauses and looks out at the water and away from me for too long. When he turns back, I see some of the pain I feel inside residing in his irises. "You weren't mine, so I no longer had a right to care about you."

You had already decided you were leaving whether I was with you or not. "And if I hadn't been?"

"Then I would've had a reason to stay."

What? He had been moving on. Without me. Even though Cole told me time and time again that Jason had moved on, should I have listened to my heart? Should I have known better and not allowed my pride to stop me from hearing Jason's side of things? He needs to know that maybe I'd been wrong. Maybe he'd been under the wrong impression all along. "It wasn't over for me, Jason. The night you saw us. It wasn't over for me until *he* told me how you'd met someone over at State. God, I felt so foolish and hurt."

"It was lies, Delilah," he says without hesitation as if his heart were speaking the words. He sits up, his expression falling from the pain—at the outer corners of his eyes and the tips of his lips. "I loved you so fucking much. What did he tell you?"

What didn't he tell me?

"Everything a best friend would know. He said you didn't want me but didn't know how to end it. How you . . ." I start to push up, to leave this discomfort, but he catches my hand.

"Please, Delilah. Tell me."

I could say I'm staying for him, but that's not the truth. I sit back down because I need to talk this through and get it off my chest. "I was used goods after dating you. Cole told me how everyone in town talked about me behind my back. Do you know what that would do to my father? Or how my mom would lose her circle of friends? I was destroyed after being with you, the has-been beauty queen."

"You weren't." Caressing my cheek, he says, "You were per—"

"Cole said he'd love me," I add, raising my chin and closing my eyes while moving out of the warmth of his touch. "He'd save my family the humiliation. He'd save my reputation, so I relented." Images of him with other women shatter my thoughts and my heart once again. When I open my eyes, my gaze hardens as the pain comes back. "Looking back now, I can see how he got me at my weakest and took advantage. You were gone. I couldn't think straight anymore. Shelby was graduating in another state. My parents had so many fights back then over the farm, me, my sister leaving. My world fell apart, and that's when he talked me into marrying him."

"God, no." An emotional toll takes over his shoulders, and they sag. Scraping his fingers over his brow, he can't even look at me. Just as I couldn't look at myself back then. I was so weak. When he looks at me, shame still fills his body and his tone. "I'm sorry I left. I'm sorry I failed you. I'm so fucking sorry, Delilah."

His apologies stun me. I'm staring at the man I thought I'd marry, and now he's sorry for everything. "You're sorry?" I gulp down my pride, realizing how much I misjudged him.

"Yes. I'm sorry I hurt you."

Too much honesty and truth of emotion is shared. It will take time to process this, so I ramble to make it go away until I have time alone to figure out why he's so sorry. "The county clerk was our witness. She took a call regarding an escaped bull on the highway in the middle of the ceremony. Cole thought I was crying from happiness, but I was devastated."

"Why didn't you call me, return my texts, or come see me? Why didn't you want to hear my side of things?"

"I thought I had. He was your best friend, so I believed him. He had no reason to lie to me."

"He had every fucking reason to lie to you because he was in love with you."

"People respected Cole back then. I was the embarrassment to my family. Cole was a second chance instead of me being viewed as sloppy seconds."

He sighs so heavy that I'm surprised he has any breath left. "Fuck that, Delilah. If I'd known—"

"See, that's just it. It seems by your reaction that neither of us did." I rest back on my palms. "I've gone over this a million ways to Friday and never could make sense of it. But here's the thing, I gave up trying to reason my way to explain things years ago." My directness is unsettling. I'm used to sitting in my farmhouse alone at night and not having to answer to anybody anymore. *Why confide true emotions to Jason? Why now?* "Upheaving the past won't change things now, so I shouldn't have said anything."

"I'm glad you did, but I want to know why you're so upset. I'm sorry things happened the way they did, and I didn't come to you, but you broke up with me and not the other way around."

"I broke up with you because you broke my heart."

"I had a full scholarship when I couldn't afford college. I had to take it if I wanted to graduate, so how did I break your heart exactly?"

My mouth drops wide open as anger rushes through my veins. Shifting, I narrow my eyes in shock. "Really?" *What the hell? How can he not remember something that's scarred me for life?*

"Yeah, really?"

I'm too wound up to sit still. I stand, walk off the dock into the grass, and start pacing under the same moon that hung high in the sky that first night I lost the love of my life. When I turn back, to possibly answer, I'm stunned into silence. His expression is one of pure curiosity as he watches me. "You don't get it, do you?"

"No, but I want to."

My emotional artillery falls like the walls I've built to protect myself. How can I stand here with weapons loaded when he sits there unarmed? The curiosity in his eyes renders him blind to our history. Does he really not remember? Something is off. For someone who's guilty, he sure looks innocent.

"Wait a minute," I start, tilting my head to the side while still staring at him. "Do you not . . . know?"

"No. I never did." He doesn't understand how much he hurt me . . . oh, my God.

My heart thumps in my chest, and I take a deep breath to help stop the erratic thoughts filling my head. "You hurt me, Jason." He hurt me.

"How?"

One word stops my pacing. "How?"

"I loved you."

Loved . . . My head is spinning, my thoughts whirling with all the angles I thought I had covered regarding our breakup years earlier. Sitting down on the grass, I look at the man he's become. He's still so much the man my heart misses. Could I have had it wrong all this time? The years we lost . . . they form a lump in my throat, but I manage to ask, "You weren't going to break up with me when you came over to tell me about the transfer, were you?"

He looks up at me, his head shaking so small as if the pain still affects him. He appears so . . . troubled, so sad, and I feel the same. He looks me straight in the eye. "No, Delilah, I wasn't. I was going to ask you to marry me."

10

Jason

I don't like to lie.

I've spent the past four years living in an abundance of them—for my protection, for the protection of others, protecting secrets and lives.

In Solace Pointe, I want to live in the truth. I want to feel the warmth of sunshine instead of sneaking around in the cover of night. *Here, I can breathe.*

But something about Delilah Rae steals my breath and my heart just from being close to her again. Even when her mouth is gaping open by an admission I promised myself I would never confess. Pushing off the splintering wood of the dock, I stand and toe my shoes off. It's time for a diversion. Drastic measures need to be taken, and if I get to see what's under that dress, all the better.

My socks and belt are stripped away, piquing her interest as she arches an eyebrow. Her mouth is open for other reasons, it seems. My plan of distraction from telling her my deepest secrets is working.

I unbutton my shirt and drop it to the pile of clothes gathering at my feet. Reaching over my head, I tug the T-shirt off as well. I'm not shy, but she's looking at me like she's never seen a man half undressed before. "Do you go out much?"

"No," she replies defensively. "Why?"

"No reason." I slide the zipper down slowly, giving her a show, and step out of my jeans.

"Why are you undressing?"

"I'm going for a swim to cool off. Even though the sun's down, it's a warm night. You should join me."

"No. I haven't been in that lake since . . . well, since we were a thing."

"A thing?" I might be pushing some buttons, but I can't deny I like her being so open with me.

"Dating, Jason. You know what I mean."

Apparently, I still know how to rile her up. I'll have her in there before she has time to decide otherwise. "I liked being a *thing* with you. How about we try it, you know, while we swim?"

She crosses her arms. "I'm not skinny dipping with you."

"Why not? Are you scared?"

"Scared?" She scoffs. "Hardly. I'm just not a teenager anymore."

"Oh, sorry for mistaking you for someone who likes to have fun."

I start on the waistband of my boxer briefs, but she says, "Wait. What are you doing?"

"Haven't we already covered this?" I push them down, and she's up and turning on a dime.

Her back may be facing me, but from where I stand, I can see her hands covering her face. "I swear to God if you're naked right—"

I dive into the water. It's cold but not cold enough to make me want to get out. When I break the water's surface, I shake my head. My hair clears from my eyes only to find hers on me.

"I can't believe you just jumped in," she says.

"I said I was going for a swim."

With a hand perched firmly on each hip, she's riled up all right. "What about our date?"

"Are we on a date, honeysuckle? I thought we were just talking?"

"You're so infuriating, Jason Koster."

"I love when you say my whole name like I'm in trouble."

Her eyes squeeze closed, but a smile follows along with her stance softening. "Old habit."

"What about old times? Come on in." This time, I can see the debate—her eyes flashing between the water and me, then behind her like her father's going to catch us. "It's only us. No one has to know." I zip my lips and wait.

"I'm not scared, if that's what you think." The debate is over, and she comes back onto the dock, looking down at me. "If you think I'm stripping down in front of you—"

"There's not an inch of your skin that I haven't seen, or licked, or tasted, Delilah Rae. So that dress, although pretty, doesn't erase the memory of what's under it. But I won't force you."

"Fine." Yup. She's riled up all right. "I'm coming in."

Mission Distraction is complete. She peels off that dress like it offended her and without an embarrassed bone in her body, she stands on that rickety dock in a mismatched bra and underwear as if I didn't think she was already the sexiest creature to walk this world.

Wriggling her hips, she asks, "Like what you see, Koster?"

"I sure do. Now get in here, Noelle."

She jumps in, and I swear she cannonballs on purpose to splash me as if that will cool down what's heating up between us. What she doesn't seem to understand is I love her moxie.

I temporarily lose her in the dark water even though the moon rises higher with each minute that passes. Her head finally pops up, and she wipes at the hair stuck to her face. A wide, carefree grin caters to her expression, and she laughs.

"Feels good, right?" I ask.

"It does." On her back, she swims away, keeping her eyes on me. "So, now that you got me in here, what are you going to do to me?"

Tease.

I lunge forward to swim after her. She squeals and takes off into the moonlight-speckled waters. I reach her feet, grab her kicking ankles, and pull. This beauty lands right in my arms, bridal style, and I hold on to her flailing body until she settles, and her laughter softens. Her breathing deepens when our eyes meet, just as mine does. But I can't will myself to laugh, to enjoy the moment, or to say anything at all.

My bravado a minute earlier gets caught in my chest, and I look at her while exposing my inner thoughts. She can still bring me to my knees with how she looks at me like I hung that moon in the sky. It's the opposite of what she's said, the pain she's shared. If I can only make her see my side, I could . . . I could what? What do I want with her?

The physical attraction we always shared still exists, the chemistry still surging between us. Why did I come here? To make amends or to hear her side? She's shared the lies Cole told her. It's time for me to make her see the truth.

I caress her slick skin, well aware that these curves are dangerous when wet.

"Jason?" she whispers.

"Mm?"

The playfulness returns to her eyes as her hands grace my shoulders. "Why are you holding me?"

"I don't have a good reason."

"Nothing at all?" Hope mixes with a coyness I've missed. It didn't matter how many times we made love when we were together, she always blushed for me right after.

"No reason other than I want to hold you again."

A look of relief crosses her sweet face, and her legs dip under the water. Then they make their way around my middle. "It would be bad if we kissed."

"Would it?"

"So bad."

"I never claimed to be good." I pull her body against mine and lean in, closing my eyes. Our lips touch, and our breaths still. Our bodies float with minimal effort. A touch turns into a caress, and I press harder, needing to feel her lips against mine again. Needing all of her against me again. God, I've missed this.

Her.

Her kisses.

Her breath mingling with mine. Her soft body against my hard one. No woman ever felt right, and now I know why. *She* was made for me. But before we get in too deep, she pulls back, leaving me breathless and turned on as she swims to the other side of the dock. "It's getting late, Jason. I think we should call it a night."

I swim a bit longer, watching as she climbs up the

ladder, thinking she needs the reprieve from me. She grabs her dress and slips it over her head, leaving the side unzipped. Coming to the edge, she peers down at me. "Whatever that was, we can't do it again."

There's no fight in her words, but more of a casual request on her part. "Why not?"

"I'm not in my right mind when I'm around you. Add in wine and it's not wise."

"Not wise for who? You or me?"

She slips on her shoes. "I blame it on the moonlight."

"The moon is an innocent bystander. It's the sunlight we need to be wary of. The light of day often reveals more truth than we need to know."

"Maybe. Guess we'll find out soon enough." She takes a shaky breath. "You're quite familiar with leaving, so you can see yourself off the property."

Ouch. "That's it?" I ask, waving my arms through the water.

"Yes. That's it."

She starts walking away, so I swim to the ladder and get out. "I can drive you back to the house."

"I know my way." She waves over the back of her head. "Thanks for dinner."

"You barely ate."

She doesn't turn back this time or respond, and I'm standing there confused, not sure what went wrong. The kiss? The conversation? The confession? *Fuck that.* This isn't the Delilah I once knew. She never ran from her problems. Is that what I am? A problem for her?

I grab the blanket and with everything inside, pick it up and set it in the back of the truck, except the wine, which I take with me. While trying to put my boxers back on, I hop from one foot to the other toward the truck to take off after her. She's not gotten far, but far enough for her not to hear me until I'm much closer.

Flashbacks of our breakup and her stubborn side whip through my mind. I'm not going to let that get the best of us again. This time, we're dealing with our issues head-on. I pull beside her, driving at the pace of her stride, and then hold the wine out the window in offering. "I have half a bottle of wine to kill. Care to join me?"

Taking the bottle from me, she takes a swig, and then says, "I know what you're doing, Jason Koster," before storming off again.

Driving again, I hang my arm out the window, dividing my attention between her and the where I'm going. "What am I doing, Delilah Noelle?"

She stops again, and points at me. "You're trying to get me drunk."

I put the truck in park and lean my elbow on the door. "Why would I want to do that? And since when do two glasses of wine get you drunk?"

"I don't drink much anymore, but you wouldn't know that since you've been off doing only God knows whatever you've been doing."

Is it me or the wine that's wound her up so much? "Hop in and I'll drive you back."

"I don't want you to drive me back. I'm perfectly fine with the stars and this wine."

"If you're so fine, then why do you sound mad?"

She stills, her chest rising and falling with her feelings trapped inside. I know her. I remember all her moods and swings that maneuvered her through them. Delilah was never a girl to complain and always dealt with everything straight on, but she's not her usual self. She's holding back, and I hate it. Popping the door open, I step out—wet boxers and all—and lean against the truck. "Talk to me."

"I can't." Her shoulders fall in defeat. When the silence becomes uncomfortable, she brings the bottle to her lips, but I catch it and lower it back down. Her eyes have lost some fire that always burned bright in the past. "We broke up. That means you have no right to make demands of me."

"I never wanted to break up, Delilah. I never wanted to make demands of you. I just wanted you."

"But you left me," she whispers.

Why does she feel I left her? *I left when she started dating Cutler.* I may have put distance between us with the transfer, but my heart stayed behind. "I'm back. I'm here now. What do you think about us ignoring the past for tonight and just enjoying our time together?"

"Is that because you're only giving me tonight?"

Fuck it. I can't hold back around her. "No, it's because I'd take all your time if you let me, but I don't think you're ready for that."

"What am I ready for?"

"That kiss you wanted earlier." I move in and close the space between us. This time, our lips don't just touch, they crash into each other's. Her arms loop around my neck, and the bottle bumps against my back. I slide my hands down the sides of her wet dress, feeling those dangerously sexy curves. Just when I feel her resolve slipping, I reach around my back and take the bottle from her.

Our lips part, and she whispers against my lips, "I hate that I missed you so much."

"There's nothing wrong with missing me. I missed you more than you'll ever believe."

A smile that endears me even more to her every time I see it appears. Leaning back, she looks into my eyes while keeping her arms securely around me. "Try me."

"Let me show you." I drop the bottle to the ground and kiss her.

And then I kiss her again, cupping her face in my hands and holding her to me. This time, our kiss is gentle, a familiarity in the feel and flow of the movement. Our lips part, and our tongues reunite with a soft caress and then more, going deeper as if staking claims that can be staked without repercussions. We both know that can't happen, but in this kiss, we pretend it can. We pretend we can do this like we used to, and the outside world doesn't exist.

Backing her against the truck, we continue to kiss, and her hands roam my backside, holding her against me. This time, I pull back, and say, "Let me take you home."

Physically, I have no way to hide my body's reaction, but I'm thinking she likes the feel of me. She holds my ass, and says, "I bet my sister I wouldn't sleep with you."

I chuckle. "As much as I love a good cuddle after sex, I love to win a bet more. No sleeping together then."

"What? No." I hear the plea in her tone as she wriggles against me.

"Oh, don't worry, honeysuckle. When I say sleeping, I mean the slumbering kind of actual sleep. I plan on keeping you wide-awake all night."

A smile slips into place, and her head falls back with laughter. "You always knew the way to a woman's heart."

"I might want your heart, but tonight, I want everything else." Nodding toward the cab, I step back. "The mosquitoes are brutal."

Taking my hand, she says, "Let's go back to the house." I

walk with her around the truck and open the door. When she's safely inside, I jog back around and steer the truck, getting us back to the farmhouse quickly. When I cut the engine, the sounds of the cicadas surround us again, the light from the front porch barely reaching us. She looks over at me, and at that moment, I can see something so tragically beautiful in her eyes. How could anyone hurt her like he did?

She pops the door but doesn't rush to get out. "Would you like to come in?"

"Do you want me to come in?"

"Yes." That's all the go-ahead I need. We meet at the tailgate with my boxers soaked through the fabric. The wet cotton of her dress also clings to her body. "What a fine pair of drowned rats we are."

She reaches for my hand, and I take it, but I also grab my clothes from the blanket in the back before we walk across the lawn. Suddenly, all the fun is gone, and we're left with the questions we should have asked and answered back on that dock. Her fight has slipped into the night, and as much as I want to have sex with her, there's too much to work through to put ourselves at risk again. The quiet between us is unnerving, the doubts coming back, so I stop on the porch just as she enters the house. "Delilah?"

The screen door slams closed between us, and she turns, surprised to see me on the other side. "Are you coming in?"

I want to so badly. So badly that I doubt myself for not taking what I want. I can't, though. Not with her. She means too much. She's the only one who can hurt me. *Again.* Instead, I sigh and look down. "I think I should go home."

Disappointment takes over her features, disappointment shaping her expression. "Why?"

"Because as much as I want to be with you, I don't want some weird thing between us. I want us kissing and laughing, making love because it feels good and because it's what we both want. So maybe we call it a night tonight?"

"That's probably best."

"Good night, Delilah. It was good to spend time with you again."

"Good night."

I head down the steps, though not in a hurry.

"Jason?" Looking back over my shoulder, I wait to hear what she has to say, every word from her too important to miss. "It was good to spend time with you, too. Maybe we can do it again before you leave town."

Leave town. When is that? It's something I need to consider. "I'd like that." I start walking again, sticks and dried leaves crunching under my feet as I cross the lawn again. I should probably get dressed before driving home. "And hey, let Shelby know you won the bet."

"I will." Gentle laughter filters to my ears. "If I won, why do I feel like I lost?"

I'm trying to do right by her. Read her body language and between the lines of what she says. Respect her and some bet she made with her sister. But I'm letting her down by not ravaging her good and proper. Women are complicated.

Dropping my clothes and the blanket into the bed of the truck, I turn back. Analyzing that body now, I see all the signs I need. Fuck my stance. Fuck her bet. *Fuck.* She still owns me after all these years. I turn around and cross that lawn like my feet are on fire and get the distinct pleasure of her smile again.

I swing the screen door wide open and step inside until I

hear her breath catch, and her eyes go wild with anticipation. "You're so going to lose that bet." Capturing her chin between my fingers, I kiss her. This time, I leave no doubt about my intentions for the night. And by how she's kissing me while dragging me toward the bedroom, she leaves none for me either.

11

Jason

The lamp crashes to the floor, the light bulb flashing before going out. I bump my knee on a table, and my big toe hits something metal. My lips leave hers as I bounce on one foot. "Fuck."

Delilah's arms are still around my neck, but her lips leave my face, and she giggles. "Sorry about that. I've moved things around since you were last here."

Looking over her shoulder into the living room, I find enough light from the kitchen to take stock of the room. It's a bad habit I'd like to break, but living like I did, it's one I needed. Even in the dark, especially in the dark, I always need to know my escape route, or I could be killed. There's a clear path to the back door if the chair is pushed in.

She turns my chin with her finger. "Hey, remember me?"

Who needs lamps when her smile lights up the room? I tighten my hands around her waist, liking the feel of our bodies pressed together too much to let her go. "I remember. I remember everything."

"Then where'd you go? I lost you."

The other meaning cracks my heart just enough to feel the ache. "I'm right here." Tucking some of her wet hair back from her face, I say, "I'm right here with you." Her body is cold, the air in the house chilling us both. I bring her to me, as close as I can hold her, and kiss her on the head. "You're going to get a cold. Maybe we should detour to the shower for a warm-up."

Tilting her head back, she can land a solid smirk herself. "A warm-up like foreplay or to actually warm up?"

"Both."

I will never get enough of her smile. I'm warmer by being at the receiving end of it, so I mentally add it to the list of things I missed about her.

"I'll get the water going. It takes forever to heat," she replies.

Just as she turns to leave, I catch her by the wrist. When she turns back expectantly, I ask, "What do you want me to do?"

Slipping her wrist from my grasp, her hand replaces it. "Come with me."

I follow her down the hall and up the stairs, stairs I remember climbing a million times when we were teenagers. We were only allowed in her bedroom with the door wide open, and if we got too quiet, her dad would start asking questions.

"What's the capital of Montana?"

"Helena."

"Do penguins have knees?"

"Yes."

If we missed one, he put us to work outside. Honestly, he was a smart man when it came to dealing with horny teenagers.

When Delilah reaches the top landing, she stops and turns around. Standing eye level with me, she holds my face in her hands, and as if someone might hear, she whispers, "I don't know what we're doing, but can we take it slow?"

Taking hold of her hips, I kiss her gently. "I'm in no rush to reach the end of this night."

"I don't only mean tonight. I mean, I guess we kind of know what's about to happen, and I want that with you. I do. I'm just worried about tomorrow."

I kiss her again, slower this time, casually reacquainting our lips. "Let's leave our cares for tomorrow and enjoy tonight. Just a little time to feel good." I can't ask for more. She deserves someone better, someone with a clear conscience and clean soul. But as I'm kissing her, I let the dark win because if I can have this chance, one last time to be with her, I'll greedily take it.

"You always did make it sound so easy."

"We don't have to make it hard either."

She embraces me, and her mouth is to my ear when she whispers, "We'll leave our worries for another day." A kiss is left behind when she walks down the hall to the bathroom.

I'm still gripping the railings like my life depends on it because no matter how convinced she is about tonight, I can't convince myself that it will be smooth sailing tomorrow.

She's the same woman I've been thinking about since the day we broke up. No one in the years since has come close. But here I am about to take a shower with her like I can walk away tomorrow not being utterly changed by merely being in her presence. *Fuck.*

It doesn't matter. I'm already walking down that hallway, every creaky floorboard announcing my approach, and pushing open the bathroom door. She's standing there in the glow of candlelight with a towel wrapped around her and her hand hanging under the water. Her blue eyes remind me of a pool in the summertime. She's giving me so much trust in this one exchange.

I can't screw this up.

I can't screw her over.

I can't take walking away from her the same way it played out last time.

If only for tonight, I have to be everything. All in. For her and for me.

Moving into the small space, I get in hers. I lower my gaze as I grip the top of the towel to unwrap her like a present.

"I'm nervous," she says.

My eyes find hers again, and I smile to reassure her. "Don't be."

Holding the towel open, I study her bare body. Every curve and shadow draws me in, her body pure perfection. The fullness of her breasts mixes with the familiar dip from her waist to her hips. The silkiness of her skin covers her feminine softness. "You're beautiful, Delilah."

A heavy breath is exhaled, and relief filters through her. "Thank you."

Her reaction is unusual. She's always been a stunning girl. She turned the heads of all the guys at school. Yet before me now is a woman who needs reassurance. In the back of my mind, I know Cutler hit her, but did he beat her self-esteem down too? *Fucker.* How could he do that?

Why did he do it?

I doubt one night will undo the damage, but if I can give her a reprieve from her battered heart, I will. I hang the towel on the hook behind me and take down my boxers while she watches. I understand the nerves. It's been a long time since we've been together, but as we're standing here, it's starting to feel as though we were never apart, and the love we once shared is within reach again.

Superficially, I like how she looks at me like she's about to drool. Makes me glad I went to the gym and got a few rounds inside the ring. I took a few blows to my stomach, but my opponent steered clear of my face. I told him I had to look good for tonight.

As much as I wished to be taking a shower with Delilah, I didn't actually think it would be happening. Reaching out, I test the water, which has warmed. My gaze roams her body leisurely. That's when I spot it. "Is that a tattoo?"

I hear the fast intake of air, and her eyes widen just enough for me to know she's embarrassed. Her hand covering the delicate skin just above her pubic bone and an inch to the right also tells me that. I'm intrigued, really intrigued, so I lean down for a better look. "What is it?"

She stops me, grabbing my bicep. "Just pretend you didn't see it. It was a mistake. A drunken night with my sister during a visit to Manhattan is to blame." She steps into the tub and under the shower spray, tilting her hips away from me so I can't see the artwork.

Following her into the tub, I ask, "Why are you hiding it from me?"

"Because I can't explain it without ruining the moment," she snaps.

I run my hands over her shoulders, leaving one hand on the side of her neck. "Hey, you can't ruin this. I want you. You want me. This right here is all good, honeysuckle."

After looking away, she takes a deep breath and then exhales. Her head goes up, hiding her face from me, and she huffs. "Fine." She angles her hips toward me, giving me an open invitation to peruse her body, which I happily do.

"What is this?" I grin while squatting down. It's only a number in black and gold—Solace Pointe High School colors. It's meaningless to anyone else but means everything to me. I run my finger over the number eight and look up.

The heat from the shower isn't causing the red that covers her face, but I pretend it is by standing up and adjusting the water to cool us off. "It's getting steamy in here." Delilah's still refusing to look at me, so I lean down to find her gaze. "I think that might be the sexiest fucking thing I've ever seen."

There's the smile I adore. The apples of her cheeks are still pink, but at least the tension she was exuding has evaporated. "Do you think I'm crazy?"

"Yes, but it's a good kind of crazy." Moving my hand over the tattoo, I rub a few circles before going a little lower and a bit over.

"I didn't know there was a good kind."

"There is when it comes to you." I kiss her lightly on the lips.

Why am I now nervous?

I've been with women, though it'd be embarrassing to admit how long it's been. It's inhumane to go so long without doing something so natural. But I couldn't afford the distraction during the job I was doing, a job that took an immense amount of attention. I was extremely focused when I worked with no break in my concentration. Too many accidents happened otherwise.

Delilah's naked body is before me, reminding me how long it's been since I laid eyes on such beauty, reminding me she was created to be my undoing. I never get nervous. I was good at my job because I was unshakeable, but this beauty has me anxious, wanting to please her.

Moving her under the water, I watch as she closes her eyes. I run the back of my hand over her cheek and then continue down her neck and lower. Her chest rises and falls with deepened breaths, her lips part so temptingly that I lean in and kiss them, my tongue connecting with hers. When I pull back, she opens her eyes, the tips of her fingers finally finding my skin. Her bottom lip finds the underside of her teeth while she runs her nails across my chest.

"Why'd you stop?" she asks.

"Because I like looking at you." When a smile crosses those sexy lips, I have an epiphany. "But I think I like kissing you more." I step closer and take her face in my hands, our lips meeting in the middle. Her nails scrape down my ribs, and I run my hands over her shoulders. Holding her to the side, I reach up and turn the showerhead, so the water warms us against the cold tile.

She's not just beauty, but brains, though I have no idea if she's lost her better senses since she let me back in her life. I may have loved her, but I never deserved her.

I was once naïve enough to believe we'd have it all if we were together. But like our love once did, that organ in my chest had died. At least I thought it had. But being with her again makes me feel alive again.

Leaning my head against hers, I close my eyes and breathe her in. "What's happening?" I ask, my voice competing with the falling water.

Her hands run over my shoulders and up my neck. A kiss to my chin, my jaw, my cheek, and finally my lips. "I don't know, but . . ." With drops dripping from my hair onto her face, she peers up into my eyes. "I've not felt this good in so long, so don't worry about me, or the past. Just kiss me again."

I do. I kiss her, covering her mouth with mine and drinking her in until a giggle bursts free from her.

"What are you laughing about?" I ask.

Shyness creeps in. Yep. We're naked in the shower together, and now she's shy . . . go figure. I laugh this time. "This. Us. It's like years ago in the best of ways."

"Yeah, I remember all those nights in the bed of the truck, in the field that time we had no other choice, and in my house." I take her hands and bring them to my lips while keeping my eyes on hers. "You're gorgeous, inside and out. If it's okay, I'm going to kiss you everywhere tonight."

Pink creeps up her chest and settles on her cheeks. She starts to raise her hands to cover herself, but I kneel in front of her instead while holding them at her sides.

"Everywhere?"

I swear I hear her gulp. "Everywhere."

"I'm, um . . . uh . . . I don't know." Her voice pitches.

"Shh." I hold her still while kissing the apex of her thighs.

"Okay." She's breathy when she speaks, and I hear the back of her head hit the tile. Determined fingers weave into my hair and tighten. When I peek up, she says, "Don't look at me like that."

"Like what?" I ask, smiling.

Her thighs clench together. "Like . . . like . . . like you want to eat me."

"I do want to eat you."

She sucks in a breath, and another giggle exhales from her mixed with a delirious laugh. Her tits also look amazing. "What's so funny?"

"You. You're staring at my girl parts."

"Girl parts?" Scrunching my brow together, I stand, resting my hand above her on the tile. Searching her eyes for any indication that this isn't the first time she's had sex since . . . I don't want to think about him, but I have no idea how long she's been separated and then divorced. Surely, she's dated since . . .

"I'm not a guy who needs to know all the gory sexual details, but let me ask you something. When was the last time you were with someone?"

"It's never been like that for me."

"Like what?"

Her gaze falls to the tub, and the strength in her voice goes right with it. I hate that she feels weak at a time when she should feel empowered. She's amazing. *Has she forgotten?* She whispers, "I've only been with two people, and you're one of them." This time, her hands find my cheek, and the day's beard growth must feel rough under her soft touch. "You always saw me so differently from who I am."

"I saw who you really were. Not Douglas Noelle's daughter. Not Jason Koster's girlfriend. Not the most beautiful girl I'd ever seen even though you were. And are. No. I always saw Delilah Rae Noelle. She's the girl I would make the world spin backward if I could just to get another chance to spend time with her. You're magnificent."

Looking up under a wave of dark lashes, she's timid when she asks, "That was then. What am I now?"

"What did he do to you?"

"Jason?"

"Yeah?"

"We're naked in the shower, and the water's running cold. Maybe we can finish this talk another time. Tonight, I want to be the girl you always remembered me to be."

"I don't need that girl when I have the woman before me." I follow up with a kiss on the tip of her nose.

She raises her arms into the air, and says, "You missed a spot." The weight of our worries lifts, and the playfulness returns. Happy to kiss that spot, I caress her breasts and kiss her neck. Her body vibrates as she laughs, then she adds, "We should really hurry this along before the water's freezing." I rub my body against hers, soaping myself up.

When she dips her soapy hands and takes hold of my erection, I waver, my eyes wanting to close, to savor, to just feel. "God, that feels so good."

"Wait until I remind you what I can do with my tongue."

I hit the knob to turn the water off and yank the towels from the shower rod. I don't see the rod falling, but the top of my head catches it. "Fuck."

"Oh, no!" Under the plastic curtain, she finds me and rubs my head. "I'm so sorry. Are you okay?"

"I'll live." With a giant bump, but I will.

"I've been meaning to secure it. It's not the first time it's fallen." She's all over me, kissing my shoulder and still rubbing my head.

With the curtain still engulfing us, I pull her hands down and look into her worried eyes. "I'm okay, and I'll fix it before I leave."

The concern trapped in her brow eases, and a smile appears. Leaning down and kissing my forehead, she says, "I'd like that. Hopefully that's not until morning, though."

"I'm hoping for at least midday." Now I'm smiling and it's probably too big, but I don't care. Taking her by the waist, I pull her close while pushing the curtain away.

"Midday already sounds too soon." Her smile is mischievous and absolutely enticing. "Come on. I want to show you something."

"Please tell me you plan on showing me to the bedroom." She wraps the towel around her, and I sigh in my discontent.

"Absolutely." She winks, her brave and beautifully confident side returning. This is the Delilah I remember. This is the side of her that I hope remains, even if I'm not around to remind her who she is.

12

Jason

When Delilah mentioned she'd remind me what she can do with her tongue, I admit, my mind recalled the best blow jobs I've ever received—*all* courtesy of her.

Lying in the truck bed under a star-filled sky.

In the cab while driving across county lines after winning a Friday night game.

Once behind the DQ.

So many times in my room, and maybe more in hers.

Our parents never knew how bad we were back in those days. Although it was always so good for us.

What I didn't expect was her tongue sliding up my neck and taking my earlobe into her mouth. When her tongue grazes over it and she sucks—*fuuuck.* She has me hard as a rock and ready to fuck. "I can't take much more of this torture, baby."

Straddling my lap, she smiles at me. "Is the foreplay too much?"

"No. It's done its job as you can tell." Taking her by the

hips, I flip her next to me and maneuver over her. Her legs part, welcoming my body as I slide into place. Slipping my hand between us, I ask, "Are you wet for me?" Sweet pink lips form a little O as the shock of my question infiltrates the fine features of her face. My cheek cocks up. "Don't tell me you don't like a little dirty talk."

"I don't know." There's a hint of excitement in her tone.

While running two of my fingers on the inside of her thigh, my gaze rises back to hers. "I want to relearn everything about you. Every inch. Everything that brings you pleasure." I reach down, running the tips of my fingers through her slickness. I kiss her collarbone as I push in, our bodies beginning a slow dance, coming together and moving apart. My emotions are too wrapped up to pretend this doesn't mean more than I've let on. It does. Being with her does. From that look in her eyes, I believe this means more to her as well. Pulling back, I touch the tips of my fingers to my tongue as she watches under lust-filled eyes. "Tastes like honey, *honeysuckle*."

"Kiss me, Jason."

I lower on the bed and place my hand on her stomach. "With pleasure." Her eyes go wide when I lick through her wetness. Memories flood my mind and taste buds. She was always so fucking delectable. Her hips begin to wiggle, and I hear her moan. My hair is tugged, but when I stop to look up, her bottom lip is under pressure and her eyes are closed.

Fucking stunning.

I make love to her with my mouth as her sweet sounds of bliss fill my ears. When she comes, she comes hard, her fingers tangle in my hair, and she calls my name as if I'm the one she prays to. I can't take any more. I'm about to explode. I'm so turned on, I've started to hump the mattress beneath me, seeking relief. I come up, sliding my body along hers as I lift myself.

"I have condoms in the nightstand," she says.

I don't care how stupid my smile looks at the moment. I reach over and open the drawer. With condoms in hand, I drop them on the bed. "Tell me these aren't the same ones from back in college."

She laughs. "No. Newer condoms."

"How new?" I ask, waggling my eyebrows. Her being prepared is sexy. I'm curious how many towns away she had to drive to buy these.

She slinks down on the bed a bit and covers her face with her hands. Speaking between her fingers, she says, "This afternoon."

"Oh no. You don't get to hide your eyes." I take her wrists and move them to the side with little resistance. I see her vibrant blues, her carefree smile, and when she giggles, I add, "You bought condoms because you were hoping to get lucky?"

"I figured better safe than sorry."

"So just anyone could have been in my place tonight, or you bought condoms to use with me?"

She rolls her eyes, but the grin gives her away.

Pinning her wrists above her head, I say, "Admit it. You were hoping to have me naked in your bed tonight." When she laughs again, I push for more. "Come on, Delilah. Tell me how much you wanted to have sex with me."

"You win," she says, trying for nonchalance. "I drove thirty minutes out of my way just to score some condoms without judgment or gossip getting around town. All the way to Cleverton."

"I may not blush like you do, but I'm flattered none-theless."

"So much talking, Koster. How about we get to the main attraction?"

I kiss her cheek. "Wow, you get feisty when you get a taste of the good stuff."

"And by taste, you mean you?"

"Abso-fucking-lutely."

"Well, get to it. I'm all warmed up, baby. Raring to go. *Again*."

Baby. I sure like the sound of that. I chuckle. "Are you now?"

"I am. So ready for more."

More. I'll have her begging for more all right. I slide a condom over my erection and hold it proudly. Women aren't impressed with large dicks. They're impressed by how they're used, so I don't need to wave it around to brag. I just need to make her feel every hard inch, filling her not just for my pleasure but also for hers. I position myself back between her legs and press the tip against her sweet abyss.

My nerves from earlier are buried under the desire I have for her. "More," I mumble, immersing myself in her heat when I slide slowly inside her. "Fuck," I exhale the word under a heavy breath. I want to say it's the sex, the overwhelming sensation of having it again, but that would be a lie. *It's her*—wet, tight, angling, moaning. *Fuck.* Delilah's heaving chest with perky tits on top, her tongue sliding over her lips, her back arching. "You feel amazing."

Her nails drag over my shoulders and then her fingers lace behind my neck, pulling me to her. "Kiss me."

I do.

I kiss her and thrust—tongues and other parts of my body going deep—claiming her in ways I haven't in years. Our breaths are exchanged, one lifeline sustained by the other. When her hands find my ass, she squeezes. "Faster."

Harder.

All of her.

I want her next orgasm, and the one after that.

I want to hear my name coming out like a curse word and to mess up that pretty hair.

I want to see her eyes wild with lust and insatiable desire for me.

I want to fuck her again—*faster, harder*—and then make slow love to her after that, feeling every damn measured movement together.

My forehead drops to the mattress next to hers, and I thrust and feel, relishing in the raw fire burning inside.

"Come with me," she urges, her body writhing beneath mine in search of her own orgasm.

Like a wave rushing through me, I come, my body and soul dragged under with her when she calls my name like it's a sin she's just confessed.

My lips part, and air enters my lungs, filling my chest. The blackness disperses, and the small room with a little lamp shining next to the bed comes into focus. Swallowing is rough because my throat is dry, but my body feels free from the confines I've felt for days, months, even years. Then I find peace in the aftermath.

Soft touches and little kisses cover me, and I open my tired eyes to find hers as bright as they were in the sunshine, and her face more beautiful in its sated state. "Hi," I say.

"Hi," she breathes, my weight causing her more trouble than she admits.

I smile and roll to the side. "Sorry about that."

"I liked it. I like feeling you on top of me with your weight holding me down."

Resting my arm across the top of my head, I peek over at her. "Why do you need to be held down?"

"Feeling this good, this light means I'll surely float away."

It's interesting how such a simple shared emotion makes me feel better. Or maybe it's her. The lightness, this peace, is something I desperately craved for the past few years. "C'mere." I encourage her over on top of me. When she's settled, her body relaxed and her head resting on my chest, I add, "I feel the same."

I can't see her pretty face, but I can feel the smile that graces it, and I can hear the happiness in her voice when she says, "That stunt you pulled this morning, stopping traffic and making demands you had no right to make . . . I'm glad you did."

Fuck yeah. My smile could probably rival hers. "I am too."

Her fingers run through the light hair on my chest. "I know I don't have a right to ask more of you," she starts, resting her chin on me so I can see her eyes. "But I'd like you to stay the night. No pressure, though."

I kiss the top of her golden locks. "I have no intention of leaving tonight."

Her smile lights up the room brighter than the small lamp ever could. "What intentions do you have?"

Repeating her words from earlier, I say, "So much talking. How tired are you?"

"What do you have in mind?"

"To show you exactly what my intentions are." I move her to the side of me and kiss her until those little mewls begin again, signaling the start of the second round.

THE SMELL of bacon and eggs rouses me from sleep. I reach

over to find the bed empty beside me, much to my dismay. I love a hardy breakfast after a night of hot sex, but I'd rather have Delilah waking me up. Maybe with her mouth on me or with my mouth on her.

Fuck.

I'm hard.

I rub over my hard cock, attempting to get it to go down, but I'm not sure that's possible with her scent all around me.

Flipping the sheets off, I get up to find my clothes clean, dry, and laid out at the end of the mattress. I pull on my underwear, still warm from the dryer. She's good, *too good*. Hopefully she washed them because she wanted to and not because she felt obligated. That bullshit about women being barefoot and pregnant and waiting on a man hand and foot doesn't fly with me. I don't need my wife to serve me.

My hand stills with my jeans halfway up.

Wife?

Where the fuck did that come from?

I pull them up and head to the bathroom. The word *wife* didn't kill my erection like I'd have thought, but my mind is spinning over the words, letting it rumble around, trying to find where it fits. I take a piss and wash my hands, but when I look in the mirror, I see myself in a light I thought I had lost touch with a long time ago. Maybe I can be who I used to be. I wasn't so bad back then. A little heartbroken. A lot ego-shattered. Losing your girl to your best friend wasn't something I could control back then, but it's nothing I should be ashamed of now.

We may not have wanted to talk last night, but we'll need to soon. I splash my face with cool water and pat it dry before heading downstairs. Passing through the living room, I follow the sounds from the kitchen and find Delilah scrambling eggs.

Her back is to me, which gives me a second to take her in. Her hair is up in a messy bun on top of her head, the delicate lines of her neck visible. She's in a black tank top that shows off the curve from her waist to her hips, leading my gaze lower to her ass—round enough to fill out that pair of cutoffs that her daddy would never approve of.

As for me? They've got my stamp of approval. Bare legs and feet anchor her to a mat with an ugly teapot design. With a hand planted on her side, she tilts her hips as if she's lost patience for how long it's taking the eggs to cook.

I ease up behind her. Sliding my hands around her waist, I kiss the back of her exposed neck. Her body tenses at first and then quickly eases. She leans her head back on my shoulder, then kisses my neck. "Good morning," I say, sliding my hands over the top of the tank until her tits fill them.

The spatula is discarded, and she spins in my arms, weaving her arms around my neck. "Good morning."

I turn off the stove and move the pan to a cold burner before pressing her ass against the counter next to it. "You smell amazing."

"That's the bacon."

"No. It's you."

"I haven't showered. I'm still dirty from last night."

With my lips against her neck, I hum. "Yeah, dirty. So dirty. I'm so hungry. For you. Want to go back to the bedroom?" Lifting her, I raise my gaze to meet hers. "Or we could test out that kitchen table like we used to joke about."

Laughter fills the kitchen, and she languidly gazes into my eyes, something more than lust filling the centers. Like . . . *love*? The word wife comes back to bounce around the vacant space in my heart Delilah left behind.

"My parents used to have a cup of coffee at that table

every morning and eat a meal there every night. They said it was the only time they were guaranteed together with the busyness of their lives."

"So that's a yes to the table?" I tease.

"That's a—"

"What the hell?" Her response is cut short when the screen door opens, and a man's voice booms. "Jason Koster's truck is out front."

13

Jason

"Morning, Billy," Delilah says as her hands press against me.

I take a step back and let her tend to the eggs in the pan like we weren't just caught. Looking over my shoulder, I see a goofy wide grin spreading across his face as the screen door slams shut behind him. I shake my head. "Your timing sucks."

"Good morning to you, too, sunshine." He sits down at the table, making himself at home like he's staying a while. "Whatcha cookin' over there, other than some delicious-smelling bacon and freshly brewed coffee?"

Replying while crossing my arms, I glare at him. "Nothing now. What brings you out to the farm?"

He chuckles and takes off his hat just as Delilah sets a plate in front of him. "I could ask you the same thing." He smiles up at her. "Thank you."

She pats his back. "You're welcome." When she turns to me, she says, "Hungry for *food*?"

I catch the food emphasis. "Starved."

"Sit down and let me feed you."

"I can make a plate."

"I'm happy to make it for you, Jason."

"Thank you." Sitting across from Billy, who waggles his eyebrows, I give him a harder glare than before. He just laughs and shovels more eggs into his mouth. After drinking some coffee, he says, "Man, your eggs are the best."

My jaw clenches. I don't like him talking about her eggs and how they're the best. I try to shake off my annoyance at how casually he walked into her house, moved around her kitchen, and sat at her table like he'd done it a million times before. She mentioned that Billy had been helping out a lot, but they're so familiar with each other. *Am I setting myself up again for a huge lot of hurt?*

She sets a plate in front of me and sits in a chair between us with her own plate. "Thanks, Billy. You're out here early."

"I'm heading to Kerbyville to pick up supplies for the week and wanted to check with you to see if you need anything other than the usual."

Delilah starts to get up, but I touch her knee. "You should eat breakfast while it's hot. I can help you guys after."

"Okay. Thanks." A soft smile plays at the tip of her lips. "Not much to get, but I'll make a list when we're done eating."

After cleaning the kitchen, Delilah and I go back upstairs while Billy heads out to the barn. "How much does Billy help you out here?"

"Don't get jealous," she says, poking me in the side when she passes. Sitting in a chair, she pulls on a pair of socks and then steps into her work boots. Heaven almighty. My memory seriously had failed me when it came to this woman. She is no girl at all. With grown-up curves and a sense about her that draws me to her like a moth to a flame, she's a fantasy come to life, easily outshining any centerfold I've ever seen.

Rolling in the hay and riding in the saddle take on a whole new filthy and oh, so dirty meaning with the vision standing before me.

"What?" she asks with her hands planted on her hips again.

"You sure do have a lot of sass with that hot ass."

Shaking those same sexy hips as she passes by me, she says, "You seem like you can handle me."

I smack her hard on her back end, making her squeal as she turns to me. I pull her by the belt loops until we're face-to-face, only a breath away. "You know I can. No seeming about it. If you want to be bent over this bed or a hay bale in the barn, then I suggest you keep doing exactly what you're doing."

Watching her lick that bottom lip is about to do me in, but then she douses the fire burning inside me. "As tempting as you make hay sound, Billy's waiting out back." She takes my hands and lifts up on her toes to kiss me. "Spend the day with me."

"That's a hard offer to turn down."

"Then don't, and I'll make sure hard is all you are later on."

Cupping her jaw, I bring her in for another kiss. This time with purpose and passion, a *thank you, ma'am, and I look forward to later* kiss. A deal struck and sealed with our lips. "I'm going to hold you to that."

She nips at my jaw and then kisses the spot. "I'm hoping you'll hold me to a lot of things later. But first," she says, walking away, "we've got work to do." I'm still standing there admiring the view when she stops and looks back. "C'mon now. Daylight's burning."

"So am I," I mumble and then laugh. She heads outside, and I sit and put my socks and shoes on. When I'm done, I go into the bathroom and scrounge around until I find a toothbrush. I bust open the package and brush before I head out to help. I feel better just in case we need to kiss at the feed store.

In the cab of Billy's dad's truck, they talk upfront. It's a nice ride, so I get more comfortable in the back seat and stretch my legs out when I decide I should text my mom. She's not been my keeper for many years, but I know she worries about me.

Me: *Hi, Ma. Helping Billy and Delilah out today at the Noelle farm. Just checking in.*

I lead with Billy, hoping that doesn't tip her off to ask too many questions.

She doesn't reply right away, but I get a return text before we reach Kerbyville town lines.

Mom: *Hope you got some breakfast out of the deal.*

Me: *I did.*

Mom: *I meant food, Jason.*

My mom's got jokes this morning. Although I'll always be her baby, as she constantly reminds me, it's nice that she treats me like a man.

Me: *Ha! I'll be home later. Let me know if you need me to stop and get you anything.*

Mom: *Have fun.*

Me: *You too. Love you.*

Mom: *Love you too, son.*

Delilah rests her arm on the seat and looks back at me. "What's so funny?"

I lift my eyes to her curious ones. "Just texting with my mom."

"That's sweet."

"I hate worrying her."

"She's such a good lady." She glances out the windshield and then back at me. "Have you spent any time with Fred Carver?"

What an odd question. "No. Just when I went to General Hardware a week or so ago. Why?"

Her eyes go slightly wide, and she turns away from me. "Oh, no reason."

"Why would I spend time with Fred Carver?" I see Billy glance over at her, and she looks at him before she keeps avoiding the question. "Delilah?"

With a heavy sigh, she angles back in the seat again. "I shouldn't have said anything."

"Yes, you should. Like now is a good time to say something."

Worry creases her forehead, the look not good enough to grace her face. "Tell me. Please."

Looking at her side, her hands twist together. When she finally looks up, she says, "Your mom and Fred have been dating. From my understanding, it's casual, but she told me she likes him."

"What?" I'm shaking my head in complete denial. "No, no way." She's not facing me, but I can see her cringing face. "Is she really?"

"Rumor has it that it's more than casual," Billy says.

"Why do I get the distinct impression that you're enjoying this a little too much?"

He shrugs. "Because I am."

"Fuck you, man."

"Hey. Hey. Settle down. She's a grown woman with needs," Delilah says.

Grabbing Billy's cowboy hat from the hook across the cab from me, I put it on and sink in the seat. I lower the brim, and say, "No. I do not want to hear about my mom's needs, so let's end this now."

Her hand taps my leg, and then she lifts the brim of the hat. "You might have to get used to the idea of her dating, but I'm surprised she hasn't mentioned him to you or that you haven't seen him hanging around."

I grumble, "He's smart enough to stay away from my mom."

The sound of her laughter fills the truck, and then Billy joins in, and says, "While you're in town."

"I'm not in a hurry."

Delilah looks at her lap, but from this angle, I see the smile on her face. Billy bursts into our moment, and adds, "It's been good to have you around again."

"It's been good to be around again." Leaning forward, I give her elbow a little squeeze. "How are you doing up there?"

Looking back, she flashes that sweet smile like she's been saving it for me all day. "Good." Her eyes tell me all I need to know and remind me of how they shined at two in the morning after we finished another round of fun under the covers.

"Can we just get it out in the open because all this sexual tension between you two isn't so subtle, if you know what I mean."

I chuckle. "No, what do you mean?"

"It's obvious I interrupted something this morning. I'm curious if what I walked in on started last night."

Leaning back, I lower the hat to cover my eyes again. "Sorry. I'm not one to kiss and tell."

Delilah is laughing, and then I hear her say, "Don't look at me like that, Billy Langston. A girl has a right to keep some secrets, even from her friends."

The truck stops, and he shifts into park. I sit up, hanging the hat back on the hook. But as soon as I shift forward to get out, he says, "You two are ridiculous. It's obvious what's going on here. Let's just hope the whole town doesn't get wind. Boy willy, they'll have all sorts of stuff to occupy their time and talk about." He hops out of the truck and shuts the door.

My eyes meet Delilah's before she gets out. We both know we can't avoid what we so easily avoided talking about last night for long. Her smile has faded. Reaching forward, I touch her arm. "Don't worry. It's going to be okay."

We're suddenly on the downward side of the high we were riding as a damper is put on our fun. It felt good to feel careless for a night, but nothing good can last forever. And then I look around, falling into my old self.

Three garage doors on the right side for large load trucks.

Two sets of double doors in the far back corners.

Four doors at the front entrance.

"Jason?"

I look behind me. Delilah is standing there with a curious look built into the tilt of her head. "What's on your mind?"

"Nothing."

"Billy wanted your help over there."

"Okay."

I start to leave, but she asks, "Where do you go in that head of yours when you disappear like that?"

"Nowhere good." Habits are hard to break.

I help load some bags of chicken feed, then slam the tail-gate closed. Billy had already loaded the rest of the supplies. While he pays, Delilah leans on the side of the truck, her boots kicked out, showing off those long, tan legs of hers.

Two cowboys walk by and blatantly check her out,

causing jealousy to run through my veins, striking deep in my chest. I step over her boots, straddling her legs, and then lean forward, caging her in. "I don't like all these eyes on you."

Her arms come around my neck, and she stares at me, seeing right through me. "I only care about your eyes on me." Leveraging herself against me, she kisses me as if she has a point to prove. Maybe she does.

I do too. I don't need to prove it here, but I'm no fool. Wrapping my arms around her waist, I lift her, and when her legs wrap around me, I kiss her deeper, getting lost in the sensual caress.

"I knew it," Billy says from behind me. "Break it up and save it for later, preferably when I'm not there."

We start laughing, the kiss broken but replaced with smiles. We don't make it out of the parking lot before he asks, "So you guys are a thing again?"

It's strange that labeling something grounds a feeling that was freeing just minutes earlier. I stare out the window. I'm not sure what to say, so I'll let her say what she needs and back her on it. But I have a feeling that conversation is going to happen now whether we want to have it or not.

"We're not going to complicate things just yet," she replies.

Lowering my head, I scrub my hands over my face. What am I doing? What was I thinking? It was supposed to be a few days, visit my mom, and then head off. To where? I don't know, but I know I have to be careful. My past could catch up to me if I'm not. And here I am, possibly dragging Delilah into my messy life as if there couldn't be any repercussions to hers.

Her hand covers my knee, and when I peer up at her, words aren't needed for me to know what she's thinking.

The crinkle in her forehead, the lilt of her lips, and the sorrow that's returned to her eyes tell me everything I need to know. I take her hand and raise it to my lips for a kiss. There's not much else I can do while trapped in this truck.

Most of the ride back is in silence, the three of us in our own thoughts. I don't mind the quiet. I've spent more time alone than with others in the past four years. Being a loner was sort of a job requirement, so I was a natural since I was looking for a way to escape. *To hide.*

I made a few friends and bonded with a woman on the last job, but that bond only went friendship deep. A deeper connection is what I've been missing. Eyeing Delilah through the space between the front seats, I'm already feeling connected to her again. I don't know if I should protect my heart, but I feel like it might be too late.

14

Jason

A small basket of eggs is just inside the barn when we arrive back at the Noelle farm. Delilah grabs it while Billy and I unload the truck. It's good to do physical labor like this. It burns off the restless energy I feel inside, the same energy I used to burn off by running away from my problems.

Billy comes up behind me and grabs the last bag as I haul some rolled-up fencing. "So between us, it's obvious you two are on again. Does that mean you're sticking around?" he asks.

"Are you asking out of curiosity or concern?"

"A little of both. She's a good woman."

I drop the fencing along the outside wall of the barn and give him a long, hard look. "You interested?"

"Nah. We're friends. Nothing more. But that doesn't mean I don't care about her or her well-being." Tilting the bill of his hat up, he wipes his arm across his forehead. "Heck, I wouldn't be out here so much if I didn't." He slides up on the tailgate and chugs from a thermos. Water drips from the cap when he pulls it away and pours some on his face, then swipes a bandanna across it.

I look back to make sure Delilah doesn't hear this interrogation. When it comes to certain things like the farm, I'm not sure I'll get the dirty details from her. "How are you running your farm and this one?"

"My family is still running our farm. My brother secured some grocery store deals. We have new equipment and hired some guys."

"What about the Noelle farm? Be honest, how's it doing?"

"Sometimes, I think she wants this place to work, and sometimes, I wonder if it's holding her back." Shaking his head, he looks at the house. I follow his gaze, and we watch Delilah chopping wood. Chopping wood is not an easy job, but she seems to be managing quite well *and* looks sexy as fuck doing it. Her body's tight with great muscle definition in her arms and legs. She was always more than this farm, though.

Billy adds, "She's pretty independent and self-sufficient, but how long can she run this place on fumes?"

"Fumes?"

"Her sister's in New York City working to save this place."

"Yeah, but she said the bank gave them an extension on the loan."

When he looks back at me, he lowers his voice, and says, "Cutler made Delilah take a second mortgage on the farm to start *his* business."

"What? When?"

"Two years ago." Scratching the back of his neck, he scrunches his face and seems unsure if he should be saying anything. "Look, Jason, don't tell her I told you this. She wears her heart on her sleeve, but when it comes to this farm, her pride gets in her way."

I look back at her. The farm works her in all the right ways, but it still pisses me off that she has to work it at all. She's always been a stunning woman, but that's the outside. Her insides are warmth to my cold heart. She makes me want to stay in so many ways. I just wonder if I'm too far gone to be the man she deserves, the man she needs, the man she wants.

Do I want this life again? This life comes with rumor mills and farming, and an honest day's work, a positive side effect. "How much debt are we talking about?"

Billy shoves off the truck and grabs the fencing at my feet. "I don't have the final numbers or anything, but I know they're well into six figures."

Shit. That's a lot more than I thought. Glancing back at her, I realize how strong she is. Who knows what else she's had to hide for so long? I hate that her pretty smile possibly hides more troubles than anyone is aware.

"C'mon," he says. "I need to fix the coop and get back to my farm by noon to get some stuff done over there."

Taking the fencing from him, I say, "You head out. I can handle the coop and anything else she needs done today."

Laughing, he lowers his cap but releases the fencing. "I bet you can."

"Fuck off."

His laughter turns hardier. "Beers later?"

"You're on. Text me."

"Do you ever take calls anymore?"

"No."

He slams the tailgate closed. "You're back in Solace

Pointe, man. Time to slow down and reconnect with the real world."

"Yeah. Yeah. You're lucky you even have my number. Not many do."

Tossing his keys in the air, he catches them, and says, "See ya at beer o'clock." He gets in his truck and starts the engine. "Call me if you need anything, Delilah."

She looks up, smiles, and waves. "Thanks, Billy. You're the best."

Billy's truck kicks up some dust. I set the fencing down and walk over to her. "Hey."

One side of her mouth lifts when she looks at me. "Hey, yourself."

"I thought I was the best."

"Aw, don't be jealous. You're the best at so much."

"Like?" I ask, teasing but curious.

The weight of the ax falls to the ground and she rests her body on the handle. "I've never known you to have low self-esteem."

"I don't, but when it comes to you, I wonder."

The ax is dropped altogether, and she comes to me, wrapping her arms around my neck. There's a sheen to her skin that makes her glow from the inside and ignites a need within me. I want this woman. Damn, I want her. I take her by the waist and lick along the base of her neck.

"Jason?" She squeals in shock but giggles. "Oh my God, you're an animal."

"I find you utterly impossible to resist. You taste divine, by the way." Despite her words, she settles into my hold, pressing our bodies together. Kissing her neck, I taste her skin again and find my way to her earlobe where I nibble. "Do you know what you do to me? Do you know how incredibly sexy it is watching you wield that ax?"

She laughs again, squirming. She's ticklish, and I love that too much. I'll definitely have to indulge my enjoyment of that trait later when we're naked. I lift her into my arms, and she straddles me. When I lick the shell of her ear, she moans, and her middle seeks pleasure against me.

"Sure is hot out here," she says.

Swinging her over my shoulder, I say, "We should go inside then," and dash for the door.

She's hanging upside down against my back, but I have a firm hold of her tight ass while she's drumming on mine. "Animal."

"You love it."

Her laughter trails behind us. "Never." She keeps laughing, though.

"Admit it. You love it." I'm about to go to her room, but I detour to the bathroom to wash my hands. I want to feel my girl on the inside, so I need to get this filthy farm off me. The water faucet is on as I scrub the dirt from my hands.

"I do love it, but you do realize I'm still on your shoulder, right?"

"I do." I dry my hands and then turn around.

She reaches down like a good girl and washes her hands. "Then you must also realize this is the weirdest foreplay I've ever done."

"Cleanliness before . . ." I don't finish that thought. Considering what I'm about to do to this woman, I don't need to drag God into it. Unless, of course, it's being called at the top of her orgasm. Then she can go right ahead and scream his name all she wants, and I'll take it as a job well done.

Slapping my ass hard, she says, "All done."

I like this time with her. It's full of fun and her sunshine.

She's just what I need, a prescription to help heal my ailments.

I make it to her room and toss her on the bed. "Okay, there you go. See you later," I tease, pretending to leave.

She grabs the back hem of my shirt, yanking me backward. "Oh no, you don't." When I fall onto the bed, her smile settles as she lies back, arms wide, legs spread. "Come here."

Not waiting another second, I land on top of her, wedging my big build between those sexy tan legs, and shamelessly squeeze her tits. Rubbing her hand along the roughness of my cheek, the smile disappears. "I like you being home."

"Is that where I am, honeysuckle? Am I home?" It's a loaded question I shouldn't have asked. I know better. I hate being put on the spot, but she makes me want to hear words I have no right to make her admit. Not this soon. It's not even been twenty-four hours in her presence, and here I am, clinging to her words as if they determine the rest of my life.

Do they?

I don't know, but then she says, "You could be," and I'm totally lost to her. Kissing her, I'm not gentle or easy, and she's not polite or reserved. She's the opposite—demanding and grabby hands—and I fucking love it.

Pushing my pelvis against hers, I'm so turned on I could fuck her through these jeans. But I want her naked, so I push up and start stripping down. I'm almost done when she lifts a leg. "Help me with my boots, cowboy."

"Yes, ma'am." Taking her by the heel and toe of the boot, I wiggle the boot until it comes off, then pull the sock off. *Why is this so sexy?* I'm quick with the other. Fuck, stripping her down to nothing is the best part of the morning.

A smirk wriggles across her face. "We should be naked already."

She's right.

Our clothes go flying, and there's my goddess—bare innocence with a good helping of vixen mixed in. I'm rock-hard just looking at her. She reaches up and grabs a condom from the drawer while I climb back on the bed, taking hold of that fine ass of hers. "I want you like this."

She stills, the giddiness from seconds earlier dissipating under my heated request. Looking back over her shoulder, she asks, "From behind or . . .?" leaving her question open-ended.

Reading people is something I've become very good at over the years. Tracking them down, reading between their lies, research, when they beg for their lives comes in handy in the most interesting ways. Like now. She's intrigued, but a little fear resides in her tone. I don't want Delilah scared. I want her turned on. I want to be the one who turns her on.

Leaning to the side, I say, "Look at me." She catches my eyes and waits. Rubbing my hand gingerly up her spine, I gently grasp her delicate neck. "We only do what you want to do, what you're comfortable doing. If you want it slow, want to make love, then we go slow. You want me to fuck you hard, fast, and so deep until your orgasm bursts free, then I fuck you. You can trust me, Delilah. So tell me. How can I pleasure you?"

The tips of my fingers find stillness where her pulse was just beating rapidly. "Breathe. For me. That's my only request," I add.

She sucks in a jagged breath and swallows. "I want all of that with you."

A slow smirk slides into place before I kiss her shoulder. "Good. I want all of that with you, too. How about we start with slow and steady right here." I dip my hand between her legs and run my fingers through her slick silkiness. Her back bends and arches when her head drops down. "When you touch me, I lose myself. It's good to be out of my mind and in your world for a little while."

Moving to the side, I hear what she needs, her body speaking to me through every reaction. Lying on my back, I look at her, and she looks at me, a small smile appearing. "Don't you want me like this?" she asks.

"Don't you know, baby? I want you any way I can have you. Tell me what you want."

"I want to see your face while you make love to me."

I lift up and kiss her while slowly moving over her. When she's lying on her back and tucked beneath me, I angle my middle. I could slide right in I'm so close. Her heat. Her sweet nectar. Fuck. I grab a condom and pull it on quickly before moving back into place. "I was just about here—"

"I know we decided slow and steady, but having you here again, feeling your body . . ." The smallest of lines form on the outside of her eyes as her happiness shines through. "I hope you don't think I'm shallow, but I really like your muscles—your biceps, your abs, your . . ." Her breathing deepens and her eyes leave mine when she whispers, "Ass."

"What was that?" I tilt her chin in my direction, and her gaze follows. "Did you say you like my ass?"

She seems to gather her courage, looking determined. "Yes, I did say I like your ass."

"That has to be one of the hottest things I've ever heard." I push in just enough to make her feel what's to come. "I want you to grab it."

Her eyebrows shoot up. "Huh?"

"You heard me. Grab my ass and squeeze to your heart's content."

"I bet you say that to all the girls you sleep with," she smarts back, rolling her eyes.

"I don't sleep with any girls." I push in another inch or so.

A gasp escapes her, and she struggles to keep her eyes open, but she does it as if on a mission. "I know that's a lie."

"It's more like let me call you an Uber."

"Now that does not surp—Oh God, yes."

Filling her to the hilt, I pause not for some grand effect but because she feels so damn good that I'm about to blow before I can make her come. Lowering my head, I whisper in her ear, "You are amazing."

She whispers right back, "I'm not doing anything but lying here."

I lift up to find her eyes. "You don't get it, do you? It's not about all the other stuff with us. It's about being together, our physical and emotional connection. I'm glad I came back."

Her eyes shine, a glassiness covering them as her expression softens. "I'm so glad you came back." Caressing my cheeks, she adds, "Now please start moving."

My body easily finds a rhythm with hers. Her eyelids close, and I lean down and kiss her sumptuous lips, parting them as my tongue meets hers, and everything deepens when I start thrusting. Just as she said earlier, it feels so good to lose myself in something bigger than my thoughts.

We hit that bliss together, our bodies wracked with pleasure and lust melding together. We lie on the bed, catching our breaths with my arm curled around her as she curls around me. This feels normal, as though we do this all the time. Nothing feels out of place. Nothing feels wrong or rushed.

Everything about being with her in this house feels how it should.

Everything about *her* feels right.

With the only girl I ever loved in my arms, my restless heart finds contentment.

Comfort.

Solace . . .

15

Delilah

I stare at the man beside me.

There's not much light in the room, but there's enough afternoon sunshine sneaking through the bent blinds for me to see the differences between the boy I once thought I'd spend my life with and the man sleeping next to me.

He's restless.

Even behind closed lids, his eyes never seem to settle. With my hand on his chest, his heart beats fast even in slumber. There are small lines that remind me more of cat's whiskers than crow's feet at the corners of his eyes. They're soft, but I see them digging in for the long haul. They look so much more distinguished on him than the ones settling in on my face from years of squinting in the sun.

Jason's nose has a small bump that wasn't there before. I like it. I'm tempted to run my finger over it and land on the lips that look like pillows where my mouth could rest easy. The stubble is thick, but not so thick that it's a beard needing to be shaved. It's hard to decide if I like this look or a clean-shaven face on him best. Both highlight the jaw that's gotten sharper over the years.

I see the clouds of the design of his tattoo so much better in the soft light of the sun peeking into the room. The artwork of the tattoo is both beautiful and sad. I hope that was him then, and he can find happiness now because I sure do love the comfort of being in his arms again.

Too soon?

I'm not sure.

Although I want to enjoy this time with him, I slip into my usual routine and start to analyze the situation to death. Why did I walk away from this man? He's never been anything but honest with me, so forthcoming with how he feels.

If given a real second chance, I won't be that stupid again. I need to trust in the journey. I won't deviate from this path if it feels this good to be with him.

"Hey," I whisper.

As if he's been awake the whole time, his eyes open, showing me those gorgeous brown eyes that always held too much emotion for him to hide from me. Despite his body's restlessness, his soulful eyes are at peace as they stare into mine. His arm tightens around me, pulling me closer. "Hey," he whispers, brushing some strands of my hair behind my ear. "Everything okay?"

Resting my chin on his chest, I look at him. "Everything's good. Better than good."

A languid smile moves into place and holds steady. "Guess we should get up. I slept harder than I thought I would for an afternoon nap."

"I'm glad. You needed it."

He bends his neck to the side, stretching it. "It's this place."

I don't beat around the bush. Neither of us has time for that. "I like having you here." He doesn't say anything, but he doesn't need to. His fingers weave through my hair, and he holds the back of my head, looking at me, studying me before pulling me to him and kissing me.

Our bodies find their way together again, and we fill the afternoon with moans, expending our desire, and satiating our lust.

Left with smiles that feel shy, although I don't know why, we take a shower and get dressed. Watching me as he puts his jeans on, he says, "I told Billy I'd fix your chicken coop."

"Do you know how, city slicker?"

Laughing, he dips his feet into his shoes and winks. "I think I can manage, but I need to start tomorrow if that's okay. I promised my mom I would change her oil today."

"You don't owe me anything, Jason. I can manage."

Coming over to me, he rubs my arms. "I know you can, but I want to help. Is it okay for me to take that job off your hands? You have plenty to take care of yourself."

My arms go around his middle as I rest my head against his chest and close my eyes. His heart is strong, and he's caring. I'm not sure I should feel so at home in his arms, but I sure do love being tucked inside them. It's safe here, like the world can't touch us, and all our problems belong to someone else. "Thank you."

He kisses my head. When we part, he asks, "Are you busy tonight?"

"No," I reply, laughing lightly. "My schedule is pretty wide open most days."

"Let me ask you something."

Here it comes—the questions I've been happily avoiding. I lean against the oak dresser, needing to brace myself against something solid. "Okay."

"Will you come to dinner tonight at my mom's house?"

"Wait. What?"

His forehead crinkles from my response. "Dinner. You. Me. My mom. Will you join us?"

That's not what I expected him to ask. I thought for sure he'd bring up Cole, but I'm so glad he doesn't let him invade our time together. "Dinner?"

"You know," he says, his hands motioning like charades as he feeds himself. "Food. Eating. Talking. That kind of thing."

I smile. "I'd love to."

A wide smile appears, but his eyes always hold a little mischievousness. "How's seven?"

"Perfect. I'll bring dessert." I start out of the bedroom, wondering if I have all the ingredients I need to bake something delicious for them.

"I always loved your desserts."

"Are we still talking about food?"

"Nope."

I roll my eyes and head for the living room. "I'm not sure I can keep up with your appetite."

"I'm insatiable *because* of you."

Stopping in the hall, I turn around and press my hands against his chest. I rub lightly over the cotton of his shirt, wanting to feel his hard muscles through it . . . yeah, I do, and I'm not making any apologies for it. But are we just undeniable physical attraction? Chemistry ready to combust? I like talking to him, but he has so much locked inside still hidden from me. I have my own secrets, too. Is it rational to want more with him when he just returned to town? To me? "What are we doing, Jason?"

His smile turns light, and his eyes darken with the

change in my tone. "We're getting to know each other. Again. That's all," he says.

I nod, and then take a deep breath before exhaling. "I come with baggage I didn't have last time around."

"We all do." When he kisses my cheek, his mouth lingers on my skin, sending goose bumps across my arms. "I lied earlier."

"About?"

"When I said I rest better because there's something about this place. I lied. It's not the place."

"What is it?"

He cups my face, and our lips meet, but he doesn't kiss me. "It's you. You give me the peace I've needed, and the emptiness inside isn't so empty anymore."

He fills the emptiness inside me as well. Our lips meet, and we kiss, exchanging the words that aren't needed.

"I'll see you tonight, Delilah."

He walks around and right out my front door like it's his own to return through. I lean against the frame and watch him through the screen door. He starts his truck and looks back at me, leaving me with a nod of his head and a smile on his face that feels genuine. Dirt fills the air behind his tires, and I watch that old beat-up pickup drive away, feeling anxious as the distance grows.

What are we really?

Are we playing a game, or is this real?

I miss him already, and it hasn't been a minute since he left.

That feels pretty darn real, to my heart at least, but I shouldn't overthink this. We need to happen naturally for it to turn into something more. More? Is that even something I should be considering? Cole will never let that happen.

He'd rather see me dead than with someone else, least of all Jason Koster.

I can't spend my life tiptoeing around Cole Cutler's eggshell of an ego. We're over. That's been made clear—in court and out. It's time I take my life back and start living again.

With more than four hours until I need to be at dinner, I wrap up some chores.

This goofy smile on my face might be the answer I'm looking for. I head out back and return to chopping the wood I'm going to need to store for winter. It's back-breaking work, but I can't afford the wood delivery service anymore. At least I no longer have to work out at the gym. The chores around here are enough to keep me in shape. And Jason seems to really like my body . . . perhaps more than before, which surprises me. I haven't felt attractive . . . well, since Jason used to appreciate me—emotionally and physically.

After the wood's chopped, I inspect the coop. I can easily fix this, but that Jason wants to help is so sweet, and I like him hanging around enough to let him take on this job. I hop on the ATV and drive around the fields to the two active ones. Paul oversees the plots with Billy, but he also lives on the acreage that bumps against the fields in a two-bedroom cottage my dad built when I was little. I used to dream of living in that little white house with its gingerbread trim and door.

Lorraine, his wife, takes care of the house, keeping it in shape despite time wanting to wear it down. She brings me food too often, but she knows how I love her cooking. She also says I'm too skinny. I'll happily take her pralines to help "widen my hips to bear children," as she puts it. They're too delicious to pass up.

She's watering the flowers out front when I drive up. "Hi, Delilah."

"Hi, how are you today?"

"It's a beautiful day," she replies with a motherly smile on her face. "I saw a truck leaving the property earlier."

Her mothering instincts go beyond a smile. I've known her since I was eight, so we've been through a lot of changes together through the years. I don't have to say much. She's happy to fill the air with her wisdom and observations, which have been comforting since I lost my mom and dad. "Your old boyfriend, the one I liked, used to drive a truck just like that."

I take over the task. As the water sprinkles across the flower bed, I keep my tone level, careful not to give more away than I have a right to. "He still does."

I don't have to see her face to hear the joy in her voice. "It was a good visit?"

Looking at her, I see her hands clasped together in front of her chest.

"You don't have to pretend. Tell me what you know."

"Paul said the truck stayed overnight."

I giggle, the usual burdens feeling lighter, almost effervescent today. "It did. Along with Jason."

"Jason," she says in such a dreamy way. "I always did like how he treated you."

"Even in the end?"

"The end? Hmm. You weren't one to reason with back then."

I've yet to process what Jason said last night. I felt like a fool. No, more than that, I felt heartsick at what I must have put *him* through. How could he come back here and want to reconnect with me? He must have hated me, especially when he saw me with Cole at Red River.

Why? Why hadn't I gone back to him and given him a chance to speak? He wasn't a selfish man. He never had been. My assumptions were based on an insecurity that I placed on myself, not from his actions. Cole is to blame for his part; he was devious. But I fell for it. Naïve. My heart hurts thinking about what I did. God, how I hurt Jason. But here he is, despite the pain he's felt, potentially offering us a second chance. He's so much stronger than I ever was.

I set the empty can down and move to sit on her steps. Resting my arms on my knees, I stare ahead at the field that meets the end of her yard. When I glance over at her, I say, "He wasn't going to break up with me. That's what he told me."

"I could have told you that, too."

Softly laughing, I reply, "You probably did. I just wasn't able to hear you through the noise in my head."

"But you hear him now?"

"I'm not sure."

She sits next to me, wrapping me in a loving embrace. "Sometimes it's not the loudest voice we hear, but the soft whisper our heart feels. Back then, the sting of *perceived* betrayal clouded your judgment and clogged your ears. Someone took advantage of that pain and twisted it for his own needs."

Although I can't remember exactly when Cole first talked to me about Jason leaving, I can recall some of what he'd said.

"I'm sure you know what guys are like, Delilah. He's leaving this town—you, me, Billy—and moving on." He reaches over and rubs my shoulder, consoling me. I'm not even sure what he's talking about, which worries me more. Is Jason keeping secrets?

My hands tighten around the handles of my cheerleading bag, and I look toward the stadium tunnel that leads to the locker rooms. Jason is long gone, the coach calling him in to talk. *Is it about leaving? Leaving school? Leaving me?*

As I worry my lip, he continues, "He's kept you on a string, someone to come back to when he wants you." He runs his hands through his sweaty hair. When he looks back at me, it's a look of excitement . . . like lust? *Surely not. I've seen this look before but dismissed it as nothing since I'm with his best friend.*

"I'm sick of the rumors I've heard about him when he's visiting State's campus. Rumors about him and other girls. You deserve better. Why do you put up with that?" he says.

I remember doubting Cole, thinking that wasn't the Jason Koster I knew and loved. But each time Cole looked at me with sympathy and held me as if to comfort me, I started to believe him. *But was it true?*

No.

That wasn't Jason at all. But somehow, I felt more confusion when I didn't hear what Jason had to talk to the coach about, or why he suddenly had to stay after practice a few times for meetings.

Was Jason lying to me or waiting to tell me what he considered good news? I know now, but I wish I had known then.

At my weakest, Cole pursued me. He'd turn up every day to spend time with me, to *help* a friend he'd said. And when I saw Jason at Red River just before he left again for college, I didn't know how to understand the look in his eyes. He'd looked angry with me and definitely with Cole. But I remember what I felt that night. I'd been just as angry. By then, Cole had told me story after story of all the women Jason had been with on every visit to other campuses. He'd told me about the *many crude jokes* he'd heard Jason say about me when out drinking with the guys.

Were they all lies? And if so, why had I been so stupid and naïve to believe him?

Because I'd been devastated. I'd believed he was leaving me and heading off to his world, a world I had no place in.

"Cole was a force to be reckoned with. He played upon my insecurities until I couldn't see anything beyond the lies he was feeding me. I owe Jason an apology." My swallow is heavy like my heart as I think about how I hurt him.

Sitting up, Lorraine pats my back. "If I still know Jason at all, I have a feeling he doesn't want or need an apology."

"What does he want?"

"The same thing he always needed. You."

"Can I be what he needs, what he deserves now? Am I stronger?" After last night, I think I am.

"Strength is found in the ashes of the fire. You've been burned, but you must rise because there's so much life ahead of you to live. Wouldn't it be nice to share that life with someone who cares for you so deeply?"

Pushing off the concrete steps, she takes the watering can from me in one hand. With her other, she covers her chest. "Trust what's in here, Delilah." Then she adds, "Paul is in the back quarter if you're looking for him," before she disappears behind the house.

Lorraine has never needed to fill her days with a lot of chatter. I think the love she feels for life is fulfilling enough. Her thoughts aren't veiled. She always makes her views heard.

I screwed up four years ago, and it cost me the future I once dreamed of. I won't make that mistake again. I stand and head for the field to find Paul and get an update on the farm.

FRESHLY SHOWERED after a long day of hard work, I'm baking with my robe on. I put the cobbler in the oven and return to the bedroom to get ready. I've timed things perfectly and am dressed when the timer goes off. Dashing into the kitchen, I hit the button to turn it off and set the cobbler on the stovetop while I gather my purse and slip on my shoes.

With one final once-over in the mirror and a big smile in place, I'm ready to go. My shoes clack against the hardwood floors, making me wonder how long it's been since I wore heels of any sort. A while. When I turn the corner, my feet halt under the arch in the kitchen.

What the hell?

I watch in horror as he scoops cobbler onto a plate, frozen to the spot.

16

Delilah

"What are you doing here, Cole?" I ask, gripping the corner of the wall next to me. Officially, he's been out of my life for two months. He finally left—*coerced* not willingly—about fourteen months ago, but I had only really begun to feel safe since the divorce. For such a long time, I'd locked my doors at night. I had looked over my shoulder more times than I could count, and even now, hearing a man yell makes me shudder in fear. But now he's on my turf, somewhere he most definitely has no business being, and I am pissed.

The metal feet of the chair screech against the floor, and he makes himself at home. Not sure how to approach the bomb—ready to blow at all times—I watch as he shovels a big bite of the cobbler in his mouth before he looks up. His eyes are the color of faded blue jeans that have seen better days. "I'm eating. You always did make the best cobbler."

"You would know," I smart back, my better sense forgotten.

"What does that mean?"

I debate on holding my tongue, but I never did abide by his rules. Most of the problems in our relationship can be summed up in that confession. "Means you were eating cobbler all over town and not caring that I knew."

The vein in his forehead becomes prominent in his anger.

Stage one.

His spoon hits the dish, clanging to the table. "You and that mouth of yours—"

"Are none of your concern anymore. I want you to leave." We stare at each other for what feels like minutes. It's seconds, but time with him always did drag, so I add, "Right now."

He stands, the veins in his neck coming out to play.

Stage two.

I remember the stages well. They were ticking time bombs leading to the finale—an explosion where I suffered the consequences.

The pop of cracking knuckles.

Stage three.

I have to stand my ground, or he'll come back. The rubber soles of his shoes stick to the linoleum as he walks, the sound ominous in his approach.

My breath shallows, but I won't cower.

"Delilah Rae Cutler. That's my fucking name on the end of yours, meaning you. Are. Mine. Always mine."

Stage four.

I flinch when his hands come at me. When I'm not hurt or hit, I open my eyes and realize I'm caged by his body, his expression laden with disgust as he snarls at me. "What do you know about Jason Koster being back in town?"

My silence must be telling, my body trembling, my breathing staggered. My throat closes in on me. He grabs my jaw as soon as I turn away and forces me to look at him. I press my hands against him and push, but his hold on me tightens, the taste of blood coating my mouth. When my eyes begin to water, he steps back and sits down to eat more cobbler.

Don't cower.

"Leave, Cole."

"Stay away from him, Delilah."

My heartbeat picks up, the fear I felt when I first found him in here returning and shrouding my bravery. "Don't tell me what to do." My voice sounds meek, and I hate it. *I hate him.* "We aren't married, and this is not your home. You need to leave right now."

Grabbing his chest over his heart, he fakes offense. "Oh, that hurt, but you know what will hurt more?"

His questions are all leading, and I don't respond. He never expects an answer anyway. He's way too impressed with himself to let me actually guess. "You," he replies. "*You* will hurt. Stay away from him. That's your only warning."

That's when his gaze travels over me. "Why are you dressed like that?" I refuse to give him any part of me. When I don't reply, he adds, "You look like a whore."

"Get out."

Laughing, he stands and grabs his plate. Tossing it into the sink, the sound of shattering ceramic fills the space. "Oops. Tastes like shit, anyway." He grabs his hat off the table and kicks the screen door open to leave. The new dent in the metal is seen before it slams closed after him.

I grab my keys from the hook, the only weapon I have within reach, then listen until I hear his truck roar away from the house.

I'm safe.

Leaning against the wall, I try to calm down.

I'm safe.

Looking at the dessert from here, I feel tears spring to my eyes. I no longer have a dessert to take, but I know my makeup is ruined as well. As much as those should worry me more, it's not my biggest concern. We can live without dessert, and I can fix my makeup.

But my dish. He knows this was my mother's. I only have a few pieces left of the original set—thanks to my ex-husband—and now I'm down another dessert plate.

I refuse to cry, despite the lump forming in my throat. He's not worth shedding another tear over. The plate, yes, but there's no point. I pick up the pieces carelessly and upset, but don't see a sharp edge, which catches my finger. "Ow." Blood pools at the tip, and when I look down, it's deep enough for me to worry. Fuck. *Fuck him.* Why does he cause me so much pain? Why does he hate me so much?

Holding my finger under cold water, I let the blood run down the drain and then wrap it in a paper towel. Taking a moment that I know will make me late, I bandage the cut.

And that's when the anger takes over, dominating every other emotion as I grab my keys again to leave.

Anger that he thinks he can come into my home.

Anger that he thinks he can tell me what to do.

Anger that he broke something precious to me.

Anger that at one time, he broke me, and I'm still putting the pieces back together.

Anger that I believed his lies.

Anger that I have nothing to offer Jason and his mother tonight.

Anger that I'm not stronger.

My head throbs with the memories of being bent, my body curled over itself as my blood puddled on the bathroom floor.

My naked body shakes uncontrollably as my mind returns to reality. This is my life; the life Cole allows me to live—bruised with fear owning my thoughts and now my body. Not again. I will never let him do this to me again. I push off the floor and avoid the mirror as I crawl through the house.

Cole left. "Going drinkin'," he'd said.

I pull my purse from the kitchen counter, the contents falling onto the floor, including my phone. Scrambling for it, I dial the only number I know will keep this secret.

"Are you calling me about the hash brown casserole?" He laughs. "You know I love your home cooking."

"Billy?"

The laughter is gone from his voice in response to hearing mine. "Delilah? What's wrong?"

"I need help."

Billy bought me a gun, but can I use it? *Will I?*

I didn't even remember I had it tonight when confronted by that monster. What good will that do me? I go to the side table in the living room and open the drawer. This time, I load the bullets, one by one until all five chambers are full. I don't touch the safety. I don't like guns and had hidden my dad's shotgun in the bedroom closet after he died. I know how to shoot, but I hope I don't have to.

I'm much calmer and run my hand over my hair, making sure it's still in place. It's a silly concern after what just happened, but I need to focus on taking one breath after the other and slowly pulling myself back together.

With a clearer head, I think about grabbing something pre-made at the market, but I'm already running late, so I go empty-handed and hope I'm enough.

MEREDITH OPENS the door before I have a chance to knock. "Delilah, I'm so glad you're here."

We hug, and then she brings me inside, but I'm quick to pull my hand back when pain shoots through it.

"Oh no, what happened?" she asks.

"A little accident in the kitchen. I'll be fine."

"Of course, I worry, but it looks like you did a good job of wrapping it. Jason's grilling out back. Hope you're hungry. He bought a ton of food today. I think he's trying to impress you."

He already has, but his mother doesn't need to hear me go on about her son. I smile when I see him. "Starved. I'm sorry I don't have dessert like I promised. I burned it."

In the kitchen, she pulls out a bottle of white wine and holds it up. "I don't need the calories anyway. But that's not like you to burn food. You're such a good cook. Everything okay?"

"Just busy." I hate lying. I really hate lying to her. She's been so good to me, but Jason will lose it if he finds out that Cole was there. "I was distracted getting ready and didn't hear the timer go off."

"No worries, dear." She hands me a glass of wine. "You look very pretty. I know Jason is happy you'll be here tonight, but I am, too."

"Can I help with anything?"

"Absolutely not. You head on out and enjoy the evening. The lightning bugs are out tonight. There's something so magical about them."

"Something so small but powerful enough to shine light through the dark is magical indeed." I open the back door. "Call me if you need anything," I add.

"Go entertain my son. I'm almost done in here."

Giggling, I shut the door behind me and whistle at him. When he looks up, he says, "Are you catcalling my meat?"

"You've got the best-looking meat around."

He takes me by the waist but moves around until my back is to his chest. Resting my head back, I close my eyes, savoring the stolen moment. He kisses my temple. "You don't mind a little PDA in front of my mom, do you?"

When I catch her spying on us, she's quick to busy herself. "I adore your mom, but I don't need witnesses."

Moving in front of me, he glances inside as if to check that the coast is clear and then back to me. "I told her about us."

"What did she say?"

He chuckles. "I told you so."

"And what exactly did she tell you, Jason?"

Leaning in, he rests his cheek against mine. "That my feelings aren't one-sided," he whispers.

"What are you feeling?"

"Everything. All at once. As if the world had dulled before you were back in my arms."

Swooning's a thing, right? Because I totally do it. "You say the most amazing things to me."

"You're amazing to me." Sliding our hands to the side, he holds my waist with his other, and we start slow dancing even though there's no music. "What's with the bandage?"

"Just a little cut. Nothing to worry about."

"It's bleeding through. I'll clean it for you." He turns and closes the grill lid before we walk inside. "Mom, can you check on the fish?"

"Got it handled, but you're not going to be too long, are you?"

He laughs, but I'm not amused. I swallow hard from

what she must think we're up to. "She thinks we're going to have sex."

"But you notice she didn't stop us?"

I elbow him. "I don't want her to think I would be disrespectful like that."

"We'll be gone five minutes. No respectful man can make love to his woman in that amount of time." Angling over his shoulder, he calls out, "I'm going to clean Delilah's cut. We'll be right back."

She doesn't reply, but I'm laughing too hard to know for sure. I sit on the side of the tub while he digs under the sink. With a small first-aid kit, he sits on the toilet lid. "Let me see your finger." He carefully unwraps the bandage. "How'd you do this? It's pretty deep. Fortunately, you don't need stitches, but it will leave a scar."

"I have plenty of those already. Most you just can't see."

His eyes flash to mine momentarily, but he lets the comment slide. *Shit. Shit. Shit.* I shouldn't have said anything. Cole's earlier visit has knocked my thoughts off balance. I have to collect myself, especially around Jason. I look away to hide the truth from him.

When my finger is rewrapped with clean cotton and tape, he kisses it. "All better?"

I'm touched by the care he's shown me. My heart's beating a little faster, my chest a little heavier with happiness. When I finally gaze into the warmth of his eyes, I whisper, "All better."

RUBBING the sides of my legs, he smiles. It's gentle like his touch. "It's okay. It's just a bandage. I didn't perform surgery." I stand and lean my head against him. The unnerved fear I felt earlier has finally disappeared in the safety of his arms. "Hey, everything okay?"

"Yes. Now."

He leans back and looks into my eyes. "Now?"

"It's nothing. I'm just feeling sentimental is all."

A reassuring smile returns to his lips. "Me too." Kissing my forehead, he chuckles under his breath. "I also told my mom we were dating. I know we said we didn't need to complicate things, but they're complicated already, aren't they?"

We hold hands between us, and I nod. "Very."

So much more complicated than he knows.

JASON'S not usually very talkative, but tonight around the firepit, he is. He's shared and demonstrated the repairs he's made around the house, mentioned his trip to the hardware store, which I promptly steered him clear of since his mother doesn't owe him an explanation regarding a certain you-know-who. And then he even talked about the motor-cycle parked on the side of the garage. That one he guided us away from fairly fast after the topic was broached. He promised to take me for a ride on it soon, though. It's a side of him I'm completely fascinated by, and I find it sexy as hell.

But then his mother, on her third glass of wine, asks him, "Are you staying?"

He glances over at me. "I'm thinking I might."

My tongue curls around the front of my teeth as I hold back from revealing my feelings. *Too soon*, I remind myself. The trouble is, I can hide my feelings, but I can't hide my smile. His mother giggles in drunken delight, and I finish my wine, feeling tipsy myself.

Changing the subject, something I'm learning he's very skilled at doing, he asks, "Are we ready for dessert? I know I am."

His mom says, "We're skipping dessert tonight." She looks at me conspiratorially as if we've just pulled off a big caper.

"Why?"

I fess up, and by fessing up, I mean, I lie while pouring more wine to forget the real reason I didn't bring the cobbler. "I burned it. It's tragic, actually."

"Damn. I'd say so. I was looking forward to it."

"I'll make another tomorrow. I promise."

His knee knocks into mine. "Well, since you promised and all."

Two bottles of wine are emptied before we decide to call it a night. After clearing the table out back, we bring the rest of the food inside and wrap it up. I'm trying to pretend I'm not feeling every drop of that wine running through my veins, but it's hard. I don't drink much these days.

Jason hugs his mom. "I'll finish in here. You go relax."

"Thank you, son." She kisses his cheek.

She comes to me, and with my face between her hands, she says, "I'm so glad you're back in his life."

"Me too."

"And mine, Delilah. It's so good to see you smiling again." She embraces me.

Meredith has always been a loving woman, but tonight, I feel closer to her than ever. "Thank you for having me over."

"My pleasure, dear." She glances at her son. "Jason, you'll see her home safely?"

I find we both struggle to keep our eyes off each other.

Hands too, but we've done a better job of that with his mom around. Though all bets are off when she's gone. "Yes, ma'am."

"Good night then."

"Good night," we say in unison as she slips out of the kitchen.

After cleaning the dishes, Jason comes over and takes my hand. "Are you ready?"

"Born ready for you."

His chuckle is deep, but he keeps it under wraps so it doesn't travel through the house. "You're drunk, Delilah."

"Not drunk . . ." I waver, trying to pinch my fingers together. "Okay, maybe a little tipsy, but you make me feel the same way."

"You get drunk on me?"

"You're a very dangerous man to my self-control."

A thumb runs over his bottom lip. "What am I going to do with you?"

Throwing myself at him, I wrap my arms around his neck. "Take me home and have your wicked way with me?" I hear the hope in my voice when I was going for sultry.

"Who needs dessert when I have other ways of satisfying my sweet tooth? C'mon. I'm taking you home."

"I want you to stay the night."

He holds the door open for me. "You couldn't keep me away, honeysuckle."

There's something in the way he says it that makes me think he might be right. Luckily for me, I don't want to keep him away.

He grabs a backpack by the door. "Change of clothes," he adds.

"You're prepared."

"Always, baby."

It's pitch-black in the country. It's not a long drive, but it's long enough for the wine to settle my mind and lull me into the melody of the night. Parking out front, he comes around and picks me up. "You don't have to carry me," I lamely protest by completely relaxing in his arms.

"I want to."

Just that simple.

I once believed I knew exactly where I stood with him. If I hadn't been blinded by feelings of betrayal and hurt, I would have realized he hadn't changed. He just opens up and tells it like it is. He says what he likes and what he wants with no room for misunderstanding.

"Bedroom or living room?" He kicks the door closed and then locks the bolt.

"Living room. Want to watch TV?"

"Sure." He sets me on the couch and then clicks on some manhunt show that is way too boring to watch. I straddle his lap, and the show is forgotten as we find ourselves tangled in love right where we are. With our bodies joined in passion, I slow down on top of him and kiss his cheek. "I hate the years you were gone."

Pushing my hair back, he stares up at me on his lap. "I never left you. You were always on my mind."

17

Jason

Delilah snores.

I think it's just from being drunk and sleeping so deeply, but I never noticed it before. It's cute when she does it, like a little snuffle-snort. My body shakes from laughter. I've tried to hold it back so the disruption doesn't wake her. I take her shoes off and work the covers over her, tucking her in and sitting beside her.

Being in her life wasn't something I dreamed possible years or even months ago. Hell, two days ago, I was coming out here just to see if she'd even talk to me, so I'm not sure I can feel settled forty-eight hours later that everything will be all right. I want to, though. For her and for me. I want her. I want this life with her.

A slower pace would do me some good and having a home base would be even better. A companion. A partner. A lover. A wife . . . It's something I never thought probable, but now that I'm in the middle of the possibilities with her, I don't want to leave.

I'm not that tired so I go back downstairs, click off the TV and the living room lamp, and grab a beer from the fridge, wanting to go out on the front porch to enjoy the quiet night.

Grabbing a beer from the fridge, I twist the cap off and flick it into the sink, landing it exactly where I intended. Amused by my minor achievement, I go to retrieve it but stop when I look down. A full cobbler dish is angled in the sink with a big scoop taken out. The remains of that scoop are splattered across a broken dish.

When I pick a piece of the shattered plate up, I notice the blood that has seeped into the jagged edges of the porcelain. I recognize the pattern of the plate as one Delilah always cherished. We were never allowed to use these floral-trimmed plates because they were her mother's. When I look up, it's easy to find the vacant spot among the display. She had to make quite the effort to eat off it. Wonder what spurred her to use that plate, and why did it end up broken in the sink with what looks to be perfectly good cobbler?

What's even more odd is that Delilah lied. I can guess all night, but I'm not getting any answers until morning from the snoring beauty upstairs. I carefully pull the pieces of the plate out of the sink and put them in a brown sack I find in the pantry.

On the porch, I sit down on the steps after trashing the bag. If that plate weren't so shattered, I would have tried to piece it back together. Much like she's pieced me back together.

I hear the bugs and see the fireflies in the field. The light above Lorraine and Paul's front door shines in the distance. I should probably go by tomorrow and say hello. I'm sure they know I'm in town, so it's rude not to stop by before too much time passes.

With my feet kicked up on the railing, I drink my beer, feeling right at home here. If I'm not careful, I could fall asleep on this porch. There's no way I want that to happen when I know what's waiting for me upstairs. Thinking about her, I decide to join her.

But lights in the distance catch my eyes before I go inside. A car speeding down the main road approaches the curve just past the farm. They're going to end up lodging that piece of shit in the fence or the field. But then it slows so much that I squat down. It comes to a stop at the end of the long drive that leads to the house.

When the lights are cut, I stand. *Who the fuck is it, and what the fuck are they up to?*

I maneuver off the porch from the other side and duck behind a tree in the yard. Making my way to the edge of the fence closest to the house, I stare. The driver remains in the car, and the inside's too dark to tell who it is from here. I'm about to sneak through the field and approach from behind, but the lights flick back on and the car drives off. But not before I get the make, model, and license plate number.

I've not seen many BMWs around the county. It's a rich man's car when most here live mortgage payment to payment. Trucks are much more practical. So was that a wrong turn or something else? With no sign of the car returning, I go back inside the house. All doors and windows are double-checked on the first floor before I go upstairs to Delilah's bedroom.

She's still sleeping soundly, which relieves me. Knowing she's comfortable gives me peace of mind. I hope she feels the same from me, that I can bring back the same confidence she once had, the confidence that motherfucking ex of hers stole.

Cole Cutler is lucky I let him go with a minor takedown

outside Red River. I'm not sure how or when, but he better hope we don't meet in a dark alley anytime soon.

I go through my nighttime routine like I live here, which makes me wonder if I eventually will. I'd never considered it since Delilah never thought she'd be living here after college, but plans change, life happens, and sometimes, we end up exactly where we were always meant to be. Standing over the bed, I stare at this stunning woman—snuffle-snorts and tattoos from drunken nights—and I'm starting to feel this might be where I was meant to be all along.

Shifting the covers on the free side of the bed, I slide her over. Her skirt scrunches up around her thighs, and I let my eyes follow the long lines of her legs. Reaching down, I toss the blanket to the end of the bed and slide down the zipper on her hip to shimmy the skirt off. I work her sweater from her shoulders down one arm and then the other, leaving her hopefully a little more comfortable in a bra and underwear. Pulling the covers over her, I lean down and kiss her head before slipping in next to her.

I don't worry about macho pride. I get right in, bumping up against her, and then spoon the hell out this woman. *My woman.*

But sleep evades me.

Headlights.

A BMW.

Stopping on the road in front of her property isn't normal in the country. Not that spot. Not this time of night. It feels off. My instincts are wired on high alert. The problem is I'm not sure if I'm dealing with a threat from my past or a present danger.

I kiss the back of her head and tighten my hold on this angel of mine. Have I put her at risk by being here? What about my mom? Was it a mistake to come home?

It's hard to think I made a mistake when I'm currently holding the one reason I survived the past few years. "Jason . . ."

My name breaks through the stormy clouds of my thoughts. "Yeah?" I reply softly.

"Please . . ."

That's when I realize she's still asleep. Sitting up, I hover over her and watch her face as it contorts in pain. *Shit.* I don't want to hurt her. Not even in her dreams, or maybe she's having a nightmare about me. I hurt her once, which I'll regret forever. If I had just told her, but my planned surprise backfired before I could fix the damage my secret caused. Her dreams should be filled with the good memories, not the bad.

I run my hand over her arm, trying to comfort her.

"No. Please. Please, Cole. Don't hit—" She balls up, her words choking in her throat as she starts to cry. "Jason. Help . . ."

What the fuck? "Delilah?" My voice is louder than I intend, firmer. I want to wake her up. *Need to.*

Air whooshes from between her lips, and her chest lowers just as her eyes open, but she remains quiet. "Are you awake?" I ask.

A hand covers her head, and her gaze finds me in the dark. "What's wrong?"

She's asking me? "You were having a bad dream."

"Oh." Her reply is flat, and she looks at the ceiling. "Sorry for waking you."

"You didn't wake me."

She glances back at me, and sadness comes over her expression, sinking into the corners of her eyes. "Can't sleep?"

"No." I lie back, wondering what is happening with her,

worried about her. Does this happen so much that she's used to the abuse even in her sleep?

"What is it?"

"I hate that you have bad dreams."

"They're just nightmares. They're not real."

"But they were."

She sighs. "Yes, Jason. They were, but they're not anymore."

I can dance around this wall she's built, but I don't want to be on the other side of it. "Can I ask you something that's rattled me for years?"

"Sure." She extends the word, dragging it out. Her eyebrows are knitted together as she narrows her eyes.

"I remember after I transferred, after we had broken up, I made a touchdown, winning the game. The team piled onto the field, tackling me with cheers in celebration. I knew you weren't there." Her body tenses, but I keep going. "I knew you weren't there, but I looked across the track and then up into the stands anyway like a bad habit I couldn't break. You know what happened?"

Hesitating at first, she takes a deep breath, then her eyes find the ceiling again. "What?"

"Delilah, you *know* what happened, so tell me."

Her body molds to my side, but she keeps her head down. "I watched you score that touchdown. I watched your team lift you onto their shoulders. I watched the crowd cheer for you. *I* watched *you*."

"I saw you. I ran as fast as I could, jumping a wall to get into those stands and work my way to the section where I'd seen you, but you were gone."

"I shouldn't have been there in the first place."

"But you were." I sit, turning my back and rubbing the

bridge of my nose as I tried to understand what happened. "You were there for me and then you weren't. Why?"

"Because Cole was playing, and I left his game to come to yours. I only needed to see you to breathe again, to feel whole, to feel what I'd missed. It was always so much better with you."

I move to the end of the bed, needing some room to think. I have no energy as the emotional toll has wiped away all my strength. "Then why'd you stay in this town? You could have left. You could have gotten as far away from him as possible. I would have helped you. Fuck, I would have gone with you."

When she doesn't answer, I turn back. She's leaning her head on the mattress, the pillow pushed behind her. The covers expose her shoulders, but she appears exposed in other ways—vulnerable—even in the dark. I want to help her, to fill in the words that hurt her too much to say, but the longer she remains silent, the more I start to realize that they won't heal but hurt us both if spoken. I'm about to end the pain she's reliving by the distance that's taken over her gaze when she says, "He didn't just hurt me after we got married."

Fuck.

Running my hand over her shin, I need her to know that I'm here how she needs me. She continues, "At first, I stayed to help my dad, but he said I was meant to fly. It was all set. I was going to move to New York with my sister, but Cole didn't like that idea and always knew just the right way to terrorize me. He threatened to set fire to the fields, and then to me, to ruin me for all others."

Guilt consumes me, and I drop my head into my hands. The pads of my palms dig into my eyes before standing and walking to the window. I hate these damn blinds. They're useless, making me want to rip them from the frame. I don't but yank the cord instead, the metal slats slamming together.

"Jason! What are you doing?"

I open the glass and climb out, my muscle memory driving me through from all the times I came and went through this window. Pacing the roof above the porch, I don't know how to make this right. I don't know how she can even allow me back into her life. When she needed me most, I didn't protect her. I've proven I can't.

How can she bear to look at me?

How can she act like she forgives me?

My feet stop, and I look back at the window as she climbs out. Standing there, she says, "Why are you upset?"

Sitting down near the corner where the trellis hangs, I look over the property, too ashamed to look at her. "I'll never fucking forgive myself for letting him put his hands on you."

"Is that what you think?" I glance at her when she comes closer and sits, keeping a foot or so between us. "You think you *let* any of that happen?"

"I didn't stop it—"

"You couldn't stop it." She reaches over, stretching across the distance that seems wider than the visible space. "Don't go blaming yourself for something you had nothing to do with and no control over."

"I loved you."

"And I loved you," she replies easily. "But it wasn't love keeping us apart. It wasn't you transferring either. It wasn't a lack of want on my part. I wanted you. Mostly, I needed you. You meant so much to me that I struggled to live life without you in it."

"But you stayed with him. Why?"

"Like you, I didn't feel I had much choice in the matter. I

tried to leave once. He dragged me from the truck before I could stick the key in the ignition. It didn't matter how hard I fought, his hands tightened around my neck, forcing me to the lake." She stops talking. I'm so tempted to fill in the space. I want to take away her pain, to tell her it's okay, but I can't. I have to let her work through this now. "We stood on the dock. While I gasped for air, he looked into my eyes and told me he would drown me before he let me leave him. He would kill me before I embarrassed him in front of the whole town like that."

I don't think she realizes her hands are on her neck, rubbing lightly as if she's soothing her throat.

"He knew," I say.

"Knew what?"

"He knew I was going to ask you to marry me."

A scoff-sob escapes her as she looks at her lap, her chest denting in momentarily. When she turns her eyes toward the sky, I can see how they shine, a layer of tears ready to fall. "Of course, he did. Cole had his eyes set on the prize long before that argument between us."

"Why didn't you come to me? Why didn't you trust me enough to tell me?"

"I believed him." She turns to me, her arms wrapped around her knees. "I believed him when he said you transferred because you didn't have the nerve to break up with me. I believed him when he told me you had been bragging about how many girls you'd been with. I believed everything because he was my friend and *your* best friend, and surely, everything he was telling me was true."

"Delilah, you have to believe me. None of that was true. I never, *never* slept with anyone else back then. You were my everything. I knew what I had; how special you were. *Are.* I've been so fucking angry with you. Through miles of travel and years apart, I never understood why you left me without another word, without giving me something I could hold on to enough to let you go. Or how you could be with him."

And that's the most honest we've been for some time. Now I know the truth. Now I know why. Even though it's not until years later, knowing still allows so much of my anger to evaporate.

He had lied to her.

"I'm so sorry, Jason. So, so sorry. I—"

"No. Don't apologize. I'm sorry you believed him then, and I'm angry because you were hurt. But you need to believe me now. I love you."

Her eyes flash to mine. "Loved? You loved me like I loved you."

I never stopped loving her, even when I wanted to hate her. My pretty girl has simply owned my heart all along.

"What about me?" I didn't mean to step up the second after the pretty girl turned Cole down. But my thoughts were voiced before I knew what I was doing.

I may have been used to throwing a ball in the spotlight, but at fifteen, I wasn't as confident off the field.

The guys looked at me. Cole stood up, offense defining his face.

The girls turned around and stared at me, except for Delilah Noelle, who smiled when she looked my way. "We barely know each other, Jason."

She had cheered for me for years, but for some reason, hearing her say my name that day was different. It was personal and made my throat thick, causing me to clear it before speaking again. "I'd like to get to know you."

With the tilt of her head, she swung her ponytail to the side. "I'd like to get to know you, too."

That was the last day I walked home with the guys after

school. Starting the next day, I walked two miles out of my way after our practices just to carry Delilah's backpack home for her. I got my truck three months later and started driving her and her sister.

I think I loved her from the minute we saw each other, and by the end of that school year, I wanted her for my forever.

"No, Delilah. I love you. Present tense. Hearts and flowers. Kisses over morning coffee and poetry down by the lake in the afternoon kind of love."

Tears spill over her bottom lids, but her joy isn't contained, and she giggles. "That's intense."

I scoot over until we're sitting together. Wrapping my arm around her, I hug her close. "That is intense and so honest that I don't even think I can look at you right now."

"What?" She squeezes me. "Why can't you look at me?"

"Because then I'm going to see that look in your eyes that tells me I told you too much."

"It wasn't too much."

Raising an eyebrow, I add, "I meant that you're going to have hearts in your eyes and a goofy grin on your face because I've given you ammo to hang over me like a carrot teasing a rabbit."

Her head leans against my arm. "You know me so well, Jason Koster. I love a good blackmail, and you've given me a doozy."

It's all fun and games, good-natured teasing, but she's still over there laughing while my stomach is tied up in knots. Apparently, she notices because she adds, "If it makes a difference, you can hang something over me, too."

"What is that?"

"I love you." *Fuck yeah.*

Free and easy.

Without stipulations.

She just lays it out there without fear . . . *Wait a minute.* "Are you saying it just because I did?"

"No. I'm saying it because I know it's true. I never stopped."

"Me either." I point at the sky. "Look. A shooting star."

"You sure that wasn't a spaceship?"

"Oh, ye of little faith. That was a star receiving our message and sending it into the cosmos."

Her happiness bubbles over, and a giggle escapes. "What does our star say?"

"Nothing heals a broken soul like the love of a true heart."

Looking back up at the sky, she teases, "Our star should write poetry." Poking me in the shoulder, she adds, "So should you, Koster. You're such a romantic."

I hold her close again, soaking in the aura of her beautiful soul. "I'm not that romantic. I just say what I feel. So, to me, poetry isn't lines strung together or words with the perfectly crafted iambic pentameter. No, that's not poetry to me."

"What's poetry to you?"

"One word. Delilah."

Jason

"Why do you sleep in your old room?"

Floating on her back with her eyes closed and her body still, Delilah replies, "I feel safe in that corner of the house."

I wade through the water, mentally running through the floor plan of the farmhouse. Her room is the farthest from the front door, the back door, and the common areas. "You never wanted to take over the primary bedroom downstairs?"

As if an unforeseen force pushes her down into the lake, she loses her balance when she loses her concentration. She pops back up before I have a chance to worry.

Glorious in the midmorning sun shining on her wet lashes and water droplets covering her skin, she swims away from me. After being here practically every day and night for more than a week, I've discovered when she turns away from me that she's either avoiding a question or hiding from me. She can't lie when looking into my eyes. Either way, it's avoidance. Simple as that.

Swimming after her, I catch her twenty yards from the dock but keep swimming to give her the space I know she needs. "I can dog-paddle all day long."

She giggles. "You're being ridiculous. Why do you want to know all the stuff that doesn't matter now anyway?"

"Because it matters to me."

"Fine. I'll make you a deal." She splashes me. "If you get to ask questions and I have to answer, same goes for you. We take turns and when one doesn't answer, the game is over. How's that?"

She may be good at avoiding those grenades of questions I drop, but I'm the king of keeping secrets. So this proposition gives me pause. Logically, though, for us to be together, she needs to know about the life I've been leading. As much as I hate admitting the bad stuff, good things came from it.

What if this is my chance to redeem myself?

What if she thinks I'm a monster?

What if she loves me more because I survived when I didn't know if I would at times?

What if she can't forgive my past?

What if she hates me?

What if . . . letting her in will free my soul from the burden of the sins I've carried with me? I swallow my pride. "Okay," I whisper. "Deal."

She swims closer but stops ten or so feet away. "When my dad died, Cole moved us straight into my parents' bedroom. I didn't want to sleep in there. I was still grieving, and it felt disrespectful. It hurt to be in that room at all, much less take it over."

"Why'd he do that?"

Smiling gently, she reminds me, "My turn, remember?" I

swim a few feet closer. "Where have you been for the past four years?"

Easy. "Alaska for a brief stint on a fishing boat."

"I knew about Alaska from your mom."

She's on to me. "The money was great, but the work was hard."

"You never minded hard work from what I remember."

It's not a question, but a statement I feel the need to address. "It wasn't the work I wanted to do. Also, it sucked being on that boat for weeks at a time. Limited booze. Horrible sleeping conditions. Fish every meal." The left side of my mouth quirks up. *No women.* "After that, I was up and down the West Coast and then crossed the country to New England. I've traveled all over between jobs and sometimes for the job."

Rolling her eyes, she retreats a few feet, which makes me laugh. "To answer your earlier question, I'm not sure. I have theories that Cole wanted to control me, and when he didn't feel he had enough power, he'd hurt me. At first, it was emotional, but then it escalated." Wading closer, she asks, "What did you do, or do now, for work and for money?"

She's tricky, that glint in her eyes reflecting her more devious side. Diving forward, I swim until I reach her legs. Her scream can be heard underwater it's so loud. Pulling her under, I kiss her before we pop back up for air together. "Ah." She sounds so satisfied my cock awakens despite the cool water.

Keeping us close, I say, "C'mere." Her limbs wrap around me, and I swim back to the dock.

"You still have to answer, Jason."

"I will, but it may take a while."

While she climbs up the ladder, I watch that fine ass.

Rubbing over my dick, I try to remind it that now is not the time. It clearly has other plans, though.

We sit on a towel with our legs dangling over the edge. I'm not going to make her ask again, but it's hard to start this conversation from a place of truth when I'm so used to hiding the details. I exhale. "I wasn't a hitman."

"What? Good God!" she exclaims, angling back as if I have cooties. "I didn't expect that. What the hell do you mean you weren't a hitman? And if that's what you weren't, what were you?"

I don't think I've ever seen her eyes both wide with curiosity while also narrowed in shock, but that's what I'm seeing, and I feel an explanation rushing to ease the lines digging into her forehead. "I was a hired gun, a soldier, or maybe a mercenary is more accurate. Not for the military, but for private citizens who needed help righting wrongs." Daring to peek over at her, I find her mouth hanging open. "Are we still playing?"

"Jason . . ."

That's all she says and turns away from me to stare ahead at the lake. Troubling her lip, she rounds down her shoulders, and the battle in her thoughts is waging a war in her body language. It's a lot to process, and I'm willing to give her time to do so, but damn, am I squirming in my skin. My heart's racing, and I'm sweating even though I'm still wet from swimming.

Sitting here is torture of a different kind than any form I've endured, and the fears I hold inside of losing her again or her never looking at me the way she did this morning in bed have become palpable. She finally speaks. "When you say hitman, did you kill people?"

Not what I wanted to hear. How do I justify what I've done to someone who has no idea of the evil that resides outside this town? "I said I wasn't a hitman." One way or the other, our pasts were going to dampen our time together. I can only hope it's temporary.

"I need you to be serious with me, Jason. Have you killed someone?"

"Yes."

On her feet, she's pacing the dock. As if her mind is spinning, her stride picks up. "You've killed someone?" she asks as if the answer will be different this time, as if she misheard me.

"It's my turn," I say, silently begging her to give me this chance. I need to bring back some of the lightness from before.

She stops, too far for me to grab her ankles and beg for mercy. "Jason."

"Delilah."

"This isn't funny. You've murdered somebody, or you killed them?"

She's right. There's nothing funny about it. Not then or now. That's why I'll spend this life and eternity in hell in misery. "Is there a difference?"

Her hands go to her head, her expression crumpled in disbelief, and she starts pacing again. When she stops, she says, "There's a difference. Killing someone accidentally is very different than murdering somebody."

"What if they murdered your friend or someone you loved? Hurt them. Tried to kill them. Then is it okay?"

"It's never okay."

I put my back to her. This will be the end of what I hoped was a beginning. The sun is high in the sky, morning turning to midday. I can feel the heat on my skin, the burning, but I don't move. A sunburn I can handle. What I can't live with is her disappointment in me, her *disgust* in me.

Closing my eyes, I remember how that bastard slept beside his wife. I remember the weight of the metal and the wood grain of the gun handle. It's slower in my memories, like a lot of things. Except Delilah. All my time with her has always been too short, gone by too fast.

I'm not sure when Delilah sat down, but her body presses to my back, her words softly spoken, "When I said I love you, I meant it. I love you, Jason. I won't stop because you're honest with me. I'll only stop if you're bad for me."

"I'm bad for you, babe. So bad you don't even know it." I hate how true those words are.

The wind blows, and the song of the birds is carried with it. I'm not sure what to say, but I confess anyway, "I hate what I've done, but I can't take it back, and I wouldn't if I could."

"Why? How can you not regret taking a life?"

"Because he took many lives, and he tried to take the life of someone I cared about, someone who deserved better than to be shot on the side of the road and left for dead. That's what he did."

She rests the back of her head against mine and sighs. I try to end her internal debate. "I'm charred inside, burned from the hell I've been living. It's probably best you know now. Save yourself, Delilah. No good can come from being with me."

"But—"

"No." I stand, moving out of her heat, her love, her misunderstanding of what needed to be done versus what we all wish we could have done if the world was a better place. As I stare at the farmland surrounding me, it's easy to believe only good exists. Even when we struggle to pay bills or crops don't produce. This place, this land, it's magical—like time stands still here—and I'm not judged as harshly as

I am beyond this property line. "I can't turn back time, and I can't take back the sins I've committed."

"You can be redeemed. You just have to believe—"

"I don't regret what I've done. It was either take him out or allow him to kill a dozen innocent people. I'll burn in hell like I've been burning here on earth, but I'll face that fire with a clear conscience."

"Jason?" She stands, her little pink bikini so damn distracting to the conversation we're having.

Grabbing my alma mater snapback, I pull it on and lower the bill. "What?"

"I meant what I said. I love you."

"I know you do, but love isn't going to be enough this time." And it's those words I now hate the most. The truth. She doesn't need the shit that is my life in her world.

She doesn't need me.

She's brave and bold, stepping right up to me with no fear of consequences. She knows I could never hurt her, even if I've hurt others. "It wasn't last time, but here we are faced with a second chance to get it right."

"We didn't survive last time, honeysuckle. What makes you think this time will be different?"

"Because *we're* different. We've seen what life is like without each other, and it's not pretty. We only get blue skies when we're together."

"I don't understand what you want from me."

"That's just it, Jason. It sounds like everyone has wanted something from you. They've trained you to believe that no one can be trusted. Whoever *they* are did quite the job on you, and for what? Their benefit or yours?"

"It's not like that."

"Then tell me what it's like because our memories may bind us, but it's who we are now that will carry us forward.

And I want that, Jason. I want to move forward with you."
She slips a little dress over her head. It's ill-fitting, hiding the
shape of her body, but she still looks so gorgeous.

The gravity of this conversation strikes my heart when I
see the depth of concern for my soul residing in her eyes.
"This is hard to process," she says. "I'm trying to understand
what would turn the man I used to know into somebody
who could harm someone, instead of saving him."

"Save him?" I walk to the end of the dock and spin the
hat around. When I turn around, she's on the other end, and
once again, I feel the distance between us. "You're not
understanding. This is not a man you can save by taking
him to church or introducing him to the Bible. This was a
monster that would hurt you if it hurt me. He killed an
innocent kid just for being in the wrong place at the wrong
time. A kid who came to help out his friend. He was shot
without a chance to plead for his life. Killed only to hurt
other people."

This is the most I've talked in forever, and it's taking a
toll. My patience is gone. I shouldn't have to justify what
I've done, but I will because it's her. "I needed money. I
came off the ships in Alaska and was robbed, gun to my
head, by one of the other crewmembers. I thought I was
going to die." I scoff, shaking my head as I scan the horizon.
"We didn't get along on the boat. He taunted me the whole
time, calling me too good-looking to be working a real
man's job and accused me of being pampered in life. First
night off the boat, we walked to the closest brothel. We got
drunk. So fucking drunk." I don't turn back because her
silence is telling. *Fuck it.* She wants to hear the ugly side of
my life, so I give it to her in the details she's seeking. "I left
when the guys started going to the back with the girls. I
made it outside to the alley before I was hit from behind

and knocked to my knees. Ten thousand stolen right from my jacket pocket with the barrel of a gun pressed to my head."

"Oh, Jason," she says. I need to see her reaction, so I finally brace myself for the expected disgust. But that's not what I get. Sympathy is woven into the lines of her expression. That's not what I want.

No one has ever loved me the way she has. I can't lose her—*not again*—and that gives me the strength I need. "I will tell you anything you want to know. I just don't want to lose you in the process."

"I don't either, but I can't handle secrets. Tell me what happened."

"They said, 'Say a prayer, pretty boy.'" But what I thought were the last words I'd ever hear didn't bother me. Neither did the money. I didn't care about anything at that moment because all I could think of was how I would never get to see you again and tell you how much I loved you. So tell me what can I say that will keep you here, and by here, I mean in my arms at night and waking up to you in the morning? I want to talk about our day in the evenings and swim in the lake at noon. I want you. I want this life with you. I want whatever life you want, Delilah. I just want you in mine. Any part of you that you're willing to give, I'll take like a greedy thief in the night."

She runs into my arms, wrapping her body around mine. Her tears run down my bare chest, and I embrace her fully, never wanting to let her go. "I love you. I love you so much." When her blue eyes look into mine, she asks, "Why didn't you come back for me?"

"Because the next day, I called my mom and found out you were getting married before I could catch a flight. I was too fucking hurt. Too angry. Too disappointed. I'd lost you,

Delilah. You were no longer mine. And my heart broke that day."

"I didn't owe it to me, but I wish so much that you would have called." *I didn't see the point. She was marrying another man, for fuck's sake.*

"I didn't want to bring you anymore pain, especially on your wedding day."

Her feet touch the ground, but her arms stay around me. "So much has changed yet so much is still the same, but I see you. I see how you hide inside your thoughts. I see how you watch, how you tick the boxes everywhere we go. I see you putting on an act that you're the same guy we used to know. I see you, Jason Koster. The real you. That's the man I love. Your secrets don't scare me, but the reality of what they are, do. I can't turn my love on and off for you. There's always a steady stream when it comes to us, but I need time to understand, to learn more about the life you left behind. It doesn't have to be today, but promise me that you'll never lie to me, and you won't keep your secrets bottled up inside."

"I'll make that promise if it means I get you."

"I'm not a prize. I never was. But I like who I am these days, and I like you too much not to give you the benefit of the doubt."

My body relaxes, knowing this isn't the end and that maybe we can get past this.

She's so damn strong or stubborn. Either way, I'm in love with this woman and so damn grateful. "I want to hear more, but maybe we can finish this over lunch. I'm starved, and I never expected to actually hear what you've been doing," she says.

"If it makes you feel better, it wasn't all bad. I was a stuntman in Hollywood on two films. And a bodyguard for a visiting dignitary in San Francisco for a couple of weeks, which is how I met the woman who became my boss for almost two years."

Her mouth is hanging open again. I lift her chin to close her mouth, but she asks, "How close were you to this boss?"

"It wasn't like that. It was strictly professional."

"Stuntman, mercenary, and bodyguard. Is that all?"

Despite the sarcasm of her question, I continue, "Oh, and I worked at a mini-mart for a few months in a small town in the mountains."

"Okay. This is a lot to process."

"Not the stuntman or the mercenary, but the mini-mart is what took it over the top?"

She laughs, rubbing her temples. "Anything else I need to know right now?"

"I was shot once."

Her eyebrows rise in surprise, and she takes a deep breath to release the tension. "Good Lord. I did not see that coming. Are you okay?"

Turning toward the truck, I wrap my arm around her shoulders, and we start walking. "I'm better now."

19

Delilah

Sitting in the kitchen eating lunch, we've not suffered from a lack of conversation. "Is that scar on your leg from when you were shot?"

"Yes." He bends down and rubs over the spot. "It was just a graze that became a story to tell."

"It's still pink. You were shot recently?"

As I watch him shift in the chair, his discomfort is still noticeable. He doesn't avoid any of my questions, though. I've made a few observations over the past two weeks that I've determined are fact as of today. Jason is not the carefree boy from my youth when his biggest worry was a game of football on a Friday night.

He's now a man who has struggled and fought with many demons. And most likely alone. As much as I hate that he's capable of killing someone, I've learned that sometimes things in life are not as black and white as we've grown up to believe. How many times had I wished Cole dead after he took out his "justified anger"—as he called it —on me?

After exhaling and sitting back, he says, "A couple of months ago."

My throat tightens, and I grip the sides of my chair. "You came back because you were almost killed." I'm not asking, but I can see I've stumbled onto the truth.

He nods. "Even though this is only a graze, there were times I didn't think I would live to see daylight. Near-death experiences make you grateful for another opportunity to make things right in your life."

I relate to this too well. "Your turn."

"Tell me about the tattoo. You didn't have that when we were together. What made you get it when we weren't?"

It's a fair question. I was just hoping for more time before addressing it. But how can I complain when he's already opened up so much to me? I can't. After the heaviness outside this morning, I'm just going to be straightforward and rip the Band-Aid off this sore subject. "Cole had been pressuring me to get his name tattooed somewhere on my body."

Jason growls under his breath. "He was pressuring you?" His gaze lengthens over my head as he slowly exhales. I can see the way the muscles in his arms tighten and would be willing to wager that his hands are fisting under the table.

His reaction gives me pause to continue. Although his jobs had nothing to do with me, this has everything to do with him. "Back then, I didn't understand how he was twisting things to make me his, but it makes so much sense to me now."

"You used the word prize earlier. You were a prize to him. He used to tell me how lucky I was to have you, but he didn't mean having a girlfriend. He meant *you* specifically."

"He wasted no time, Jason. One moment, I only saw him when out with you, and the next, he was over every night offering a shoulder for me to cry on. That's when the stories started about you and the other girls, although he'd already whispered a few before we broke up. He told me story after story about how much he had loved me for so many years, and how he was so disgusted that you, his best friend and my boyfriend, would cheat on me. That no woman of his would ever know such betrayal. That he would look after me because no man around here would look at me twice after being with you."

"Delilah . . ." It's as if his frustration and pain have collided, and he pushes up, letting the feet of the chair skid against the linoleum. With his hands pressed to the edge of the sink, he stares out the window. His anger feeds the shame I feel inside for falling for it. But then he turns around, and says, "You had no reason to doubt him."

"I had you. That was reason enough." I shake off my own pain. "No one came near me once I was with him, so I guess I proved his theory true. He was an enemy in disguise." I've never spoken these words out loud and for good reason. "I feel like such a fool."

"Trusting someone isn't a flaw. You saw the good in him—"

"And the bad that wasn't true in you. Why are you defending him?"

"Defending him? Is that what you think? I'm not fucking defending him. I'm defending you. You were told lies from a trusted ally."

I didn't have to believe him, but we're going in circles. Jason gives me more credit than I'm due. Pushing my plate away, I look down at the years of scratches on the table. "He came home drunk one night. That wasn't unusual. It must be hard to live in the lies of screwing over the people who once cared about you. Anyway, the guys had been teasing him that he got your sloppy seconds." Just saying that phrase makes me feel cheap. "That's what I was relegated to in this town. Not the girl who made good grades or who was a cheerleader. I wasn't even a former beauty queen to them anymore. I was Jason Koster's sloppy seconds." I cringe when the words reach my ears again.

I dare to peek up at him. His breathing is deep, his arms crossed defensively, but worry is seen in the depths of those whiskey-colored eyes. Before he can say anything, I do. "We had a huge argument. That was the first time he ever slapped me. He'd been rough before but had never gone that far."

"Hitting a woman doesn't make him a man or more powerful. It makes him a coward." His knuckles whiten from gripping the counter on either side of him. Our eyes meet, and I stand before him wishing I could change everything that tainted us back then. I can't, so I'll live, survive like I've been doing. "I'm here, and I'm okay."

His silence is eerie as his gaze shifts from me to the table. He's still, so still I almost back away, but I'm not afraid of him. I want to soothe that anger away. Just as I reach for him, he says, "Do you know how much it kills me that you were ever touched by him? In any way. I will never understand how he could hurt you like that." It hurts to see him in so much pain, especially because of me.

I cover his hands and tilt my middle to rest against his legs, wanting this connection to give me strength. "You're not to blame. I know you want to take fault because you weren't here, but I don't blame you. That sits squarely on my shoulders. I'm still so angry with myself that I got mixed up with him in the first place."

"Because he twisted shit around to look like a hero. He took one fight between you and me, a fight that never should have happened, and worked it to his advantage. But if I would have fought harder for us—"

I'm hugging him, my head against his chest, but I can't keep my eyes off him for long, needing to see every reaction and emotion flickering through his eyes. The anguish he wrestles with, the guilt that seems to fill him, comes in waves of rage, and I feel it too. I understand. I've been there. I'm still in that catastrophe, if I'm being honest. "We can't go back and change those things."

My arms are around his neck, and his hands find my lower back. I always did love our size difference. Even though he's still hard in all the right ways, we fit together like two puzzle pieces. "I never stopped thinking about you. I never thought I had a chance of getting you back. If I'd known you weren't living the life you wanted, I would have been here. If I'd known he hurt you, I would have killed him."

"Don't say that." Though if I admitted my darkest secret, it would be one and the same. "What am I going to do with you?" When his arms tighten around me, I have the same thoughts I'm sure he does. I crack a smile. "We can't solve our problems between the sheets."

He tilts his head to the side, a smirk spreading across his lips. "You sure about that?"

"Despite the heavy topics, I've not been this happy in years."

He runs the back of his fingers along my cheekbone and then kisses the corner of my mouth. "We'll get through this together." I love how much he loves touching me, looking at me like I might disappear if he's not watching. I never felt this with Cole. I doubt I ever loved him, or him me. When I look at the adoration on Jason's face when he looks at me, how he cherishes me as if there is no other choice but to do so, I see the difference.

I love him. Soul deep.

"What happened with the tattoo of his name?"

Not every detail is needed. Knowing the danger this man can be, I realize it's best to keep this on the surface. Playing with the hem of his shirt, the same damn shirt that's hiding the good stuff underneath, I reply, "After he hit me, he told me I would get it done or he'd hold me down and do it himself." Jason's hands aren't tight, but I feel his fingers flex around my waist. "I had already planned to visit Shelby the following weekend, so I promised I'd get one while there. Shelby and I were blowing off steam, laughing and drinking. I never felt better than when I was away from him. One night, when we got drunk, we passed a tattoo parlor. I took his threat seriously and decided I would stick to my side of the bargain. I would be in control of anything permanent added to my body. I think you can see the error in my thinking while drunk."

Exhaling loudly, I know how bad this sounds, but I tell it how it was. "I told them to tattoo my husband's jersey number."

Understanding passes through him and all the tension that was straining his muscles moments before eases. The figure eights he was drawing on my back stops, and he says, "Eight is a long way from twenty-two."

"It sure is, but like I said, I was drunk."

"You keep saying you were drunk. Did you tell them my number on purpose, or was the alcohol to blame?"

"I blame the alcohol?" Closing my eyes, I shake my head.

"Are you asking me?"

"No. I do blame the booze."

He smiles. "You know what I think?" I don't reply, instead wanting him to figure it out on his own. "I think the number eight may have accidentally slipped out, but you didn't correct them. I have a tattoo. They don't just ink you without a final go-ahead."

The gold centers of his brown eyes are bright with happiness. I want to kiss him, but I don't want to hide behind a distraction, even if he's hard to resist. Tapping the tip of his nose, I say, "You're enjoying this too much."

"You're right, but as much satisfaction as I've found in this, I imagine it didn't go over so well once you got home."

"April fifteenth. The day most people dread because their taxes are due, but for me, I thought it was the last day I would ever breathe."

When it gets heavy, Jason needs room to process, and now is no different. He walks to the back door, but instead of looking out, he lowers his hands. The rise and fall of his torso matches the pace of his heavy breaths. As if something possesses him, he suddenly opens the door and walks out. The door is still open, and I catch the screen door before it slams shut. "Jason?"

"How can I not kill him? How do I stand here and listen to the pain he's caused and not want to destroy him? Tell me, Delilah, because I'm so close to following through."

I step outside and sit on the top step. "I know you are. I was too at one point." I laugh humorlessly to myself. "At many points. As for you, I need you too much to let you spend your life behind bars over me."

He stops and looks back at me. "Billy said he took you to the ER once . . ."

"Billy shouldn't have said anything."

"Why?"

"Because you can't fix it. This anger coursing through

you . . ." I take his hands to try to settle his anxious energy. "It's fruitless. It happened, and nothing can be done about it now. I'm divorced. He's out of my life." I think back to finding him in my kitchen. "Hopefully for good."

Taking my face between his hands, he looks into my eyes and studies them as if he's discovering new colors inside. "You don't believe the lies you tell yourself. Why would I?"

"I'm not lying."

"Okay, then you're fooling yourself into believing you're safe when you're not."

He sighs, appearing to calm down. Backing up, he goes to the back steps and sits down. "What kind of vehicle does he drive?"

His question is so far out of left field that I struggle to link the train of thought. "Um, a Ram. A black Dodge Ram truck."

"Shit," he says, looking disappointed.

"What?"

His body language changes, his shoulder span, a bit wider, harder like his jaw is. "I don't think it's a big deal, but I saw a car parked in front of the farm one night. I thought it might be Cutler."

"Was it a BMW?"

His stare hits me hard, and he stands. "Yes."

"I forgot. He has a BMW, but he rarely drives it except for work meetings. He bought it when we were together, but we couldn't afford it, so it became another source of contention."

"How often does he drive by?"

"I don't know. I've not seen him drive by, but I'm not really watching for him."

"The divorce has been finalized for a few months, but

have you seen him since then?" When I hem too long, he says, "Tell me, Delilah."

Trust. Honesty. Security. No secrets. That's what love is. "He came by the other day. It was the first time since I saw him at the courthouse."

Steepling his fingers together, he runs them up the bridge of his nose, struggling to contain his rage, but trying his best. This I can relate to. "He's a fucking dead man already, so be honest with me. You didn't burn the cobbler, and you didn't break your mom's plate. That's when he was here, wasn't it?"

I feel ashamed that I didn't handle myself better that night. Will Jason see how weak I really am and leave? "I told him to leave. I don't think he'll be back."

"He'll be back. He's obsessed with you, but I also think he'll be back because I am. He hates losing, but to me, it's as if his whole world revolves around securing that victory."

"He needs to hold it over your head."

"We won't let him." The vein that was bulging at his temple eases, and he asks, "Why didn't you tell me that night at my mom's?"

"I knew you'd be upset."

"Not with you."

I cross the yard and lower my voice. "I knew you'd go after him, and I don't want you getting hurt because of me."

The laughter comes from deep within, too big to hold inside. "Trust me, baby, he can't hurt me."

"He's volatile. Angry and possessive. He's an alcoholic who makes everyone else pay the price for his failures. He'll start a fight with you."

"Let him. I can handle Cole Cutler."

"Things are finally starting to settle down with him." I pause and look away momentarily. He knows me too well and can spot when I'm lying, so I try to hide my eyes, but I can't hide forever, and I have to share my worries with him now. "Don't start a fight with him. Promise me," I plead.

"I promise I won't start a fight with him, but I will finish one, once and for all. This has been going on too long. It's time to put an end to it." Pulling me into an embrace, he hugs me and then dips me. With my head resting in his hands, and my heart on the line, he says, "And I promise you right here, Delilah Noelle, I'll give you the ending you deserve. The one we're owed."

He kisses me slowly as if we have all the time in the world. Maybe it's possible for us to find the peace we're both searching for. It sure feels it when we kiss like this.

When I'm lifted upright, he adds, "There are so many things I want to make right, that I want to make you proud of me for, that I want for us in this life. Thank you for giving me the chance."

His lips take mine, crashing our hearts, our love, our bodies together in a frenzy of passion. He gives all of himself in this kiss, and just like the first time I kissed him, I fall madly, head over heels in love with this man. It's easy to promise my life to him with words, but we're deeper than that. It's not about the words or confessions, sins or pasts.

It's about the kiss.

This one right here. It's felt deep through my body and reaches my toes. This man. *This. Man.* He kisses me with such desire I realize all others don't matter. *This* kiss is the first kiss of our forever.

20

Jason

I'm fired up, but I keep the hurricane of anger hidden from her. I have to. Delilah deserves peace after all she's been through. I sit back in the chair in her room, my leg bouncing from the unsettled emotions twisting inside my gut. I need to move, to fuck, to drink, to beat something up . . . but I'm home.

I have to temper how I've been trained to react. I don't want people here to see the cold mercenary I've become. She returns and spins. "What do you think?"

"I like that one."

Her hands fly to her hips. "You've said that about the last two dresses."

"I like them all. You look good in everything."

Coming over to me, she leans down to my eye level, and her hand presses on my knee to steady it. "Jason, it's going to be okay. I'm okay. You don't have to worry about me."

"I worry. That's not something I can change. It's not something I want to change."

She stands up with a sigh before turning on the heel of her boots and heading for the door. "I'll wear this one. Let's go. We both need a night out."

Although I can see the worry in her eyes when she passes by, maybe she needs me to let it go. I won't, but I'll put on a happy face for her tonight. "Yes, ma'am."

It doesn't take long to reach Red River. The ride is mostly quiet. We know we're making a statement when we walk in there together. People will talk to our faces and then behind our backs. Word will get out, but it needs to. I want this night out with my girl, but I also want to tempt the snake out of his hole. Cole Cutler needs to know I'm not going anywhere, and he better not come anywhere near Delilah.

I help her out of the truck and hold her hand protectively in mine as we walk down the sidewalk to the busy bar. Just before we reach the doors, she pulls me to a stop. "Hey?"

Turning back, I see her eyes are gloriously bright blue with the setting sun shining on them. Wisps of her blond hair blow in the light breeze. The pink of her lips draws my gaze, and I bend to kiss her. She never says anything, but between her grip on my arm and the way she snuggles into me, I hear her unspoken words in every heartbeat. Stroking her hair down her back, I whisper the words she reassured me with earlier, "It will be okay."

I kiss her temple before she pulls away and tugs me toward the door. "Come on, cowboy. Let's give 'em something to talk about."

Cocking an eyebrow, I say, "You're on."

She laughs. "I cannot wait to show you off."

I take hold of the door and let her pass in front of me. "I'm more than a pretty face," I tease, not so dumb to the fact that women find me attractive. There's only one woman I'm drawn to, and I'm feeling fucking fantastic that I get to show her off as well tonight.

"You're right," she replies, tapping my chest. "You have a great ass too, and arms. Oh, and thank you for letting me pay homage to all eight of those ab muscles last night."

I slip my hand under her hair and rub the back of her neck. "I let you pay homage to more than my ab muscles. Any chance for a repeat performance?"

"A very good chance."

Guess getting caught in our own world is something we do more than just out on the farm. Patsy Cline is crooning from the jukebox in the back, but other than that, the place has gone quiet. Even the pinball machine has stopped dinging. I scan the area, always aware.

Five booths.

Twenty-one people.

Ten barstools.

Eight taken.

I need to stop doing this. It's a bad habit that needs to be broken. *I'm safe.* No one's going to get me here. The past is in the past. It's time I live in the present.

It's easy to get caught up in the stares and dropped jaws, to walk out of here like we don't belong or that we can stop the gossip before it begins. But I don't want to. We walk to a tall table in the center of the bar, and I pull out her chair. She whispers, "They're not talking at all. What do we do?"

She sits down with a big grin on her face. "Give 'em a hot minute to get used to us again and the chatter will begin."

The bar returns to life like we never walked in, conversations continuing with only a few sideways stares. McGilley calls, "Good to see, Mrs. Cut—*Ms.* Noelle. It's been a while."

"Sure has, Mr. McGilley."

"First drink is on me. What are you having?"

I laugh, reaching across the table with my palm up. When she slips her hand in mine, I say, "I got her covered. Thanks, though."

Delilah blushes for me, but then says, "Two bottles of your best."

Sliding off the stool, I tap the table. "Be right back."

McGilley sets the bottles down and eyes Delilah over my shoulder. "She never comes in anymore."

"Maybe things are changing."

"For the better, I'd say."

The lines deepen around his eyes and the smile is more sympathy than happiness. Like any good bartender, he prefers to listen over talking, but something's on his chest that he needs to get off, so I stay. "Say what's on your mind."

When he stretches his hands wide before me, you'd think he was working a farm instead of a tap by his calloused hands. "If you ever get the chance, tell her we're sorry."

I wasn't expecting that, but it's felt deep within me because I understand on some level. On another, though, this town stood by and witnessed it. "You should tell her yourself."

He nods. "Beers are still on me tonight."

I hold one up. "Thanks."

When I turn around, Billy's pulled a chair up like he intends to stay. He flicks the bill of his cap and grins. "What's up?"

Setting the beers down, I reply, "Night out is all."

"Cheers to that."

We toast and then drink. "Good week?" I ask him.

"Got caught up in an auction for a calf midweek, and everything went to shit after that. Been meaning to mention the county fair is coming up in a few weeks."

Delilah says, "Wow, I haven't been in years. I want to go." With her chair closer to mine, she rubs my leg under the table. "Maybe you can win me a giant bear or something I can cuddle with."

"I thought I was your cuddle bear?" What the fuck did I just ask? Cuddle bear? Billy looks disgusted, so I'm quick to add, "God, forget I ever said that. That is seriously *chop your balls off* talk."

"I thought it was cute," she says through her laughter. "Cuddle bear."

"No. We're not doing that. That name is not happening." I down my beer. "McGilley, another round please."

Billy finishes his beer, and then says, "It's good to know that even the great Jason Koster has a soft side."

"No," I say, "it's not great to know. Nobody needs to know that."

Delilah's still laughing. "He doesn't, Billy. He's hard all over. Trust me."

Billy stands. "This conversation has gone south fast, and I don't need to hear it. I think there's a lonely girl over there looking for company."

Shoving his shoulder, I follow his gaze. "She's staring straight at you, so I think she found her next victim." He walks off just as Sabrina Smith shows up with a straight face and an ax to grind. "Well, if it isn't Miss Freeland County herself. What brings you out, Delilah?"

"Sabrina," she replies, giving her the courtesy of acknowledgment but not much else. It's entertaining to watch. Anyway, we both know Sabrina came over on a mission. Sabrina has always been fairly harmless, but she's bold enough to get on your nerves fast. It's almost impressive how quick on the draw she is tonight. We just have to wait until she's bored with us. Looking around the bar, I wait until her scrutinizing glare lands back on me. "No hello, Jason?"

"Hello."

"After all we shared, too."

She loves to tell lies about us hooking up. It never happened, but years after high school, she still holds on to them like they'll turn into reality if she continues dragging it out. Delilah shifts, causing me to give her the attention she deserves. I don't want her uncomfortable, so I reply, "Nothing ever happened between us, Sabrina. Your memory seems as foggy as ever."

"It did, too. You're just choosing to hide the truth—"

"Sharing a microscope in biology our sophomore year doesn't count as intimacy. It was an assigned partner project. I had no choice."

She rubs Delilah's shoulder with a satisfied smile on her face. "See? He remembers. Anywho, where's that handsome husband of yours, Delilah?"

I'm not having this insanity ruin my night out with Delilah. Whispering, I warn her, "This town may let you pull this bullshit with them, but you won't with us. I'll let you walk away without embarrassing you in front of everyone, but this is your only warning. I want you to stay away from Delilah and from me. You see us coming, you cross the fucking street. Do you understand, Sabrina?"

Her mouth was gawking open by the word "bullshit," so I know I got her attention. "Well," she starts, raising her chin in stubborn defiance and fluffing her hair. "A microscope is the only thing I ever intend to share with you, Jason Koster. Your meanness is noted." She scoffs as she walks back to her booth and the poor sucker stuck with her for the night.

I'm still shaking my head in annoyance when Delilah says, "I've noted a few things about you myself."

The beers arrive right on time. I down some of the cold lager, and ask, "And what might those be?"

Leaning over the table, she looks to her left and then to her right before returning her gaze to me. "The impressive size of your—"

"Delilah." It's not the name that has her tensing. It's the fucker saying it. I see how her shoulders cave forward and that chin that was held high lowers.

My heart starts pumping against my chest, my hands fisting. I stand, turning and come face-to-face with my ex-friend. "Turn around and walk away, Cutler."

"Me, walk away? That's my fucking wife."

The word cuts deep, but I'll never bleed for him. Delilah stands behind me with her hand on my back. "Ignore him, Jason."

Cower? For him? No fucking way. I owned this town once, and I will again if it means putting him in his fucking place. Taking a step closer, I bump my shoulder against Cole's, and I say, "Don't you ever fucking call her that again. And if I see you within ten miles of that farm, or *my* girl, I will fucking end you."

With our eyes locked on each other, we remain in an unwavering silent standoff. McGilley finally yells, "Break it up, boys, or hit the streets."

Cutler ignores the bartender. "You need to check yourself, Koster. That woman—"

"She's not *that* woman. She's her own woman. She's whoever she fucking wants to be." And goddamn do I hope she chooses me.

My words seem to cause him to choke, and that's when I'm unfortunate enough to get a whiff of his breath, which is alcohol laden. "What the fuck are you talking about?"

I'm shoved but don't budge, and I'm definitely not taking

the time to explain things. "I suggest you go back to wherever you came from and don't come back over here."

"You heard him, Cole. Back off." Delilah wraps her hand around my forearm. "Jason, let's leave."

That's when I see it. Not her, but the look he gives her, the one that comes loaded with threats he intends to carry out—hate darkening his pupils as his eyes narrow—latched onto her. "Leave?" His shoulder punches forward as he grits. "Together? What'd I tell you about him?"

What he told her? He's so lucky I don't level him right the fuck now. I step in front of him and give my last warning. "Don't look at her. Don't talk to her. Ever. Again."

Billy comes over and tries to pull Delilah to safety, but her hold on my arm tightens. "Jason," she pleads as she comes around me. Her fear has disappeared as she faces Cole and says, "You and I are done. You need to leave us alone."

He reaches to touch her, but I knock his hand away. Cutler shifts and then faces me. "You got a death wish, Koster? Cuz I'm happy to fulfill it."

"You're drunk. Go home."

"Fu—"

"Hey. Hey," Billy cuts between us. "C'mon, guys." Looking at Cole, he says, "Stop causing trouble where there is none."

"He needs to stay away from us," I say.

"You do realize I own half that farmhouse you're fucking my wife in?" He laughs, but it's more maniacal than humorous.

Speaking of death wishes, he's close to making his own wish come true. "*Ex.* You seem to be forgetting that important detail."

Cole swings, but Billy pushes him back on his ass. "Time for us to go," Delilah says, taking my hand.

Before we leave, I add, "Put it on my tab, McGilley."

"Sure thing, Jason," McGilley replies.

Before the door closes behind us, Cole yells, "You're my wife, Delilah. A piece of paper doesn't define us."

Outside, I glance down the sidewalk and then at her. "Are you okay?"

"I want to go home."

I wrap my warmth around her, hoping to ease the fear that's causing her hand to shake. I don't blame her for being shaken. I thought I was about to come to blows with Cutler, and I was willing to because it's clear he's gotten into her head again. *And she put up with that asshole for how long?* "Okay."

While walking back to the truck, I scan the area. Everything looks normal, except the car parked next to my truck.

Instantly recognizing it, that car stands out in this town.

Shit.

21

Jason

Up ahead, leaning against the passenger door is someone I never thought I'd see again. When I stop walking, Delilah asks, "What's wrong?"

"Nothing." I lower my voice so only she can hear me. "Will you wait in the truck for me?"

"You're scaring me, Jason."

My gaze slides to her. "I don't mean to. Everything's fine, but I need a few minutes, okay?"

"Okay." She walks ahead, staring at the man as she passes. When she looks back over her shoulder, I catch her eyes and give a smile I hope reassures her. As soon as Delilah is tucked safely inside the truck, I cover the last few steps. I always expected my crimes to come back to haunt me. I just didn't see them coming back tonight. Crossing my arms, I ask, "What brings you to town?"

Cruise, an old ally, isn't uptight, but he seems particularly at ease tonight. He comes over and offers his hand. "You left in a hurry."

Happily, I shake it. "You been missing me?"

"Ha." He smiles and steps back to give me space, always a respectful friend. "Kind of."

Chuckling, I drop my guard. "Yeah, I get it. I'm a likeable guy. I was underappreciated in the Kingwood world."

That makes him laugh. "Probably so, but it was easier not to trust than be stabbed in the back."

"Understandable." I glance at Delilah, who's watching us through the window. I give her a nod to put her worries at ease. After my confessions, I don't think she's feeling as comfortable as we are about this encounter. "Is this a social visit?"

"Not really. Got some time?"

I can trust him, so I tell him to follow me to the farm. When I hop into the cab of the truck, Delilah asks, "Who is that?"

"An old friend." I reverse the truck and put it into drive.

"Who is he, though? Why is he showing up here at almost nine o'clock at night looking for you? Please don't lie to me."

"I don't lie to you, Delilah. I told you more than I should already." Cruise is behind me as we head out of town. "We used to work together."

She gasps an octave too high for the small space of this cab. "Killing people?"

Resting my hand on the bare skin of her thigh, I give her a gentle squeeze. "I don't think he's killed anyone. You can ask him when we get to the farmhouse."

"He's coming home with us?"

I glance between her and the road. "He's one of the good guys, Delilah. You don't need to worry about him."

"Are you one of the good guys?"

"Depends who you ask." I wink at her.

That gets me a punch to the arm and has me laughing. "I'm asking you, Jason."

"Yes, I am. Why are you so serious?"

She rolls her eyes and sits back. "How are good and bad defined in your world?"

Man, she's laser-focused on this. "The same as in your world but with bloodshed."

She turns away and looks out over the dark fields dotted with the occasional farmhouse. "That's dark."

I grip the steering wheel, tempted to turn on some music and not have this conversation. Avoidance isn't an option for us anymore. "That's why I came home."

"Why *are* you home? You didn't come back for me. You thought I was still married."

"I wasn't living the life I wanted. I missed my mom." Checking my rearview mirror, I mumble, "I missed you."

The warmth of her hand penetrates the cotton sleeve of my shirt when she reaches over. "I shouldn't have, but I missed you, too. Jason?"

I glance over. "Yeah?"

Her fine features are barely visible in the dark, but I see her eyes on mine. "I have to tell you something."

"What is it? I want to know everything about you."

She laughs. "You make me sound so interesting when I'm the same as I always was, stuck in the same town where you left me."

"I hate that you think I left you on purpose. I left dejected, but guess what?"

"What?"

"Together, two broken hearts can be whole again." I ask, "What's your confession?"

"I feel silly telling you this, especially knowing I'm to blame for the mistakes I've made."

"We all have things we'd like to change. Some we can. Some we can't. Doesn't matter as long as we grow from the experience." I smirk, though she can't see me.

After a soft laugh, she says, "I used to fantasize about being married to you and how glorious each day would be. We would have a family and run the farm but go on great adventures around the world. I never even made it to Paris."

"I've not been to Paris, either. How about we go together?" I turn onto the property and drive up the dirt road to the house. "And there's nothing wrong with fantasizing about a future together. We were dating, and it was serious; it's only natural. I had the same dreams."

"It was when I was married."

Oh. Wow. I shift the truck into park and cut the engine. With my arm draped over the back of the seats, I angle toward her. "Your fantasies are how it should have been." And how it will be if I have my way.

"Thank you for never making me feel ridiculous or dumb."

Cutler is a fucker.

Checking the rearview mirror, I watch as Cruise parks behind us. We should go in. Both of us move to get out, but before we do, I say, "I think you're incredible and so smart. I've never seen you as anything less than magnificent."

"Jason," she says, barely above a whisper, "you're so good to me, good for me. I'm never prepared for your words."

"They're not words, Delilah. They're the truth."

"How did I get so lucky?"

"It's not luck, it's love." I get out and come around to her side. "Come on. I want to introduce you to my friend."

CRUISE HAS CHANGED in the short time I've been gone. What he's gone through has darkened his already reserved demeanor. Guess he has more demons than he started with as well. He's a quiet guy, but Delilah has a way about her—everyone opens up to her. Laughing, Cruise is on the tail end of a story about getting his ass kicked in an alley by a drug lord and his gang. "King just looks at me and laughs."

On the edge of her seat, she is fascinated. "He laughs?"

Staring down at the bottle of beer in front of him, he picks it up, swirling the liquid inside. "That was before we knew what we had gotten ourselves into."

"What had you gotten yourselves into?" Delilah asks.

His eyes shift from her to me. "We were lucky to have Jason on our side."

She knows she's not going to get the details she's wanting. Cruise, like me, is a pro at leaving secrets good and buried. Delilah stands and walks behind me. Rubbing my shoulders, she says, "I'm going to bed. I hope you consider staying the night, Cruise. We have a spare bedroom down the hall with clean sheets and a view of the lake that's beautiful to wake up to."

"You drive a hard bargain. Thank you for the hospitality."

"It's getting late," I add.

"We shouldn't let the night slip by without talking."

Delilah says, "Well, on that note, I'll leave you to it." Bending down, she kisses my neck, then whispers in my ear, "You okay with me going to bed?"

Tilting up, I see her waiting for me to answer. "You don't have to ask me for permission." I wrap my hands around her neck and bring her closer until our lips meet in the middle. "I'll be up shortly."

"I'll keep the bed warm."

As soon as I hear those creaky floors upstairs, I lean forward. "As fun as it is to reminisce, why are you really here?"

"We miss you."

"King doesn't miss me."

"No, he doesn't, but the rest of us do. I'm here with a job offer."

Never saw that coming.

I'm impressed he found me, in all honesty, and now he's thrown a job offer on the table. "I'm surprised you need my help."

"It's always good to have backup."

"Backup for you?" I can't help the chuckle. "Saving your ass is more like it."

"Right. That's the job offer." His sarcasm game is strong. "Saving our asses when our asses need saving."

I can match him. "Here's some advice: stay away from criminals and psychopaths with a vendetta, and you'll be fine."

"I'm told to offer you double your old salary." The social part of the visit is put to rest, and the business is finally at hand.

The money is tempting, but I've earned more than I can spend in this lifetime. Anyway, Delilah is more than enough reason to say no. "I'm out of that line of work. I'm settling into this life with that beautiful creature upstairs. It's a slower pace here, but it's good for clearing my head. And when it's really quiet, I can hear the cicadas buzzing, frogs croaking, water rolling over the lake, and Delilah's snores. They're not loud. It's actually kind of cute because I just like the sound of her next to me."

"I'm not sure what to say to that. I do think she might kill you if she knew you told someone she snores." He chuckles.

"Yeah, she might, but it'd be a damn good death coming from her."

"I don't know what's happened to the guy I knew a few months back, but you're not him. Whatever this place has done to you is good." He laughs. "You're almost tolerable now." He stands and cracks his neck to the side. "I'm going to bed. I'll be out of your hair by morning."

"You can stay a few days. I have plenty of manure for you to shovel."

His laughter gains strength. "I know you don't know much about me, but manure is not something I'm familiar with or looking to shovel to entertain you. Thanks for the offer, though."

"Anytime."

He heads for the archway but turns back before he leaves. "You're always welcome back. Delilah's welcome, too."

"Thanks, but I'm wanting a solid future with her, man. Not sure working for King can offer that."

Nodding, he says, "Understandable. Night."

"Night."

CRUISE STUCK TO HIS WORD. He was long gone by morning, leaving Delilah disappointed. She probably hoped she could gain more insight into me if he stuck around a little longer. And she probably could have. I slide my hands around her waist from behind and kiss the nape of her neck. "Now you're stuck having to listen to me telling you all the stories."

"But you hold back."

"I don't hold back. I just don't share the ugly details you don't need haunting that pretty head."

"I've told you. I can handle the truth."

"Okay. Here's some truth for you. I once stood guard outside a dressing room while an A-list actor fucked two women. It took him ten minutes to get off during a fifteen-minute break. He rehearsed his lines while doing it. When he returned to the set, he nailed the scene. He nailed them too, but—"

"Ew, Jason"—she spins in my arms—"it's not even nine in the morning."

Laughing, I ask, "Is there a better time of day to tell a story like that?"

"Yes, like when I've had wine or at least lunch. Or not at all. That's not a good story."

"I didn't say they were all good. I said they were ugly. I learned a lot about people and how they operate. How power is used and abused, and the way money twists the human psyche to make them greedy. It's not like that here. It's still good. You're still pure."

"I'm not so innocent."

"None of us are, but we don't have to live like it's the apocalypse either."

Rubbing against me, I can tell she's working up to get more intimate. "I am so glad you came back." Her hand wraps around my morning erection. "What do you think about—?"

"Yes. Just like that."

"Really? I was thinking my mouth might do a better job."

I still her hand. "Don't let me keep you then."

After enjoying each other for breakfast, we work our way downstairs for actual food an hour later. "What time did Cruise leave?" she asks.

"I heard him leave around five." It was good seeing him, but nothing felt quite right with him around. It was as if he carried in a cloud of darkness I thought I'd left behind.

I start to laugh when I see what he left me on the kitchen table. A sealed envelope propped against a bag of Oreos. Delilah passes me and grabs the cookies. "I love Oreos. Can I have one?"

"You can have as many as you want." My gaze goes to the envelope. Taking it in hand, I recognize the name on the front—*Eric,* my old alias—making me smile. I open it, pull the note out, and read:

GLAD YOU FOUND *a reason to stay.*

A friend once told me that everything is sweeter when you've found your reason to stay. *She was right.*

22

Delilah

Jason and I have been playing house for weeks, happily avoiding the outside world as much as possible. We don't venture much beyond the property line, except to run errands for the basics or visit his mom. Though it's been nice when she comes around here as well.

Billy also hangs out with us, sometimes to help and other times to drink a few beers. It's a peaceful existence.

Too peaceful.

Peeking out the window, I spy just the guy I need to talk to and run into the barn to find Billy. "Billy?"

He comes out from the area where we keep old equipment. "Yeah?"

"Have you heard from Cole lately?"

"Saw him yesterday at the gas station. What's up?"

"He doesn't usually take his ego getting bruised so lightly." I dig my teeth into my lower lip and look back at the house where Jason is showering.

Sitting on a stump of wood my dad used for a chair, Billy

takes off his cowboy hat and runs a hand through his hair. "Are you talking about what happened at Red River between him and Jason?"

"Yeah." I lean against the frame of the open barn door and cross my arms over my chest. "I've been worried, living every day like he's about to strike. Is he?"

"You don't have to worry, Delilah. You have Jason around. He's not going to let Cole step foot on this farm."

"I don't want Jason fighting this battle. I don't want Jason near Cole at all. It won't end well. You know that."

"Jason can handle himself. I saw him pin Cole to the ground by a neck hold in like two seconds flat. The guy's got a lethal side."

You're telling me. "When did that happen?"

"When Jason first arrived in town. Same place. Red River."

Jason didn't tell me. *Why?* We both look back toward the house when we hear the screen door slam closed. My heartbeat picks up. Pushing off the barn, I point at Billy. "I'm serious. I don't want Jason and Cole near each other. You'll let me know if you hear about Cole coming out here?"

"You know I will."

Finding some relief, I smile. "Thanks. I appreciate it."

Just as I turn, Jason walks toward the barn looking as devastatingly handsome as always. "You sticking around, Billy?" He's far enough away not to have heard us talking.

"I was thinking about it. I was also thinking about getting laid."

"Billy." I shake my head and pretend I was tending to the rusted tools hanging on the wall. "Gross."

"Really? Are we fifteen? A man has needs, Delilah. I'm assuming a woman does too, so I'm going to go help one out with those needs tonight."

Jason's laughing too hard and smart enough not to get involved in the conversation. I start back for the house, but I stop and go back. "You can't say stuff like that in front of my sister when she comes to visit."

Billy swipes a piece of hay and jabs it in the side of his mouth, smirking. "Why not?"

I shake my head at his ridiculousness. "Because she's used to men with class."

"Annnnnd?"

"And," I say, then huff, frustrated he doesn't get my drift without me spelling it out. "And do you have a tie?"

"Delilah." Now Jason joins in, chuckling under his breath at me. "Leave the poor guy alone."

"What? I'm just asking if he has a tie."

Billy responds instead, "Yes, I do. Why, are you trying to set me up with Shelby?"

"Because I like you, and I love her, and I think you guys might work well together."

"Your sister has hated me since I was eight. I don't think she's gonna go for you trying to set us up."

"That's not a no. Anyway, nobody even remembers you pushing her into the mud."

"Except you."

And my sister. "Doesn't matter," I reply. "We're not kids anymore. Right, Jason?"

His hands are up, and he's backing away. "I'm not getting involved in this one since it predates my arrival in Solace Pointe."

Rolling my eyes, I turn back to Billy. "Wear the tie for dinner on that Friday night. Okay?"

Yanking the hay from his mouth, Billy huffs. "Am I going to church?"

"No, but if you play your cards right—oh God, what am I

saying?" I laugh at myself for setting my sister up like this. Lord help me if she figures it out. "Just wear something nice —not too dressy but not straight off the farm."

"Some women like straight off the farm, but I have a feeling your sister is not going to like this setup one bit."

"What's not to like? Four friends getting together to hang out and catch up is all good stuff."

"Guess we'll find out. As for these tools, I think I can clean 'em up and sell them. You don't use them, and Paul has his own."

"If we can make some money, let's sell them. Every penny counts right now."

Jason nudges me. "Speaking of money, I wanted to talk when you have a few minutes."

Although I'm curious to know what he wants to talk about specifically, I don't push for more with Billy standing here. "I'm free now."

Billy gets to work, pulling the tools out from the corner, and I join Jason as he walks to the back of Billy's truck. "I've been meaning to talk to you as well, but you go first. Is everything all right?" I ask.

"Yeah, it's good. I'm good. You?" *This is awkward.* Dragging down the tailgate, he motions for me to sit.

I hop up and let my feet dangle. "I'm good. Since we're all good, I wanted to ask about the fair again. With Red River not working out how we planned, how do you feel about going?"

He moves between my legs, covering my bare thighs with his large hands. "I'm fine with it. The reality is we can't stay holed up here forever."

"I don't want to be controlled by my ex." The tips of his fingers dip under my cutoffs and then work around to my ass. I've discovered he's such an ass man.

"I fucking hate that you even have an ex." Taking me by surprise, he brings me in for a kiss. It's possessive and greedy, abrupt and lustful. My body's temperature rises as does my need for him.

"How do you turn me on from one kiss?"

"Because you know what follows." He lifts me off the hot metal and rights me on my feet again. "You want to go upstairs?"

Looking back at Billy, I debate briefly but decide against it. "He works for free to help me out. I think we should finish the chores."

"I'll wait, but I can't promise I'll be good."

"Good because I love when you're bad."

His hands span my lower back. I love being engulfed by him. But thinking about him holding me to the fire with Billy, I also respect him. It wasn't a callout to hurt me or shame me, humiliate me, or demean me in any way. I've not held the same level for anyone since my father. "Hold on to your britches, Ms. Noelle, because I put the *bad* in bad boy."

"Bad boys are my weakness."

"Then I'm one lucky bastard."

I'm the lucky one, but I'll let him own the title for a bit. "We should finish the chores so we can have some fun sooner rather than later."

"I like the way you think."

"I like everything about you."

The tips of his fingers slide inside the waistband of my shorts, and my body responds instantly to his touch. In the heat of the day, he manages to make me shiver from desire while goose bumps pebble my skin.

Billy comes out of the barn. "I'm taking off."

I back up a few steps from Jason, who says, "Your timing really fucking sucks."

"*Thank you* would be nice. Don't mind me. You guys can roll in the hay or whatever it is you're wanting to do. Just don't tell me about it and don't make me watch."

I close the tailgate for him. "Thanks for helping out."

"You're welcome. About the fair tomorrow—"

"We'll be there," Jason replies, surprising me. "Want to ride together?"

He shakes his head. "Nah. I'm hoping to bring whoever I meet tonight to the fair tomorrow."

Laughing, I say, "You've really thought this through."

"My needs come with plans. I'm not a love 'em and leave 'em kind of guy, despite what you hear around town."

"Noted," I reply. "Then we'll see you there around six?"

"I'll be there with the football team. I promised to kick their asses at the carnival games."

Jason adjusts his hat. "You're stooping to new lows if you're betting against high school kids."

"They're big dudes these days. Anyway, I'll let them win. Builds their confidence before the game this weekend. Also, I got roped into judging the Mutton Bustin' race."

Elbowing him, I tease, "You old softie."

"Guess they figure the all-time winning champion in Freeland County will make a good judge."

He's got me in a corner, but then he says, "And cowboys tend to screw up their marriages. I bet there will be a lot of hot single moms there." *And then I'm reminded why we never hooked up.*

"Ugh. I thought you were bringing a date."

"Date, not wife."

"Again. *Ugh.* Why'd you have to go and ruin it? I'm going inside."

I leave the guys laughing in my wake. Inside, I grab the iced tea container from the windowsill after noticing the deep, bright color it's turned from steeping in the sun all morning. Jason comes in the back door just as I finish filling two large glasses.

"It's not sweet," I warn.

"That's okay," he says, coming to me. "I haven't had sweet tea since I moved away from here." He licks the side of my neck. "And you're sweet enough for me."

"Ahh," I sigh, giving him easier access. "And sweaty."

"I know. It's fucking sexy as hell." His hands wander as my eyes dip closed.

"We shouldn't," I whisper in all the ways that counteract how I'm feeling.

His breath breezes across my skin when he whispers, "You sure about that?"

He makes it hard to tick through my list of chores, much less even remember what they are. "I have so much to do." I tug him closer.

"I want to do you." His voice is muffled as he sucks on my neck.

Anxiety takes over the pleasure, and I push back. "Jason, stop."

Shock and hurt run across his face as we're forced apart. "What?"

Realizing too late what he must think, I move closer again, reaching to close some of the distance. He takes my hand, clasping it between his. I whisper, "No. No. I don't mean this. Or us, but if you leave a mark . . ." I stop myself from continuing that thought for worry of upsetting him.

"If I leave a mark, so what? Who's going to care?" It dawns on him before I can answer, and his puzzled expression hardens. "Because of Cutler?" He knows the answer without me filling in the silence. "It's none of his fucking business what we do. He's your ex, Delilah. He doesn't have a place in our lives, much less a say."

Gripping the counter behind me, I'm not scared of Jason. His kind heart always puts me front and center, but I am worried about him. The one person who could push Jason too far is the one who would love to do it. Revel in it, in fact. And I'd lose Jason all over again because let's face it. Cole would never survive an encounter with Jason if it came down to it. I have no doubt about that. "I know. I just don't want to incite him. If he sees a hickey on my neck, he'll flip out, and who knows what he'll do."

"The fuck?" Wild eyes stare into me as his hands fist at his sides. I've never seen him this angry and never at me before.

"You don't understand. You weren't here when tiny things would set Cole off. *I was. Alone.*"

"You're right. I wasn't." He grabs the door and walks out, leaving me standing there with my mouth open. He's never been afraid to take a conversation head-on. This isn't like him, not how he usually is with me.

I hate that I've upset him, but years of brainwashing still rears its ugly head sometimes. I run out the front door just as he approaches his truck. Catching myself against the porch railing, I ask, "Where are you going?"

"I need my bike."

"Don't leave. *Please.*"

My words or maybe the plea in my tone stop him. With his back to me, he says, "I need to take a ride and clear my head."

"Jason, look at me."

When he turns back, his soulful eyes reveal such pain, and I hate that I'm the cause of it. *Again.* "I'm sorry I upset you. I don't want any more trouble with him. I just want you. Please don't be mad at me."

His shoulders lose their tension as he returns to me. He stops on the bottom step like he did that first day he showed up here after the rain. His respect for me has been shown in many ways. We may have moved fast once we reconnected, but he took each step with care for my feelings. Even now, he remains a few steps lower. He doesn't try to intimidate me like Cole. Jason humbles himself before me, and it's a genuine sign of respect I'm still getting used to.

We also still have so much to discuss—our wants, our needs, our new dreams for the rest of our lives, but when we do talk, he communicates *with* me, not *over* me. "I'm not mad at you, Delilah. We're not fighting. I've been here every day like I live here, and reality just hit me. We can play house and pretend, but this *isn't* my farm. And as long as you're worried about him and how he'll react to my presence, it's as if you're not really my girl. I'm not giving you an ultimatum. I'm here for you however I can be, however you want me to be. I don't care if I lose to him in football or in a fight or whatever. That's all shit that's built on ego and pride. But when it comes to you, I can't be second to him. I won't be. Not again."

"You're not. You never will be." I move down until I'm equal in height, in standing, a partner, not a queen who needs her subjects to bow before her. Equal in all ways that matter. I keep my hands to myself, but it's a struggle when all I want to do is caress that furrowed brow until the tension is released. "You never were. I don't want him near you. I don't want you hurt."

"How many times do I have to tell you I can handle him?"

"He's not the same person you used to know. You moved

past the glory days of your football years. *He didn't.* Two things matter to him—his ego and me—and you've effectively taken both from him since you came back."

"You're divorced. He can't hold on to you anymore."

"He's an alcoholic with a gambling problem. He didn't want the divorce. I petitioned for it after I got a temporary restraining order. The judge granted me a quick divorce, but that restraining order was lifted the same day because the good ole boy judge admired Cole's football record." I can't stand the space separating me from the man I love. Even inches are too much to bear. *I hate that Jason has come home to this. To me, with this dreadful baggage.* "It's not a matter of *if* he'll try to get me back or hurt me. It's *when.* And I don't want you caught in the crossfire."

He finally breaches the divide, holding me without pressure. "I'm not afraid. He can come after me as long as he doesn't come after you. I won't let him hurt you, Delilah. You're my everything."

My heart beats erratically in my chest. The immense amount of love I have for him has always been set to its own frequency. Taking this stunning man by the jaw, I hold him in my hands. "Were you always this foolish?"

"Only for you, honeysuckle." We kiss, and I sigh, melting against him. "I might pay him a visit to put things to an end."

"He's not a reasonable man."

He winks. "I have ways of helping him see the light."

"Do I want to know what that means?"

"No, it's better if you don't. It's safer that way. In the meantime . . ." He kisses my neck. "Want to go for a ride on my Harley?"

Now that is an offer I can't refuse. "Absolutely."

23

Jason

The wind whips around us. The road's wide open. I could keep riding. I could steal her away from this life that's holding her back. Would she stop me?

Would Delilah want to keep going or turn back?

We're both caught in a whirlwind we can't control, and it sucks. I know she loves me. She doesn't have to tell me, though she does often enough. She shows me. I see it in her pretty blue eyes. I feel it in the way she touches me and how she cares for me.

I love her.

Goddammit, I love her so fucking much. I'm an asshole for lying to myself for so long. I pushed any thoughts of her, memories, and emotions that threatened to surface back down, in no place to deal with something that always ended without her.

I won't take this second chance for granted. I won't lose it either. I'll protect her. I'll protect this relationship so it can set when we take our last breath. Not a second sooner.

I cover one of her hands with mine before returning it to the handlebar. Having her on my bike, wrapped around me, was yet another fantasy I never thought would happen. Here we are, though. Trust in me to care for her—to keep her safe—has been handed over without question.

Delilah took the helmet and put it on before I had a chance to insist on it. "Share this piece of you with me," she said. An hour later, we haven't made it far, but we've crossed county lines. I veer onto a small, hidden-from-the-highway dirt road. I don't think she'll remember when I brought her here back in college, but it felt like a good time for a revisit.

The river comes into view, and I love the sight of the mountains with the gray and purple of twilight. We dismount, and she sets the helmet on the bike before wandering toward the edge. "You brought me here a few times. I always remembered the beauty but could never find it without you."

"Why were you looking for it?"

Standing at the water's edge with her back to me, she says, "I thought if I could find it, it would lead me back to you."

When her head tilts down, her shoulders shake with a sob that seems to come from out of the blue. I know it's just been building inside her, though. I go to her as she covers her face with her hands. Holding her from behind, I whisper in her ear, "My heart was always with you. Our beat was just silent until I returned." I move around to hold her as she cries on my shoulder. "I'm not mad at you, honeysuckle." Stroking her hair, I whisper, "And I'm not leaving."

She looks up, the tears that puddle on her lower lids running over. "For now?"

"I'm thinking about forever. What do you think?"

Her smile—small and full of insecurity—is not one that should ever reside on her face. "Do you mean that?"

"If that means staying on the farm or moving to somewhere new, I want to be with you."

She sighs, her tears finally drying as she wipes away the last of them. "There's so much debt, Jason. It's already dragging me down. I can't saddle you with it."

"Remember how I wanted to talk about money?"

"Yes, but I didn't." Moving to the water's edge again, she crosses her arms defensively over her chest. I wish she knew she didn't have to be on guard with me about anything. She glances back at me over her shoulder. "I may not have been the one who grew that debt, but it's mine to erase and basically impossible. Every time I feel pride in what I've accomplished there, another bill arrives to remind me of my failures."

She stands there as if she has to take on the world on her own. "I'm right here with you. I'll help however I can, but that means we have to discuss it openly. Every dirty detail of the debt needs to be exposed. It's the only way we can tackle it."

"Money brings out the worst in people. It's not something I want to include in our relationship because eventually, you'll be drowning just like me. How would I be able to live with myself if I did that to you?"

That's not the Delilah I know. She's never been one to focus on the negatives, but after what I've learned regarding the human condition, she's right. "It doesn't have to be that way."

"I don't know anymore, Jason. I just know that my dad died trying to pay it off, and Cole thrived on building it up. Neither had a good outcome."

"I'm not Cutler. As for your dad, he shielded you from

the hell he was living in to protect you. I love you, Delilah. Let me help you end this burden." We remain next to each other, letting any discomfort evaporate into the beauty of nature.

"How?" she whispers so softly I almost miss it under the sound of the wind brushing across the top of the water.

"I've been thinking about our future and the farm. I have money—"

She's shaking her head before she speaks. "I'm not letting you spend your money on the farm, if that's what you're suggesting."

"Wow, I didn't even get the offer out. Is it pride that keeps you holding so tightly to a sinking ship in the face of a life raft?" I take her hand, and despite her unease in the conversation, her fingers lace with mine. "Tell me, Delilah, what if I want to help?"

A heavy sigh prefaces her head tilting to lean on my shoulder. As if the wind inspires her, she turns to me. "I don't know what kind of money you made or have, for that matter. It's not something I've thought about since you came into my life." She shrugs. "I think I thought you returned because you were just like me and everyone else in this town, living day-to-day. But more importantly, whatever money you have, you have more than earned. You were shot. You've done unimaginable things for that money—"

"Is it too dirty to use it for a good cause?"

She scoffs with a ridiculously adorable grin as the sunshine enters her eyes, causing her to squint and finally face me. "I'm not that high and mighty, Jason. I meant that you've had to sacrifice so much to earn every dollar."

"Everyone who works makes sacrifices."

"Usually not with their life."

"I didn't think I would, but shit happens. Things go

wrong. Bad people sometimes get ahead, but they don't win."

"What happened to them? I know one died."

"They all died." The confession doesn't shake her, her expression remaining one of indifference. I walk to the edge of the water and squat down. Picking a weed, I rub it between my fingers before tossing it to the ground. "You have more questions, so let's just address them and move past this."

"Why did that note from Cruise say Eric on it?"

"Because it wasn't from Cruise. It was from my old . . . boss, a friend. Acquaintances. I don't know what to call them. I consider them friends and allies more than anything else."

"So it's like an inside joke?"

"It was an alias at one time."

"Eric," she repeats, trying out the name. "You chose Eric. It doesn't suit you."

Chuckling, I ask, "And Jason does?"

"Yes. To me, it's just a part of who you are. Like Cuddle Bear." Laughter escapes her sweet grin.

I huff. Am I ever going to live that down? "You can call me that if you like."

She bumps up against me playfully. "Okay, Cuddle Bear."

Wrapping my arms around her waist, I ask, "Anything else you're wondering about?" Digging the toe of her shoe into the ground, she keeps her gaze lowered. "What's wrong?"

"When you tell these stories about being shot or working on movie sets, I feel like you've lived a whole lifetime without me. You went on adventures and saw the country. You lived a life I thought I'd be sharing with you. I worry I won't be enough for you. That you'll get bored and—"

My eyes widen. "You feel left out because I was shot?"

That earns me a half smile. "Not that. You know what I mean."

"Nothing compares to being on that farm with you no matter where or how far I traveled. If I could change things, I would. I would come back after college for you."

"You swear?"

"On my life."

"No, not on your life. I'm not willing to risk that."

We start walking along the bank. "Okay. On Cutler's life."

She bursts out laughing. "That shouldn't be as funny as it is."

"You have a dark side, Ms. Noelle."

Elbowing my side, she says, "It's from hanging around an assassin."

"Let's go with bodyguard. It's fitting. So you successfully avoided digging deeper in to the topic of finances, but I also wanted to talk to you about something else."

"All right."

"I know you're recently divorce—"

She startles, catching me off guard. "Oh, my God. Are you going to ask me to marry you?"

"What?" A hand flies to my hair, and I run it through. "No. Wait. I mean—" The heartbreak on her face does me in. I rush to cup her face in my hands. "Why are you crying? Don't cry."

"I'm sorry. I thought you meant you were going to ask me." She looks away, embarrassment coloring her cheeks. "Forget it. Forget I said anything."

An ache grows in my chest at seeing the pain on this

woman's face. "If you'd say yes, I'd marry you right now." Beautiful eyes the color of bluebirds peer up at me. She wears her heart on her sleeve for everyone to see. It's battered like mine but filled with so much love to give. "I would."

"I'm a recently divorced, almost bankrupt farmer in the middle of nowhere. My spirit has been bruised along with my body. I have a lot more scars than I had when I was wearing that Freeland County tiara. I feel older than my years because of them. And here you come, riding back into town, and screwing up my plans of being a spinster for the rest of my life."

"You know why? Because when I heard you were single again, all the plans I made suddenly seemed secondary. Scars don't scare me. I have a lot of my own. As for your divorce, I say this is my lucky day. It's as if Cupid himself had a say in the matter. I also think you're more stunning than the day we fell in love."

"Which time?"

"Both. Age doesn't hold a candle to your beauty. But who cares if we get lines and both age if we're living a good life and growing old together?" Taking her by the hips and wiggling them back and forth a bit, I say, "I'm not sorry about ruining your plan to grow old alone."

"Why are you so good to me?"

"Because you deserve good. Lots of it, and I intend to give it to you for the rest of your life."

"I love when you give it to me."

Leading her back to the bike, I say, "Speaking of giving it to you . . ."

WITH MY ASS pressed to the leather, Delilah slides down my erection. Once she's fully seated, her head falls back, and her hair sways across my thighs. When she tilts forward, she says, "I will never get tired of how good you feel inside me."

Fuck. "Show me how good I feel to you."

"So good," she rasps, rocking her hips on top of me.

My stomach muscles tighten from the sound. "I'm not gonna last long, babe."

She moves faster, her eyes closed, her nails digging into my shoulders. "Don't come yet. I'm so close."

She's an angel under a halo of blond hair. A vixen who knows how to command her pleasure. "You're so fucking gorgeous."

"God, yes," she releases on a sharp-edged breath, her body tremors and her hands squeeze like that perfect pussy of hers.

"Fuck." I grab her by the hips and hold her down while I thrust until I'm emptied of everything held deep inside—my emotions, my secrets, my cum, my sins. *Everything* is given to this goddess who rules my world and is healing my soul. I drop my forehead against her chest, trying to catch my breath.

When I look at her, her gaze is on me. She runs her fingers through my hair. "I'd marry you if you asked, but I only want you to ask when you're ready. Not for me but for you. We're not in a hurry. I'm not going anywhere."

"I love you." We kiss, and things feel settled between us in the good kind of way. It's dark, and the stars are out, ready to guide us home. "We should get back."

"It's a shame to leave somewhere so beautiful. Thank you for bringing me here again."

"I'm glad we came." I wink, amused by the double entendre.

"So, do you always carry condoms in your pocket?"

"Only when I'm with you."

"Good answer, Mr. Koster. Good answer."

Once we're dressed and back on the bike, ready to go, I lean back, and ask, "You ready?"

"Ready for anything."

I'VE BEEN BACK LONG ENOUGH to have stopped by to say hi, so here I am walking along the far side of the field, ready to remedy the situation.

The little house looks to be in good shape. Paul and Lorraine always did take care of it. I find Paul on top of the smaller tractor, cutting the weeds lining the road. He shuts it down when he sees me and leans on the steering wheel, wearing a smile that time recorded in the deep lines surrounding his mouth. "I was starting to wonder if you were ever going to stop by."

Kicking the large tire, I gaze up, using my hand to shield my eyes from the sun. "I should have come sooner."

"Yeah, you should've." He climbs down, and we shake hands. "It's good to see you, son. How are ya?"

"I'm good. Staying out at the farm and helping Delilah with chores. You?"

He sits on the step, shadowed by the tractor, and takes off his hat to wipe his forehead. "Keepin' on with the keepin' on. Heard you were hanging around these parts."

"Yeah," I say, looking toward the farmhouse in the distance. "Never thought I'd be out here again—"

"But here you are." He grins. "She's always been a good girl."

"She has." I shove my hands in my pockets, the conversation awkward when I don't want it to be. "I wanted to come by and say hi because things are getting serious with Delilah."

"Gettin'?"

"Maybe already are."

"That's what I thought, considering that truck of yours seems to be permanently parked over there." He stands but puts his foot on the step, the lightness already making room for the talk I knew was coming. "It's not been easy for her. If you're planning on leaving anytime soon, then best be doing it now. She doesn't need another broken heart."

"I'm not leaving anytime soon." I glance over when a car drives by. When I turn back, I look him in the eye. "I'm going to marry her this time."

"She deserves better than she's gotten. She was left in a bad state last time."

"I carry that regret heavy on my shoulders every day. If I would have known—"

"Don't let it weigh you down too much. I was right here and . . ." His gaze goes to the ground between us, and for the first time in my life, Paul looks . . . *regretful*. His body slumps. "We can't change what's happened." The dark of his brown eyes hold more than memories but are still optimistic. "I know you well enough, Jason, to know you'll make things right by her. But if you don't, we own two shotguns, and Lorraine and I aren't afraid to use them."

"I'd forgotten how you never messed around."

"My days are long, but there never seems to be enough hours. I don't have time to beat around the bush." He reaches forward, and we shake hands again. "Since you're hanging around, feel free to come give me an afternoon off here and there," he jokes.

"I will."

Sitting atop the old tractor, he says, "Make sure to say hello to my wife, or she'll give me a hard time. She's not home right now, but she's been dying to see you."

Delilah is fortunate to have them nearby. They care about her. They were there for her when I wasn't, and I'm thankful she has them in her life. "She could have come over anytime. Both of you. You're always welcome. You know that."

"Eh, I told her to give you and Delilah some time to grow together. I see it worked."

Chuckling, I reply, "It sure did."

24

Jason

"Welcome to the Freeland County Fair and Rodeo."

The greeting screeches through the speakers as I park the truck in a field of cars and get out. I scan the area, but it's massive.

One main ticketed entrance.

One gate to exit.

Too many ins and outs surrounding this place.

I hate large events because danger lurks everywhere. The lack of safety here is disconcerting, and I'm supposed to walk my girl right in there like it's not. So much can go wrong quickly. Reminding myself that I grew up coming here and the people are good, I try to believe it's safe. It's not the locals I'm worried about. It's my past showing up. Shit can get crazy fast without warning.

Pushing these thoughts down isn't going to be easy, but maybe that's yet another penance I'll pay for living the life I have. Delilah's a reminder of the good in people. Don't I deserve the good for the bad I've seen?

When I come around, Delilah slips out. The short skirt of her dress slides up while her boots land on the gravel with ease. Long, tan legs teasing my dick. *As always.* Looking around, I'm tempted to take her here. There aren't many people around, but enough that we might be noticed since it's only six o'clock, and the sun is still high in the sky.

I settle on a compliment. "Have I told you how sexy you look in that dress?"

She's blushing when she looks at me from under the brim of her cowboy hat. "We're not having sex here."

My hands go up in surrender. "I wasn't going to suggest it." Damn, she's got my number.

"I know you, Jason Koster. I can see it on your face, and the way you're looking at me."

Grabbing her around the waist, I pull her against my hard-on. "I can't help that you do things to me."

Her hands slide under my shirt, her nails scraping lightly against my stomach and arousing me even more. "I'll tell you what. You win me a prize, a *big* prize, and we'll fulfill that fantasy of yours."

"The one with you bent over the hay bale?"

"That's the one, cowboy."

Fuck yeah, I'll win that prize.

Her pupils dilate. With a mischievous smile on her face, she runs her tongue over the corner of her mouth and then bites her lip. *Fuck.* My cock hurts from being restrained in these jeans.

The sexy confidence she had when we dated has returned. She's so damn tempting and maddening when she teases, but the reward when I'm deep inside her is worth the foreplay. She makes it to the end of the truck bed and turns back. "Well, c'mon now. We have a prize to win."

I shift the best I can within the confines of the denim.

"Let's get a move on." She saunters off, but then looks back and winks. "Good times await, stud."

———

I'M COMPETITIVE, to say the least.

With the offer she made on the table, there was no way I was going to lose. I don't care how much money I had to spend on these carnival games, but I feel set up. She doesn't want the biggest stuffed panda from hitting rigged milk bottles or the pink Care Bear tossing darts at balloons. *Nope.* Delilah Rae has set her sights on the grand prize—$500 cash—in the county sharpshooting contest.

Well, if this isn't my lucky day. I sign up for the tournament against hunters and gun owners who shoot for fun. Everyone in the state pretty much has a gun on his or her property, but they've never had to use it like I have. I'm feeling confident I can win this contest. Billy was taken out in the second round of the previous bracket, leaving me with a warning about the competition.

I'm not intimidated. Shooting isn't only about hitting the targets. It's about accuracy. When I see Cole Cutler hanging out at the judge's table, laughing and working them over, it's no longer about the money for me. It's about dominance and instilling fear in him. Delilah isn't his, and he needs to learn boundaries. Damn do I hope I'm put up against him.

When I spot Delilah, I stop to watch the show. Holy. Fuck. Her tongue dips out, whipping some of the spun sugar into her mouth before she licks her lips. Her eyes dip closed as the sweet confection coats her mouth. I'm on the move. She smiles when she sees me. "Are you signed—"

Interrupting her question, I kiss her. I take possession of that sweet mouth and when her lips part, our tongues dance among the sugar, savoring her. quick to grab her to steady her wobbling legs. Her eyes slowly open, her lips still parted. "Oh my," she says breathlessly.

"That's for teasing me."

"If I get kissed like that for teasing, expect a lot more of it. Just saying." She giggles as her free hand finds mine. Her eyes dart to the gathering crowd, and she adds, "When I said I wanted a big prize, it doesn't have to be this one."

"I'm all signed up. I'm in it to win it, baby."

She lifts up and steals a kiss. "For the record, you're pretty sexy yourself." When she lowers back down, her smile is wiped clear from her face and the laughter stops. I know what's changed her disposition. *Cutler.*

He makes a show of his presence, strutting around the place like the reigning king of the county. Fuck him. He's so fucking cocky. I can't wait to knock that chip right off his fucking shoulder. As if my wish was a command, an announcement blasts through the speakers. "Bracket Four report to the stage. We've got our very own hometown hero, Jason Koster. Former Freeland County quarterback and homecoming king."

I hear the laughter. A lame title is better than none, so what-the-fuck-ever. A gentle squeeze to my bicep causes me to flex, and she gets the full strength of what lies under this T-shirt.

Delilah stands behind me, and with a seductive whisper, she says, "I should call you king."

The life I left behind comes racing back, and I duck my head, squeezing my eyes. They aren't bad memories on the whole, but some, like the restless nights, were the worst. I'd like to forget those forever . . .

I know how to protect someone, how to risk my life for theirs for money, but this penthouse is secure. My mind allowed to wander back to a time that was simpler.

King and Cruise don't know what to make of me, but they need me and know it. What started out as a job has become more. I care about these people, and Ali—I don't let my mind go there.

It's a job.

That's all, *I tell myself and attempt to fall asleep again.*

When that doesn't work, I get up and head down the hall. I click on the coffeemaker and start snacking on Oreos left on the counter. As I stare through the large windows, my head begins to clear as the sun rises. It's always easier in the daytime to handle the dark crimes I've committed.

My mom would be devastated by the choices I've made, and I wonder what Delilah would think of me?

Turning to my side, I say, "Nah, I don't need the trouble that comes along with a name like that."

My ass is slapped. "Okay, Cuddle Bear."

Chuckling, I roll my eyes. "Shh. We'll keep that one between us."

Although the humor still lingers in the air, worry starts to darken her irises when she glances toward the stage at Cutler's name being called. "Cole Cutler, owner of Cutler Cabling and former running back for Freeland County High School."

"You forgot to add the one who got the girl!" Cole shouts.

I glance over my shoulder as he approaches. *He's such an asshole.* I want to add, the one *who lost the girl,* but it's best if I keep quiet. My shoulder is shoved, and I turn, his throat in my hand within seconds. "Don't fuck with me, Cutler, or you'll get a repeat of what happened outside Red River." I shove him back to the sound of Delilah gasping.

Chuckling like the asshole he is, he says, "A bit touchy for a wife-stealing wife-fucker."

The announcer says, "Gentlemen, save it for the shootin' contest. You have five targets ready to take these bullets of anger off your hands."

He's right. *Delilah deserves better from me.* I turn to find her in the crowd behind me, worry creasing her brow. She comes to me once the fucker is gone and takes hold of my arm. "You don't have anything to prove, Jason. We can walk away, go ride the Ferris wheel, or I'll get more cotton candy and we can take it into the bedroom with us for some sweet fun."

But that giant check for five hundred dollars hanging high above the announcer's head gets my attention. Cutler needs money, and he's got the skills to win this. That is, of course, if I wasn't here to make sure he doesn't. "It's okay." I kiss her, and she wishes me luck. I don't need luck. This is fun and games.

At the podium, a case is presented to each of us. The rules state we don't get to choose our weapon, much to my dismay. I hate revolvers, but that seems to be the choice for this contest. Even worse, Cutler gets an Uberti handgun, a better handgun over the Smith & Wesson .357 I end up with. I shake my head. His is made for competition. My gun is made for collectors, not precise shooting. *Fuck.* I refuse to lose, but it may be harder to win with this weapon.

I take the gun out of the case and check the chambers. Five bullets. Five targets. The fastest and most accurate shot moves to the final bracket. Four winners of their brackets will shoot to win. I have to take Cutler out first. We're led to the line. Cutler wins the coin toss to see who goes first. I cross my arms and take a few steps back.

He walks to the line and kicks up some dust. When he's given the go-ahead, he shoots. It's an impressive showing for such an asshole. He used to kill every can with a BB gun when we were young and took turns shooting. If he'd win one round, I'd win the next. We were always good at pushing each other.

The paper targets are changed, and Cutler's are brought to the judges.

I'm told to step to the line. As soon as the signal is given, time stands still. The colors that once surrounded my target turn a gray gradient, allowing me to focus on the bull's-eye. My arm flies out steady, my elbow locked to absorb the recoil. With narrowed eyes, I focus dead center on the target. The first bullet flies from the chamber, and I turn just enough to send the second toward its intended destination.

Third.

Fourth.

Fifth.

It's too fast to process the damage done properly. I lower my arm as the gray fades away, and the sound of life returns. As if the whole damn world is muted, not like the noise and chatter from before, I look behind me and am greeted with silence. The rowdy rodeo goers are staring—some with their mouths open, some closed but with their eyes wide, and some sport both. I see the rise and fall of Delilah's chest, her eyes meeting mine. Barging through the gawkers, she comes toward me. "Jason?"

"What?" I ask, not sure if she's okay or if I'm in trouble.

"That was the most incredible thing I think I've ever witnessed," she whispers, "in my life."

"From my shooting?"

"Yes, your shooting." The exposed top of her chest is flushed. "Holy damn. I see now."

"What? What do you see?"

A sexy grin slips onto her lips. "I see why you were so good at your job."

"Former job," I correct.

Her hands flail. "Whatever. Do you want to leave early?"

Now I smirk, utterly amused. "You turned on, baby?"

"So much."

"I was just messing around out there." I try to see my targets, pretending I don't know that I hit the center of the bull's-eye. *Every. Time.* "We used to shoot BB guns for fun."

"That wasn't messing around, Jason. What you did was pure skill." We return to the podium together. "Your face. I've never seen you look like that."

"I wake up every day with the same ugly mug. Nothing new here to see." I try to distract her by making a big deal about putting the gun back in the case.

It doesn't work because she's still staring at me. As soon as the case closes, her hand covers my forearm. "I'm serious. I want you so badly right now."

"I would have shown you what I can do with a gun sooner if I would've known how turned on you are by it."

The announcer interrupts our foreplay, "Wooooweeee. Holy cow! Would you look at those targets! Our hometown hero just might maintain that status. You've been cut, Cutler." A snicker echoes across the range, causing the crowd to join in at Cutler's expense.

"You fucking rigged it, Koster!" he shouts. I turn around, and he charges, tackling me to the ground. *Shit.* He swings, but I flip him to the side with a good shove to his chest and knee to the groin. I'm on my knees and get a solid punch in before I'm grabbed and yanked backward by two dudes each the size of the Hulk. Fighting a guy who's been drinking too much to hold Cutler back, the fucker hits me with an uppercut before I can free my arms and fight back.

But when I do . . . I land heavy on top of him. Two punches and the sad sap is groaning in pain and hiding his face like it's worth protecting. This time, security pulls me back. Yanking out of their grip, I raise my hands, shrugging my shirt back in place. "I already stopped."

Jeffrey Whaley, our town deputy, cuts through the crowd. "Why am I not surprised it's the two of you fightin' again?"

"Because Cutler can't seem to keep his insecurities under wraps," I reply.

Whaley grabs me by the elbow and the twin Hulks back away. "You're out of here, Koster."

"What the hell? He fucking started it."

Deputy Whaley never saw things for how they were. He preferred to pick and choose who his criminals were. Today, I guess I'm the bad guy. "Shut it, or I'll take you to jail."

Delilah pushes through the crowd. "Jason was defending himself, Deputy Whaley. All these witnesses can back him up."

"Step back, Mrs. Cutler."

"It's Noelle," she corrects with fire in her eyes.

He stops and eyes her. Releasing my arm, he says, "You jump from one bad decision to the next. Cut your losses on this one before I see you in jail right along with him."

"No." She steps in front of him, proving his point, and crosses her arms over her chest. "You have the wrong guy, and I'm not going to let you get away with this."

"Well, there's nothing you can do, *Ms.* Noelle, so step aside."

As proud as I am of her, I can handle it. "It's okay, baby. He's not going to take me in. I'll be back."

Seeing her all fired up like this, fires me up in ways we can't act on. She's feisty and fierce. Her hands are on her hips, and she's passionate when she raises her voice. "Actually, Jeff Whaley, it's not okay—"

Cole grabs her arm and tugs her toward him. I'm in

action to take that fucker down once and for all, but she's already swinging and lands a perfect right cross, his jowls shaking under the impact.

Deputy Whaley sighs, and then yells, "Take her into custody."

25

Delilah

I'm not scared.

I probably should be, but I'm not.

I'm never scared when I'm with Jason. You would think having been so close to Cole when he flew at Jason, I'd be rattled. *I'm not.* And even though I'm leaning over a cop car handcuffed, I'm not worried. *Not one bit.*

His cheek is pressed to the same trunk as mine, both of us staring at each with smiles on our faces. "Maybe you shouldn't have told him his wife's famous blue-ribbon recipe was a rip-off of your mom's," he says.

Laughing, I reply, "Maybe, but it's true. Shows what cheaters the Whaley family have always been."

"Commit a crime and you walk away with a warning in this small, fucked-up county. Expose the truth about an apple crisp, and you get a night in jail. Sounds about right."

"They won't book us," I say. "They have nothing on us."

He stares at me like he's seeing me in a whole new light.

Oh wait . . . he is, and asks, "Since when did you grow a pair of balls the size of Kentucky?"

"I'm just tired of it all. Tired of being called Cole's wife. Tired of being called a whore to my face from rumors spread all over Solace Pointe. Tired of hiding who I want to be. Tired of hiding us. I'm so fucking tired of all the bullshit. Do you ever just get tired of it all, Jason?"

He smiles. "Yeah, that's when I decided to come home."

"But this is my home. I have nowhere else to escape to."

We're both lifted by our shoulders and brought around opposite sides of the car. Our heads are pushed down as we're loaded into the back of the cop car. The doors slam closed, and we look at each other. Blue and red lights illuminate the night around us when Jason leans forward, and says, "Marry me, Delilah." Not a question. It's a plea followed by a smile and nudge. "Fuck this town and marry me. We'll live like the shunned in our private paradise by the lake. We'll fish and fuck, raise a family, and pour so much love into that farm and each other that no one will have cause to say anything bad."

Although my heart feels full—of love, welling emotion, and him, his sweet dream should come in a trade-off. "I don't want to marry you to stop gossip."

"Then marry me to start it. I'll walk down Main with you on my arm, proud as the day is long. You're my girl. You always were. And you always will be. Let me be your man long past forever. Will you marry me, Delilah Rae Noelle?"

Jason, Billy, Paul, and my daddy are the only men who've never used my married name, which surprisingly the town refuses to drop. There's a lot to be said for men with manners. Besides manners, Jason's the man I was always meant to be with. I may be newly divorced, but I was never truly married. Not in my heart anyway. The answer is easy, coming forthright just like Jason is now. "Yes."

Leaning together with our hands trapped behind our backs, we meet in the middle, but words aren't necessary. Our kiss confirms the promises we're not afraid to voice, but don't need to be said.

The deep and steadfast love we have for each other is felt in this kiss. A million yeses exchanged. An eternity of I love yous whispered through caresses.

The driver's door opens, and Deputy Whaley folds inside. "Geesh, stop that or I'm gonna have to hold you in separate cars."

Jason's laughing, and then he licks his bottom lip, making me wish I was the one licking it. He then bites that bottom lip as if the secret he's keeping from Whaley might escape.

Whaley says, "I don't know what's gotten into you, Delilah. Dragging my wife and her blue ribbons into your mess can land you in a cell for the night. You can't blow that low and not expect to pay the price. What if my wife finds out?"

"What if the women's auxiliary club finds out she's been stealing blue-ribbon recipes long before last year? Isn't she up for re-election of the Fourth of July Extravaganza Director this year?"

"Is that a threat, Ms. Noelle?"

Jason stares at me wide-eyed, and mouths, "You're such a badass."

But Whaley ruins the moment by adding, "Your father is probably rollin' in his grave right now. What would he say if he saw you cuffed in the back of my car?"

Angling my chin up in defiance, I reply, "He'd be proud I stood up for what was right."

His dissatisfaction comes in a huff before he turns his attention to my partner in crime. "I blame you, Koster. When you weren't on that football field, you were causin' trouble. If my vote mattered, I'd have that billboard down by the highway demoed and burned for the homecoming bonfire."

"Well, Deputy," Jason starts, "I actually wasn't in trouble much, but you did go to Kerbyville High, so maybe it's the rivalry that makes you hate me so much."

"I do not hate you." Whaley's voice rises. Looking at us in the rearview mirror, he says, "I'm gonna let you go with a warnin', but you better be leaving Mr. Cutler alone and mindin' your own damn business. Do you both hear me?"

Jason replies, "Loud and clear."

"Did ya hear me, Ms. Noelle?"

"I heard you."

"Good," Whaley says. "Just head on home and stop causin' trouble where there is none."

When I look at Jason, he's already looking at me. A small smile is seen as the flashing lights drift across his face. "Even though I didn't win the money, I totally won the grand prize," he whispers.

I'm about to tell him the money doesn't matter, but the doors open, and we're helped out of the vehicle. Facing each other over the roof of the car, he smiles at me, and I smile back. This is not the way I expected him to ask me to marry him, but now that we're on the other side of it, it was perfect for us.

We don't talk until we're out of eavesdropping distance. As I rub my wrists, his hand lands on my lower back, and he guides me away from the cops. His lips are near my ear when he says, "I had that shooting contest in the bag. How about a consolation prize on the way home?"

Sneaking a peek of him, I see the confidence embedded in that grin. "What'd you have in mind?"

———

THE WINDOWS ARE DOWN, and Blake Shelton's "Every Time I Hear That Song" is playing through the speakers, floating into the night. With a palm on each thigh, he slowly spreads my legs apart. We've had a lot of sex since he's been back, but it's hard to get used to how he looks at me—my whole body under deep inspection as he studies every inch in the moonlight. *In awe.*

I lift up, my eyes meeting his briefly before his gaze lowers again, and he kisses that spot where my most private parts meet the top of my thigh. My head drops back on the blanketed bed of the truck, and I happily sigh while closing my eyes.

"You're amazing, Delilah." He kisses me again—deeply with intention as his tongue sinks inside me. "Your trust is a beautiful thing. I promise never to abuse it."

I sigh in relaxation, my muscles and mind getting lost at this moment, getting lost in him again, something that's so easy to do. Blame it on the moonlight or his magical tongue, or maybe a combination of both, but my orgasm comes fast and hits hard, my back arching as he holds me still. When I catch my breath and come to life again, I whisper, "You're so bad." My body is a puddle of blissful goodness. "You're going to send me to an early grave of ecstasy."

"Hey, honeysuckle?" When my eyes connect with his, he says, "I may be bad, but I'll always make you feel good." He maneuvers onto the truck and lies next to me. Looking over, he takes my hand, rolls to the side, and kisses me.

It's naughty and rough, raw, and God, so crazy. "I feel so

carefree with you, like we could disappear into that star-filled universe and never look back."

"Is that what you want? Do you want to leave here, leave the farm?"

Turning my eyes to the night sky, I lean my head against his shoulder. "I don't know what I want other than a redo."

"How about we start with an *I do*?"

I smile, my happiness bubbling to the surface through giggles like I'm a teenager. "Sounds good to me."

We lie there a little longer before grabbing the blanket and shutting the tailgate. The music is loud, the wind whisking in through the windows. I haven't felt this free of cares in years. It's deliciously addicting. My calf is warmed by Jason's hand, his touch comforting.

My protector—of heart, body, and soul.

When we enter the city limits of Solace Pointe, I rest my head on my arm to watch the town roll by. I've seen these same buildings my whole life, passed under this stoplight a million times, and every time I do, I wonder what it's like to be somewhere else. To get . . . away.

My sister knows. She got a job offer right after college and stayed for the money. Almost every time we talk, she tells me she wishes she were back on the farm feeding the chickens and swinging on that rickety porch swing.

I'd trade the quiet of the country for six months in the city. Big dreams die in little towns.

Jason runs his hand over my thigh, pushing the skirt of my dress up, his heat searing my skin. I glance his way, and he says, "You seem sad."

"Not sad. Confined to a life I didn't choose."

"What about us?"

"You're the best part of my reality." *My recovery and next chapter.* I angle my back against the door and prop my boots on his lap. "Tell me a story about one of your adventures."

Goose bumps are left in the wake of his hand as it runs over my knee. "I once drove from Seattle to San Diego. That's some beautiful country out there."

"What's the ocean like?"

We pull up the drive to the farmhouse. "There's nothing like a sunset over the Pacific Ocean. I'll show you one day."

I have no doubt he will. He's a man of his word. "As much as I want to travel and see the world, I feel like you've brought some of it back with you."

Taking my hand, he kisses the top. "I'm going to give you the best life, Delilah, the one you always wanted. You'll never want for anything. I want you to share your dreams with me."

"I'm too broke to dream outside my means."

"Dreams are free. What does your heart long to do?"

"I love the farm. I've always seen myself living out my life here, but I've always dreamed of seeing the Eiffel Tower, and I wonder what it feels like to dig my toes in the sandy beaches of Southern California. Although I don't need to be rich to be happy, I do wish to see what's beyond these county lines."

"I have money."

I slide across the truck bench. "We've already talked about this. I don't want to take your money."

"I've saved it for my future, and you're my future, Delilah."

"Future Mrs. Jason Koster." I lift and kiss his neck. "I like the sound of that."

26

Delilah

A bottle of wine, two beers, and three BLT sandwiches later, Jason is dancing with me in the kitchen.

We're happy.

We're stuffed.

We're drunk.

We're high on life.

We're turned on.

That's nothing new. I've never felt so alive, or is it more that I never recognized how empty I felt prior? Like a summer storm rolling in right before a picnic, he wrecked all my plans. But in his destruction of my perfectly planned life, he gave me a sunrise of hope.

His hands tighten on my thighs, causing me to gasp in pleasure. With his lips to my ear, he whispers, "I suspect you wear these dresses to tempt me into sinning."

"Is it working?" I ask through broken breaths.

"It's working." He moves, going deeper. "The fair was

fun, but if I could spend every night buried inside you like I am now, I'd never leave this farm."

"We were arrested. That wasn't fun."

Laughing against the back of my head, he says, "We weren't arrested, but fuck, you sure do know how to use that smart mouth of yours sometimes."

"Too much?"

"No, it's fucking sexy as hell."

Currently pinned to the counter in front of the sink, my skirt is bunched above my ass. My panties are in shreds on the floor. His shoes push against my boots while he pushes into me.

Again.

And again.

Closing my eyes, I chase the darkness that alights with fireworks of desire. Fuck, I want it. Like him, I want it so badly I can taste it—salty sweet—from an hour earlier when I made Jason fall apart, dropping his guard and getting off as he watched me take him deep in my mouth.

He's close.

His thrusts are becoming erratic.

I'm close.

The thought of him being turned on turns me on. So much. My fingers sting from the pressure of holding the edge of the counter so hard. Leaning onto my elbows, I feel his fingers dig into my hips as he comes. Mine follows fast. My mouth falls open, releasing a rough moan as his name drags through my body's vibrations.

Reaching behind me, I fist his T-shirt as my breath returns to steady. Opening my eyes, I scream, pushing off the counter in front of me.

Those eyes.

The eyes that have haunted me.

"Shit." Jason jumps, tugging his jeans up. "What happened?"

Pointing toward the window, I say, "Cole. Cole. Co—"

"Cutler? What? Where?" Jason spins me around to face him. "Where, Delilah?"

"Out back. He's out there, Jason. I saw him. I saw him watching us."

He's running out the back door before the words leave my mouth.

Was Cole real or an apparition? Is he here? Surely, I'm hallucinating. I run to the front door to look for his car, and when I swing it open, I'm charged—one hand covering my mouth and the other holding the back of my head. I scream, but it goes unheard beyond the palm of his hand. My eyes are wide while Cole pushes me deeper into the house.

"Shut up," he demands between gritted teeth.

I'm grappling for anything I can grab while being shoved too fast to comprehend what's happening. I'm shoved backward into the hallway, my back hitting the corner before we clear it. Anger has swallowed his reasoning with none left to be found in his eyes. There's no stopping him. He pushes harder as I wince in pain. With his hand over my mouth, my attempts to scream are squashed again. My eyes water, and fear for my life takes over as I try to grab his wrists to pull them away.

Cole's body is hard, harder than natural. As I stare into his bloodshot eyes, the pupils are pinpricks, his strength extraordinary.

He's not drunk.

He'd be sloppy.

He must be high on something.

I scream as I claw at his arms, but nothing deters him. With the strength of an army, he pushes me into my parents' room. The door is locked, and I'm shoved to the ground. "You think you can make me look like a fool and get away with it? Is that what you thought?"

Scrambling away from him, I feel my back hit the bed, and then my hands go up in surrender. "Listen to me, Cole—"

"No!" I'm whacked with the back of his hand, and my ears start ringing. "I told you to stay away from him, and what do I find out? He's living here, and you're fucking him." He stands over me, fury surging through a vein in his forehead, making it bulge. "You let him treat my wife like a whore in the kitchen. Is that what you want? You want to be treated like that?"

"He's going to kill you when he finds us."

"Do you let him fuck you in *our* bed?" His eyes dart to the mattress before returning to me again. "Like I used to fuck you?" Reaching for his belt, he starts to undo it.

Red-hot panic runs up my spine. The sound of his belt through the loops. His rapid breathing. The crazed look in his eyes. Too many memories flash before me, and I become paralyzed with fear. But somewhere in the alarms of my brain, I hear Jason's voice through the noise. *"If I see you within ten miles of that farm, or my girl, I will fucking end you."* Jason's here. I *feel* him near. He knows my house like the back of his hand.

I look back at Cole, who's not in his right mind. I won't be able to reason with him, but I won't die on his timeline either. While his hands are busy, I grab one of his legs and yank it forward, sending him to fall on his backside. He's too quick to recover for me to get far, my boot grabbed as I lunge away from him. With my body free as he holds me, I push off the wood floor to get to my feet. We both are upright at the same time, but he rushes me again in another onslaught. Jumping onto the bed, I roll to the other side and start running, but he grabs my hair and yanks me to the ground, my head hitting the floor when I land.

My vision is spotty, a solid thought elusive. I struggle to stay alert, darkness wanting to overwhelm as my body is dragged into the bathroom.

Fight.

I try to kick my feet, but my socked foot slips because I can't find traction on the floor. The water is turned on in the tub, and I'm dragged closer, my whole body controlled by one of his hands. "Cole!" I scream, tears streaking down my face, my heart racing. The pain in my scalp becoming too vivid to handle. "Please."

"Please what? You ruined everything. Everything was for you."

"Please stop." He steps into the tub, pulling my body over the edge with him. As he slides down the tile, he cradles me against him, my back to his chest, his hand squeezing my neck, cutting off my ability to breathe.

Fight.

I tug at his arms, though I find comfort in the cool water as it creeps up the sides of my body. Every flail sends water flying over the edge as I fight for my life. Pushing off the other end with my feet, my body is slammed harder against him, the air punched from his lungs.

Black spots color my vision, the bright light of the bathroom beginning to dim under the pressure of death. Trying to recount how long it's been since Jason ran out the door, I realize that time evades me under the struggle, and he may not be able to save me.

I always thought death would follow a filtering of flashing memories, the ones that made you happy through the years one lived, feel alive, and loved. I was lied to. Every regret I've had in life is given a front-row seat to my breaking heart, the memories forefront in my mind, the ones I would change . . .

I should be grateful for the time Jason and I had together. I'm not, though, because I'm in love with him. From a distance, my heart shatters to the ground as I watch him be the hero of the game. When he's a few feet in front of me, he stops, reading my inner emotions. He's always seen me too clearly.

I'm not ready to hear the words. I'm not ready to wake up tomorrow and know he's not mine anymore. Is Cole right? I can't hold him back, and if I don't go, he'll stay. I don't want him to give up his dreams for me. His focus needs to be on football, not on a small-town girl from back home. "Hi," he says, catching up to me. "I got the transfer."

"Yeah, I know." *I try to sound disinterested to cover the sobs that ache to be set free.*

"Hey!" *I look back to find he stopped a few feet back.* "What's wrong?"

I choose to stare at the ripped-open envelope instead of the golden-brown eyes that will weaken my knees and my resolve. Stick to what's best for him. Cole warned me, "Don't become a hindrance he'll regret one day. He'll get rid of you as soon as he transfers anyway." *Think of Jason. Protect my heart.*

Water covers my head, drowning the memories with the remainder of my life. The only way to express the immense love I'll carry with me comes between coughing his name, "Jason."

I push one more time, putting all the strength I can muster behind the effort. As water falls over the edge of the tub, it hits me. Cole's muscles have softened, his hold on me released. As air enters my lungs, I cough even harder but scramble to escape. When I fall over the side, my shoulder hits the ceramic base of the toilet and my back the cold tile.

He mutters, "I'm sorry. I'm sorry. I'm sorry," through sobs that fade into the sound of the water draining from the faucet. Cole reaches for a gun on top of the toilet just as Jason kicks the door in. The gun goes flying across the small room and spins on the tile.

Quick to grab it, Jason takes me under my arms, pulling me free from the room. His face is fuzzy, his voice muted. "Say something, Delilah."

Despite almost drowning, my throat is dry, and I roll to the side to cough. "You came for me."

As my vision begins to clear, I watch as he kneels to lift me. I've never gripped him so tight, so desperately clinging to him. Setting me on the bed, he has the gun aimed at the door while whispering rapidly, "Go to Paul's and wait for me. Tell him what's happening."

My boot is tossed next to me, and as I put it back on, I reply, "We'll go together."

"No. I'll handle this. Go!"

I take off running. The front door now wide open, I push against the front screen door, then run down the steps and across the lawn. I don't stop until I reach the field just beyond where the porch light reaches and hidden behind dead vines, I stop to catch my breath.

Tires grind against the gravel of the dirt driveway, and I peek over to see a car I don't recognize. The windows are too dark to make out who's inside, but when a door opens, a large man dressed in a short-sleeve dress shirt gets out and looks around. I drop to my knees, keeping my head lowered until I feel it's safe to take another peek. *Who is he?*

I overhear him on the phone say, "I'll take care of him." Nothing about him is familiar, so I know he's not from around here. He lingers on the porch, nodding, as he holds the phone to his ear. "Consider it done."

My gaze darts back to the door where the love of my life is about to be ambushed inside. Jason needs to get out, so I have to warn him. But how? Paul and Lorraine. I need to call Whaley and get Paul's help.

Taking his time, the man opens the door and goes inside. I start running away from the house, but don't make it halfway through the field before I hear a gunshot explode inside the house, stopping me in my tracks. My breath stops in my chest. *Jason.*

My thoughts volley between the two houses. What do I do? I can't lose Jason, so I turn around and back toward the house. Just when I reach the edge of where the floodlight shines, another shot causes me to duck and press myself to the side of the siding. My breath comes hard, and I try to regulate it so I'm quieter, keeping the sobs stifled inside.

The silence inside has me clamping my eyes closed, willing the tears to stay at bay. I have to fight. I have to fight for Jason and the future he promised me.

He's my forever, and I'm his.

I refuse to lose him. Not today. *Not ever again.*

27

Jason

"Holy shit." I'm pressed against the wall of the bathroom. With the gun cocked and ready, Cole cowers at the end of the barrel. I'm not sure if who's in the house or who to be aiming my gun at. Someone's not shy about making an entrance, and it sounds like something made of glass took the brunt of it.

Cole weeps with his knees tucked to his chest. "I don't know what I'm doing, Jason."

"Keep your voice down." He's a fucking mess. "Do you know who's out there?"

"I wanted to die. I wanted to die with her."

I have a good mind to put him out of his misery. The fucker shouldn't live. He caused all of this. Lost years. *Her pain.* And then he tries to kill her. Drown her. I want to take him out so badly, but the two warning shots fired in the living room tell me he's not the one I need to worry about.

The door to the bedroom is still open, but I managed to

hit the lights before ducking back in here. I have Cole's gun. One bullet in the chamber. *Fucker.* I'm guessing he intended to play a game of Russian roulette. My gun is in the truck out front, but that means getting out of here undetected to retrieve it. That might not be possible with this sack of shit still shivering in the tub. "Cutler," I whisper between my teeth.

He's useless as he dips lower, not even making an effort to save his own ass. My body stills when I hear the floors creaking through the house, my mind ticking through the escape routes of this house.

Front door through the living room.

Window to the roof up the stairs.

The back door in the kitchen.

I've become complacent. My mind rushing to the obvious instead of what I can actually get to undetected.

Two windows in either corner.

One larger one at the end of the hall.

Small horizontal window in the shower.

Fuck.

The windows in here are my only chance to get out. I just hope there's not a surprise waiting for me outside. When I hear another set of footsteps, I run. Needing all my strength, I set the gun on the bed, unlock the latch, and try to pull up.

Fuck!

The window is stuck. Yanking again, it doesn't budge. I run my finger along the seam, and that's when I see it's been painted closed. *Who the hell would do that?* Glancing over to the other window, I see the same thing.

Fuck.

Fuck.

Fuck.

I grab the gun and head to the door. Backing up to the wall, the gun is against my chest, my finger loose on the trigger.

One bullet.

One.

Images of Delilah carefree swimming in the lake, as if there was nothing that could stop her from loving life, are tattered dreams of seeing her that free again. *She deserves sunshine and happiness. A long life filled to the brim with it.*

She's who I'm living for, so I hope she's long gone. Please to fuck, let her have listened to me this one time. If she made it, Paul will keep her safe.

I suck in a slow and steady breath that fills my chest, and then round the corner, running to the window at the end of the hall. I'm glad I'm not wearing boots because the rubber of my sneakers dampens the sound of my feet as I run. The fucking wood still creaks, giving away my precise location if you know the house as well as I do. The latch is released with one hand, and I reach down, pulling it open and dive out. I hit the grass and roll before maneuvering to the side and pressing my back against the chipped paint of the house.

My breathing is too loud. My body too slow to remember how to move when under fire. I've let myself go, trusting I was safe. Will I ever be? Have I brought danger here? Are they here to take me out? *Or worse, Delilah?*

I eye the large trunk of an oak tree. It will give me a better vantage point of the house and get closer to my truck.

Three.

Two.

One.

Running with all my strength behind me, I grab the tree and bring myself to a stop. The farmhouse has been quiet since they called out, "Come out. Come out," and fired the two shots. I can't see any movement through the open curtains of the living room, but I stay still anyway, needing time to think. Scanning the location of the truck, I have a good forty feet to cover just to reach it. Why'd I have to park in the wide open with nowhere to hide?

Fuck.

I keep to the shadowy parts of the lawn but am swift. If someone wants me dead, this is prime time. Skidding to a stop behind the tailgate, I duck down behind it, listening for any commotion outside or action inside. *What the hell are they waiting for?* If it's Cutler they're after, surely, they can hear him sniveling in the bathroom. The guy's a blubbering mess in that bathtub, for God's sake.

But if this is my penance for the sins I've committed, it's going to be hard to escape. If I manage it tonight, when will the next attack take place? How did I ever believe I could find peace? Instead, I've put my heart at risk. Even my mom. *Fuck.*

I should have never come back to Solace Pointe. I led these monsters right to the only place I've tried to protect. I can't get caught up in this loop. I need to clear my head and concentrate.

I hurry to the front of the truck, thankful I've disabled the internal light and that damn buzzing that comes on each time I open the door. I click open the driver's door and grab my gun from inside a blanket shoved in the corner behind the passenger's seat. Dropping to the back near the tailgate with both guns in hand, I focus on my breathing and set my mind in the right state. With long draws in and slower exhales, my heart rate finally steadies as well.

In the distance, across the field, I see the shining beacon of Paul and Lorraine's front porch. With her safe, I take a gun in each hand ready for the battle ahead. One bullet in Cole's. Six in mine. I'm definitely not as prepared as I like to be, but I'll work with what I have.

There are seven opportunities to take down this intruder. Adrenaline pumps through my veins as I make mental notes on the vehicle from its color, make, and model to the license plate. Ready to take this guy out, I position myself so I can't be seen from the house and peer through the truck windshield at the brightly lit front porch.

What. The. Hell?

As if I'm seeing my nightmare come true, Delilah runs onto the porch. *Shit.* I run to the front of the truck both guns ready to fire. "Delilah!" I whisper-yell.

But she's too determined and makes it through the front door before she hears me. I run faster, not waiting for a perfect moment to take these fuckers down if her life is on the line. My heart is beating a mile a minute as I hear shots fired, but thank fuck no scream follows. *What is this guy after because he just entered the wrong fucking house?*

I take the front porch steps by three and have the screen door swinging open by the count of four. The lights go out when I hit the floor and slide between the couch and the coffee table. Crouched down, I listen for sounds in the house besides the door screeching with a loud bang when it closes.

A tap on my ass causes me to jump and turn around, aiming both guns right into the blue eyes of my girl. "You scared the shit out of me, Delilah," I whisper, lowering my guns. "What are you doing?"

"I was coming in to help you. Thank goodness with you scaring so easily."

I roll my eyes. "Funny. I told you to go to Paul's and wait for me."

"I was on my way, but then I heard gunshots and came back." Her eyes are glassy, and she takes a shuddering breath. "I thought they were going to hurt you."

"Now they'll hurt you instead. Not a good trade-off. There's no sense wasting time arguing over something we can't change. I have to get you out of here."

Footsteps draw our attention, so we still our bodies to listen. Glancing back at her, she points upstairs. I mouth, "You sure?"

She nods.

Leaning in, I kiss her cheek and then keep my voice low against her ear. "I'm getting up. You go to Paul's and do not stop for anything. Do you understand?"

"Stay alive." Kissing me, she whispers, "For me. I love you."

"I'll do my damnedest. I love you. Now go."

As soon as she's moving, I'm up, covering her as she runs back out the door, catching it with my foot before it clangs against the frame again. Then I hit the wall that leads upstairs, my guns ready to fire. Studying the staircase, I'm out of options. If they hear me going up there, I'll be dead before I hit the landing. My other choice is to wait them out. I choose the second option as it seems to support me living longer.

Now I need to find the closest exit. The living room has no coverage, so I head for the kitchen. As soon as I do, I turn, staring right into the cylinder of a silencer. *Fuck.*

"Drop the guns," he says.

I don't recognize this asshole, so I don't know what he's capable of. I set the guns down because unfortunately, escaping isn't an option when you're staring into the eyes of the Grim Reaper. "Who are you and what the fuck do you want?"

"First off, save your questions. I'll give you all the information you need, and in return, you'll give me what you owe my boss."

"Which is?"

He looks annoyed by my follow-up, but replies, "$57,850."

"You must have come to the wrong farm because I don't owe your boss, or anyone else, jack shit."

He laughs under his breath. "Likely story. Look, don't make this difficult. I'm just here to do my job."

"Which is?" I repeat the earlier question, thinking I might be able to tangle this guy's mind enough to distract him.

"Collect the money or serve a death sentence, Cutler. So pay up or say goodbye."

"Cutler?" I can't even find relief because leave it to Cutler to endanger all of our lives. "You have the wrong guy. He doesn't live here."

"If we had a dollar for every time we heard that—"

"If you're going to hold me accountable for him, I want to know why he owes you money?" Figures that fucker is responsible for this shitstorm.

Prodding the gun to my chest, he says, "This is his address, so if you're not him, damn, sucks for you because I can't exactly let you walk away." Tilting his head to the side, he leans in enough for me to memorize every rotten feature of his ugly face. "So tell me. Who are you?"

I've learned how to play this game. They like dirt and to feel like you're akin to them, one of them, not above. Their egos are too fragile for that. Keeping calm under pressure, I say, "I'm the guy fucking his wife." The bitter aftertaste of those words lingers on my tongue. "Ex-wife."

"Ex?" He sighs but doesn't lower the gun. In fact, he nudges my nose with it. *Asshole.*

"Too bad. It seems you're in the wrong place at the wrong fucking time."

I hear the cock of the gun and hope to God Delilah is safely across that field. If I'm going down, it's not something I want her to bear witness to.

A floorboard creaks, drawing his attention. Maybe Cutler will come in handy. Using the distraction, I jack my knee into his groin as hard as I can, causing him to fall just as he pulls the trigger. The bullet narrowly missing my ear when I drop to retrieve my guns. Both of us wrestle until I win, pinning him and standing over him with both guns aimed down—one at his head and one at his dick.

I kick his gun across the floor and then toe him in the shoulder. "Why does Cutler owe you money?"

"Shit card players shouldn't enter backroom poker tournaments."

"Stand. Slowly. Keep your hands up and visible." I could shoot this guy in the head right now, but what do I do with Cutler? I'm going to have to deal with him differently despite my desire to end him.

"Look, buddy. I get that you're not Cutler. It's a simple mistake. No harm, no foul. I'll just get out of your way so you can get back to fucking his ex."

"You would have never let me walk out of here, so let's not pretend otherwise. Now that the tables have turned, what do I do with you?"

Before I can decide the next step, Cutler comes barreling down the hall screaming and pounding his chest. *What the hell? Has he lost his ever-fucking mind?*

It happens fast, and I'm flipped to the floor. The guns scatter with us scrambling after.

I grab one and turn on my ass to find a gun already pointed at me. The sound of the bullet discharging echoes through the air. I close my eyes and wait for the hit.

28

Jason

Cole groans in pain, dragging himself to sit. "I've been shot. You shot me!"

This is going to be a bloodbath. I'm stuck in a standoff with my hand steady on the gun I'm aiming right at his heart. His gun aimed right at me.

"Shut up," I growl. I hate Cole . . . even saying that fucking name. I also may want to kill him, but I'm not going to let this guy kill him for me.

Knowing there's no way out of this mess, I keep flashing my mind back to Delilah. *Delilah and I didn't fall in love slowly. Nothing came slow when it came to us. We fell fast and hard. I can't lose her.*

The door opens, and my eyes flick to find her standing with a gun aimed at this dick. Why will she never listen to reason? "Get out!" I yell.

Out of the corner of my eyes, I see her flinch in response. The guy in front of me grins with pure evil in his eyes and turns his gun on her.

"Run!" I say. I work my way up until I'm standing, ready to take that bullet if he shoots at her.

He laughs. "I'm not afraid to shoot a woman in the back."

I believe him. He's trapped and is going to hell soon enough, so he might as well try to drag an angel with him. "You shoot her, and there's no reason for me to keep you alive."

She doesn't move.

"Tough guy, huh?" His aim doesn't shift while she stands frozen in the spotlight. "Come here, doll," he says to her.

"Don't listen."

She glances at me. "What do I do . . . Eric?"

Cole knocks his head against the wall, and whines, "Who's Eric? Help me, Delilah. I've been shot."

As if she just spotted him, she looks his way, her hands starting to shake. "Oh, my God."

For Delilah, I'll die any day of the week. But for Cole, fuck that noise. "It's barely bleeding." Even wet, his pants make it look worse than it is. "You're going to live," I say.

The asshole shifts, practically belly laughing at this scene. "This is the ex? Damn, I'd be fucking her, too, pretty boy." He gets to his knees, keeping the gun on her.

The term grates my nerves, drudging memories of that gun to my head back in that alley years ago. My body tenses, and I grind the warning, "Sit back down or I'll make you hit that floor."

Despite the odds against him, he's emboldened and gets to his feet. Nodding toward Cole, he says, "So this must be Cutler."

"I don't want to die," Cole cries. "I'm sorry, Delilah." Cole is moaning. "Shoot them, Koster. Shoot them." The asshole needs to shut the fuck up.

My finger twitches, causing the other asshole to blink. I'll win. I can have a bullet between his eyes before he has a chance to blink. My target is in focus, the room starting gray.

"Eric?" The sweet voice of an angel wipes the gray away and brings me back to her. My eyes slide to Delilah's. "Remember how you said it was us or them?"

I will never forget the night I killed that man. "I remember." I don't want her dead, but I don't want her left to be tortured by these guys either if I'm killed. We're stuck in this damn standoff like we have no chance at that happiness Delilah and I have talked about.

"This is one of those times," she says. Why is she referencing our conversation about why I had to kill someone? Without regret. "A situation like this is why you made the decision you did, right?" There's no tremble to her tone. Her confidence is fierce.

I glance around at the predicament we're in. His hand is shaking. Mine is not. He doesn't want to shoot me. What kind of money collector is this clown?

When I look back at Delilah, she's not scared. She's not shaking. She's strong, stronger than I thought possible. I reply, "Just like this."

"I understand why you did it now."

The guy says, "Clue me in. Did what?" When Cole groans in pain again, the asshole yells, "Shut the fuck up," and then shoots him.

Delilah screams as another shot slices the air. I follow through and take the shot, aiming to injure but not kill. I'll spare his life this time. I'm on my feet and over him. Cole blacked out, and I can tell Delilah's going into shock. She's going to be in shock, but I need her to stay focused. Just for a little while longer. "Call 911," I say.

She nods, but it's lifeless, so I repeat, "Call 911."

"Okay," she replies, her eyes leaving them to find mine. "Okay." When she hurries into the kitchen, I see the mess this guy is making. Why does blood always have to be so messy? "You look like you might bleed out. This is where I give you a choice. You can either make sure you never come back to this town or within fifty miles of this town, or I kill you and feed you to the fishes out back before the cops arrive. Choice is yours."

Grabbing his leg in agony, he replies, "My boss will kill me, so I'm already a dead man."

"Fish it is." I stand and aim the gun at his head.

"Wait!" His hands lift in surrender. "I have a wife and three kids. I won't bother you again. I won't come anywhere near this town. I promise."

Squatting down, I look him in his beady eyes. "Why should I trust you?" He squirms under the intensity of my glare.

"It's Cutler I was after. I have no beef with you or the ex-wife. I promise. We have a deal?" *We'll see what sort of deal you get with the sheriff's department.*

"I'm going to let you live this time."

His head thumps on the wood. "Oh, thank God."

"Thank me." I turn my attention to where it needs to be right now and the sirens sounding in the distance. Red and blue lights flash across the fields and invade the living room. It's going to be a long night, and I just want this nightmare to be over. *I need to get to my girl.*

"THIS GUN IS STILL REGISTERED to your daddy, Delilah. You need to file the proper paperwork to put it in your name."

The farmhouse has been shot up. Holes are in the walls,

the floor, and in people. Cutler is in the ambulance on his way to the hospital, and the gambling ring criminal otherwise named Brooks is also on his way to the hospital. Naturally, Whaley's more concerned about the proper paperwork for the gun Delilah used to come save me. She's my hero.

"I'll take care of it this week," she says, twisting her mouth in annoyance.

Although Delilah's dress has dried from the warm night air, Lorraine wraps a blanket around her. I know Delilah is going to experience a whole range of emotions, but right now she's running on adrenaline. When you're up that high, the fall back to reality is sometimes chilling.

I take her hand and turn it palm up. Placing a kiss on it, I let my lips remain, closing my eyes, grateful that I've been gifted this life with her. When I lift back up, I ask, "Are you okay?"

"You don't need to worry about me. I'll be fine."

She's not a good liar, and at times like this, I appreciate that fact. Wrapping my arm around her shoulders, I hold her while we finish giving our statements.

In towns like Solace Pointe, the whole jail staff comes out for a looky-loo, so we're grateful we don't have to go down to the station. Three hours of questioning is quite enough. Delilah's exhausted, so I wrap this up. "We're done, Deputy. If you have more questions, you'll have to contact our lawyer and set up a formal interview."

"Sounding like a big shot there, Mr. Koster. You've been involved in these kinds of situations before?"

"No," I lie. "I just know my rights."

Whaley scratches his chin. "Well, I think we have enough to file our reports. If we don't, we'll be in touch."

"What about your men inside?"

"They'll be there all night. I suggest you find another place to stay for a few nights while we do our investigation."

After a heavy huff, Delilah's shoulders fall. "Great. Just great." She slides out of my grasp and walks toward the field. Standing at the edge, she crosses her arms over her chest and stares into the darkness. She's struggling, and I get not wanting an audience. "Thank you, officers." I join her side, wishing I could make this all go away like it never happened, but sometimes bad shit happens. I hate that the outside made its way to the inside of our little piece of paradise. "Whaley said we could go."

"Where can we go?" It's not resolve but resignation I detect in her tone.

I try to take it away and offer an opportunity. "Anywhere we want."

"Lorraine said we could stay with them. She has a sewing room with a foldout couch."

"Billy called. They wouldn't let him on the property, but he said we're welcome on his farm." I move closer, keeping my eyes ahead.

"Your mom called me." Taking my hand, she holds it between us. "She said she wants us to come over."

"Tomorrow. How about I take you to a hotel so we can decompress?" We've had a lot happen, and we've told the story more times than I care to tell again. "A room of our own."

"Can we treat ourselves and get one with room service? I'm hungry. By the time we reach a hotel, I'll be starved."

"You can order the whole menu if you want."

A sliver of a smile ripples across her face. I'll spend the night coaxing the full one out because she deserves to smile.

An hour and a half later, we're standing in our room, and she's staring at the tub, her tone full of disappointment.

"Normally, I'd take a bath to wind down." Coming to sit on the bed next to me, she says, "I think I'll skip it tonight."

Almost drowning in one makes her reaction reasonable. *Fucker. He's stolen that from her as well.* "Sorry I wasn't there sooner. I thought he'd run, not gone inside. I was checking the perimeter."

"I thought he was on drugs. Now I'm thinking he was on a mission." Resting against my chest, she drapes her arms over my middle.

My arm curves around her back, holding her to me, our warmth exchanged in the embrace. "He only had one bullet in his gun, Delilah." I don't mean to sound ominous, but his intentions were clear.

"He was going to drown me."

"And then kill himself."

"His life is shit. He's shit. I hate him so much."

Swearing doesn't come natural to her. The words are distorted, dripping from a place that should never reside inside her heart—*hate*. Sitting up, she presses her palm on my chest over my heart. "What if you wouldn't have found me in time?"

Caressing her cheek, I lean forward and kiss her. "You saved yourself. I have no doubt after the courage you showed tonight that you would still be here."

"In your arms?" It's an odd question, but the whole night was odd.

"I have everything to live for now, so no one's taking me out that easily."

Her smile returns, the light in her eyes smothering the dark that tried to win, tried to take her hostage.

A knock on the door signals room service. I hop up and let them push the cart of food inside. After tipping, we're left alone with enough food to feed a small army. Her eyes are wide, and a huge smile appears. When my stomach growls, I rub it, and ask, "Was the drive worth it?"

"It was definitely worth it." When she grabs a bowl of spaghetti, I can tell by the way she settles back on the bed and starts flicking through the channels that she's content . . . for now.

I've been paid a lot of money over the past few years. It gave me financial security for the rest of my life and then some. But living within the confines of darkness, at times existing just outside the law, I didn't have this. *Contentment*. With her, *my* girl, I've found it. Peace. Solace. This is something no paycheck ever provided.

I'll take this life over the last every day of the week and twice on Sundays. I reach for the steak because there's no time like the present to enjoy a few of the finer things in life.

29

Delilah

I can't breathe.

I savor the fiery orange on the inside of my lids. Orange means life.

Flailing my arms to find anything to hold on to that will give me the leverage to save myself is useless. I'm held under, drowning in his arms.

. . . The horror I felt at that moment has worked its way into my veins. It's attached itself in ways I can't remove. I was so close to that slice of paradise with Jason that even though we survived and still have that future, I don't think I'll be able to easily let last night go after almost meeting death.

I thought I was doomed to spend eternity tangled up in Cole and death, hate, and hell.

Jason stirs, and I look back. Just the sight of him, the fact that we're alone in this room has me smiling, though. He once told me he was a soldier, a mercenary of sorts, but when I look at him, I only see my dark-haired knight. His sleep is steady, his features finding peace, as his body lies bare for me. The sheet is tangled around a leg, exposing parts of him that I'm the only one privy to these days.

How can he possibly be that hard when he's sleeping? Men will always be a mystery to me. It's a mystery I'm happy to solve over the next sixty, seventy, or more years. I'd love to live a long life with him. The years we were apart, when he was doing those things he doesn't like to talk about, will pale in comparison to the years we'll spend together.

One day, *they won't matter at all.*

One day, *last night won't matter.*

We survived. Together. That's all that will matter when our souls leave this place.

I shut the blinds and crawl back into bed next to him. Careful not to wake him, I untangle the sheet and cover us both up. How does he sleep so soundly? Even after what could have been a horrific tragedy.

Is the peace that keeps his features gentler in the moonlight his acceptance that the world has bad people in it? He's just learned to deal with it?

If he had his way, my life would remain pristine and untouched by the outside world. It's good in theory but not realistic. I'm human, which means I'll make bad choices . . . breaking up with Jason and trusting Cole hopefully the worst. It also means I have a chance to start over, clean the slate, and move on. Move on is what I intend to do. I feel so incredibly fortunate I get to move on *with* him this time.

I run my fingers lightly over his arms, appreciating the dip and rise of the muscles beneath. Is it wrong to want to get lost in something wonderful after the events from earlier?

His eyes open. "Delilah." My name languidly rolls off his tongue as if we have more than one lifetime together. In no great hurry, his hand reaches for me.

"Make me forget for a little while."

Our gazes stay locked long enough for him to read me like a book. He sits up and sweeps my hair behind my shoulder. His hand remains and slides down the strap of my pajamas. His lips are warm, wet, and delicious against my skin until I'm left with the cool air of the room breezing across the trail he's left.

He removes my top, and when his palms cover my breasts—kneading and squeezing—I close my eyes, enjoying how my body responds to him. When he moves on top of me, I open for him, opening myself and letting him in —mind and soul.

And when he reaches for a condom, I cover his hand. "I need to feel all of you."

I need his weight, his lips on mine, the rough tips of his fingers scratching across my skin. I want him to mark me as his. I don't need to feel pretty to the world, to wear a tiara and smile anymore. I just want him to find me beautiful when I'm not wearing makeup and my hair is a mess. I only want to be how he sees me already, the real me—the bare and bold me. The *me* I am with him.

His mouth moves along my neck, kissing and sucking, and I feel every last one of them all the way to my core. My hand slides into the back of his hair, keeping his close, loving the feel of us together—ravaged and real, carnal and lustful.

He warms my neck as his fingers flame the fires of desire between my legs. "Take me," I whisper in his ear.

"I want all of you, baby."

"Take every last bit of me. I want to forget everything outside this room."

The stubble of his beard has grown in overnight and scrapes against my chest, leaving me to crave more of the sting left behind. I love it. It's not pretty, fitting for how I feel. He looks at me, his eyes gently drifting back and forth between mine, studying me. He says, "Sometimes the bad helps us remember the good. Let me be that good for you." *He is good, knowing exactly what I need and how I need to be loved.*

"Leave no part of me untouched."

He thrusts, his desire for me driving him deep inside me. My back arches and my head goes back, leaving my neck exposed. Jason pulls back and thrusts forward while his lips find my throat again.

Wrapping his arms under me, he uses my body against his, uses me for his pleasure while heightening mine. Our bodies start to sweat, sliding with ease and creating more. The sounds of our love are the only sounds I hear. The troubles from the night drift away as I quickly find the ecstasy in his arms instead.

"I love you," I exhale with every breath. "I love you. I love you."

Our bodies slow until our souls sigh in satisfaction. His head rests on my chest and I hold him there, never wanting to let go.

Time doesn't stand still for us. It ticks by as we lose minutes or days, like the years we lost that we'll never get back. This time, there's no true loss because it's time I've spent losing with him. Allowing the ugly of the day to fade away, together we find our own haven, and I've found solace in his arms.

Moving to lie next to me, his hand covers my cheeks. Despite the sheet being tangled again, he kisses me gently. With my lips against his, I kiss him back with such care for this man I love so deeply. I fall back on my pillow and weave my fingers through his hair. He knew what we were deciding when we didn't use a condom. "Thank you."

"For what?"

I would welcome a baby into this world if it were his, if he was there with me to prove that when lives are meant to be entwined, they twist themselves completely into eternity. "For loving me without conditions."

"Let's get married as soon as we can."

All those years he'd believed I hated him, that my soul wasn't somehow tied to his. But here he is, forgiving me when I can't forgive myself. Could I be so kind if the roles had been reversed? My heart would be too damaged to repair if I had seen him with another woman. This man before me is the most generous of beings. And like he once said, maybe my true heart now can heal the broken parts of his soul once and forever. "I'm sorry."

"What are you sorry for, honeysuckle?"

"For assuming instead of trusting. I did more than break my heart. I broke yours, and that's harder to live with."

Taking my hand, he places it over his heart. "You healed this broken heart and settled my restless soul." He brings my hand to his mouth and kisses each finger. He takes my left ring finger, closes his mouth around it, and then slides it out slowly. "If you could have any ring, what kind do you dream of?"

"I don't need rings or jewelry. I have everything I need right here."

Smiling, he chuckles. "Oh no, you don't. You don't get off that easy. I want everyone in Freeland County and wherever we travel to know you're mine."

"And you'll wear one because you're mine."

"I will flash that ring every chance I get, proud to say I'm the lucky bastard who gets to go home with you every night."

Dawn peeks through the window, and we slide farther under the covers. "I'm not ready to get up."

"Paul will manage the farm. Let's stay a few extra days."

"Here at the hotel?" *How fun would that be?*

"Here in this bed. We'll eat like kings. We'll binge bad TV—"

"And make love. All night and all day."

Snuggling closer, I rest my head next to his on the pillow and try to steal a kiss, but he catches me before I sneak back to my side. "Better get used to this, honeysuckle." Slipping his arm under me, he molds me to him. "I plan to hold you like this every night for the rest of our lives."

My eyelids dip closed, my body finally heavy with sleep, or maybe it's that peace he found earlier. I turn, and he spoons me, wrapping his arm over me. "I can handle it." His breath is warm on my neck, but it's even and comforting. Cocooned against him, I feel safe, and say, "You saved me."

"I didn't save you. You saved yourself."

"I'm not talking about last night."

No more words are needed. We both sigh in content-ment and close our eyes.

Just as I'm finding sleep, he whispers, "I'm going to make up for every minute we were apart. I promise to give you the fairy-tale ending."

My lips turn up, happiness filling me, and I tighten my hand around his as I drift asleep.

THE HOTEL WAS A NICE REPRIEVE, a little escape in the middle of chaos. Returning to the farm is difficult at first. Not because I'm scared. I'm not. This place holds way more good memories than bad, but dealing with the aftermath of physical damage is stressful. "I don't know where to start," I say, rubbing my temples.

"We just start. Pick something to fix and see it through."

Billy inspects the bullet hole in the floor of the living room. "You turned and the bullet landed here?"

Jason is standing on the other side of it with his arms crossed and nodding. "Yup. Pretty much."

"Damn, dude. Did you shit yourself?"

I laugh when Jason scrunches his nose, and replies, "No."

Billy's hat is off, and he's scratching his head. "What'd you do then?"

I peek back at Jason before I enter the kitchen. "I shot him."

"Whoa."

We had a cleaning crew from Kerbeyville clean up the blood on a referral from the police. It makes it easier to deal with a mess of broken lamps and a few holes.

Following up his astonishment, Billy asks, "What did you do while you were gone again?"

"Fishing boats in Alaska. A little time in New England. A few other cash-in-hand jobs."

I guess that's the story we're sticking with. His past doesn't matter anymore. Like he said, he doesn't have regrets. I don't either. Guess it took being in his shoes to finally understand why. I do. Us versus them. I hate that there's even the necessity to think this way, but when push comes to shove, I'll fight for us. Just as he did.

Looking out the window doesn't bother me. It should, considering that's how the beginning of that night began, but Cole's been released from the hospital straight into a rehabilitation facility. He's facing time for his alleged ties to an illegal gambling ring.

He doesn't rule my mind or control my life anymore. The people of Solace Pointe are no longer blind to who Cole Cutler really is. I doubt he'd be able to get within a mile of my farm now that they know the truth. I finally feel . . . free. *Vindicated.*

I let myself rest, leaning on the counter. Warm lips caress the back of my neck as his hands slide around my hips, coming to rest across my belly. After kissing the shell of my ear, he whispers, "You think we have a baby in there?"

I cover his hands. "I hope so."

30

Delilah

Shelby Noelle always did stand out in a crowd. As much attention as I got for my good grades and looks growing up, I'd simply followed in her footsteps. She's two years older than me and won everything from homecoming queen to Miss Freeland County, prepping me for the roles. But she was also something I wasn't—*outspoken*.

After picking her up from the airport more than an hour away, Jason and I have been peppered with questions from the back seat of the car we borrowed from his mom. Everything on updating her on the farm to more personal questions like, "Where are you sleeping if you're not staying in the house?"

"We put a bed and a few essentials in the loft," I reply, already knowing how she's going to react.

"The loft of the barn?" she exclaims but then laughs. "Good Lord, Delilah. You two are literally rolling in the hay."

"Sort of."

Jason's adds, "Definitely."

She laughs, and then adds, "I lost my virginity out there."

Jason's shaking his head. "Peter Monroe was an asshole."

"He was, but man, did he know how to—"

"Eww," I say, hoping she doesn't finish that thought. "Don't even go there."

Under lots of laughter, she rubs my shoulder. "I think you're old enough to handle the truth, Delilah."

"I'm pretty sure you don't want to hear too much of my truth." I glance at Jason, giving him a little wink.

"Actually, I want to hear everything." Her tone turns sentimental. "You don't know how terrified I was when Jason called me and told me what happened."

I sigh, exhaling heavily. I'm still not sure I'm happy he called her. On the one hand, I get it. I do. He did it because my family should know. On the other hand, I knew it would worry her unnecessarily. "I'm fine."

"Now," she adds, "but that might not have been the case."

"We can play out fifty different scenarios, but the only one that exists is the one where we survived. Let's not rehash it." We can bicker all we want, but I don't want to spend my time with my sister like that. "We're here. All is good."

"Okay," she relents. "You haven't changed much, Jason. Charming my sister just like you always did."

He's changed so much, but those changes are hard to see when you're looking at our *hometown hero*. He's more than that. He's my savior in so many ways, the king of my heart. I won't correct her, though. He's fine lying low and letting everyone else fill in the blanks. Now that I understand the deep-seated reasons behind his calm demeanor, he deserves even more respect. Jason doesn't need the glory. He never did. Not when he played football and not now.

He quietly goes about putting himself on the line for others, protecting what he cares about, and loving me like there's no tomorrow. I don't mean for my swoony mewl to slip out, but it does.

After grieving the loss of my parents, missing my sister, the fear of losing my home to debts, and the abuse— emotionally and physically—I survived at the hand of Cole, it feels good to feel this happy, to find happiness with this man I've loved for what feels like my whole life.

He's changed.

I've changed.

Our once naïve young love has changed.

And I like us better. I'm better just from him being back. We're moving forward together with our eyes wide open and on even footing.

Jason reaches over, his hand covering the one resting across my stomach. In this sweet moment, it's easy to remember the most valuable lesson my sister taught me: looks don't matter. It's what's in your heart that counts.

We came from a long line of beauty queens, but they all had something else in common—they loved with their whole heart, and they lived for their families. With one hand on my stomach and Jason's nestled on top, I've never felt closer to my roots, and for the first time, I truly under- stand what Shelby meant.

Jason Koster has good looks down to a science, but it wasn't his looks that drew me to him. Not then and not now. It was his heart. It still is. He's given me his heart to protect, and I will with all that I am. I peek back at my sister, and say, "We're getting married."

The back of my seat is grabbed, and she pulls herself forward. "What? You're engaged?" Her eyes dart to my hand.

"We are."

"When? How? Oh, my God. My baby sister is getting married." Her accent has lessened since she's lived in the city the past couple of years, but every now and again, I hear it. Like now. "Delilah Rae, how could you keep this secret from me? Tell me everything, and you owe me a pie big time. You so lost that bet."

Jason's too busy laughing to get in the middle, so I reply, "Not even a week ago. I wanted to tell you in person. As for the pie, I already have one cooling in the kitchen."

"Yum." She hits Jason on the arm. "Well, look at you coming back to town and sweeping my lil' sis right off her feet all over again. Took you long enough."

Turning onto our property, he says, "It's good to have you back, Shelby."

"It's good to be back. So. When's the wedding?" Side-tracked, she leans so far forward she's practically in the front seat with us. "Oh wow."

"What?" I ask, looking through the windshield to see what I'm missing.

"This place. Doesn't matter where I go, or how long I've been gone, there's no place like home. Pictures do not do the farm justice. I miss being here so much." As soon as the car stops, she jumps out and heads to the side of the property to see the lake.

Jason looks at me, his hand gently rubbing my shoulder. "You okay?"

"I'm so much more than okay." His smile sends my heart soaring. "I've never felt happier."

"Glad to be a small part of that."

The engine is off, and he's about to get out, but I stop

him. "You're more than a small part of it. I know I shouldn't rest my happiness in other people, but it's good to have a place to rest it for once."

Leaning over, he kisses me and then rests his forehead against mine. "I will always be a place of rest and peace for you, babe." He pulls back, but stops to add, "I didn't know I could be this happy either. But that's what you've gifted me along with a place to rest my soul in peace." Caressing my cheek, he stares into my eyes.

Sometimes, I wonder what he sees when he looks so deeply into my eyes, and sometimes, I just like the feeling of his need for me. Well, I always like that, so . . . "How hungry are you?" We have company, so I guess we need to remember we have an audience.

He cracks a smile. "Starved." Hopping out, he hurries around to help me out.

It drives him nuts when I take away an opportunity for him to be chivalrous. He ribs me over it, but he also knows that sometimes I'm okay standing on my own independence. I take his hand, though, because I appreciate having his support, too. He allows me to feel safe and secure being me. *The me I like.*

When we reach the corner of the house, he says, "I'll take her bags inside. You should spend time with your sister."

A small look is exchanged, love filling in any space between us, and we both smile.

When the tips of our fingers part, I walk around the house to find Shelby standing with her hands clasped in front of her chest. She reminds me so much of my mom who used to do the same thing. I stand next to her, looking out at the water. The wind blows and sunlight sparkles like stars across the tops of each ripple. "It never gets old."

She glances over with a gentle smile, and then wraps her arm around mine. "You're pregnant."

My body shifts, but I don't move away. "Why do say that?"

"I can see it. Your eyes. Your skin. Your happiness. The way you hold your stomach without even realizing you're doing it." The lake holds nothing to the glistening in her eyes.

"Nothing's confirmed."

"But you know, don't you?"

I nod. I do know. I feel the shift inside me, excited to watch it bloom. "Mom and Dad would be so happy for you, Delilah."

"What about you?"

A tear slips down her face. "I'm happy you found a love to last a lifetime."

I embrace her as tears slip down my cheeks. Leaning my head on her shoulder, I sniffle. "Thank you. That means more to me than you know."

After our mother died, Shelby not only looked after me like a sister but also a mother. It's a role she shouldn't have had to take on, but she did, putting her needs behind mine. When we look back up, we laugh—feeling a little silly and a lot sappy. "You've done so well managing this farm on your own. Maybe you should take this time for you and Jason." Pressing her hand lightly on my belly, she adds, "And for your family. The farm will always be here. Go see the world you've always wanted to explore."

"Jason has seen so much, but he says he wants to see it again with me."

Turning back toward the lake, she wraps her arm around mine, her head on my shoulder this time. "It's your turn, Delilah."

"You sacrificed a life here to help keep this place afloat. We still have so much debt to deal with."

"Let's walk to the dock."

I follow her as she meanders, taking her time, as if she has all the time in the world. Slipping off our shoes, we sit on the edge with our legs hanging off and our toes dipped in the cool water. She leans back, closes her eyes, and raises her face toward the sun. "The farm has been paid off."

I'm about to mimic her position, but instead, I bolt upright from her words. "What do you mean? How?"

With one squinting eye and the other open eye on me, she says, "I think that's a discussion you should have with Jason."

"Why do I need to talk to Jason?"

Patting my leg, she says, "Just talk to him, and then we can talk again."

The sound of tires traveling down the drive toward the house draws our attention to a truck. It parks and when the door opens, Shelby's eyes go wide. "Good Lord. Who. Is. That?"

I burst out laughing while turning my gaze back to Billy as he unloads some bags of feed. "*That* is Billy Langston."

Now she's upright. She might even be sticking her chest out if I'm not mistaken. "No way. That cannot be Billy."

Shrugging, I laugh again. "I told you he wasn't that lanky kid anymore."

"Yeah, but you didn't tell me he looked like *that*. Good gracious, he could be mistaken for a Hemsworth."

"Yeah." I nod and look back at him just as he lifts the front of his shirt, exposing those defined abs and wiping his face free from sweat.

Shelby's jaw drops open. "Nope, not lanky at all."

I say, "Mistaken identity has happened a time or two for

Chris from what I hear." Cupping my hand to the side of my mouth, I yell, "Hey, Billy."

A large bag goes flying onto a pile, and he looks up. Tipping the brim of his cowboy hat up, he smiles. "Hey, Delilah." I can tell the moment he realizes who's sitting next to me. He walks over as Shelby stands and starts straightening the bottom of her shirt as if he'll care if it has a few wrinkles.

Billy runs his hands down the front of his jeans as he comes closer. "Is that you, Shelby Noelle?"

A lip bite and a fluff of her hair. She's already a goner for this cowboy. "Sure is, Billy Langston."

My, oh my. Look whose accent has suddenly made a comeback. If you were wondering, the answer is Shelby's. Billy has a way of doing that to the ladies—you know, making them all gooey inside and flipping their worlds upside down.

Except me. My heart knows where it belongs. I've found my home with the most thoughtful man I've ever known inside the house. This second chance is one I'll never take for granted.

While they start chatting, I slip my shoes back on, and when I pass him, I pat his arm. "Don't forget about tonight."

Shelby asks, "Are you joining us for dinner? We're making a big homemade meal with all the fixins'."

"I'd be a fool to miss it, Ms. Shelby."

I think I hear her swoon. "Well, don't go getting all dressed up for me. What you're wearing now—this T-shirt—is such a good fit. Feel free to come as you are." Oh goodness. Is this what flirting looks like? I walk away, grinning. I think I'll give them some time to get reacquainted.

I find Jason sitting in the bedroom by the window. He's propped on a large trunk, and it's clear from his posture he's heavy in thought with his shoulders down. Leaning against the doorframe, I scan the room, wondering what he's staring at. "What are you doing up here?"

His eyes find mine. "Thinking about life."

"That's heavy."

Chuckling, he looks down again, fidgeting with loose threads of his black jeans. "Yeah, kind of."

I go inside the pink room and sit on the end of the bed. "Shelby told me the farm is paid off."

Almost expecting him to tense, I watch his shoulders for the subtle movement, but it doesn't come. He's relaxed, and I find comfort in that. When he finally looks at me, he says, "You would have never taken the money."

"Because it's yours. You put your life on the line for it."

"Don't you see, Delilah? There is no me without you. If I can do something to make yours and your sister's, Paul and Lorraine's, and my mom's life easier, I will. Spending it on the farm feels like a good way to spend some money."

I go to him, leaning down and hugging him. "Thank you. It's not enough, but it comes from the heart."

"You don't owe me anything. I'm happy to do it. I'm happy I *can* do it." He adds, "I also bought my mom's house and paid off her debts."

Now I smile. "You are an amazing man, Jason Koster. Thank you for everything you've done."

"I'm only amazing because you love me."

"I always will." We sit there a moment longer before he says, "Now that it's paid off, what do you think about Shelby taking the farmhouse? I was thinking we could build the home of your dreams a few acres down, around the lake."

Thrown for a loop, my words get caught in my throat. I just end up staring at him. "This is a lot to process. I think we should talk about money like you wanted to."

"Okay. I'll start." He stands, his hand covering the side of my neck right before he dips sideways to kiss that ticklish spot behind my earlobe. Then he whispers, "I have a lot."

A lot? I tilt back, seeking his eyes. When I find them, I ask, "A lot of money?"

He smirks with a nod. "Yes. I have a lot of money."

"Do I want to know how much?"

Pulling back, he remains in front of me, but this time, his hands pace the length of my waist. "Since it's half yours, I think it would be wise for you to know. That way we can make decisions on how to spend it together."

My mind is struggling to wrap around this massive turn of events. "You're giving me half your money?"

His arm works its way around my lower back as he teases. "You're not going to make me sign a prenup, are you?"

Rolling my eyes, I laugh. "Not likely, Richie Rich."

"Then we share everything fifty-fifty. How's that sound?"

I pull him close, as close as we can embrace. "Equal in everything. That sounds like heaven on earth." Tilting back once more to find a mischievous glint in his eyes, I say, "But to be clear, what you're saying is you're rich."

He chuckles. "What I'm saying is *we're* rich. *Beyond rich.*" Resting his head against the top of mine. He adds, "And the best is yet to come, honeysuckle."

Not a prediction.

A promise.

31

Delilah

Some matches are made in heaven. And some are made right here in our little parcel of paradise.

Billy's been here every day since Shelby's arrival. He was here before Jason came back too, but his help hasn't been needed as much since Jason started taking on more of the upkeep and maintenance of the farm.

He's here for the second time today, though, because he forgot to "check on something left in the barn." Sitting in the loft, I hear him muttering to himself and look down to see him pacing, psyching himself up to ask her out on an official date. I smile but remain quiet. Unfortunately, Jason doesn't. "Stop fucking around and just ask her."

I whack Jason's leg. "Don't tease him," I warn while laughing. "The man is clearly crazy about my sister."

Billy's gaze darts up. "Oh, man. What are you doing out here?"

Jason calls from his reclined position on the bed. "Making love to my woman. Ask Shelby out and get it over with. I'm tired of watching you two dance around the obvious."

I look over the edge at Billy again, and laugh. "Sorry. We should have told you we were here. It wasn't nice of us to eavesdrop. But since we're all here, Jason's right. I think she'll say yes, but you have to ask."

"Any advice?" he asks.

"She loves sushi."

His nose scrunches. "That raw fish?"

Jason chuckles. "Yep."

I glare at him. "You're being bad today."

"I am. You should punish me. With your mouth again."

"Oh my God," I whisper, "behave."

"What's the fun in that?"

I'm about to tackle him and show him how punishing my mouth can be and then let him punish me with his, but then I remember Billy is still here like his whole life is depending on some tidbit of insight I can give him regarding my sister. He says, "So catch a fish out back and give it to her?"

Jason says, "Go away, man. I have business to take care of."

"But I need help," he replies.

I peek over the edge again. "Just ask her. No gimmicks. No pretenses. No games. Just be you, Billy. She'll appreciate the sincerity."

"You're right." He appears empowered as he walks with purpose toward the house. "Wish me luck."

"Good luck," I call after him. *Shelby's about to be the second luckiest girl in Freeland County.* When he's out of sight, I crank the fan up and turn back to Jason who looks devilishly sexy and smug lying there waiting for me. "About that punishment—"

"Punish away, baby."

I do, and then I let him reciprocate, but it's more making love and lust, punishment of the *good* kind.

BROOKS WAS CHARGED with aggravated assault, attempted murder, tax evasion, and fifteen counts of illegal gambling with no bail. I'm not sad in the least.

Us versus them.

He pled not guilty. Not surprising but he's still an asshole.

As much as I wish we hadn't experienced the nightmare of that night, it brought me to an understanding. Taking Jason's hand as we watch him be charged, I have no regrets. I would put my life on the line time and again for the ones I love.

Cole Cutler is asked to stand. His assigned lawyer stands behind the defendant's table with him nervously tapping his fingers against the tabletop.

My hands don't shake. Anger is stronger than the fear he used to instill in me. The judge reads the charges, and then asks if he understands what he's being charged with. With his head down, he replies, "Yes."

The judge asks, "What do you plead?"

Cole's lawyer whispers in his ear while I anxiously await his answer. I take a deep breath, holding it. Cole nods, looks at me, and then to the judge. "Guilty."

The gavel strikes, causing me to jump. I whisper to Jason, "Did he plead guilty?"

"Yes." This is what we wanted when we walked into the courthouse this morning, but the shock of it happening is staggering. I sink back in the seat, not sure what to do with myself or these welling emotions inside me. Jason's chest deflates, and he exhales his relief. However, something in his body language surprises me. Grabbing the bench in front of us, he lowers his head.

I pop back up, rubbing his back. "What's wrong?"

"He was my best friend." When his eyes land on mine, he asks, "How could a person I once trusted be so intent to destroy our lives?"

That is a question I've given so much thought to but avoided thinking about in the aftermath of kicking him out and our divorce. I think I was still so shell-shocked about what I'd been through and doubtful that he'd ever really be gone from my life. *And now I know that fear was well founded.*

There's no obvious reason for his actions. *Greed? Hate? Sadness?* "Jealousy."

My marriage to Cole never felt real, not in the ways that count. Marriage is love and beauty, support and friendship. I was betrayed, tricked into believing I deserved less in life. He had to beat me down to keep me from seeing the truth. But I see. So clearly, I see what could have been versus what became. One rash decision changed our lives forever, and I'll always carry half that blame.

But Jason's forgiven me, so I need to start trying to forgive myself. It's not about how long it took us to find our way back to each other. It's that we found our way despite the detour.

Jason nods silently, but then moves to leave, taking me with him. His mother catches us in the hall, hugging us to her. "Is it over?"

"They were charged," he says, assessing the courthouse exits. I wonder when he'll truly be home and not need to know how to escape, if necessary. "Not sentenced. He pled not guilty, so he'll go to trial."

She looks from him to me and back to him. "What about Cole?"

"Cutler pled guilty and will go straight to sentencing. We have to wait."

Meredith replies with a smile, "Well then, how about dinner tonight?"

We have dinner with her at least once a week, when she's not busy with her boyfriend, Fred Carver from the hardware store. Jason starts grumbling, but I place an arm on him and reply, "We'd be happy to. Will Fred be there?"

"Yes. I think it's time for my guys to spend some time together."

"You're killing me, Mom."

"Oh, you'll live. I have needs too—"

"No." He rolls on his heel, turning his back to us. "I do not want to hear about your needs when it comes to stuff like this."

"Maybe we'll have a double wedding," she teases. I love that she gives him a hard time. It's good for him.

I joke, "Our girl is all grown up."

"Don't you start in." Walking backward toward the doors, he says to her, "We'll see you tonight."

"Love you, Jase."

"Love ya."

I catch up to him, laughing and smacking his ass as I pass. He's quick, though. And good with his hands. Correction: *great* with his hands. I'm scooped up in his arms outside the courthouse, kissed, and carried to the truck. I'd fight, but it's a good way to travel—all bundled up in his arms.

When I'm set down, my back rests against the truck, and he cages me in. As always, I'm ready to make out right here on the sidewalk, but it seems he has other plans. "I want to take you somewhere."

With how he's looking at me right now, he can take me anywhere.

Needless to say, time hasn't tempered our attraction or the chemistry between us.

I DIDN'T EXPECT to be sitting across from Sabrina Smith inside Solace Pointe National Bank, but here we are. Cole's name has been removed from all the farmhouse paperwork and put fully into mine and Shelby's name. "It's surreal," I say to Jason, who's sitting next to me.

Rubbing my leg, he nods. "It's how it should be."

Sabrina, in all her snooty flair, stands abruptly and taps the papers on the desk. "I'll need to get my manager to handle your paperwork, Jason."

When she leaves the cubicle, I whisper, "What is she talking about?"

Matching my tone, he replies, "Wait for it." *By the look in his eyes, this ought to be good.*

The bank manager, Worley Hiccolms, comes in and heartily shakes our hands. "Mr. Koster. Ms. Noelle. Good to see you today." He glares at Sabrina. "If you'll excuse us."

"Sure," she says, playing it off like she's not nosy and desperately wanting in on whatever this is.

Worley smiles like a Cheshire cat and pushes a piece of paper across the desk toward us. "Ms. Noelle has been added. We can update after the nuptials if there is a legal name change. If you could both sign here, she'll be granted full access to the safety-deposit box and the two bank accounts."

I bump my knee against Jason's. He says, "Life is unpredictable. I thought it was a good idea to get you added sooner rather than later."

The bank manager says, "It's good to take precautions. Now, if you'll sign here and here, you can be on your way, and we'll take care of the rest." Jason has me sign first, and then he signs on the line beneath mine. Worley stands eagerly. "I want to personally thank you for trusting your financial interests with our fine establishment."

They shake hands. "Thank you. Don't get robbed."

"Eh, we're insured."

We all laugh politely through a round of goodbyes until we reach the sidewalk. I ask, "What was that about?"

"I guess he's just happy to be working with us."

"Jason?" My hand goes to my hip. "Be open with me. How much money are we talking about? Worley doesn't treat everybody like that, so I'm assuming a lot. Twenty? Fifty? A hundred thousand?"

We reach the truck. With the door open in his hand, he says, "We can go inside and get a statement if you'd like."

"No." I climb into the cab. "Just tell me."

He shuts my door and drags this out. Adding to the drama while he walks around to the driver's side, he smiles smugly when I watch him through the windshield. When he slips into the cab of the truck next to me, he starts the engine.

"Jason, tell me."

"You sure you want to know? I know how you get weird about money."

"I'm not weird about money," I reply defensively, but then ease into the seat, resting my elbow on the door. "Well, maybe I am. I've never had enough to know if I get weird or not."

His arm is on the back of the bench while he reverses. "Well, after paying off the farm and Mom's house, there's two point eight million in the accounts."

"What?" I shout, whacking his arm. My throat dries, and I start coughing.

Patting me on the back, he looks over, but I see the wry grin on his face. "Are you okay, baby?"

I clear my throat. "Two point eight million dollars? U.S. money?"

"No, in Oreos. Yes, dollars."

Leaning back, I can't even fathom that amount of money. "From jobs?"

"Yes. I was paid well."

"That much is more than well, Jason."

He shrugs as he pulls out and starts driving. "I was very good at what I did."

"I would say so."

"This is a lot to take in. I get it. Every penny I earned was for this life, *for us*. I know that sounds unbelievable. You were married. I shouldn't have thought of you as more than someone else's wife. I think deep down my heart knew where it belonged. I knew. This is where I belong. Right here with you. Call it kismet or luck, great timing, or great fortune. Doesn't matter as long as I have you."

Our hands reach out and find each other in the middle.

This is love.

Pure.

Soul-enriching, life-affirming, deep-seated, raw, messy, and real love.

Getting a second chance to be with this generous and kind soul is more than kismet or great timing.

It's destiny.

I WALK into the barn and climb the ladder to the loft. We can't live up here forever, and definitely not through the winter, but it's been fun. It's been the escape from the house we needed after that night we were attacked.

When I reach the top, I spot a large gift box on the middle of the mattress. Sitting down next to it, I take it, smiling before I even lift the lid. I don't understand the present inside, but maybe the note can explain. I pull the card from the envelope and read:

DEAR DELILAH,

FOR OLD TIMES' sake, please wear this uniform and meet me at the stadium one more time. I'll be waiting for you at 8 p.m.

LOVE YOU,
 Jason

HOLDING the note to my chest, I blink back tears. But it's hard when every day I'm given with the love of my life is a blessing.

I set the note aside and reach for the uniform. Laughing, I stand and hold the skirt to my hips. Not sure if this will still fit, but I'm willing to squeeze into it for Jason. With the top and bottom part of the uniform in hand, I rush back down the ladder and into the house.

"Shelby?" I run to the hall and call upstairs, "Shelby? Where are you?"

"Stop yelling, Delilah. I'm in here," she calls from the other room. It's been great having my sister home. Working remotely is allowing her to rediscover her love for country life. With the farm paid off, she gets to decide her future and whether she returns or stays. Secretly and not so secretly, I hope she stays.

I rush into the kitchen, my boots coming to a halt against the linoleum. Holding up the outfit, I ask, "Will you help me get ready?" A smile already sits on her face when she turns around with an iced tea in hand. Like me, she can't hide anything in her eyes. "You know what this is about, don't you?"

"Maybe." She shrugs before setting her glass on the table and taking me by the arm. "Come on. Let's get you ready."

32

Jason

Billy drives his fists down on my shoulders. "All done."

Suited up in my old football uniform, the jersey is stretched across my broader shoulders. "It's been a long damn time since I wore pads."

"You're a big dude, you know that?"

Chuckling, I bend down to tie my shoes. "Yeah. I'm aware." When I stand, the cleats add some height. "Shorty."

"At six one, I'm not usually considered short."

"Eh, don't worry. We're not playing football anymore. What time you got?"

"Ten till eight."

"I'm going to head out there."

We shake hands, but I bring him in for a chest press. "Are you hugging me, man?" he asks.

"Maybe. Just go with it." He remains, and I inwardly laugh. "Thanks for everything you've done to take care of Delilah over the years." We step back, and I grab the helmet. Holding it under my arm, I make sure I have everything else

I need. "Thank you for tonight, too." *I want everything just right for her.*

Giving me a middle-finger salute, he replies, "Aye aye, captain." Some things never change. The smart-ass. When we enter the tunnel that leads to the field, he stops. "Good luck out there."

"Thanks, but I never need luck." *I just need her.* We walk in opposite directions. By the time I reach the field, the sun is starting to set. I scan the field and then the bleachers.

Six field exits.

Three on the far side.

Three behind me.

Ten exits up the bleachers.

Five on each side.

I make my way to the fifty-yard line, put my helmet on, and wait. This afternoon, the rest of the pieces of my life fell together . . .

Delilah and the farm are free from Cutler forever. It didn't take much to get him to sign. I recommended it might be safer for him in jail than roaming free if he didn't. I simply rubbed my neck and bam, he signed. I'm just here to pick it up.

I expected the coward to give in, but I didn't expect to happen so quickly. Sitting across from Cutler, I don't say anything. I'm not sure what to say anyway, but he does. "You were a good friend to me, Jason."

I scrub a hand over my jaw. "I was."

"I'm sorry. I loved her." The fucker knows nothing about love. Never has.

"No, you didn't. If you did, you wouldn't have laid a finger on her. If you truly loved her, you would have wanted to see her happy, which she was with me."

"I'll tell her I'm sorry."

"Don't." I stand. "Don't ever contact her again. This paper-work is all she needs from you."

The guard releases the door, and I walk out. With glass dividing us, he yells, "I'm sorry."

He will be sorry. Where he's going, there are no friendships, no future, or direction. He'll understand a little of the hell I went through. Then maybe, he'll be sorry. But right now, the asshole doesn't have a clue.

. . . The bright lights flick on, lighting up the stadium and surrounding area. The scoreboard comes on next. The final score from that night years ago lights up the board. It was a good game for me, one of my best, so it's fun to relieve that memory before things went to shit.

I spy Billy looking over the field from the announcer's booth and give him a thumbs-up.

When he returns it, I know he's spotted Delilah. The second she comes through that tunnel, it's as if the night becomes a lot brighter.

Shelby was helping me on the inside and got her here as promised. When Delilah sees me, she stops, wearing a wide smile I can see clear across this field. As much as I want to greet her, I don't. It has to be perfect. For her. So I stay. When she heads to where she used to cheer, I know the plan is coming together. I continue to wait, and she keeps peeking my way.

The bass drum echoes from the tunnel, the other drums joining in. Our alma mater marching band kicks in, filling the stadium with music. Marching between us to the end of the field and then looping behind me, it's quite the produc-tion, but she's worth it.

With her hands over her mouth, she bends over in laughter.

She shakes her pom-poms like old times, enjoying every

minute. With a fifty-piece marching band backing me, I take a deep breath and exhale slowly.

I'm nervous. I shouldn't be, but I realize that this isn't about second chances. We already have that. Tonight is about righting wrongs.

Dragging my tongue over my bottom lip, I fix my eyes on her and start walking. I glance up to see Shelby next to Billy in that booth. And I know if they weren't making out right now, they'd totally be cheering us on as well.

Delilah. The name alone means delicate, but she's anything but fragile. Her inner strength fortifies how strong she is outward. Smart, she's running her farm better than most of the neighbors in this county. Adapting as needed and cleverly creating a new financial plan when the other wasn't working. When she had no one, she survived to create a new life. She's the sun to my revolving world. And I don't want to live a day with her light shadowed.

She shifts her weight from foot to foot, nervous like me. For some reason, that makes me feel better knowing we're both invested as deeply in each other. Not that I didn't know that already, but her reaction gives me reassurance. Then I focus on my target—a blond with big blue eyes, wearing her heart on her sleeve and a number patch near the hem of her skirt.

I take the helmet off and carry it by the face guard at my side. Just ten feet separate us when the world comes back into color—vivid and electric. And there in the center of my universe stands the only girl my heart ever recognized as its own. She's as gorgeous as she always was, that uniform a fantasy come to life. Again. Damn, she knows how to work her assets to her advantage. Shapely legs and that top all filled out. My mind goes to the gutter instead of the speech I had prepared. Shit. I'm blank. I walk right to her and wrap my arms around her waist, picking her up. Her legs wrap around my middle and her laughter fills the air right before the marching band begins to play again. Bending down, she kisses me.

This is how that night should have gone.

"You're all I ever wanted, Delilah Rae Noelle."

As I set her down, her laughter is replaced with glassy eyes as she struggles to hold her tears back. "Me too. You're all I've ever wanted, Jason Koster."

I drop down to my knee and take her hand. "Three thousand fans crowded into this stadium every Friday night to watch our team play and hopefully win. We usually did."

She reaches out to touch my chin before taking her pom-poms in both hands again. "You were named MVP all four years in school."

"But it's not the trophies or the accolades I remember. When I look back on my life, my highlights reel plays our love story."

"Oh, Jason," she sighs with a gentle smile, her body leaning toward me as if keeping the distance is torture for her.

"I remember everything about you—from the purple shirt and denim skirt you were wearing the first time I saw you to the kiss you blew me from atop of the parade float junior year. No victory was ever won without looking for you in the crowd. Your approval. Your support. Your love. That's all I needed, so although life may have taken us in different directions and knocked us off course along the way, it still carried me right back to your door. This is our chance to put us back the way we were always supposed to be. Delilah Rae Noelle, marry me. Travel the world with me. Have babies with me. Hold my hand even when you're mad at me. And I promise I'll kiss you even after we fight. I'll take the middle-of-the-night feedings, so you can sleep. I'll protect you. Always. But . . ."

I get choked up. It was bound to happen when you feel this deeply about something or someone. "I'll love you in this life and the next. I'll give you the world and the universe, the stars above, and will make love to your body and your heart. Will you marry me?"

Throwing her arms around my neck, her pom-poms are dropped behind me as she sits on my bended knee with her head tucked into the nook of my neck. Her cries are soft but shake her shoulders, but when she lifts up, she says, "Yes. A thousand yeses, Jason. I want to be your wife, partner, the mother of your children, and your forever."

Jumping up, I bring her with me and spin around. We kiss again, and when our lips part this time, Billy comes over the loudspeaker, and asks, "What'd she say?"

I give him a thumbs-up.

Shelby and he cheer just as the band starts playing our school's touchdown song. Marching across the field, they form a circle around us to Delilah's utter delight. I set her down, still holding her hand but spinning her out like we're on the dance floor. When she stays away too long, I say, "C'mere." Caressing her face in my hands, I kiss her good and improper, the way she likes to be kissed.

"You sure did go to a lot of trouble for a girl who already said yes."

"You once asked for a redo. I want to make all your dreams come true."

She tilts her head to the side, eyeing me with a sweet smile on her face. "You succeeded, stud." Plucking the eight on the front of my jersey, she adds, "You always did look good in a uniform."

"You look so incredible I'm already planning a quick

escape route to get you home and in bed so I can make love to you all night."

Spinning away from me again, she shows me the back. "It's all rigged with safety pins. This skirt is way too tight." She's linked the sides together. There's at least two inches keeping the sides from meeting.

"You're sexy as hell anyway."

"I've put on a little weight since you've returned, a few love pounds. I'm not worried, but it will be more."

"More?"

She bends down and picks up one of her pom-poms, flashing me her fine ass while doing it. These pants are feeling tighter already. When she turns back, she grabs something dangling from the center of the black and gold. "Yes. More."

I'm so confused until I see the stick, a white stick with two pink lines that she's holding out for me. I take it, the poofy ball coming with it. My thoughts fumble to register what this is, even though I know exactly what it is. She calls my name. "Jason?"

"Yeah," I reply, glancing at her and then down at the stick again.

"We're having a baby."

It wasn't just one time we didn't use condoms. We stopped using them altogether because we wanted this. We *want* this. I drop my head but keep my eyes on her. "You're pregnant?"

"Yes." Her smile is even prettier than seconds before.

My heart starts beating for a new reason. A baby. "I'm going to be a dad?"

Cozying up to my side, she laughs. "Yes, you're going to be a dad."

I wrap an arm around her and kiss the top of her head.

"What about the wedding? Do you want to get married sooner?"

"It doesn't matter when. It only matters that we're together."

The band had stopped playing and have almost disappeared from the field altogether, but who could notice when I'm having a baby with Delilah Rae, my honeysuckle. She wraps her arms around my neck and tilts back, letting me bear the weight as she smiles toward the moonlight. Technically, it's under the stadium lights, but for her, I get all the light to shine for her. "I was in town earlier, and I overheard Janice spreading gossip at the pharmacy."

"And what gossip was she spreading?"

"Well," she starts, raising one eyebrow, "rumor has it that you're bad for me."

"Shouldn't believe everything you hear. Sometimes a little bad can be good for a girl."

"I'd say." She kisses me, and I kiss her with all the love she deserves.

"You know they're going to gossip about me knocking you up before marriage?"

"Let 'em. They don't matter. Only we do. And this baby. We're going to give this baby the best life ever."

Bending down, I kiss her bare midriff. "Hey baby, it's your daddy." Delilah's fingers run through my hair, holding me there. "Do you know how much I love your mama?"

I take her hand while I still hold that stick in the other, ready to confess the last of my secrets. "I have more money than what's in Solace Pointe Bank. Your name is on all four accounts. I was going to give it to you as a gift when the paperwork came in, but I guess we should figure out how to manage it together to make sure our family is always taken care of, and we can re-file all the paperwork."

"More money? I don't understand, What paperwork?"

"I don't really have a lot of faith in small-town banks. I was protecting our financial interests by spreading it out across the US and one account in Switzerland."

"Wait, what are you saying?"

"We're really fucking rich."

Her brows knit together in disbelief. "Since my name is now on it, how much are we talking about?"

"Fifteen or so."

As much as I love surprising her, I don't like shocking her. "You're not talking thousands, are you?"

"Nope, sweet face, I'm not."

After looking up at the stars for a few seconds, she finally looks at me. "It's not stolen?"

"No. All earned with my blood, *literally*, sweat, and hard work." I run my hands over her waist, not able to resist her soft skin. "You have full access. And that's it, no more secrets. You know everything now."

Her hands slide under my jersey, her warmth penetrating my skin. "I guess I should confess my final secret to you, too."

She's never been one for secrets, or so I thought. "What secret?"

A devilish grin is followed by her dipping the top of her skirt down. "You know my tattoo?"

"Yes." I stop her hand and look around. It's way too low to expose in the middle of this stadium. What can I say? I'm a jealous bastard. "*My* number eight that's nowhere close to twenty-two?"

She giggles. "That would be the one."

"What about it?"

With both hands, she tugs me close, and whispers, "I wasn't drunk."

A grin grows across my face. "Have I ever told you how sexy that tattoo is?"

"Nope." A little hip wiggle punctuates her reply.

"How about I show you?"

Boy, do I.

I show her three times, in fact, before the rooster crows the next morning.

33

Jason

I shift for like the tenth or twentieth time in the five minutes I've been sitting here. Maybe there's still time to bolt. The door opens. Guess not. I stand, unsure what I'm supposed to do or what I should say.

"Jason, good to see you." We greet each other with a handshake.

"You too, sir." I sit back down as he sits in his chair on the other side of the desk.

"Stephen is fine."

"Yes, sir." *Habit.*

"Look, son, I'm glad you finally came by. It's been a while since we've had a chance to talk."

"Yeah, I think maybe the last time was when I was fifteen. It was a warning about masturbation and the dangers of it."

He starts laughing. "Yeah, for the parents' sake, we give all the boys around that age the same warning. If not, imagine the mess on their hands."

I think the minister just made a joke. *Am I allowed to laugh or was that a slip up*? "So we don't go to hell for it?" *Checking, just in case.*

Leaning forward, he lowers his voice. "Look, masturbation is natural, but you don't want it to control your life. Do you have a masturbation problem you'd like to discuss?"

Shaking my head, I'm horrified and squeak, "No. I'm all good in that department." Having lots of sex out of wedlock, though, currently. I'm pretty sure he's well aware. Clearing my throat, I finish by saying, "That's not why I'm here."

"Why are you here?" He leans back in his chair, giving me a full view of the cross on display above his head.

"You might have heard the rumors."

"I was happy to hear that the angels played a hand in bringing you and Delilah together again."

I'm not sure how to say what I want versus what I should with him. "Is everything between us confidential?"

"Yes. Unless it's illegal. I can help you repent to the Lord, but not keep you out of jail. What is it, son?"

Resting my forearms on my legs, I whisper, "I'm seeking forgiveness."

"Forgiveness from God?"

I glance toward the stained-glass window. "I've done things I'm not proud of, but I don't regret them either." Turning back to him, I add, "But I also want to spend eternity with Delilah, so I'm coming to you for help."

Steepling his fingers, he studies me. "Hmm. Interesting quandary. Can you elaborate?"

"Not really. I can tell you that I didn't carry God with me while I was gone. I'd lost faith and left Solace Pointe to find if there was still good in the world."

"Did you find what you were looking for?"

Sitting back, I cross my ankle over my knee and think

about his question. "I found some good but needed faith to find the rest."

Mimicking me, he pushes back in chair. "Ironic, isn't it?"

"I had nowhere to go, but my motorcycle led me back home."

"Back to town or to the Noelle farm?"

I smile. I can't help it. "To Delilah."

"And what did you find once you were there?"

"Myself."

He nods with an all-knowing smile. "You don't need to seek forgiveness, Jason. You needed to follow your heart, and you did. That's where good lives and will always lead you exactly where you're supposed to be."

I BLAME the sun for shining in my eyes and causing them to water. Not the gorgeous woman walking on the arm of her sister down a pink rose-petal aisle. I'll never admit otherwise.

Yup, the sun. That's my story, and I'm sticking to it.

Billy nudges me. "Are you crying?"

"Are you?" I snap back.

"Maybe." He shrugs it off. "A little."

"My soon-to-be wife is beautiful."

With our eyes ahead on the ladies, he says, "I like Shelby."

"Yeah, I know."

"Really?"

"Yes, it's obvious. Apparently to everyone but you." I elbow him. "Now can we get back to *my* wedding?"

He nods. "Yeah, sure. Sorry."

The music wafts through the air from the trio playing by

the barn. My eyes stay fixed on my flower, my honeysuckle, my Delilah, her shoulders exposed as the lace hangs down on the sides. The dress flows around her, and the flowers circling her head make her look like a goddess. *My goddess.*

"Do you think Shelby likes me?" Billy starts in again. "She flirts with me, and we hung out a few times, but—"

"Shut up, Billy." I laugh. Right before the girls reach us, I whisper to him, "She likes you, or she wouldn't give you the time of day. You guys need to seal this deal, once and for all. Make your move at the reception. Chicks love weddings." I turn back in time to take the hands of my sweet woman. "Hi."

She whispers, "Hi." Her hands aren't shaking, and her voice is steady. She's confident like the girl I always knew her to be. The difference is, she's not *that* girl. She's a woman who acknowledges the challenges of her past and is choosing to focus on the future. She's as kind as she is beautiful, accepting me with open arms despite my past. I begin to tell her all the reasons I love her, but it's the last one that means the most to me. "When I think of love, I think of you, Delilah. Home is where the heart is and my heart is wherever you are, my wife and soul mate. You gave me a reason to stay, and in return, I pledge to you my love in this lifetime and every life after."

Emotions trickle across her face but end in a smile just for me. "You showed up here on a motorcycle in the pouring rain. If that wasn't a love song in the making, I don't know what is. There you were, Jason Koster, looking at me with eyes that carried the years' worth of burdens, breaking my heart. What you didn't know is I had a broken heart, too. You carried half of my heart with you all those miles you traveled and all the seas you sailed. We didn't have to be together to know we were no good apart. Two halves only make a whole when the puzzle pieces fit, and we fit. Forever-more, our souls will be whole because we found our way back to each other."

"I always did enjoy a good love song. Care to finish this melody together?"

"I do."

34

Jason

"Then what did he say?" Delilah asks, drawing figure eights in the sand.

How am I expected to finish a story about a minister when she's dressed in a skimpy bikini? She's way too distracting, and some guys were eyeing her earlier. I almost kicked their asses for ogling my wife like that.

I've discovered it doesn't matter what she's wearing, though. Whether she's wearing a fancy dress in Paris or she's mostly naked on the beaches of California, they stare everywhere we go.

Makes me miss the privacy of the farm where I'm the only one who gets to ogle.

Lounging back on the sand, her baby belly is barely a pooch. I actually think that's from the hot dog she had at lunch, along with the salad, the large glass of water, and two scoops of ice cream. I don't argue though. She's insisting it's what our baby boy needs.

I'm kind of hoping for a girl. She'll be a badass like her

mom and learn to throw a football like her dad. Guess we'll find out in about five more months. In the meantime, it's been one long honeymoon. Shelby took a leave of absence to handle the farm while we're gone with the help of Billy. He and Paul manage the fields like they always have. Billy is happy on the farm with Shelby for now, but Paul and Lorraine are going to love the vacation to Hawaii we've booked for them. They've been friends to me and parental figures to Delilah. It feels good to be able to give back to the people who have given us so much.

The floor plan for our home on the other side of the lake is approved, and the construction is underway. We'll be able to settle in before the baby comes.

There's a lot to be grateful for, and I owe it all to the woman next to me. "Who?"

"The minister, Jason."

"He said I'm exactly where I'm meant to be."

Waggling her finger at me, she says, "Come over here." She's irresistible.

I kneel between her legs and then drop my hands on either side of her head. I've traveled the world with this woman. Nothing compares to her natural beauty. "What is it, sweetheart of mine?"

"I've been thinking. Even though we've both been to hell and back, we're finally living the life planned for us all along. We're living our destiny."

"I have no doubt."

Lowering myself down, I'm careful about putting too much weight on her. When I kiss her, a little moan is shared. "Want to go back to the hotel?"

"Can we order room service?"

I stand and offer her a hand. Coming face-to-face, I wink. "Anything you want."

"Anything?"

"Any. Thing."

She's quick to grab her bag and head to the car. Kicking sand up with her feet, she grants me with her gorgeous face when she looks back over her shoulder. "Good. I have a few ideas."

"Do they include me or food?" I grab the blanket, dusting the sand off as I hurry to catch up with her. "What are you craving?" Fuck the blanket. She looks too delicious to keep my hands off. I scoop her into my arms, putting her into a fit of giggles.

"I'll give you a hint. I brought your jersey with me."

"You want me to put it on?"

Tapping her chin on the side of the SUV we rented, she twists her lips. Such a tease. "I was thinking more along the lines of me wearing it for you . . . with nothing else underneath. What do you think about that?"

Holy fuck, as if I couldn't desire her more, she goes and concocts the best plan in history. Since I'm still lost in those images, she says, "I also have a new cheer I want to show you. That doesn't include any clothes at all."

I open the door for her, and reply, "They didn't make me MVP for nothing. You're about to see how I score a touchdown."

Slipping inside the car, she smirks, "I'm hoping this includes a few tackles and first downs, hotshot."

Once I'm in the driver's seat, I start the engine. "You ready to back up all this big talk?"

"I can back it up."

"I know you can." Taking her hand, I kiss it. "Hey."

Delilah is the definition of the purest love. Sure, she's being playfully sexy, but there's so much more to her that challenges me to be a better man. I'll strive every day to meet that demand. She replies, "Hey."

Feeling much like the shy kid I was once around her, I hesitate, but then I lean into my personal sanctuary, touching her cheek. "After the adventures we've had, traveling to all these places these past few months, have your dreams come true?"

"Don't you know, sweet man? I didn't have to travel the world to make my dreams come true. I just needed to be with you." She leans into my hand. "Do you think the farm can give you long-term peace to calm your restless soul?"

"It's never about the farm, or the lake, though both are peaceful places. It's always been about you." I kiss her forehead, and whisper, "I'd lost myself, but I found my way home because you gave me a reason to stay."

She takes my hand from her cheek and lowers it to her belly. "Now you have two."

"How do you feel about three?"

Though her eyes go wide, she doesn't say no. "Is that why we're building a five-bedroom house?"

Moving my hands to the top of her belly, I rub gently. "No, that's for the fourth baby I was going to beg you to have down the road. That's why we're building five bedrooms."

"You want four kids, Jason?"

"I want a big family, sweetness." I sneak in a kiss attack on her neck, making her laugh.

"You keep that up, and we might end up with a football team."

"That's the plan."

Tilting to give me more access, she also caresses my neck. "Oh Lord, help me. You are my complete undoing."

I lean back to get a good look at my girl, her hair hanging over her shoulders, looking so much like the day we began. Kissing her palm, and then the side of her mouth, I whisper, "I was undone the moment I laid eyes on you, honeysuckle."

I THOUGHT I knew what love was. It's all tied up in a pretty package of silky hair and soft skin, a smile that warms me all the way on the inside, and a soul that cares for me despite my bad deeds. Delilah holds every emotion I've ever felt—happiness, heartbreak, protectiveness, possessiveness, compassion, and ecstasy. I've never been able to identify everything I feel for her with a single word.

It's an overwhelming emotion—soft, rounded on the corners, but sharp-tongued, fiery and passionate, pure and comfort, desire and lust, kindness and genuine . . . *safe.*

Complicated to describe.

Easy to feel.

Perhaps heaven is the best word for it.

The day I meet my daughter, my head clears, and things aren't so complicated anymore. All these feelings—jumbled inside my heart in a mass of emotion—become clear when I look at Delilah with tears in my eyes. I still need more than one word to describe what my wife gives me that day:

Love.

Hope.

Faith.

Faith Noelle Koster is born on a Sunday morning in early spring. She comes into this world screaming, but as soon as I hold her in my arms, she stops and coos. This little human might be small, but she is mighty. When her tiny fingers wrap around one of mine, she does more than hold my hand, she steals my heart.

Two days after we arrive home with our bundle of joy, I wake up before five in the morning to find the bed next to me empty. I quietly pad down the hall and find my wife sitting in a rocking chair holding our newborn. Watching her in this sweet moment, I'm reminded how I once thought I didn't deserve this life. I didn't believe that a sinner like myself deserved solace from the wrongs I committed.

But here I am, living proof that sometimes, the bad guy simply needs to find a reason to be good. Sometimes, their souls aren't completely black but just a little singed around the edges. Sometimes, it just takes seeing the light to make it all right.

I walk into the room and catch Delilah's eyes. Her early morning smile is one of my favorites, though she argues she's tired and has dark circles. I don't see anything less than beautiful. "How'd I get so lucky to be your husband and Faith's father?"

When she reaches for my hand, I kneel next to her chair and take it. She says, "It was never about luck, babe. It was destiny."

Destiny.

JASON KOSTER

If you'd like to spend more time with Jason Koster, you can find him in SAVAGE, where he was first introduced. I fell in love with this man the moment he walked onto the page. That was when I knew I had to give him his own happily ever after.

SAVAGE is now available here: *https://geni.us/SavageAm*

TURN THE PAGE to read the Prologue and Chapter 1 of this epic romance for Free.

SAVAGE

Welcome to the mysterious world of the rich and the damned in this gritty, modern day fairy tale. Two star-crossed lovers will either find their destiny or meet their fate in a world where demons come in the form of familiar faces and pawns aren't just players, but deadly.

She was my destiny.

I was her downfall.

We were a match made in hell.

But when we were together, that hell was pure heaven.

The moment I laid eyes on her, I knew she would pay the price for my sins. I wasn't much older than she was, but old enough to know better. Old enough to know she would be good for me and I was bad for her. But I pursued her anyway. Back then I had hope that maybe she could change my future.

Maybe together we could change our fate . . .

PROLOGUE

The sun shouldn't be shining

Considering the pain I'm feeling, it's too bright.

Too happy.

Too blue.

The periwinkle sky reminds me of the only blue I want to see. Brilliant blue eyes, not found in the heavens, but here on earth.

The world dims momentarily. "Where's your boyfriend?" the man asks.

How did I end up here? *Like this?*

I know. I just don't want to admit the truth. *Even now.*

Closing my eyes to block him out, I search my mind for the answer. "He'll come for us," I whisper.

Us.

A sharp slap to my face sends my head to the right. I'm too stubborn to scream, to give him any further satisfaction, even as the taste of copper coats my mouth. Curling to the side, I hold my stomach, attempting to protect the only thing that matters. I haven't told Alexander. I haven't had the chance. I was going to, but an unforeseen detour brought me here.

Grief begins to envelop me, but I try to hold on, just a little longer. Reaching out, I touch the red pooled in front of me, wondering if that's someone else's blood. *It can't be mine.* There's too much to be mine. I'm alive, but now I'm wondering for how long.

"Where's King?" is shouted, but I'm too tired to answer. Even if I could, I don't know where he is.

He didn't answer his phone. I allowed him to ride away, and the memory of his face causes my breath to stutter in my throat. As I cough, and blood splatters my present, I wish I could change the past. I wish I could go back to the beginning and relive our love from the start.

I would do so many things differently. Despite how we ended, I wouldn't change *us*. I wouldn't change our love.

His life is full of lies—the kind he tells and the ones he lives. Lies that have become mine and will haunt me as I learn to live without him. Those lies still haunt me as if they are mine to survive.

He once told me he would give me the life I dreamed about—the ending I deserved—a happy ending—but with rocks cutting into my skin and a stranger kicking the life from me, I start to wonder if all hope is lost.

Until I hear that familiar sound—the distinctive sound of a Harley's exhaust foreshadowing my knight in leather armor.

It doesn't matter how long it's been since I've seen him.

It won't matter what bad has happened between us.

Our love will never die, even if I do.

"I told you he'd come for us."

Knowing he'll be here soon, I close my eyes, and dream of the fairy tale we once had . . .

CHAPTER 1

Alexander Kingwood IV

This is my favorite way to wake up.

Often pretending to be asleep, I spy on her as she climbs out of bed, finding peace watching her day begin. Life is better with her around.

Simpler.

Happier.

A kiss to my face. Location varies from the tip of my nose to forehead, the occasional closed eyelid before she sneaks out of bed, tiptoeing into the bathroom and then back out. I struggle to stay still this morning, needing her in ways that aren't quiet. The night clogs my throat, my voice still gruff. "Come back to bed."

Standing at the dresser, digging through the top drawer where she keeps some of her things, Sara Jane looks back at me with a smile at play on her lips, simultaneously giving me a peek at some side tit. "I thought you were asleep."

I stretch my arms up and grab hold of the top of the headboard behind me. "I'm up." Her back is smooth. The curve from her waist to her hips defined more with each year that passes. Her ass sits high and tight above her legs. Her body caught at the other end of transitioning from a girl's into a woman's. Giving her a solid once-over, she knows what's on my mind. "Come back to bed," I repeat the request without a plea. She'll come. She always does for me.

Sara Jane is not just good to me. She's good *for* me. She's kept me from burying myself or being buried more than a few times. My pretty firefly has seen me through my highs and lows and now stands by my side as the one constant in my life, the only person I can truly count on.

Her lace panties slide down her thighs and she returns. She knows what I want. She wants it too, so I don't have to put on a big production or sweet talk her back into bed. Settling on top of me, she slides down over my cock, ready for me, slick with desire. Slow and steady feels like a good idea this morning. I hold her hips, keeping my grip light as she fucks me.

Her hands press to my chest and she leans down to kiss me. Before she has a chance to pull back, I grab her face, making sure our eyes meet, and I hold her gaze. "You know how much I love you, right?"

Softness covers her expression as she smiles. "As much as I love you, Alexander."

Alexander. Hearing her say my name keeps me grounded to her and planted in reality. She's the only one who calls me that, the only one I *allow* to call me by my full name.

When she sits up, she begins to rock, her head dropping back, her hair long, the tips running over my thighs. Her tits are amazing, full with weight to them. For someone so small, she was blessed in all the right places. My pretty little firefly has changed a lot since we first met. If possible, she has become even more stunning.

The first time I saw her, I knew she would be mine. Nothing would keep me from her. Something wild and untamed stirred deep inside just from the sight of her.

Cruise hadn't understood. He'd been busy talking about some cheerleader he scored with the night before, but my mind had drifted, which had been standard anytime the chicks from school were brought up. I'd lost interest in the easies by tenth grade. But after what happened two weeks before, I'd struggled to find pleasure in anything. My taste buds had dulled, and life lacked color.

Except for that damn blue polka-dot umbrella and the girl standing beneath it, who stole my world from under me. She was sunshine on a rainy day, a rainbow against gray clouds, hope in a Catholic school uniform. She was why poetry was written and art created. I could deny I became a fool for love the second I saw her, but it would be a lie. She made me want to be a better man, a better person in life. She made me think twice about the direction I was heading. But we both knew better. Our course was already set, our love a sweeping storm that would brew for years before raging.

Her hair hung down, darker because it was wet, soaked as if the umbrella hadn't protected her. Her eyes were wide with innocence as she ate a candy bar like it was the best treat she'd ever tasted. Her skirt . . . damn that short skirt. I saw the man in the car next to me staring at her and I wanted to beat the shit out of him for looking at her like she could be his next tasty treat. That fucking pervert was around my dad's age. *Fucking asshole.* She couldn't be more than seventeen.

I was tempted to go over and cover her bare legs with my jacket. The girl was oblivious to the attention she attracted, and I almost felt I should become her protective knight in shining armor. I wanted to kick my own ass for that thought. So fucking lame. Until she looked my way. My throat went dry and my lips parted. The humid air wouldn't save me. I was lost to this girl from that moment on.

She looked away, and the sweetest of pinks colored her cheeks. *Damn.* Her purity shined like a beacon. I've never been one with a need to take a V-card to feed some locker room pride. Nah, I didn't need to prove anything to anyone, least of all some jock-asses who bragged about every girl they bagged. But when she dared to look my way again, a deep-seated desire stirred. I wanted her.

It was a carnal reaction I felt in my gut, but it had nothing to do with sex. Sure, sex crossed my mind, but its images were blurred like visions of déjà vu.

With no justifiable reason, right there at a busy intersection in the suburbs north of downtown, I became determined to be everything she would ever need. I would risk it all just to talk to her. If she'd never been kissed, I'd kiss her so she never desired to kiss another man. If she was still innocent in other ways, I would earn her trust and not just make love to her, but create it, a bond so strong she'd never need anyone else. I would be her first *and* last love. That day as the rain came down, I made sweet Sara Jane Grayson my mission. With nothing left to lose, I vowed to steal her heart and own her soul.

As I watch her moving on top of me, buried deep inside her, I hope I've changed her for the better. Three years ago, when our worlds collided, she changed me.

She collapses on my chest and I hold her tight as our bodies relax after the intense release. Fingertips tap across the tattoo that honors her, the one she hates. To be fair, she doesn't want me to have any, but she calls this one an ugly bug. There's nothing ugly about the firefly. Just like her, its strength is illuminated in the darkest of times.

Lifting up, she rests her chin on my chest, and asks, "What are you doing today?"

In any other room, in any other house, with any other couple, this question would be so easy to answer. But it's not in another place and we're not just any other couple. We're complicated and my life is twisted. I try hard to spare her from getting caught up in my tornado. My self-destructive ways have become worse, but I don't mention most of that to her anymore. Instead, I respond like we are one of those other couples, where answers are easy, and life is simple. "I'm going into the office, and have a meeting with my father. I'll pick you up on campus later."

Sitting up, she maneuvers away, but I'm quick and grab her wrist. When her sweet, soulful eyes—that melt me like butter—reach me, I add, "More."

"More?"

"I love you more."

A smile slips into place and she pokes me in the chest. "You're not so tough, Mr. Kingwood." It's a game she likes to play, to pretend that some of my bad isn't as bad as her mind imagines.

I play along because despite the light she brings into my world, I only bring darkness into hers. The smile she evokes from me comes naturally though. "Nah, I'm not so tough."

Leaning back down, she kisses my cheek and then gets up to shower. I watch that ass I'm so fond of until she disappears into the bathroom. My phone vibrates on the nightstand. It's been going off for at least an hour. We both ignored it, but I can't any longer. Reaching over, I grab it and glance at the messages.

The sigh is automatic as soon as I see the text.

Cruise: *When are you coming in? Your dad is flipping out.*

Me: *I'll be in shortly.*

Cruise: *Fucker.*

Me: *You know it, Sucker.*

I toss the phone on the bed and head into the bathroom. I open the shower door and look in, eyeing her. "Perfect timing."

Sara Jane laughs and her hands go up. "Oh no, you stay back. I can't be late again or I'll be counted absent."

Taking the soap from her hands, I step in and run the bar over the silky skin of her breasts and down farther until the bar is dropped and my fingers are between her legs. "If that's the worst that can happen . . ."

"Damn you."

"You love it, baby. So much. Just like you love me."

Her eyelids dip closed when her shoulder blades hit the white tile wall. I lean over her and kiss her breath away when my mouth covers that little O her lips are forming. Hands press against my chest then slide up to grab hold of my shoulders, pulling me closer.

Soap and sex covers her as I glide my tongue up until it's discovering every curve and alcove of her mouth. I want to fuck her. *Again.* So fucking hard that she forgets she has classes altogether. She forgets the outside world. She forgets everything else, everything but me. Pressing my cock against her hip, I push as my fingers fuck her pussy. I'm trying to be good, trying to make it about her. Only about her, but she makes it damn hard when she grabs my cock with both hands and starts to get me off.

"I want to fuck you." My words are minced under the water's spray as I lean my head against the wall and take the shell of her ear between my teeth.

"God, Alexander." Her body folds against mine, her

orgasm close enough to feel her tightening around me. "Why do you do this to me?" Her question is loaded, and I'm not sure it only concerns our sexual deviancy.

"It's what you do to me. Turn around." I take her by the ribs and spin her toward the wall. Her hands go against the wall in front of her and she parts for me. Such a good girl.

My dick is big and she's small, so I bend down until I feel her wet heat with my tip. I bite her shoulder lightly then thrust hard. Her cry echoes off the walls with her hands braced higher up. I take her hips and fuck, lost in her, lost in the sensations of her sweet little pussy.

My fingers dig deeper as our bodies gyrate together, slicker by the second. I close my eyes and let the water rain down over me as movements become erratic, compromised by the slipperiness. Close. So close. I will never have enough of her, never satisfy the heavier urges my heart craves. So I stake claims for her, but more for me. "You're mine. You know that?"

"I always have been." Her words are strained and then sucked back in as she takes another deep breath.

"Mine. Fucking mine. Always. Say it."

"Always yours, Alexander."

"King," I demand, fucking her harder. She knows what I want. It's something she only gives me when I'm at my best, in my opinion, *worst* in hers.

She won't say it. I know her too well to know she won't play into that game. And I'm coming too fast. "Fuck," I shout and pull out, my cum covering her lower back and dripping lower. Backing away to the corner, my breathing is harsh as I stare at my painting with pride. I shrug. "What can I say? You feel too good." She rinses her body and steps out of the shower without a word.

She's pissed off.

I won't make apologies just yet. She felt too good to be sorry. Lazily, I clean up and shut the water off. I step out and grab a towel from the rack. "Come on. Don't be mad."

"Easy for you to say. You came."

Her feistiness is a turn-on. If I didn't just fuck her, I'd try again. This time I'd fuck that damn sexy mouth of hers. "I'll make it up to you."

"I think you've done enough. Now I'm late for class and wound up."

I take the ends of the towel wrapped around her and tug her to me. "Don't be mad." I kiss her on the head, and then give her the smirk that will win her over, easing her irritation. "I'll make it up to you tonight. I promise."

"I have a group project to work on tonight. I'm going to stay on campus." She backs away, not looking at me while running the towel over her hair.

My brow cinches as I watch her. "Hey, are you really upset?"

"I'm not happy."

When she still doesn't look at me, I nudge her. "Don't be like that."

That gets her attention. She stands straight up, throws her hand on her hip, and narrows her eyes. "Like what, Alexander? What am I being like?"

"I know where this is going, and I'm not doing it. Don't start a fight where there is none."

"I learned from the best. It's what you do every day."

"Not with you." When she turns her back on me, I lose it. "I'm warning yo—"

Spinning on her heels, she points at me. "You're warning me? I'm not one of your lackeys, Alexander. Stop trying to make King happen. I don't call you King, and I never will. So don't you dare warn me about anything."

If she were one of my *so-called* lackeys, she'd be knocked right the fuck out for that. Seeing her with wet, messed-up hair, a towel wrapped around her, and her finger poking my chest, I stand down, deciding to give her the respect she demands. "Fuck, you're scary, Firefly."

Her hand falls to her side, and she rolls her eyes, but the smile I wanted to see is there and brings one to my mouth. When the tension in her muscles loses its momentum, she says, "You're ridiculous. Get dressed. We're both late."

Advanced Review Copy

Thirty minutes later, I kiss her before we open the door. I straighten the backpack on her shoulder and wrap my other arm around her. She whispers, "Be civil with your father."

"It will be a struggle, but I'll try. For you, I'll try." Stepping back, I hold a few fingers up pledge style, not sure if it's supposed to be two or three. "Scout's honor."

"You were never a scout," she corrects and laughs, stepping into the hall. "But try. Okay?"

After slapping her ass, I wink. "I always do."

FREE in KU! If you would like to continue reading about Alexander and Sara Jane, click here:

https://geni.us/SavageAm

WE WERE ONCE

Read the Bestselling Book that's been called **"The Most Romantic Book Ever"** by readers and have them raving. We Were Once is now available and FREE in Kindle Unlimited. https://geni.us/WWOAm

"This is hands down my favourite book so far of 2020" - *Amazon Review*

"This is why I read romance." - *Kris, Literary Misfit, GR*

"If there is one book that you need to pick up it is We Were Once. My favorite book of the year!" - *Beckyrae99, Amazon*

"A sweeps you off your feet kind of book." - *Liz, Amazon*

"An EPIC love story!" - *Amazon Review*

"Their story was flawlessly written and heartfelt." - *Amazon Review*

READ THE PROLOGUE & CHAPTER 1 FREE - Turn the Page

WE WERE ONCE - PROLOGUE

I've never died before, but I recognize the feeling.

WE WERE ONCE - CHAPTER 1

Chloe Fox

"Promise me you'll protect Frankie with your life, Chloe."

Glancing sideways, I find it hard to take this seriously. "Um . . ."

My mom hugs Frankie to her chest like the son she never had. "You'll give him a good home, feed him, and nurture him?"

I think this is taking it a little too far. "It's a plant, Mom, not a human."

"It's not just a plant. It's a bonsai tree. They're fickle creatures—"

"Technically, it's not a creature. It's a miniature tree."

"Creature or not, promise me you'll take care of it, Chloe. This isn't just a plant. This little guy can provide harmony and calm to your place."

"Mom, I got it." I attempt to pry the potted plant from her, but when she resists, I ask, "Do you want to keep Frankie? He'd love New York City. You can take him to

Central Park or a show on Broadway. A quick trip to MoMA or the Statue of Liberty—"

"Very funny." She shoves him toward me. "Take him. I bought him for you."

"We can set up a visitation schedule if you'd like?"

That earns me an eye roll that's punctuated with laughter. "You might think I'm being dramatic, but I can already tell this is what your apartment is missing. I wish you'd let me decorate it more. So, mock me if you must, but that little guy is going to bring balance to your life."

"It's a lot of pressure to put on a plant, don't you think?"

"Little tree," she corrects stubbornly as if I've insulted the thing. Crossing her arms over her chest, she raises a perfectly shaped eyebrow. "You want to be a doctor, Chloe. Treat it like a patient. Water, attention, and care. The basics."

Holding the plant in front of me, I admire the pretty curve to the trunk and branches. It's easy to see why my mom picked this one. "I'll try not to kill it like the plant you gave me last year." I set the plastic pot down on top of a stack of textbooks on the coffee table. "But you have to admit that I gave that ivy a great send-off."

"You did. Right down the trash shoot." She laughs again, but I hear the sadness trickling in.

"Why are you getting upset?"

The green of my mom's eyes matches the rich color of the leaves when she cries, just like mine. "I think the bonsai has had enough water for one day. Don't you think?" I ask teasingly to hide how much I hate the impending goodbye.

She laughs, caressing my cheek. The support she's always shown me is felt in her touch. "I've had the best time with you over the past few weeks. I'm going to miss you, honey."

Leaning into it, I say, "If everything goes to plan, I'll be in the city next year, and we can see each all the time."

"You've worked hard. Now it's time to enjoy your senior year." Her departure pending, we embrace.

"I enjoy working hard, and my grades still matter this year if I want to get into med school."

A sympathetic smile creases her lips when she steps back. "I'm sorry you feel you have to be perfect all the time or that you feel medical school is the only option for you. It's not. You can do—"

"It's what *I* want." This subject was the final blow to her marriage to my dad. They disagreed about a lot, but my schooling and future were the sticking points. I don't want to relive it.

Moving to the couch, she fluffs a pillow, but I have a feeling it's only out of habit. "Seeking perfection is the easiest way to find disappointment." She eyes the pillow, satisfaction never reaching her eyes. Standing back, she swings her gaze my way. "Happiness is a much nobler mission."

After she divorced my father, she put it into practice. After leaving Newport for Manhattan two years ago, she's happier than ever. "I know you have big plans, Chloe, but you're only young once. Go out with Ruby. Have fun. Kiss boys. You're allowed to do what you want instead of what others want for you. You're allowed to be you."

Be me? The words strike me oddly. "Who am I?"

"Ah, sweet girl, whoever you want to be. New experiences will allow you to see yourself through a new lens."

I sit on the couch, blocking her view of the pillow she just fixed. "Is that why you left Newport?"

"Yes, I wanted to discover me again. In Manhattan, I'm not Norman's wife or the chair of the preservation society.

I'm not running an eight-thousand-square-foot house or hosting garden parties. In New York, I get to be Cat Fox and Chloe's mother. Those are my favorite roles I've ever had."

Working with my father might have been great for my résumé, but back home, I'll always be compared to the great Norman Fox. I'll live in his shadow if I return to Rhode Island and won't ever stand on my own accomplishments. So I understand what she means a little too well. She seems to think she was saved. *Is it too late for me?*

"Do you know who you are?"

"I'm learning every day. All I'm saying is life is happening all around you. Look up from the books every now and then."

Turning around, she takes one last glance around the apartment. "You need a pop of color in here. I can send sofa pillows."

I get what she's saying. She's the queen of décor and has strong opinions regarding my life. She'd love to not only throw some pillows on my couch but also put a man in my life.

She never understood that good grades are much more rewarding than spending time with boys who want nothing more than a one-night stand. "Don't send pillows," I say, grinning.

A sly grin rolls across her face. "You can snuggle with them, or a guy—"

"You want me to date." I sigh. "I get it."

"College guys aren't the same as high school boys." She takes her purse from the couch and situates it on her shoulder as she moves to the door.

I roll my eyes. "Could have fooled me."

"You just haven't met someone who makes your heart flutter."

"You're such a romantic."

Kissing my cheek, she opens the door, and says, "Take care of yourself, honey. I love you."

"Love you, too." I close the door and rest against the back of it, exhaling. After two months of working at my father's clinic and then staying with her in the city for the past two weeks, I'd almost forgotten what it was like to have time to myself and silence. Pure, unadulterated—

Knock. Knock.

I jump, startled from the banging against my back. Spinning around, I squint to look through the peephole, and my chin jerks back.

A guy holding a bag outside my door says, "Food delivery."

"I didn't order food," I say, palms pressed to the door as I spy on him.

A smirk plays on his lips. Yup, he flat-out stares into the peephole with a smug grin on his face. Plucking the receipt from the bag, he adds, "Chloe?" The e is drawn out in his dulcet tone as if it's possible to make such a common name sound special. He managed it.

I unlock the deadbolt but leave the chain in place. When I open the door, I peek out, keeping my body and weight against it for safety.

Met with brown eyes that catch the setting sun streaming in from the window in the hall, there's no hiding the amusement shining in them. "Hi," he says, his gaze dipping to my mouth and back up. "Chloe?"

"I'm Chloe, but as I said, I didn't order food."

He glances toward the stairs, the tension in his shoulders dropping before his eyes return to mine. "I have the right address, the correct apartment, and name. I'm pretty sure it's for you." He holds it out after a casual shrug. "Anyway, it's getting cold, and it's chicken and dumplings, my mom's specialty that she only makes on Sundays. Trust me, it's better hot, though I've had it cold, and it was still good."

He makes a solid argument. All the information is correct. I shift, my guard dropping. I'm still curious, though. "Your mom made it?"

Thumbing over his shoulder as though the restaurant is behind him, he replies, "Only on Sundays. Me and T cook the rest of the time."

"Who's T?"

"The other cook." He turns the bag around. Patty's Diner is printed on the white paper. Then he points at his worn shirt, the logo barely visible from all the washings.

"And Patty is your mother?"

He swivels the bag around and nods. "Patty is my mom."

My stomach growls from the sound of the bag crinkling in his hands, reminding me that I haven't eaten in hours, and chicken and dumplings sounds amazing. Only "culinary cuisine," as my dad would call it, was acceptable when I was growing up. Comfort food didn't qualify because anything with gravy instead of some kind of reduction was a no-no.

Grinning, he pushes the bag closer. "As much as I'd love to stay here all night and chat about the mystery of this delivery, I have other food getting cold down in the car. You're hungry. Take the bag and enjoy." He says it like we're friends, and I'm starting to think we've spent enough time together to consider it.

I unchain the door and open it to take the bag from him. Holding up a finger, I ask, "Do you mind waiting? I'll get you a tip."

As if he won the war, two dimples appear as his grin grows. The cockiness reflected in his eyes doesn't take away from the fact that he's more handsome than I initially gave him credit for.

Handsome is a dime a dozen in Newport. Good genes passed down long before the Golden Age run in the prestigious family trees of Rhode Island. So good-looking guys don't do much beyond catch my eye.

He says, "I can wait." I pull my purse from the hook near the door and dig out my wallet. He fills the doorway, snooping over my shoulder. "Where are you running to?"

Huh? I look up, confused by the question. "Nowhere."

Following his line of sight, I realize what he's referring to just as he says, "The treadmill. That's the point. You never get anywhere."

"It's good exercise."

"Yeah," he says, his tone tipping toward judgmental. "You're just running in a circle. Stuck in place."

"I'm not trying to go anywhere. I'm—"

"Sure, you are."

When I answered the door, I wasn't expecting to have my life scrutinized under a microscope. "Why do I feel like you're speaking in metaphors?"

"I don't know. Why *do* you feel like I'm speaking in metaphors?" His tongue is slick and his wit dry, which is something I can appreciate, even when it's at my expense.

Handing him a ten, I say, "Hopefully, this covers the therapy."

He chuckles. "I'm always happy to dole out free advice, but I'll take the ten. Thanks." Still looking around, the detective moves his attention elsewhere. "Nice bonsai."

"Thanks. My mom gave me Frankie."

"Frankie?"

I tuck my wallet back in my purse and return it to the hook. "The little tree?"

Eyeing the plant, I can tell he wants to get a closer look by how he's inching in. He says, "Bonsais aren't miniature trees. They're just pruned to be that way. It's actually an art form."

"You seem to know a lot more about it than I do," I reply, stepping sideways to cut off his path. "Are you a plant guy?"

"I like to know all kinds of things about plants. Mainly the ones we eat. I wouldn't suggest sautéing Frankie, though."

"Why would I sauté Frankie?" I catch his deadpan expression. "Ah. You're making a joke. Gotcha." I laugh under my breath. "You're referring to food."

"Yeah."

I take the door in hand as a not so subtle hint. "I should get back to . . ." I just end it before the lie leaves my lips. I have no plans but to study, and that sounds boring even to me. "Thanks again." I'm surprised, though, when he doesn't move. "Don't let me keep you from those other deliveries." *Hint. Hint. Hint.*

He remains inches from me, and I look up when he says, "Thanks for the tip."

"You're welcome."

Shoving the money in his pocket, he rocks back on his heels. "Hope you enjoy the food."

Pulling the door with me as he passes, I remain with it pressed to my backside. "I'm sure I will."

"Anytime." I barely glimpse his grin before he turns abruptly to leave. Then he stops just shy of maneuvering down the stairs and looks back. "You need balance in your life."

Shock bolts my eyes wide open, and my mouth drops open as offense takes over. Standing in my discomfort, I consider closing the door and ending this conversation. But

I step forward instead, leaning halfway out. "Maybe you need balance."

Through a chuckle, he replies, "The bonsai. You said your mom gave you the plant. She thinks you need balance in your life. Mine gave me calm. Mom knows best. That's all I'm saying."

Pulling the door, I take a step back, glancing at him one last time. "Thanks, professor," I remark.

"Have a good life, Chloe." His laughter bounces off the walls of the hallway.

I shut the door, bolting the lock and attaching the chain, not needing the last word. "I will," I say to myself. After a quick peek out of the peephole again to verify he left, I set the bag next to the stack of books and take a second look at the plant. "By the way he was looking at you, I thought he was going to plant-nap you, Frankie." He sure was all up in this little guy's business.

Must be a biology major.

I begin to unpack the bag, trying to ignore how his presence and the faint scent of his cologne still linger but notice how it feels a few degrees warmer. "I wouldn't blame him," I tell Frankie. "You're a beautiful specimen."

Getting up, I lower the thermostat before trying to figure out who sent the food. With perfect timing, my phone begins buzzing across the coffee table. I race back to catch a text from my best friend: *If you hear from me in ten minutes, call me right back.*

Quick to respond, I type: *Another bad date?*

Ruby Darrow, the heiress to the Darrow Enterprises, and I have been close since we roomed together freshman year. I can't wait for her to move into her apartment next door. Her return message reads: *I'm not sure. If you hear from me, then yes. Yes, it is.*

Me: *I'm on standby.*

Ruby: *Because you're the best.*

I take my duties as her friend very seriously, so I set the phone down next to the bag and pop open the plasticware. When my phone buzzes again, I'm fully prepared to make the call, but this time it's not Ruby.

Mom: *I had food delivered for you. Did you get it? Chicken and dumplings. I'm in the mood for comfort food and thought you might be, too.*

I wish I would have known ten minutes ago. Eyeing the bag, I smile. I can't argue with her choice of dish, but I'm just not sure if the pain in the ass delivery was worth the trouble.

Even a baseball cap flipped backward didn't hinder his appearance because, apparently, I just discovered I have a type. Small-town hero with a side of arrogance. *Jesus.* This is Connecticut, not Texas.

Despite his appearance, I wasn't impressed. Dating cute guys has not worked out well for me in the past. The local bad boy doesn't fit into my plans or help with my "balance" as he points out I evidently need.

So rude.

I balance just fine. School. Trying to think of more, I get frustrated. I'm at Yale for one reason and one reason only— to get into the medical school of my choice—and to do that, I need to keep my brain in the game. The school game, not the dating game. "What does he know anyway, Frankie?"

Returning my mom's text, I type: *Got it. Thank you.*

Mom: *Promise me you'll live a little, or a lot, if you're so inclined.*

She's become a wild woman in the past two years. I'm happy for her, but that doesn't mean I have to change my ways to fit her new outlook on life.

As I look around my new apartment, the cleanliness brings a sense of calm to me. After living in my parents' homes over the summer, it feels good to be back at school and on my own again.

Me: *That's a lot of promises. First, caring for Frankie, and now for my own well-being.* I laugh at my joke, but I know she'll misinterpret it, so I'm quick to add: *Kidding. I will. Love you.*

Mom: *Hope so. Live fearlessly, dear daughter. Love you.*

Feeling like I dodged another lecture on "you're only young once," I smile like a kid on Christmas when I find a chocolate chip cookie in the bag. With just one bite of the food, I close my eyes, savoring the flavor. "Patty sure knows how to cook."

I click on a trivia game show and spend the time kicking the other contestants' butts as I eat.

Soon, I'm stuffed but feeling antsy about the dough sitting at the bottom of my stomach, so I get up and slip my sneakers on before hopping on the treadmill. I warm up for a mile with that bag and the red logo staring back at me, so I pick up the pace until I'm sprinting. "I'm not trying to go anywhere. It's good exercise," I grumble, still bothered by what the delivery guy said. A bleacher seat therapist is the last thing I need.

I start into a jog and then a faster speed, though my gaze keeps gravitating toward the bag and the red printing on the front—Patty's Diner. The food might have been delicious, but I can't make a habit out of eating food that heavy or I won't be able to wear the new clothes my mom and I just spent two weeks shopping for.

I barely make four miles before my tired muscles start to ache. I'm not surprised after a day of moving, but I still wished I could have hit five. I hit the stop button and give in to the exhaustion.

I take a shower and change into my pajamas before going through my nightly routine—brushing teeth, checking locks, turning out the lights, and getting a glass of water. I only take a few sips before I see Frankie in the living room all alone. My mom's guilt was well-placed. I dump water in the pot and bring it with me into the bedroom. "Don't get too comfortable. You're not staying here."

Returning to the living room to grab my study guide for the MCAT, I hurry back to bed and climb under the covers. But after a while, I set the guide aside, behavioral sciences not able to hold my attention against my mom's parting words.

Classes. Study. Rest. Routines are good. They're the backbone of success. I click off the lamp, not needing my mom's words—*live fearlessly*—filling my head. Those thoughts are only a distraction to my grand plan. *Like that delivery guy.*

Want to read more (FREE in KU):
https://geni.us/WWOAm

EVEREST

If you love romantic suspense, fantastic banter, and chemistry between characters, you must read EVEREST. You are going to fall in love with Ethan and Singer. Read their story now. https://geni.us/EverestAm

FREE in Kindle Unlimited

FOLLOW ME

To keep up to date with her writing and more, visit S.L. Scott's website: **https://geni.us/slscott**

To receive the newsletter about all of her publishing adventures, free books, giveaways, steals and more: **https://geni.us/intheknow**

ABOUT THE AUTHOR

To keep up to date with her writing and more, her website is
https://geni.us/slscott to receive her newsletter with all of
her publishing adventures and giveaways, sign up for her
newsletter: https://geni.us/intheknow

Instagram: https://geni.us/IGSLS

To receive a free book now, TEXT "slscott" to 77948

For more information, https://geni.us/slscott

Printed in Great Britain
by Amazon

78906036R00222